Thomas E. Lightburn served twenty-two years in the medical branch of the Royal Navy, reaching the rank of Chief Petty Officer. He left the service in 1974 and obtained a Bachelors (Hons) degree at Liverpool University. After teaching for sixteen years, he volunteered for early retirement. He then began writing for *The Wirral Journal* and *The Sea Breezes*, a worldwide nautical magazine. He interviewed the late Ian Fraser, VC, ex-Lieutenant RN, and wrote an account of how he and his crew crippled the Japanese cruiser, *Takao*, in Singapore.

Thomas is a widower and lives locally pursuing his favourite hobbies of soccer, naval and military history, the theatre, art and travel.

Published work

The Gates of Stonehouse
(Vanguard Press 2005)
978 184386 203

Uncommon Valour
(Vanguard Press 2006)
978 184386 301 4

The Shield and The Shark
(Vanguard Press 2006)
978 184386 350 2

The Dark Edge of The Sea
(Vanguard Press 2007)
978 184386 400 4

The Ship That Would Not Die
(Vanguard Press 2008)

The Summer of '39
(Vanguard Press 2009)
978 184386 561 2

A Noble Chance
(Vanguard Press 2010)
978 184386 647 3

Beyond the Call of Duty
(Vanguard Press 2011)
978 184386 714 2

The Russian Run
(Vanguard Press 2012)
978 184386 840 8

Deadly Inferno
(Vanguard Press 2013)
978 184386 736 4

THE HIDDEN ENEMY

Thomas E. Lightburn

THE HIDDEN ENEMY

Vanguard Press

A CIP catalogue record for this title is
available from the British Library.

ISBN 978-178465-132-9

*Vanguard Press is an imprint of
Pegasus Elliot MacKenzie Publishers Ltd.*
www.pegasuspublishers.com

First Published in 2016

**Vanguard Press
Sheraton House Castle Park
Cambridge England**

Printed & Bound in Great Britain

Acknowledgements

I wish to express my sincere thanks to Ex Master-at-Arms, Robert Grenfell, who served in the RN for 24 years. Rob is now a Yeoman Warder of the Queens Bodyguard at the Tower of London. Without his expert knowledge of type 23 frigates, this book could not have been written. My gratitude also to the medical staff of HMS *Lancaster* for their kindness in allowing me access to the sick bay and relevant information about modern medical techniques. I would like to thank Petty Officer Medical Assistant Andy Jewitt and WO Medical assistant Lorraine Connolly for their invaluable information regarding the medical routine for personnel on board HM Ships; Sue Sullivan of the *Navy News* for providing me with a detailed picture of a type 23 frigate, Doctor S.K. Mukherjee for his medical expertise, Robert Nicholson for his help with the manuscript, Justine Robinson for her computer knowledge and the staffs of the Imperial War Museum and Greenwich Library.

CHAPTER ONE

Lieutenant Janet Martin unlocked the door of the office and went inside. The time was 0730 on Monday 8 July 2013. Janet carefully removed her smart tricorn cap and hung it on the hat rack. The office like many in administrative building of Royal Naval Barracks in HMS *Nelson*, Portsmouth was quite spacious. At the far end leading into her boss's sanctuary was a door marked 'Senior Planning Officer ' Well polished brown, linoleum covered the floor, and two strips of neon when switched on, flickered wildly before giving a clear white light. A pastel painting of Portsmouth's Guildhall, and old portraits of admirals, long since passed away, broke the monotony of the walls painted a dull shade of cream. In a corner was a stainless steel sink above this was a framed mirror. Next to this was a small cupboard on which lay a tray of cups, saucers, a tin of instant coffee and an unopened carton of semi skimmed milk. A bulky green metal filing cabinet rested in one corner. Close by were two well-worn armchairs, a glass-topped table with an assortment of magazines.

Feeling slightly hung over, the product of a too many pink gins in the wardroom the previous evening, Janet opened one of the bay windows overlooking the parade ground. Looking up at the clear blue sky she felt the warm sun caress her face. Turning around, she sat down at her desk. In front of her was a leather-bound, pink blotting pad, a buzzer and inter-com, a batch of pencils and biros in a pink, plastic container and a black, hard-backed book marked 'Diary'. Close by a computer and printer rested on top of an oaken sideboard. She reached across and switched on both.

After making a note of her boss's morning appointments, she gave a rueful smile. First on the list was Commander John Hailey, commanding officer of HMS *Dawlish.* She had met him a four months ago at a cocktail party on board his ship. He had the same dimpled chin and disarming smile reminiscent of Cary Grant, an old Hollywood heart-throb. She sat back in her chair remembering his six-feet plus dark, good looks, his broad shoulders and thick, well-groomed, shiny black hair greying at each temple. But most of all she recalled his dark blue penetrating eyes that sent a shiver of delight running down her spine whenever he looked at her. She also recalled reading in the newspapers that he had recently gone through a messy divorce from Annabel Sutherland, a well-known actress she had seen several times on television.

After their brief conversation she had felt somewhat disappointed when he excused himself and joined another officer and his wife. However, after being introduced to a tall, handsome, fair-haired officer named Ray Noble, who was the ship's Executive Officer she immediately lost interest in Hailey.

Janet was twenty-three, with a First Class English degree obtained at Oxford, and had been in the service just over a year. She stood five feet four with a fresh complexion, clear blue eyes and a sparking smile that displayed a set of small even white teeth. From her black leather shoulder bag, she took out a round eggshell- coloured powder compact. She opened it and looking in the small mirror, turned her head from side to side ensuring her shoulder-length chestnut hair, worn in a chignon was still in place. She then added a slight touch of lipstick and dabbed a quick application of powder on her cheeks then closed her compact. Satisfied with her appearance, she replaced the compact, zipped her bag and placed it on her desk. A glance at the wall clock showed 0830 - it was time to prepare her boss's mug of coffee, strong with two spoons of sugar.

A few minutes after 0840, the door opened and in came a medium sized man in his early-fifties. Under his left arm was a folded copy of *The Times*, and in his right hand he carried a brown leather brief case. As he usually did each morning, the perfumed aroma of face powder caused him momentarily to glance disapprovingly at Janet. He then removed his cap, displaying a layer of thin greying hair surrounding a small round bald patch.

Captain George Storey joined the navy in 1975. He came from a long line of naval officers whose antecedents dated back to Nelson's time. After commanding several warships including HMS *Endurance* of Falkland Islands fame, he was appointed Director of Naval Planning and Fleet Disposition. The four gold rings he wore on both sleeves indicated rank and among the row of medals the D S O and K G B, showed ample evidence of his respectful position in the service. He had been happily married to Hilda for twenty-eight years and had a son, Simon who was a stockbroker.

'Morning Janet,' he said crustily while delicately sniffing the air. Janet had been his secretary for almost a year during which time they had developed a pleasant working relationship.

'As usual, the place smells like an Egyptian bordello,' he added, screwing up his small, grey rheumy eyes. His voice was deep and resonant, and as he spoke, the fleshy jowls under the chin of his round, pale face wobbled like a jelly.

'I'm sure you know more about those establishments than me, sir,' Janet sarcastically replied 'Coffee in five minutes.'

'Any appointments?' the captain grunted as he opened his office door.

'Commander Hailey, sir,' Janet replied, 'at nine thirty.'

'Oh yes, I remember, send him in as soon as he arrives, and I'll have that coffee when you're ready.'

The captain's office, situated on the fourth floor of the administrative building, was bathed in early morning sunshine and smelt heavily of mansion polish. A wide, bay window offered a perfect bird's-eye view of HMS *Victory* and the imposing Semaphore Towers a large, red-bricked building incorporating the head office of Admiral Fearnley, the Naval Base Commander and the Queen's Harbour Master.

The room was tastefully furnished with a black, leather Chesterfield and two matching armchairs, thickly piled, dark blue carpet, and a high, stuccoed ceiling from which hung an elegant crystal chandelier. In one corner rested a glass cabinet, containing an assortment of bottles of alcohol and glasses. The walls were lined with leather-bound books and photographs of warships, old and new. Nearby the curved surface of a large globe encased in an oak stand, shone like a brass ball, and on the wall behind a wide mahogany desk, was an ornately framed coloured photograph of Queen Elizabeth and the Duke of Edinburgh.

As he sat down, Janet came in and placed a steaming hot cup of coffee on his desk.

'Thank you,' muttered the captain giving Janet an approving glance. He then took out an old brown meerschaum pipe and a pouch of Old Roan tobacco. After filling it, Janet picked up a heavy-looking brass lighter and, with a grimace, handed it to him. In a matter of seconds a cloud of blue pungent smoke billowed in front of him.

'Filthy habit,' Janet remarked, shaking her head disapprovingly while walking towards the door.

'Don't go on so,' the captain growled removing his pipe. 'You're beginning to sound just like my wife.'

Janet simply shook her head in disgust and left the room.

Taking another puff of his pipe, the captain unlocked a side drawer and took out a large buff-coloured envelope marked 'TOP SECRET'. He broke the seal and removed a fairly slim, four-page document. Holding his pipe in one hand he used the other to pick up his cup and take a deep gulp. He replaced the cup and began to study the pages. In doing so his lips tightened into a firm line. The information contained in the report was quite alarming. The sharp sound of the buzzer on his desk disturbed his concentration.

'Commander Hailey to see you, sir,' came the clear voice of Janet. Much to her disappointment when Hailey knocked and came in he didn't show any signs of remembering her. He simply gave her a warm smile and introduced himself.

'Good morning, sir,' Janet said smiling, 'go right in. The captain is expecting you.'

Hailey's cap was neatly tucked under his left armpit, and he carried a brown leather briefcase.

Looking up from his desk, the captain's pale fleshy features creased into a warm smile. 'Good morning, John, nice to see you again,' he said pushing himself from his chair.

Hailey placed his briefcase on the floor and they shook hands. The captain sat down.

'Do take a seat, and smoke if you want to,' the captain said nodding towards a silver cigarette box and matching lighter.

'Thank you, sir,' Hailey replied, 'but I don't smoke.'

Storey sat back and folded his arms over his ampler waist, 'first of all,' he said, smiling benignly. 'Let me congratulate you and your crew for the work you did in the Caribbean; the three tons of cocaine and a ton of cannabis you captured from that Columbian tramp steamer will eventually save many lives.'

'Thank you, sir,' Hailey replied modestly. 'But, most of the credit for that belongs to Lieutenant Somersby and his Royals. They searched the ship and found the drugs concealed on bags marked flour at the bottom of one of the holds.'

'Yes, I read that in your report and was most impressed,' the captain answered placing his pipe on the rim of a heavy brass ash tray half full of bits of black tobacco.

Hailey sat back in his chair, crossed his legs and said, 'I'm afraid, it'll take a few more ships from ourselves and the Americans to really get to grips with the drug smuggling problem, sir.' Hailey paused momentarily, then went on, 'During the three weeks the ship was in dry dock I sent the first and second parts of the watch on seven days leave, the rest are going today, but I'm sure they wouldn't mind a few more runs ashore in Barbados.'

Storey pursed his lips, sat forward, picked up his pipe and took a few puffs. Immediately another cloud of smoke surrounded his face.

'No doubt,' he replied dryly, while wafting the air with a hand. 'According to your report, all your defects, including the problem with the electrical supply to your diesel engines, have been dealt with. I take it that's correct?'

'Yes, sir,' Hailey replied, adding confidently, 'sea trials will take place when the port watch will have returned from leave.'

'How long do you think this will take?' Storey asked.

'Two days at the most, sir,' Hailey replied confidently.

'Splendid,' answered the captain. He then leant forward, removed his pipe and placed it, still smouldering, in the ashtray, then went on. 'As I'm sure you are aware, the Armilla Patrol operates east of Suez. This consists of six frigates and two RFAs. These ships have to cover an area stretching from the Horn of Aden to the Persian Gulf.' (An RFA is a Royal Fleet Auxiliary.)

'What about the Americans and our European allies, not to mention the Chinese?' Hailey asked, his voice full of concern. 'Surely it's in their interests to help as their supply of oil comes from the Persian Gulf.

'Most of the American ships are engaged patrolling off the coast of South Korea,' the captain answered with a frown. 'As you know the North have been testing nuclear weapons. The Chinese and the Scandinavian countries have several warships in and around the Gulf, but it's a large area. More importantly, we only have nineteen warships in commission. As a member of NATO, we have to provide cover for the Atlantic. Then there is the Falklands to consider, as well as supplying ships for the Fishery Protection Squadron. So you see our so-called fleet, is spread thinly on the ground...' A knock at the door interrupted him.

The door opened and Janet came carrying a tray, two cups and saucers plus a shiny silver coffee pot.

'As it's almost ten-thirty, sir,' she said, giving a depreciative glance at the smoke filled atmosphere, 'I thought you'd like coffee.'

'Splendid idea, Janet,' said the captain, reaching for his pipe, 'perhaps you could be mother?'

Janet laid the tray down on the captain's desk, poured the coffee and handed them to the officers. 'Do you take sugar?' she asked Hailey.

'Two spoonful's please,' he replied.

Janet did as he asked then walking to the bay window, she opened it, and with a touch of sarcasm, said, 'I'd better let some air in here before you both suffocate.'

'Typical woman,' muttered Storey, rolling his tired grey eyes, 'nag, nag, nag.'

A wide grin spread across Hailey's face as he thanked her before taking a good sip of his drink.

As soon as Janet left the room, the captain took a puff of his pipe then picked up his cup and took a deep gulp of coffee. 'Ah, that's better,' he said with a satisfactory sigh. Resting his pipe in the ash tray, he went on, 'The Defence Committee, of which I'm chairman, have formed what is called a Fleet Ready Escort.' He paused noticing the curious expression in Hailey's eyes. 'In effect, this is a single warship, maintained at high readiness for deployment anywhere in the world. Of course, this includes the Gulf area.'

Hailey raised his eyebrows and gave the captain a quick sideways glance. 'Rumour has it that pirates have captured a Swedish cargo ship and are holding the crew to ransom. Is that correct, sir?'

'Humph,' retorted the captain, placing his pipe in the ashtray, 'you seem to be well informed. Who told you that?'

'I overheard a few stokers talking earlier today,' Hailey answered, somewhat cynically. 'Apparently they heard it on CNN.'

Storey sat back raised both hands and grinned. 'So much for secrecy, eh? However, your stokers are quite right. The Gulf of Aden and the Arabian Sea makes that region a vital economic conduit and is an indispensable international shipping lane.' The captain paused as Hailey finished his drink.

'Indeed, sir,' Hailey replied gravely. 'Seventy-two percent of oil supplies flow through it from the Gulf and Middle East.'

'In your opinion, Commander,' said Storey, leaning forward and placing both hands on the desk. 'Which area in the Gulf is the most vulnerable?'

'The Strait of Hormuz, at the mouth of the Persian Gulf, sir,' Hailey immediately replied. 'It is very narrow and could easily be blockaded by a determined enemy. The result could be catastrophic to the economy of many countries.'

The captain sat forward and tapped the document in front of him. 'This is a top secret report from the Emirates Centre for Strategic Studies. Not only does it stress the links between piracy and groups belonging to global terrorism, it also states that the Taliban is receiving weapons including rocket launchers and mines from the Muslim Brotherhood in Egypt.' The captain paused then, furrowing his brow, added, 'the mines are especially dangerous. Intelligence informs us that they're called flat mines. Each one contains a new explosive called Trysin. It's twice as powerful as TNT and could easily sink or seriously damage a large ship.'

With a puzzled expression on his face, Hailey said, 'Why are they called flat mines, sir?'

Storey picked up his pipe and took another deep puff, then once again dispersing the smoke with his free hand, replied, 'because they float just below the surface and are usually camouflaged to look like bits of flotsam. As such the boffins tell us they can be hard to detect on the radar.' He paused momentarily and stared disapprovingly at his pipe. 'Damn thing's gone out,' he muttered, placing it back in the ash tray. 'Anyway,' he went on, sitting back in his chair and placing both hands on his desk, 'so far Al Qaeda haven't used the bloody things as it thought they're too expensive to make in bulk, nevertheless you'd better mention it to your PWO.'(Pronounced 'Pea-woh) and staff.

'I will indeed, sir,' Hailey answered forcibly. 'But besides ourselves, how many other countries have warships patrolling that area?'

'Quite a few,' the captain answered flatly, '*Doncaster* is on station along with an American destroyer and a Spanish frigate. But the pirates enjoy the confidence of the locals. This makes it bloody difficult to track the blighters down.'

Hailey uncrossed his legs, leant forward and with a look of expectancy, said, 'I take it, sir, *Dawlish* is the next Fleet Ready Escort warship?'

'This hasn't been decided,' replied the captain,

'So when do we sail?'

'After your sea trials, you are to restore and re-ammunition,' the captain answered. 'I'm sorry I can't be more specific, but my advice is be prepared to leave as soon as possible. I've enjoyed meeting you,' he added as they shook hands, 'and I'll send for you should any emergency arise.'

'Is there a time limit on this, sir?' Hailey tentatively asked. 'I mean, if there aren't any problems abroad, do we just sit and wait?'

Storey pursed his lips and replied, 'I'm afraid so. With the world in the state it's in, rest assured sooner or later you'll be needed.'

CHAPTER TWO

A dark blue utilicon (nicknamed a 'tilly'), with the letters RN painted white on both sides, was waiting outside the administrative block to take Hailey back to his ship. The time was a little before 1200. Hailey rolled down the window of the passenger seat to allow the warm July sun to caress his face. With a wry smile he remembered it was on a similar July evening in Portsmouth, eight years ago, that he met Annabel. Hailey was a young lieutenant serving as navigating officer on board HMS *Roebuck*, a survey vessel. He and several officers had been invited to a cocktail party on board the aircraft carrier *Illustrious*. Hailey remembered thinking how large the wardroom was compared with the one in his ship. Even the armchairs and settee covered in standard multi-patterned chintz looked bigger and a damn sight more comfortable. The room was well lit by neon strips attached to a low-slung deck head, painted like the bulkheads, in glossy pale cream. Officers in their mess dress and women wearing attractive evening gowns, stood in groups making polite conversation, their voices clearly audible over the gentle hum of the generators.

At the after end of the room above a well-stocked bar, a forty-inch plastic television set was secured to the bulkhead. Under this was a cabinet containing a CD quietly playing a Chopin nocturne. Stewards, male and female wearing smart white jackets, hovered nearby, waiting to refill glasses. The gentle hum of the ship's generators filled the air.

The atmosphere was warm and tinged with the agreeable aroma of perfume. Hailey and his fellow officers were greeted by the ship's executive officer, a tall, dark haired commander with heavily tanned features.

'Welcome on board, gentlemen,' he said pleasantly. 'Do help yourself to drinks.'

It was while Hailey was shaking the commander's hand he saw her. She held a long-stemmed glass in one hand and was surrounded by a group of young officers. She had her back to him and all he could see was her short, chestnut-brown hair curling around her milk-white shoulders. It was when she half turned to smile at an officer he vividly recalled how stunning she looked in a long-sleeved bright yellow dress with a plunging neckline. A small set of pearls complemented her slender, swan-like neck and each time she smiled her captivating emerald green eyes sparkled seductively.

While half listening to the commander's voice, he watched as she laughed, flinging her head back and flashing a set of white even teeth. Her pear-shaped face and porcelain features stood out among the darker complexions of her admirers, who were obviously captivated by her. Hailey guessed her age to be in her mid-twenties. She was without a doubt the most beautiful woman he had ever seen.

The executive officer excused himself, and moved on. Hailey then turned to one of his own officers.

'I say, Harry,' Hailey said, nodding towards the woman, 'I wonder who she is.'

'Great Scott, old man!' exclaimed Harry, 'don't you recognise her, that's Annabel Sutherland the actress, surely you must have heard of her. She's starring in *Private Lives* at the Old Vic in London.'

'I'm afraid not,' Hailey replied looking intently across the room. 'Not all that keen on the theatre.'

At that moment she turned, sighed wearily and with a bored expression glanced across and saw Hailey staring at her. Much to his surprise she excused herself and carrying her half-filled glass in her left hand, walked slowly towards him, smiling faintly as she did so.

'Do you always stare at someone you don't know?' she asked in a clear well-modulated voice.

'I do beg your pardon,' Hailey managed to say, noticing how her eyes shone under the wardroom lights. 'It's just that . . .'

'Annabel Sutherland,' she interrupted, sensing his embarrassment while proffering her hand. Her palm felt soft and warm and as she looked at him, he remembered feeling like a nervous schoolboy. Almost immediately they were surrounded by several more young officers, all of whom were intent on engaging her in conversation.

'Really, gentlemen,' she said tossing her head back and smiling, 'I am flattered by your attention.' Then diplomatically added, 'Perhaps you'll excuse Lieutenant Hailey and myself. If you need an autograph, I'll see you all later.'

Following a brief visit by the captain of *Illustrious*, a tall sharp-featured man with a receding hairline, two officers vacated their settee allowing Hailey and Annabel to sit down. For the next half hour they sat in deep conversation oblivious to their surroundings.

She told him her career began with RADA, then touring with a repertory company and later a contract with the BBC. After several TV plays, she auditioned for the part of Amanda, in Noel Coward's *Private Lives*. 'And the rest as they say is history. What about you?' she asked staring deeply into his dark blue eyes. How long have you been in the navy?'

'Four years,' he replied, after finishing his drink. 'My parents were both civil servants and wanted me to follow in their footsteps, but I needed to get away and see the world.'

'And have you seen much of it?' she enquired, with obvious interest.

'Mostly the coasts of Great Britain,' he replied with a sight grin. 'You see, I specialised in hydrography, and before you ask,' he quickly added, 'that involves charting coastlines, sounding the depth of seas, the study of tides and currents. *Roebuck* is my second ship, the first was *Gleaner,* a minesweeper.'

'It sound very exciting,' Annabel replied, taking a sip of her drink. 'But tell me, do you like the theatre?'
Hailey raised his eyebrows and slowly shook his head. 'I'm afraid not,' he said, feeling somewhat embarrassed. 'Being at sea doesn't give me much time for . . .'

Placing her hand over his and giving it a firm squeeze, she quickly interrupted him, 'then you must come up to London and see me at the Old Vic,' she said smiling. 'Can you do that?'

'Err . . . Yes,' Hailey hesitatingly replied, 'it so happens I have a long weekend due to me. I was intending going to Manchester to see my parents, but . . .'

'Then it's all settled,' she replied, keeping her hand in his. 'Come on Saturday night. I'll leave a ticket for you at the box office and we can have a supper afterwards. How does that sound?'

'Splendid,' Hailey answered, feeling his face redden, 'I'll book a room at a hotel and . . .'

Once again she interrupted him. 'I shouldn't bother,' Annabel replied. 'I have a flat in Chelsea that has a spare room. And don't look so frightened,' she added with a coquettish smile. 'I'm not going to bite you.'

Six months later, they were married. A month later, after leaving *Roebuck,* he was appointed to HMS *Shelby*, a type 42 frigate. For the next six months, he was away in the Mediterranean. Following a quick refit, his ship was at sea on and off again for another five months. While he was away, Annabel accepted an offer from Warner Brothers in Hollywood for a screen test. He arrived back in the UK to only find she was still in America. When she returned home, he remembered how excited she was, telling him she had been given a part in a movie starring Clint Eastwood.

Despite Hailey's protestations, she was determined to go back to America.

'This could be my big break,' she cried defiantly. 'And nothing's going to stop me. You have the navy, and I have my career.'

How right she was he told himself. Blinded by love, he had failed to realise they were living in two different worlds. Now it was too late. The end of their marriage began when she returned to Hollywood, where it had been reported that she was seeing a famous actor. The story made headlines in the gossip columns in England and America. Reporters accosted him, hoping for a tit- bit of scandal. Luckily, they weren't allowed in the dockyard where he was able to seek sanctuary on board his ship and the understanding of his fellow officers. Even members of the crew seemed sympathetic to his plight. Annabel's movie took longer to make than she thought during which time he filed for divorce. A month later he was awarded a decree nisi on the grounds of adultery.

CHAPTER THREE

The thick, Hampshire voice of the driver interrupted his reverie. 'Here we are, sur,' he said stopping the tilly near the bottom of *Dawlish*'s metal gangway. 'Wish I 'add me time in the Andrew all over again. Yer ship looks like a right trim craft, so she does.'

'Thank you, driver,' Hailey replied. Gathering his briefcase, he slid the car door open and climbed out. (The term 'Andrew' is said to refer to a Lieutenant Andrew Miller a highly successful press-gang officer in the 18th century.)

Dawlish was moored portside to the quay. For a few moments, Hailey stood at the foot of the gangway. His eyes took in the ship's graceful lines, and the large Union flag hanging limply from the jack on the end of her sharp bow. He noted the rigid inflatable boats (RIBs) stored in pods on the upper deck plus fifty-eight rafts that opened automatically when launched. A series of reinforced, nylon hawsers, stretching like umbilical cords, secured the ship to the wharf. Her pennant number, F 229, painted in bold black lettering, stood out starkly against the pale grey of the ship's side.

Hailey was only too aware that *Dawlish*, bristled with modern technology and had a complement of nineteen officers, a hundred and eight men and twelve female ratings.

The decision by the MOD to allow women to serve on board HM Ships was at first a contentious one. Many thought they might they might not cope with ship life and the arduous discipline. Superstitious diehards even considered women at sea bad luck. However, opinion soon changed when, some twenty years ago, women successfully served in all capacities on board HMS *Brilliant,* a type 23 frigate.

On the fo'c'sle the barrel of the Vickers 4.5 inch gun thrust defiantly from a rounded turret. This, plus the twin sets of four deadly Harpoon and vertical Sea wolf missile launchers near her flight deck, reminded him that

Dawlish had more hard-hitting, accurate firepower than the mighty *Hood* in World War 2. *Dawlish* and her contemporaries were more than a match for any would-be enemy.

He raised his eyes, taking in the enclosed bridge where he had spent most of his time at sea. Directly in front of him was an array of screens, switches, dials and telephones. Another chair a few feet away to his left faced the console. This was an electro-hydraulic system in which the quartermaster, using a small wheel, could set a lever which could steer the ship and control her speed. If the captain wanted the ship to maximise its speed, he would usually telephone the engineer officer to confirm this. Whenever the ship left or entered harbour or in times of emergency, the console was manned by Chief Coxswain Jock Forbes.   During normal sailing the chair was occupied in six hourly watches by Petty Officer Harry Lyme, and Leading Seaman Mickey Finn.

In a cramped recess behind the bridge was the pilothouse. This was the province of Lieutenant Paul Gooding, the ship's Navigating and Meteorologist. He had a first-class honours degree in geography and *Dawlish* was his first ship. Slotted on a shelf above a small, wooden desk was a series of nautical charts covering the world's oceans and sea lanes. Close by, a shaded bulb provided a blue light when the ship was darkened.

Directly aft of the bridge, rose the stately steel foremast with its attendant cables and technical attachments dwarfing the bulky main engine and gas turbine vents immediately in its rear. Then came the squat flat-sided funnel, designed to reduce radar contact. Filling half of the flight deck and looking somewhat out of place amongst this mass of modern technology, was an oblong shaped steel hangar housing a HMA8 Lynx Helicopter, nicknamed by the crew the 'Flying Bug'. Finally, from the stern, the White Ensign suddenly caught the breeze and flapped loudly as if to welcome him back on board. Yes, thought Hailey, remembering the tilly driver's words, she certainly is a right trim craft.

The tall, broad-shouldered figure of Lieutenant Commander Ray Noble, the ship's Executive Officer, stood to attention at the top of the gangway. Alongside him stood the Master-at-Arms Jerry Knight, a tall, thickly set man with keen, penetrating pale blue eyes and dark curly hair. 'Bogey,' as he was nicknamed, was the ship's policeman responsible for the disciplinary matters on board the ship. Standing close by was PO Jack Whitton, a small, thin-faced, two-badge seaman Duty Petty officer and Quartermaster Bud Abbott, a portly, ruddy-faced able seaman holding his silver bosun's call to his lips. As Hailey stepped onto the deck, Noble, Knight and Whitton snapped to attention and saluted as Abbott piped their captain aboard.

Nearby Able Rating Lottie Jones, was using a handful of cotton waste to polish the ship's bell. Her working rig consisted of a blue shirt and dark blue trousers and shoes, known as 3Cs. Her short bark brown hair was neatly tucked under a round cap. Upon hearing the pipe, she immediately stood to attention.

After returning their salutes, Hailey gave Noble, an uncomfortable look and in a firm voice, said, 'Good morning Number One, you'd better come with me to my cabin and I'll fill you in about the meeting with the captain.'

Although Noble's official title was Executive Officer, old customs die hard, and he was still referred to as the First Lieutenant.

'Any news about our future, sir?' Noble asked, as he walked away.

'It looks like we're stuck here for some time,' Hailey answered warily, 'but follow me to my cabin and all will be revealed. '

The captain's day cabin was situated two decks below the bridge. It was comfortably furnished with a settee, two armchairs both upholstered in floral chintz. The bulkheads, like the wardroom were pale green and the strips of neon from a low slung deck head provided shadow-less lighting. A dark blue carpet embossed with the small, ubiquitous gold anchors covered the deck. On the wide, leather-bound desk rested a telephone and an assortment of files. Behind the desk, secured to the bulkhead, was a framed coloured photograph of Queen Elizabeth and the Duke of Edinburgh. A forty inch television was secured into the port bulkhead. Under this secured on a small desk was a computer and printer. Close by, packed on a wooden shelf, was a row of official books and folders secured by a crosspiece. There were two doors, one of which led into a small, but well equipped galley, the other into the captain's sleeping quarters, a spacious room consisting of a wardrobe, a set of shiny oaken drawers on top of which was a bunk covered by a white duvet. Above a headboard, hung a voice-pipe leading directly to the bridge. Then came an overhead lamp which invariably remained on when he fell asleep. This was Hailey's private quarters; a sanctuary where he could think and deliberate on the many decisions he had to make.

Hailey's personal steward, Paddy Flannigan, a tall, dark, sallow-faced two badge PO from Londonderry, was waiting for them.

'Would you and the First Lieutenant like some coffee, sir?' As he spoke he displayed a set of uneven tobacco stained teeth.

'Not at the moment, thank you, Flannigan,' Hailey replied dismissively. 'And I'd be grateful if you would leave us alone. Which means, no listening through the galley door.'

'To be sure, as if I would do that sir,' Flannigan replied, his pale blue eyes creasing into a humorous grin.

For the next half an hour, Noble sat intently as Hailey described his meeting with Captain Storey.

When Hailey had finished, Noble sat forward in his chair with a frown furrowing his brow. 'You mean to say, sir,' he said, shaking his head in disbelief, 'we'll be at a mere twenty-four hour notice after which we could be sent anywhere in the world?'

'That's about the size of it, Number One,' Hailey replied, 'I suggest you personally inform the rest of the officers and mention on Daily Orders that for the foreseeable future we will remain alongside the wharf.'

With an air of resignation Noble replied, 'Well, it's a pity Cynthia is in Sardinia on a fashion shoot for *Vogue* magazine and wasn't due back for at least two weeks. By that time we could be half- way across the world.'

'Ah, the lovely Cynthia,' Hailey replied with a sly smile. 'Isn't it time you made an honest woman of her? I thought you two were engaged. You really ought to marry her and settle down.'

Cynthia MacLean was a beautiful, leggy, twenty-two year old model, with shoulder-length blonde hair and eyes the colour of the Mediterranean sky. Noble had met her at a cocktail party in London a few months before *Dawlish* sailed for the Caribbean, and they were immediately attracted to one another. During weekends, or whenever they could, they stayed at her flat in Holland Park, making passionate love far into the night.

'Cynthia and I are not actually engaged, sir,' Noble casually replied. With a touch of uncertainty, he added, 'Maybe one day we might, anyway the navy still has the highest divorce rate of the three services.'

Realising the implication of his words, Noble immediately bit his lip.

'You don't have to tell me that,' Hailey answered dispassionately.

'Sorry, sir,' Noble hastily replied, 'I didn't mean to . . .'

'Forget it,' Hailey answered flatly, adding, 'I'm sorry I can't be more specific about our movements, but if I were you, I'd make sure my tropical kit was ready for use.'

CHAPTER FOUR

Most of the conversation between Hailey and Noble when they met was overheard by Lottie Jones, ostensibly polishing the ship's bell. As both officers disappeared through the hatchway, 'Secure. Hands to dinner,' came over the ship's tannoy. A few minutes later Lottie, giggling with excitement, made her way to the female quarters. She was carrying two large cardboard boxes containing small cans of beer, collected from the NAAFI. (An organisation running canteen shops for service personnel in ships and shore establishments.)

The issue of rum had long been abolished, due mainly to the recommendations to Parliament by Admiral Sir Peter Hill-Norton. In his opinion, he felt that, after drinking rum, ratings might not be capable of handling the new and sophisticated computer equipment that was being introduced into the service. The government agreed and the last issue of rum was on 31 July 1970. Ratings called this a 'black' day, and mock funerals took place throughout the feet. On board HMS *Tyne,* a submarine depot ship in Devonport, the crew lined the quarterdeck and removed their caps as the Officer of the Day tipped the remnants of the rum issue over the side into the harbour.

In lieu of the rum, ratings were issued daily at 1200 with three cans of beer (usually Courage Export), ostensibly to be drunk during dinner hour. However, many ratings kept one or two vans in their lockers for later consumption. The cans were made of light aluminium and could easily be flattened, stored and landed for recycling. Senior ratings had their own bar and could imbibe in three small measures of spirits or three glasses of beer.

Situated up for'd next to the petty officer's recreation space, the girls' mess was reached by a wide steel stairway leading down from the upper deck. This was home to twelve girl ratings, aged between nineteen and twenty-one. In charge of them was Sadie Thompson, a tall, twenty-three year-old buxom, two-badge Petty Officer.

The mess was quite spacious. A well-scrubbed wooden table occupied centre stage, resting on a pusser's blue carpet. (Everything belonging to the navy is referred to as being 'pusser'.) Framed paintings of local scenery on the bulkheads painted a pleasant, pastel yellow, rested between a forty-inch television set. Under this was a highly polished oaken cabinet containing a DVD and an assortment of discs that gave the place a somewhat homely appearance. Side lights, pale green lampshades, complete with matching tassels added a touch of femininity. Three sides of the room were lined with settees upholstered in brown leather, and near the door was a bulky fridge. The sleeping quarters accessed via a side door, consisted of bunk beds covered with white duvets, tall shiny metal lockers together with an en-suite bathroom and toilet, referred to as the 'heads.'

'Guess what girls,' gushed Lottie placing the box on the table. 'I overheard the captain tell number one, that after the sea trials, we won't be going anywhere for the time being.' As she spoke the corners of her saucer-like pale blue eyes, wrinkled in to a wide grin. 'Maybe we'll be given some more leave.'

'And pigs might fly,' remarked Radar Operator Diana James, an extremely attractive brunette with a well-developed figure. Several ratings, senior and junior had tried their luck with her. So far she had managed to reject their advances, saying she was 'saving herself.' A suspicion eventually circulated on the lower deck that she might be a lesbian. A suspicion that would be eventually prove to be unfounded.

'Don't be so pessimistic, Di,' Lottie replied. 'From what I heard, it could be sooner than you think.'

At that moment Logistics Assistant Jilly Howard came into the mess. 'So much for the "no touch" rule,' she sarcastically remarked as she poured out a mug of tea from a bulky, aluminium teapot. 'That randy, sod Tosher White, pinched me bum on the way here. When I turned around he just grinned and gave me one of his innocent looks.'

'Serves you right,' replied Lottie, sitting down and opening a can of beer and licking the froth, 'you're always egging him on. Remember what Sadie told us. The lads are only human, so don't encourage them.'

The girls' mess was segregated from the rest of the crew, and a 'No Touch' rule for either sex was laid down in the ship's standing orders. Anyone found guilty of breaking this rule was usually dismissed from the ship. However, once ashore things changed. In most foreign ports, the crew had all night leave and liaisons were inevitable.

'Oh well,' sighed Jilly, reaching for a can of beer, 'as Shakespeare wrote, "love laughs at locksmiths". '

'Be careful some lecherous bugger doesn't discover where you keep your key, then,' said Medical Assistant Susan Hughes. As she spoke, her eggshell blue eyes set in a round, pleasant face broke into a salacious smile.

By this time the girls most were sat down, eating their dinner or relaxing on the settee, smoking while watching a rerun of *Strictly Come Dancing* on the TV.

'That Anton Du Beck is essence,' Lottie sighed girlishly. 'And those tight trousers her wears, well, I ask you,' she added coyly.

'I suppose the sequined dress that Flavia whatshername has nearly got on accounts for the bulge between his legs,' Jilly remarked, wiping her mouth with a serviette.

The last girl to enter was Communications Technician Kate Harrison who had just come off duty. She was a twenty-year-old petite, dark-haired girl with clear-cut, attractive features. Normally, she was lively and very talkative. Today, however, she refused a can of beer offered to her by Jilly Howard, and without saying a word, sat down and began toying with her food.

'You're quiet today, love,' Jilly remarked, glancing enquiringly across the table at Kate. 'You look a bit peaky. Are you feeling all right?'

'I'm OK,' Kate answered wearily. 'Just a bit tired, that's all.'

'Are you sure?' enquired Jilly, 'it's just that . . .'

'I told you,' cried Kate, angrily placing her fork onto her plate and standing up. 'I'm all right.' She then hurried out of the mess into the sleeping quarters. She flung herself down on her bunk and stared up at the underside of the mattress above her. No, she told herself, biting her lower lip, I'm not all right.

Her period was overdue by a few days. Normally she would feel discomfort in her lower abdomen. So far this hadn't happened, and she was worried to death. The thought of being pregnant sent shivers of fear running through her. Like all the female ratings, Kate was well aware of the consequences of falling pregnant. After being downgraded P3P (a non-drafting medical category), she would be discharged ashore to Portsmouth then granted maternity leave. During this time she could choose to leave the service or take a maximum of one-year maternity leave before re-joining the navy. If the worst came to the worst, Kate knew instinctively she couldn't face leaving her baby and returning to the navy.

Kate lived with her parents in Bridlington. She closed her eyes, and remembered the warnings her parents had given her when she told them she wanted to join the navy. Years ago, Henry, her father, a tall, forty-four year-old balding man, had been a purser in the merchant navy.

'I hope you know what you're doing, lass,' he had said cautiously. 'We had women on board when I was at sea, and I saw what went on. Remember, it's a man's world you're going into so be bloody careful. Nature being what it is,' he added guardedly, 'contact with the sailors is unavoidable and at sea, well . . .' He paused and shook his head, and looking sternly at Kate, went on. 'Anything can happen.'

Kate's mother, Hilda, a short, fair-haired woman, was ardent churchgoer. Remembering that Kate had been conceived on board one of her husband's ships, she gave her warning stare, and said, 'if you get pregnant don't come running home to me. I know what sailors are like.'

For the umpteenth time Kate regretted herself for allowing her boyfriend, Peter Walker, to make love to her. It happened on the last night before the ship left Barbados. Peter was a Leading Physical Trainer, nicked named 'Clubs' by the crew. He was tall, with a good physique, and clear brown eyes that creased up at each corner every time he smiled. Their relationship began in Portsmouth a few weeks before the ship sailed for the Caribbean. Kate sensed he wanted sex but managed to console him with a series of heavy petting. Not that she was a prude. She had lost her virginity when she was fifteen, in a flurry of gasps and groping hands, behind the toilets at school. The whole thing was an anti-climax that left her feeling dirty and disappointed. But now, after meeting Peter, she had developed feelings she never knew before. At sea, their so-called courtship became frustratingly intolerable. A quick kiss in the 'heads' and a few lovelorn glances was all they could safely manage.

When they went ashore in Barbados, she instinctively knew what would happen. Darkness had fallen, and overhead, a full moon was surrounded by a panoply of twinkling stars. From a winding ribbon of a white beach edged with clusters of lazy palm trees stretched a placid dark sea glistening in the moonlight. Kate remembered thinking it looked like a romantic scene from a travel poster. Walking hand in hand their feet sank into the warm sand. Peter was dressed in a loose open necked white shirt, dark slacks and trainers. She wore a short, MacDonald tartan button down skirt pink blouse and flat-soled shoes. A perfect dark spot under a group of overhanging palm trees provided seclusion from a few other couples strolling nearby. With undue haste, borne out of weeks of frustration, their arms went around one another, and when they kissed she thought her lips would bruise. Her skirt had risen almost to her waist and she felt Peter's hand tremble as he removed her flimsy thong. She in turn, hastily undid his trouser belt and carefully unzipped him. In a matter of minutes they were practically naked. She remembered a feeling of sheer ecstasy as Peter, breathing heavily, eased himself on top of her and nervously thrust his penis into her soaking wet vagina. In a matter of seconds, passion overrode performance, as they both climaxed together. Shortly afterwards, they made love again slowly with mutual passion. Afterwards, they lay in each other's arms silent and satisfied, feeling the warm breeze caress their faces. An hour later, fully dressed and hand in hand, they returned to the ship.

With a worried sigh Kate decided not to tell Peter her period was overdue. Who knows, she told herself, it could be a false alarm.

CHAPTER FIVE

Hailey was in his cabin sitting at his desk flicking through the signal log. The time was shortly after 1400. After knocking on the door, Noble came in and removed his cap. With a tired sigh Hailey looked up and sat back in his chair.

'Do sit down, Number One,' he said, leaning forward and placing both hands flat on his desk. 'I've received a phone call from Captain Storey. He wants to see me again the morning. He sounded rather urgent so I expect we'll know what the future holds for us then. When I return, I propose to hold a heads of department meeting in my cabin. I'd be grateful if you'd let them know.'

'Very good, sir,' Noble replied. 'Any guesses as to where we might be going?' he added with rueful smile.

Hailey shook his head and wearily replied, 'Your guess is as good as mine.'

Noble stood up, put on his cap and left.

Situated on the port side, two decks below the bridge, the wardroom was well furnished with e comfortable looking brown leather armchairs, side settees and a few small well-polished wooden tables. A dark blue carpet, embossed with tiny gold anchors covered the deck and in the middle, a long oaken table shone from under six sets of stud lighting. A forty inch television was secured to the port bulkhead which, like the rest was painted a standard pale cream. A CD and DVD player rested on a small, oaken table. Close by was a mail rack, a cabinet containing an assortment of keys, and a table on which rested several officers' caps. At the far end was a well-stocked bar behind which hung a coloured portrait of an elderly Queen Elizabeth and Duke of Edinburgh. Next to this was a door leading into a galley. Like all modern warships, there were no portholes and air generators provided ventilation.

Lunch had finished, and many of the officers stood around in groups smoking and drinking coffee. Everyone had changed out of civilian clothes into their daily working rig. This consisted of black trousers and shoes, with white shirt and tie worn under a dark, navy blue jersey with the insignia of rank on each shoulder. The gentle hub of the generator filled the air and the atmosphere was warm and alive with animated discussion.

'My guess is after our little jaunt in the Caribbean, we'll stay in Pompey for a while, what say you Liz, any word from above?' The well-modulated plummy voice belonged to Lieutenant Commander Bob Henderson, the ships Principal Warfare Officer. His six feet frame, dark wiry hair greying slightly at each temple, hovered over the petite figure of Lieutenant Elizabeth Hall. Liz was standing nearby, next to Lieutenant Commander Shirley Mannering, a tall, fair-haired Warfare Specialist Officer.

'Sorry to disappoint you, Bob,' Liz replied, her soft violet eyes, staring directly into his, 'but I'm only the captain's secretary, and as such I'm not privy to his private thoughts.' She paused and with an all-knowing expression, added, 'By the way, how is your wife and family?'

'Fine, thank you,' Bob answered, taken aback at her question, 'I do believe you're from York. How is that fine old cathedral?'

'Still standing,' Liz answered with a touch of sarcasm. 'Now, if you'll excuse us, Shirley and I have something private to discuss.'

'Of course,' Bob replied, with a condescending air, 'girl talk I suppose,' and walked away to join a group of officers.

'What was all that verbal sparring about, Liz?' Shirley asked giving her friend a searching look. 'Don't tell me he was . . .'

Liz gave a short, throaty laugh. 'Not really,' Liz replied, lying to herself, 'anyway, he's married with two children.'

'The married ones are always the worst,' said Shirley as they accepted a cup of tea from a female steward.

Shirley was twenty-six, five feet plus, short brown hair and attractive pale blue eyes. Her sparkling, intelligent grey eyes offset her plain, but well-formed- features and slightly overweight frame. She and Liz had a cabin next to one another and over the past months they had become firm friends.

Liz was two years younger than Shirley. Barefooted she stood five-feet-five, with a full figure. After obtaining a Science degree at York University, she took a sabbatical and against her parent's wishes, declined a teaching post and along with Charles, her boyfriend and fellow graduate, toured Europe. This whetted her appetite for travel. Liz and Charles parted ways and she joined the navy. *Dawlish* was her first ship. As secretary to the captain, she was privy to many secret documents; a task that gave her immense satisfaction.

With a sly smile, Shirley answered, 'Many of the other officers are married but it doesn't stop some of them making the odd suggestive remark.'

'I suppose we bring out the beast in them,' grinned Liz, 'some,' she added, glancing accusingly across at Henderson, 'more than others.'

Since joining the ship six months ago, Liz had tried as best she could to avoid Henderson, but on a ship the size of *Dawlish*, this was virtually impossible. Not that there was any ill feeling between them, on the contrary, she was attracted to his good looks and physical presence. Whenever they did meet, she always felt a tingle of excitement run through her. Anyway, she told herself, the 'no touch' rule applied equally to officers as well as the rest of the crew.

Henderson finished his drink and joined a group of five officers who were laughing and talking while sipping tea.

'Had a good leave, sir?' enquired Gooding. As he spoke his small, grey eyes broke into a weak smile.

'Yes, thank you, Pilot,' Henderson replied, looking around at their faces. 'You lot seemed to have enjoyed yourselves.'

'I say, sir, any news about what we'll be doing now that the defects have been sorted?' The speaker who asked was a Lieutenant John O'Grady, the ship's communication officer.

'Personally I hope we're here for a while, sir,' said Midshipman Damian Parker-Smith, a tall, lean young man with a mop of untidy dark hair.

'You see, sir, that's because he's in love,' added Midshipman Geoffrey Dunlop, glancing at Henderson while digging Parker-Smith with his elbow. 'Apparently he met this popsy in Liverpool and . . .'

'Oh do shut up, Dunners,' Parker-Smith interrupted, feeling his cheeks redden, 'I told you that in confidence.'

'My guess is we'll be off to sea sooner than we think,' added Assistant Engineer Lieutenant Richard (Dicky) Vellacott, a stocky, dark-haired, twenty-four year-old Cornishman.

Henderson, smiling benignly, listened patiently to their remarks, then, clearing his throat, said, 'We'll all know soon enough. The captain has an important meeting in the morning, after which I'm sure all will be revealed.'

CHAPTER SIX

A few minutes before 0900 the next morning, Hailey stood outside Captain Storey's office. Feeling an air of anticipation, he quickly cleared his throat, knocked on the door and went in. Janet was standing at a table holding an electric kettle. She turned, smiled at Hailey and in a pleasant voice, said, 'Ah, Commander Hailey. The captain is expecting you, Please go straight in, you're just in time for coffee.'

The captain was sitting hunched up at his leather bound desk studying a white paper marked 'TOP SECRET'. The warm, stuffy atmosphere was made worse by a curling cloud of blue tobacco smoke hovering above the captain's head. In his left hand he held his usual, heavily stained meerschaum pipe emanating a thin trail of tobacco smoke. As Hailey entered he lifted his rheumy grey eyes, leaned back in his chair and impatiently wafted the air with a hand.

'Good morning, Commander,' he said, his voice deep and resonant. With each syllable the jowls of his pale, fleshy face wobbled slightly. 'Do come in and take a seat.'

'Thank you, sir,' Hailey replied sitting down on comfortable leather armchair and placing his briefcase nearby.

At that moment, Janet came in carrying two mugs of coffee. She placed them on the desk and waving her hand in the air, muttered something about the smoke polluting the atmosphere, then left.

'Impudent rascal' grunted, Storey, laying his smouldering pipe in a heavy looking brass ash tray, 'one day, I'll have her sent to sea. Now, I expect you're wondering why I've sent for you again, so I'll come directly to the point. The powers that be have detailed your ship to be the Fleet Ready Escort vessel.'

Hailey wasn't overly surprised. He sat back in his chair and crossed his legs and replied, 'I was half expecting you to say this, sir. I know that

37

Daring, the navy's ultra-modern destroyer, is due to sail to the Falklands, and what few warships that remain are either in refit or scattered around the globe on patrol duty.'

'Yes indeed,' the captain replied, furrowing his brow. He picked up his pipe, sat back in his chair and took a puff, sending an inevitable cloud of pale blue smoke bellowing around his face. He removed his pipe and continued, his voice stern but calm. 'This is the drill. After your sea trials you are to be on short notice for deployment anywhere in the world. As I mentioned during our previous meeting you are to be fully stored with food, fuel and ammunition.'

'I take it, short notice means twenty-four hours' notice, sir?' Hailey asked cautiously.

'That's correct,' Storey answered firmly. 'This should give you ample time to flash up your engines.' The captain paused, picked up his pipe, took a puff then continued. 'In case of emergencies, no long leave is to be given. Each rating must report their mobile telephone number to the Master-at-Arms. This includes the home telephone numbers for those who live locally. Anyone going ashore who hasn't a mobile phone is to let the QM know where he or she is going. Your number one can deal with the officers. Having recently returned from the Caribbean, your crew should be up to date with their vaccinations. Any questions?'

'No, sir,' Hailey confidently replied. 'I anticipated hearing something like this and I'll be convening a heads of department meeting as soon as I return to the ship.'

'When will you sail for sea trials?' the captain asked knocking the drum of his pipe into the ashtray. In doing so he sent a thin trail of tiny sparks and smoke into the air.

Stroking his chin pensively, Hailey answered, 'on the twenty-second, sir, two days after the port watch returns from leave.'

The captain heaved his burly frame up from his chair, signifying the meeting was over. Hailey did likewise.

'That's about it then,' Storey said as they shook hands. 'Let me know if any problems arise from the trials.'

'Very good, sir,' Hailey replied, he then picked up his briefcase and left the room.

Hailey returned to the ship at 1200. Waiting near the top of the gangway was the First Lieutenant, PO Jack Whitton and Bud Abbott. Returning their salutes, he glanced at Noble and said, 'meeting of heads of departments in my cabin at 1400, Number One.' Without waiting for a reply he made his way to his cabin. As he did so, 'Secure. Hands to dinner,' came over the tannoy.

Shortly before 1400, eight officers, led by Bob Henderson, entered Hailey's cabin. Behind him came his assistant, Lieutenant Peter, 'Tug' Wilson, a tall, dark-haired officer. In a matter of minutes they had settled down in the chairs provided by the wardroom steward.

'Good afternoon, everyone,' Hailey said, looking at the expectant expression on their faces, which, over the past year, he had come to know as well as his own. 'I'm sure you are all eager to know why I've asked you here, so here goes.' For the next twenty minutes, everyone listened intently as Hailey in a clear concise voice, recounted his meeting with Captain Storey. 'Now I'm sure you've got a few things you'd like to ask,' he said, lowering himself behind his desk.

'What time will we sail on the twenty-second, sir?' asked Henderson, his keen brown eyes firmly focussed on Hailey.

'Zero eight hundred, Bob,' Hailey replied, 'Special sea duty men will be required at zero seven hundred,' he added glancing sharply at Noble.

Supply Officer, Lieutenant Commander Martin Rogers, a medium sized, fair-haired officer, frowned, 'If we're not sure when we'll be needed, sir,' he said in a deep resonant voice, 'how much food should I order?'

'I can't answer that,' Hailey replied pursing his lips, 'but I suggest you order the maximum of everything and act accordingly.'

'I take it my marines will be practising deck landings from the helicopter again, sir?' Asked Lieutenant John Somersby, a heavily tanned twenty-two year-old officer, giving Flight Commander Jerry Ashcroft, a quick enquiring glance. Ashcroft was thirty-four. After passing out from Greenwich College he volunteered for the Fleet Air. He saw active service during the Falkland War on board HMS *Illustrious* and was now a senior helicopter pilot.

'Indeed, you will, Johnny,' Hailey answered. He then noticed Ashcroft's dark blue eyes staring directly at him and said, 'Any problems with the Lynx, Jerry?'

'No, sir,' Ashcroft replied confidently, 'the beast had a complete overall at Lee-on-Solent.'

'What about your department, Norman?' Hailey asked, looking enquiringly at Engineer Lieutenant Commander Bosley, a small, thirty-five year-old officer with a pale complexion.

Bosley had obtained a First in nautical engineering at Oxford, and against his father's wishes for him to join the family law firm in Leeds, joined the navy. Bosley natural talent for engines soon gained him promotion. *Dawlish* was his third ship. The engine spaces with their gas turbines, electrical motor, massive gear boxes, were a mechanical wonderland in which he felt perfectly at home. He likened the ship to the human body with the bridge it's brain, the engine room its heart and the diesel oil the ship's life blood.

'My Rolls-Royce Spey engines will be ready whenever you want them, won't they Dicky,' he replied, running a hand through his thick dark brown wiry hair while glancing at Vellacott.

'Yes, sir,' Vellacott answered with a distinct Cornish accent, 'the chief stoker and his team have been practising regular drills and are top line.'

'I don't doubt it for a minute,' Hailey replied, lighting a cigarette and smiling warmly. 'Now, Doc,' he went on looking at Surgeon Lieutenant Glyn Smyth, a tall, fresh-faced doctor with inquisitive grey eyes. 'How is your department, 'all the jabs up to date?'

'Yes, sir,' replied Smyth, smiling, 'and I've sharpened up the scalpels!'

'What about you Pilot, everything in order?' Hailey. His question was directed at Gooding.

'All in order, sir,' Gooding replied, 'the Sat Nav has been tested and is in full working order. I've even got charts of most parts of the world in case of problems.' (SatNav, short for Satellite Navigation, is a computerised navigating system used throughout the navy.)

'Well, that's about it, gentlemen,' said Hailey, standing up. 'Pass the word to your respective staffs. If and when I know more about a possible mission, I'll let you know ASAP. Now please carry on.'

Theories about where *Dawlish* might be sent spread around the ship like wildfire. Even the officers wondered what might happen

'Quite frankly, Number One,' Hailey remarked, 'my guess is the eastern meddy.' The time was 1600 and 'secure' had just been piped. They were in Hailey's cabin, ostensibly, discussing the ship's future destination. A copy of *The Times* lay open in front of Hailey.

'What makes you think that, sir?' Noble asked.

'According to the latest reports,' Hailey replied, tapping the newspaper, 'Syria's president Bashar al-Assad's government forces are being forced on the defensive. Apparently, the rebels are very well armed and are at the gates of Damascus.'

'And I take it Russia is continuing to give aid to Assad supplying him with guns and so on?' Noble asked, relaxing back in his chair.

That's right,' answered Hailey. 'As you know, Obama and Cameron are reluctant to send arms to the rebels as it is thought Al Qaeda has infiltrated the government forces.' Hailey paused and gave a worrying frown, and continued, 'Remember what happened when we supplied the Mudjahadeen with weapons to fight the Russians in 1980?'

'Indeed, sir,' replied Noble. 'When the Mudjahadeen became Al Qaeda, the rockets and small arms were used on us. But what makes you think we'll be involved?'

'Rumour has it,' answered Hailey, 'that weapons are being shipped from private companies to the port of Al Ghaydah in Yemen, which, as you know, is an Al Qaeda stronghold.'

'Ah, I see what you mean, sir,' said Noble, nodding his head in tacit agreement. 'That's where you think we'll come in,' He paused then, with a worried sigh, went on, 'But, surely, sir, that'll cause a diplomatic incident with Yemen.'

'I doubt it,' Hailey replied confidently. 'I am informed by the powers that be, that Yemen will deny all knowledge, even though it is well known they support the rebels. Mind you, Number One,' Hailey went on, 'it's only guesswork. There are so many hot spots in the world we could be sent, for

41

instance, patrolling the eastern med or helping the Americans off the coast of North Korea.'

'You're right there, sir,' Noble said, stubbing his cigarette out then sitting back in his chair and folding his arms. 'But most of the officers think there'll be some sort of crisis in the Persian Gulf.'

'Well, wherever it's going to be,' Hailey gravely replied, 'we'll have to be ready to go there.'

CHAPTER SEVEN

During the next week, the crew were kept busy ensuring the ship was ready for sea trials. Hector Pascoe, a tall, wiry Chief and his team of air engineers, checked and re-checked the loading systems for arming and disarming the Lynx helicopter. Assistant Weapons Officer, Lieutenant Harry Thomas and his staff made sure the four deadly Sea Wolf, anti-air missiles, the anti-ship Harpoon rockets and the two ant-submarine torpedoes were in full working order. Under the eagle eyes of Chief Gunnery Instructor Digger Barnes, his men practised drills on the 4.5 inch Mk8 gun, the two mini guns and the general purpose 30mm machine gun. Digger's brawny bull-neck and muscular physique gave him the daunting appearance of an all-in wrestler. Needless to say nobody argued with him.

In the constantly darkened Operations Room, situated directly below the bridge, Bob Henderson was leaning over his personal orange-glowing radar screen. Glancing around he smiled confidently, noticing the communication, radar and weapons electrical ratings were engrossed checking their instruments.

The Ops Room was the tactical nerve centre of the ship. It is from here that Henderson will, if necessary, order, 'Secure for action. Assume Weapon State Monty.' The WE ratings operating their computers would then load all weapons including the Sea Wolf missiles. The order, 'Weapons State Golf' would then be received meaning the weapons were ready to be activated. As a young boy, Henderson he recalled listening to his father, a retired admiral who was gunnery officer in World War Two, talk about gunnery practice.

'What with all your technology,' his father would say, puffing gently on his old briar pipe, 'you people have it easy. In my day, I had to spend hours up in the director platform, scanning the horizon with a pair of binoculars, searching for the enemy. Now,' he went on, 'a powerful long range radar does the job for you.'

'And a damn sight more accurately,' Henderson had tactfully replied.
On Friday 19 July, port watch returned from leave.

'I'm afraid one of the radar operators is sick on shore with a broken
leg,' Noble said, standing in front of Hailey's desk. 'The Master-at-Arms
tells me he' won't be fit for duty for at least a month. In view of the
uncertainty of our movements, I think we should apply to barracks for his
relief as soon as possible.'

'I agree, Number One,' Hailey replied. 'And remember, week-end
leave only for those off duty and they are to give details where they can be
reached, including mobile phone numbers.'

The door of the drafting office in the Royal Naval Barracks in
Portsmouth opened and in came a tall, strikingly handsome, twenty-year-old
rating with well-groomed jet black hair and deep-set, intelligent brown eyes.

The date was Thursday 18 July, the time 0900. Sitting behind a desk
cluttered with paper, was a three-badge regulating petty officer whose
expanding waistline and high-coloured cheeks, were the result of too many
hours spent drinking pints of Bass. Behind the RPO, a female rating sat at a
desk using a computer. She looked up and gave him an appraising smile,
then continued working. Nearby several male ratings were also working at
their computers.

'Communications Radar Operator Ashir Al Hassar, PO. You sent for
me?' the rating said, nervously, wondering if he was in some sort of trouble.

'Yes, I did,' the RPO gruffly replied. With a tired sigh he sat back and
stared inquisitively at the, broad-shouldered figure in front of him with a
swarthy complexion. 'If you don't mind me asking, lad,' the RPO tentatively
remarked, 'you look a bit, err . . . foreign like. Where are you from?'

'Clerkenwell in London, PO,' Ashir replied, adding, 'my parents came
here from Pakistan twenty years ago.'

'And how long have you been in the navy?' The RPO asked, sitting
back in his chair and folding his arms across his protruding waist.

'Eighteen months, PO,' Al Hassar replied. 'I finished my radar course
at HMS *Collingwood,* a year ago.' He didn't add that he found the mastering
complexity of modern technology easy and had come top of his class. At
primary school and later at the local comprehensive he had developed a gift

for mathematics and English, and obtained GCE A levels in both subjects. Almost as an afterthought he added, 'Err . . . where am I going on draft to?'

'HMS *Dawlish*,' the RPO replied curtly. 'A type 23 frigate. She's tied up alongside Fountain Lake Jetty. Pack your kitbag and take it to the baggage store. After completing your leaving routine, take a short weekend and join her on Sunday,' he added, handing him his drafting card plus tie-on labels for his kit bag.

The RPO's words sent a thrill of excitement running through him. This, he thought, was the chance he had been trained for. He couldn't wait to tell his parents.

'When is she sailing?' Ashir asked nervously.

'Haven't a clue,' the RPO answered sharply. 'It doesn't say anything about that on the draft note. *Dawlish* has recently had a complete overhaul. I see this is your first ship, so if I were you, I'd make sure my tropical kit was up to scratch.'

Two hours later, having completed his leaving routine, Ashir was in his cabin packing his gear. The door opened and in came Slinger Wood, a small, stocky seaman specialist who shared his cabin. The time was just after 1200 and 'Hands to dinner,' had been piped over the barrack's tannoy.

'Don't tell me you've got a draft chit, Ash?' Slinger enquired, lighting a cigarette.

'That's right,' Ashir replied, pulling the chord tight on his kitbag, then closing it with a small padlock. 'HMS *Dawlish*. I join her on Sunday'

Later that afternoon, Ashir collected his draft order and short weekend pass. After supper he met Slinger and several other ratings in the bar.

'A mate of mine, Bud Abbot is on *Dawlish*,' a communication technician remarked, lighting a cigarette. 'He tells me the electrical system on the diesel engines have been overhauled.'

'To hell with the fuckin' engines,' chimed in a small, portly leading cook while wiping froth from his upper lip. 'I hear they're girls on board, so you'd best keep it in your trousers.'

'He won't have any luck,' said another rating, 'they've all got padlocks around their cunts.'

'It's a pity you haven't got one around your filthy mouth,' interrupted an attractive blonde logistics assistant who, unnoticed by the speaker, was standing nearby. After glaring contemptuously at him, she tipped a half full glass of beer over the front of his trousers and casually walked away.

The following morning, Ashir caught the 0900 train from Portsmouth Harbour Station and using his mobile phone, immediately contacted his parents. Doing his best to contain his excitement he told them the news about *Dawlish*. It had been a few months since his last weekend leave and they were overjoyed when he told them he was on his way home.

'Oh, Ashir, my son,' his mother cried, 'It's so good to hear you. Here is your father', she added, trying her best not to cry while passing the telephone to him.

'Come home quickly, Ashir,' his father said eagerly, 'we cannot wait to see you.'

Ashir smiled. It felt good to hear his parents speaking Arabic.

Ashir arrived at Waterloo shortly after 1100. He wore jeans, a blue bomber jacket, an open- necked white shirt and trainers. In his left hand he carried a service issue suitcase containing uniforms and spare clothing. After taking a crowded Northern Line tube to Euston, he caught a Hammersmith and City to Clerkenwell. Emerging from clammy claustrophobic atmosphere of the tube station, he felt the warm July sun fan his face.

It was a short walk to where his parents lived at number seven Briset Street, a small, red-bricked terrace house in a narrow thoroughfare off the busy St John Street. The house, like those on either side, didn't have a garden, only a set of wrought iron railings and gate.

The door opened and he was greeted by his father, a tall, dark-skinned man whose large, black beard almost hid most of his strikingly handsome face. It was evident that his son had inherited his father's looks. The pristine white, long-sleeved, ankle-length cotton dishdasha he wore failed to disguise the portly bulge of his stomach. On his feet was a pair of well-worn leather sandals. Behind him stood a small, stout woman dressed in a black, cotton garment known in as a hijab. This was a baggy, long-sleeved apparel that covered her body from head to toe except for her face. Muslim religion bade her wear the niqab in public, (a combination of the hijab except for it only allowed her eyes to be seen.) Indoors, only her husband and loved ones were allowed gaze upon her full countenance, therefore a headscarf, the same colour as the hijab, covered her head and neck exaggerating the full shape of the face.

Peering round the bulky shape of her husband, she smiled lovingly at her son and lovingly stroked his face.

Hussein and Fatima Al Hassar had come from Pakistan in 1993 and opened a haberdashery shop. They were both Sunnis, differing dramatically from their neighbours, Iran who were mainly Sh'ites. Ashir was born two years later.

The family became regular visitors to the Finsbury Mosque. It was here they listened to the fiery sermons preached by the imposing figure of Mullah, Abu Hamza. Using a metal hooked appliance in place of a right arm, lost while fighting for the Mujahedeen in 1972, the preacher's strident and convincing voice decried the presence of the British and her allies in Iraq and Afghanistan. It was during these meetings that Hussein and his family became highly influenced by Hamza's lectures. They soon became involved in subversive activity aimed against the British Government who they were convinced were the enemies of Islam.

'Ashir,' cried Hussein, placing his arms around his son and drawing him close, 'Salaam Ailaecum.' (Peace be upon you.)

'Ailaecum- a- Salaam,' (And unto you be peace.) Ashir answered, feeling his father's beard scrape his face.

Ashir then broke away from his father allowing Fatima to embrace him.

'Come, Ashir,' she said taking his hand, 'I have prepared your favourite beef stew.'

'That wonderful smell is making my mouth water,' Ashir replied, smiling while sniffing the air. He knew the beef would be halal. (Meat prepared from a cow, slaughtered by opening a vein in it the animal's throat and allowing the blood to drain away.)

'It will make change from having to eat the unclean food of the infidel,' Hussein said, as they entered a small kitchen.

Ashir gave his parents an affectionate smile then went upstairs. His room hadn't changed since he last saw it four months ago. The same red lampshade hung from a low ceiling, an unlit gas fire, a multi-coloured carpet covered the floor and on the pale yellow walls hung pictures of Allah. A

47

narrow, wooden framed bed on which lay a silk coverlet embroidered with a red sickle moon lay in the middle. Close by was a small bedside table on which rested a copy of the Koran bound in red leather, the same colour of the Prophet's beard. Opposite this was a wardrobe and long mirror. Then came a solitary, high-backed wooden chair resting next to a small chest of drawers. Ashir slowly walked to the window, parted the net and looked out onto a backyard where as a boy he had played games. He turned, looked around and smiled nostalgically, everything he saw were old friends welcoming him home.

After removing all his clothes he picked up his toilet bag and went to the bathroom. He carefully washed his body and cleaned his teeth and rinsed his mouth in purification and returned to his room. From a drawer he took out a pristine white, neatly folded dishdasha. With a feeling of pride he slipped it over his head allowing it to fall just below his ankles. He gave a contented sigh feeling the how cool the plain cotton material felt on his skin. He then removed a white silk prayer mat and spread it on the floor facing where he estimated Mecca would be and knelt down, his forehead touching the carpet.

The next ten minutes was devoted to silent prayers to Allah, asking forgiveness for mixing with the infidels and adopting their customs and way of life. He ended by asking that his mission, whatever it was would be successful. He then stood up, put on a pair of goatskin slippers and looked into the mirror realising because of the close-knit community on board a ship, this would be the last time he would wear traditional Arabic clothes. He muttered 'Allah Akbar', (God is good) and left the room.

A few minutes later, he and his parents were sat at a table in a kitchen equipped with the latest gas cooker, washing machine, spin dryer and microwave. Ashir finished his meal and used a piece of bread to mop up the remaining gravy from his plate. Reaching across the table, he poured a glass of water from a jug, and with a satisfied sigh, sat back in his chair. Sitting opposite him, Hussein sipped a cup of tea, a serious expression etched on his face. Fatima stood with her back washing pots and pans in a stainless steel sink.

'Now, Father,' Ashir said, wiping his mouth on a small serviette. 'What is this special task Allah has me?'

'Before I tell you,' Hussein replied gravely, 'are you still prepared to do what is necessary?'

With a defiant expression in his eyes, Ashir stared at his father and replied, 'Yes, I am.'

'May Muhammad, 'peace be upon him,' muttered Hussein, 'bless you.' He paused again then continued, 'As you know, it took special dispensations from the Hikam to allow you to adopt all the habits and customs of the infidel in order to convince them that you were one of them.' (Hikam, which was also known by its Arabic name of Harakat Isiah Shabaab, was a secret, fanatical movement dedicated to establishing an Islamic state in Britain.)

'I understand, Father,' Ashir replied, 'although I have managed to do this, I hate it. But Allah has deemed it so, and I must obey.'

From the age of ten, Ashir's primary school teacher, proselytised in glowing terms, saying that dying for Allah would bring immortality to true believers of Islam. When he was older the same teacher told him when he died he would dine in Paradise on the finest foods and indulge himself with forty beautiful virgins. It was this intoxicating mix of pleasure and religion that convinced Ashir where his future lay. The fiery lectures of Abu Hamza convinced him and several other young men that the teachings of the Koran allowed them a dispensation from Allah to kill the infidel. With Ashir's radicalisation complete, all that was needed was a plan for him to carry out Allah's will.

At one of the secret meetings it was Abdul Ali Shahim, the local leader of Hakim, that suggested Ashir join the Royal Navy. Abdul was at tall, thin-faced man with a sallow complexion and shifty brown eyes, set in a round, fleshy sallow face. He had recently been released from Belmont Prison after serving five years for inciting riots and aiding and abetting young men to go to Iraq join Al Qaeda. Abdul was revered by his followers who contrived to keep his whereabouts unknown to the authorities.

'He's a clever boy and could easily blend in with the sailors and adopt the infidel's customs,' said Abdul, looking sternly, first at Hussein then Ashir. 'Especially if he's sent to a warship.'

Hussein stood up and placed his hand on Ashir's left shoulder. 'There is something I have to give you, Ashir', he said grimly. He gave Fatima a serious glance then left the room and went upstairs.

'We are very proud of you, Ashir,' Fatima said, her eyes moistening as she laid her hand tenderly on Ashir's shoulder. 'And we know Allah will be pleased with what you are going to do.'

'Whatever it is, Mother,' Ashir replied, 'rest assured I will do it and honour you both.'

Hussein returned to the kitchen, a gleam of defiance in both his eyes. Fatima and Ashir immediately saw he was carrying a small brown cardboard shoebox. They watched as he sat own and slowly placed it on the table. Hussein opened the lid and took out a bulky parcel sealed in brown, waterproof paper.

Ashir stared, wide-eyed at the package, his heart beating a cadence in his chest. 'Please, father,' he pleaded, 'tell me what my task is.'

'This, my son.' Hussein replied, gently tapping the larger of the packages with a hand, 'contains Trysin. It is an explosive twice as deadly as Semtex. There is also six detonators, each with a timing device.' He paused and with a steely glint in his deep-set dark eyes, gently passed the package containing Trysin across to Ashir. 'Conceal it carefully, my son, then, at a moment of your choosing, blow up your ship and send the infidels to hell. You will die and as he Koran teaches us, you will become a Shahid, a martyr, and dwell in Allah's Paradise forever. However, my son,' he paused, allowing the severity of his words to register with Ashir. 'Some time after your ship has sailed, text me and say. "I am keeping well. Love Ashir." That will tell me all is well. If there is a problem, write, "Missing you both. Love Ashir." Understand, my son?'

'Yes, Father,' Ashir nervously replied. 'Perfectly clear.'

CHAPTER EIGHT

Promptly at 0800 on Monday 22 July, *Dawlish*'s crew began preparing to leave harbour. The Union Jack flying from her bow caught the offshore breeze and billowed slightly as if bidding farewell to Portsmouth, albeit only for a few days. On the foc'sle, a cable party of ten ratings, including three girls, glanced expectantly up at the bridge. All of them wore Number 4 working rig. This consisted of long-sleeved blue shirts, blue trousers, steaming boots and caps with chinstraps down. In addition each one carried a knife and marlinspike in a leather scabbard.

Hailey was on the bridge sitting in his chair watching the activity on the fo'c'sle. In front of him, was an array of dials and screens that made up the bridge integrated computer system. Behind him Gooding was checking charts in the pilothouse. Next to him, his runner, Able Seaman Sandy Powell, waited patiently for orders. Nearby, Quartermaster Seaman Pete Price, stood pensively by the ship's tannoy. Close by Jock Forbes, was sat at the console. All personnel wore dark blue trousers and matching pullovers with shoulder epaulettes denoting their ranks.

'Prepare to single up.' Hailey shouted. A few minutes later he added, 'Let go the head rope,' then, peering through one of the bridge's nine, four-inch, Perspex windows, he watched as Midshipman Peter Dunlop passed the order to Chief, 'Harry' Lyme.

'Look lively, there,' yelled Harry as he watched the cable party along with Seamen Specialists Jackie Parker and Betty Morgan, haul inboard the deceptively strong dark blue nylon hawsers. Using a quick figure of eight pattern, they expertly secured them around the twin bollards.

'Head rope gone, sir,' Dunlop shouted down his intercom while glancing apprehensively up at the bridge.

'Head rope clear, sir' reported Lyme, peering over the guard rail.

'Fenders in,' Noble shouted, moving onto the port wing. Using the bridge telephone he contacted Sub Lieutenant Julian Morris, and ordered his flight deck party to haul in their ropes. A few minutes later came the officers' sharp reply. 'All clear aft, sir.'

'Hands to Cruising stations, Number One.' said Hailey glancing at Noble.

'Very good, sir,' Noble replied. Seconds later the strident voice of Pete Price echoed over the tannoy conveying the order around the ship.

'Set Lever 40, Chief,' said Hailey, his voice clear and calm. Forbes immediately moved a small lever to the appropriate mark on the console. This sent an electrical signal to control the hydraulic pumps that turned the rudder.

'Half ahead both,' ordered Hailey.

In the engine room, Bosley gave a cursory nod to Vellacott, who pressed a large white button next to the speed indicator. Straightaway the combined diesel-electric and gas (CODLAG) system started. The whine of four Paxman Valenta 12CM diesel generators combined with the two Rolls-Royce Spey engines came alive, gradually surging to 40 per cent of their combined 11,000 horsepower.

Almost immediately, the 4000 ton frigate moved imperceptibly away from the quayside. The movement disturbed a row of seagulls perched high above on the yardarm, flapping their wings, they squawked violently and flew away.

The sea was a calm, gunmetal grey and high above a few scattered cotton wool clouds flitted across the pale blue sky. Away to port the high-rise buildings of Gosport formed a backdrop to the ferry terminus and the masts of the town's marina. Hailey watched the Gosport ferryboat, painted an eye-catching pale cream and green, make its way across the harbour. Some distance behind, the Isle of Wight Ferry began to slow down as it approached the terminus adjacent to Portsmouth Harbour Station. Hailey's attention was immediately drawn to the bulky shape of a cross-channel Brittany cruise liner passing within two hundred yards on *Dawlish*'s port quarter.

'Damn things are a bloody nuisance,' Hailey muttered impatiently. 'The sooner we clear the harbour the better.'

'Makes you wonder what the harbour was like packed with battleships, aircraft carriers and God knows what, during the war, eh sir?' Noble said, ponderously shaking his head.

'You sound like my father,' Hailey replied. 'He commanded a destroyer in the last war and was forever telling me stories of near misses as they left port due to those very ships you mentioned.'

On the quarterdeck, Able Seaman Sandy Powell looked away to port at one of Portsmouth's main attractions - a 170 metre tower with a sweeping metal arc resembling a billowing ship's spinnaker, rising spectacularly from Gunwharf Quays. Years ago this area was HMS *Sultan*, a base for minesweepers and a training establishment for marine engineers. Now it was an attractive modern shopping centre with a variety of boutiques and restaurants.

Sandy turned to his oppo, Shady Lane, and said, 'To think many people in Pompey objected to the spinnaker, thinking it was too expensive and would spoil the city's skyline. Now, it's one of the first places visitors flock to see."

Just then Harry Tate abruptly interrupted them. 'Stop nattering you two,' he growled, 'and make sure those fenders are secure.'

With the dockyard fifty yards on her port side, *Dawlish* gradually increased speed.

Nelson's flagship, HMS *Victory*, flying her famous Trafalgar signals from her yardarms, jutted defiantly in the air behind Semaphore Towers.

'Attention on the upper deck, face to port,' was piped.

Straightaway the ratings, marines and officers fallen in on the flight deck and fo'c'sle snapped to attention. The officers then saluted.

Hailey and Noble had already moved to port wing. Feeling the prying eyes of Rear Admiral Fearnley on them, he and Noble also stood to attention and saluted. 'This is the bit I always hate,' Hailey muttered from the side of his mouth. 'It make me feel like a fish in a bowl.'

'At least the old bugger didn't pick up anything, sir,' Noble replied.

'Signal from tower, sir,' said Communications Officer Pincher Martin, 'message reads, "thank you, carry on".'

Dawlish slowly gathered speed. On her starboard side what used to be HMS *Dolphin,* the navy's main submarine base, but was now a museum, could be clearly seen. Close behind, the slate grey roofs of the old naval hospital at Haslar shone in the early morning sun. On the opposite side, Southsea, with its fairground, pier, grassy parks and war memorial slowly faded way as *Dawlish* cruised past Fort Blockhouse, built in the last century as protection against French.

'That ugly looking thing were a battery in 1918,' remarked Buck Taylor, a tall, ruddy-faced, three-badge Leading Seaman from Portsmouth. 'Now it's a leisure centre owned by the fuckin' council. My Uncle Jack works there as a guide.' Taylor was in the group fallen in on the flight deck. Jean Rochester, overheard him and quickly turned around. As she did so, the shoulder-length, blonde pony-tail hanging from under her cap swished uncontrollably in the air.

'Sounds like he's got a good number,' she said, stifling a yawn, 'maybe when I leave the Andrew your dear uncle could get me a job as a guide.'

'A bloody girl guide most like,' Taylor replied sarcastically.

The tannoy booming, 'special sea duty men fall out,' obliterated Jean's obscene reply.

Meanwhile, in the hangar, Hector Pascoe, was overseeing his small staff of mechanics as they worked on the Lynx helicopter. On the flight deck twelve marines, stripped to the waist, were being put through a series of arduous calisthenics by Leading PTI Peter Walker.

Betty Morgan, suddenly stopped using her squeegee to clean the deck and nudged her friend, Jean Rochester, and said, 'that big boot neck with ginger hair could practice push-ups on me anytime.'

'After you with him,' Jean replied with a sexy sigh.

'Pack it in, you two,' shouted PO 'Dusty' Miller, 'or you'll be working during the dog-watches'.

Leading Medical Assistant Dixie Dean, opened the sickbay door and began seeing 'the dead, the dying and lead-swingers,' as he called sick parade. Nearby, Susan Hughes, sat at a desk working her computer

Wally Hardman, a portly, overweight chief cook and his team of chefs were labouring in the heat of the main galley preparing dinner, cottage pie, covered by layers of mashed potatoes.

In the ships office, Liz Hall concentrated entering lists of stores, ammunition food and medical supplies into her computer. Suddenly, she stopped a look of surprise on her face, 'My goodness, twelve gross of condoms,' she cried glancing indignantly at Supply Officer Lieutenant Commander Martin Rogers. 'Surely we don't need that many, sir!'

Rogers was a tall, fresh-faced officer with a first in English. 'How the dickens should I know,' Rogers testily replied, 'when we were in the Caribbean, I spent most of my time looking for rare species of shells and studying the flora and fauna.'

'Of course, sir,' Liz replied, rolling her eyes, 'I forgot.'

Below one deck, Kate Harrison sat quietly in the Communication Office. Her period still hadn't stated and she was sick with worry and finding it hard to concentrate on her work. Night after night she had agonised what to do if the ship was suddenly placed under sailing orders. If this happened she would be forced to report sick before being sent ashore, probably to the hospital in barracks. The thought of leaving the navy she loved, and in particular Peter Walker, would break her heart. But with a baby to look after, she would have no choice. Thinking about this upset her so much she removed her earphones and stared blankly at the panel.

'Is there a problem, Harrison?' asked Lieutenant O'Grady standing next to her.

O'Grady's strident Irish brogue brought Kate back to reality. 'Err . . . no, sir,' she nervously replied. 'I was just adjusting my headset.'

In the constantly dimmed, windowless Operations Room Bob Henderson was studying his personal radar screen. The Ops Rooms was the nerve centre of the ship. It was here, when at action stations, that Henderson and the captain would fight the ship. The gentle whine of the engines was almost inaudible and the atmosphere, pleasantly warm. One side of the long room was occupied by weapon technicians checking their computers and monitors that controlled the fighting mechanisms throughout the ship. One computer showed the weapon technicians practising loading a Sea Wolf missile (range 1-10 km) and Harpoon launchers. Henderson and his assistant Lieutenant Tug Wilson stood nearby quietly talking. He and Henderson were waiting impatiently for the weapons loading procedure to be completed.

'Bit bloody slow, Tug,' Henderson grunted, 'better have a word with the weapons technicians.'

On the other side of the room facing the weapons technicians, radar and sonar operators sat facing their control panels. Each panel looked similar with a few rows of coloured buttons, small switches and flickering dots representing ships. At sea, each operator was able to scan an area of ninety square miles. Hovering nearby, Chief Petty Officer Spud Murphy watched over proceedings. He wore earphones with a narrow bulbous mouth-piece enabling him to receive or pass on information from those ratings on duty.

Upon entering the Ops Room, Ashir blinked several times. With the exception of the bright orange screens, the room was in darkness.

Before reporting for duty, Henderson had summoned Ashir to his small office next to the Ops Room.

'Stand easy, lad,' Henderson said, 'according to your report, you came top of your class,' he added, glancing at a computer print-out on his desk. 'Well done. I see this is your first ship?'

'Yes, sir,' Ashir replied, nervously shuffling his feet.

'Remember this,' Henderson said, leaning forward and folding his hands. 'Teamwork is essential. On a small ship, everybody depends on everyone else. In a way, it's like a close knit family. Get to know your mess mates and learn from them. If you have any problems, don't hesitate to ask either myself or the chief. Understand?'

'Yes, sir, and thank you,' Ashir had replied before being dismissed.

Murphy met Ashir as he entered the Ops Room and was told he would be sitting next to Diana James.

'She's one of best operators,' he said quietly, 'so pay attention to what she tells you, savy?'

'Yes, thanks, Chief,' Ashir nervously replied.

Diana overheard Murphy's lecture to Ashir. She glanced up and saw a tall dark, six foot plus rating standing behind her.

Earlier, at breakfast, Jilly Howard looked at Diana, and dabbing her mouth with a serviette, said, 'I say Di, have you seen your new radar bod, he looks like Omar Sharif.

Now, watching as Ashir sat down, she thought Jilly's remarks were more than accurate.

'Diana James,' she said, flashing a Colgate smile as they shook hands.

'Ashir Al Hassar,' he replied, feeling how soft and warm her hand felt. He couldn't help but notice her chestnut coloured hair tied in a bun, her clear, porcelain features and large, captivating brown eyes. 'But I'm called Ash.'

Looking curiously at his swarthy features, she asked, 'If you don't mind me asking, Ash, are you English?'

Ashir was used to being asked this and quickly told her his background.

'Your first ship?' Diana enquired.

'Yes,' Ashir replied, switching on his monitor.

'Well, if you need any help, please ask,' Diana answered, doing her best not to stare at him.

Ashir's experience with girls was limited by his religious beliefs. Of course he knew about sex. He had often overheard the groans and sighs coming from his parents' bedroom and knew what was happening. But even though the Koran forbade sex out of marriage, he couldn't help but wonder what it was like. He couldn't help but notice girls in their short skirts and skimpy clothes, walking around town, and feeling aroused. When he had such thoughts he prayed to Allah for forgiveness.

However, during his training he had a run ashore with his mess-mates and ended in a sleazy bar in Southsea. As part of blending in with them, he drank too much, and when a small, plump blonde girl appeared and sat on his knee he pretended not to mind.

'My name's Wanda.' She said seductively. 'What's yours?'

After he told her she began to stroke the back of his head and gently wriggle her bottom. Ashir suddenly felt himself becoming aroused. 'My, you're a big lad,' she cooed in his ear while sliding a hand underneath him and squeezing his penis. 'Come on,' she muttered, 'let's you and me go somewhere.'

Feeling unsteady on his feet and listening to the raucous cat-calls from his mates, Wanda helped him up. After that things became a little hazy. He found himself lying on a grassy park near the waterfront. He remembered feeling Wanda's warm, wet lips on his and feeling her unzip is flies and placing a warm hand on his erect member. Deep down he knew what she was doing was wrong but was too drunk to stop her. His excitement mounted and in a matter of seconds it was all over.

'Don't worry, darling,' Wanda said using a handkerchief to clean him. 'I understand. You lads don't get out much.'

Shortly afterwards, she helped him up and hailed a taxi. She gave him a quick kiss and told the driver to take him to the dockyard. The next morning, despite a gigantic hangover he lied, boasting to his mess-mates of a sexual conquest. But racked with guilt, he silently prayed to Allah for forgiveness, determined that it would not happen again. Nevertheless, he found the close proximity of Diana and the faint smell of her talcum powder somewhat disturbing.

CHAPTER NINE

Thanks to the courtesy of Flannigan the seat of Hailey's chair had a soft, comfortable cushion. From here, Hailey sat observing the sluggish movements of small groups of yachts and dinghies dotted around the narrow waters separating the Hampshire coast from the Isle of Wight. The sky was a cloudless blue and the sun warm and relaxing.

'This weather certainly brings them out, eh Number One?' he said with a wry smile. 'Steer ten degrees to starboard.'

'I bet you wish you were one of them, sir,' Noble jokingly replied.

'Perhaps,' Hailey said, lowering his binoculars. He then unhooked the engine room intercom. A few seconds later the stern voice of Bosley came on the line.

'Ah, Norman, captain here,' Hailey said. 'When we leave the Solent I intend to increase speed to twenty-four knots and test the engines.'

'Twenty-four knots, sir,' Bosley replied, raising his voice slightly, 'is this wise? The last time we went that fast was chasing those drug-runners in the Caribbean. So far we've only reached ten knots and that was as we left harbour.'

'I know that,' Hailey answered impatiently, 'and all being well I also intend to go to our maximum speed.'

'Twenty-eight knots, sir,' Bosley retorted, 'isn't that pushing it a bit considering the engines have just been overhauled?'

'Better to find out now if they're all right than later when God knows where we'll be,' Hailey answered deliberately, 'and don't worry, I'll take responsibility for any damage to your precious engines.'

'Very well, sir,' Bosley replied, shaking his head, 'but on your prospective fourth stripe be it,' and replaced the intercom.

'The old man's taking quite a risk, eh, sir,' remarked Bosley to Vellacott. 'I hope the engines don't break down again'

'So do I,' Vellacott replied, wiping beads of sweat from his brow.

On the bridge Hailey glanced across at Shirley Mannering, and said. 'Please have piped, "The ship will be increasing speed in five minutes. All hands keep clear of the upper deck".'

'Very good, sir,' she replied nodding towards the duty QM who immediately picked up the tannoy and carried out the order.

'Perfect weather for a damn good speed trial, eh, Number One,' Hailey remarked, using a hand to shield his eyes from the glare of the sun.

'Absolutely, sir,' Noble replied, giving him a cautious smile.

Ten minutes later, with the Hampshire coast a thin line on the ship's starboard beam, *Dawlish* increased speed from fifteen to twenty knots. Like a greyhound after its prey, the ship bounded through the relative calm of the dark blue sea. A tide race of white water streaked down either side of the ship as foamy bow waves curled over the fo'c'sle, sending spots of spray splattering against the outside of the bridge windows.

In the Ops Room, Ashir gave Diana a wary look. The large dots on his screen showed the approach of four large ships.

'Better report it to the chief, Ash, and give him the details.' Diana cautioned.

Ashir immediately did as she suggested and told Murphy who immediately informed the First Lieutenant.

'Radar reports four vessels two miles apart, approaching ten miles dead ahead plus a small fleet of yachts. The ships appear to be tankers, sir,' Noble said.

'Thank you, Number One,' replied Hailey, then somewhat glibly added, 'good to know the Ops Room are on their toes.' He then unhooked the engine room intercom and spoke to Bungy Williams. 'Everything all right, Chief?' he asked.

'So far so good, sir,' Williams replied, mopping his sweaty brow with an off-white handkerchief. 'But the engineer officer and Lieutenant Vellacott look a bit pale.'

Hailey gave a short laugh and said, 'I expect he'll become a little paler as I'm increasing speed to twenty-four knots.'

In the large, humid gas turbine generator situated below the funnel, Chief Stoker Patrick Flynn, was carefully watching the thin line silver mercury in the oil gauges slowly rising.

'Don't look so worried, Chief,' said a stoker, noting the concerned expression on the chief's face, 'the old man knows what he's doing.'

The chief shook his head slightly. 'I soddin' 'ope so,' he said, in his sharp, Scouse accent, 'cos if he doesn't, it's back to Pompey.'

Five minutes later the engines were at full capacity, delivering 23,190 kW (32,100 shp). However little vibration was felt. This was due to the quietness of two GEC electric motors driving the engines.

'Radar confirms the vessels are tankers, sir,' Noble said. 'Do you want to reduce speed?'

Using their binoculars, everyone immediately focussed their attention on the oncoming tankers.

'Yes, we better had,' replied Hailey tersely. 'As you say, Number One, maybe their radar might not be as efficient as ours. Reduce speed to twenty knots.'

Almost straightaway the whine of the engines subsided slightly as the ship slowed down.

'Well I'll be damned, sir,' cursed Noble. 'One of the blighters seems to be coming right at us, surely they can see where we are.'

'Steer ten degrees to starboard,' snapped Hailey. 'Her captain should obey the rules of the road and do the same.'

(International Navigation Laws state that two vessels approaching each other must both give way by altering course to starboard).

'That might bring us on a collision course with one of the other three tankers, sir,' warned Shirley Mannering.

'Blast!' snorted Hailey, his binoculars clamped to his eyes. 'The buggers haven't altered course, and they're still coming at us, steady as we go, Number One. Surely they must see us and give way.'

'They don't appear to be doing that, sir,' retorted Noble. 'Their captains must either be blind or drunk.'

'Or both,' Mannering added scornfully.

By this time the four tankers were two miles away; the yellow shell logo clearly visible against their red funnels.

'Jesus Christ, Number One!' Hailey cried, 'what the hell's wrong with them. Give her two short blasts on the foghorn. See if that wakes them up.'

Noble lowered his binoculars and pressed a small button next to the console. Straightaway the sharp sounds of the foghorns rent the air.

'The idiots must be deaf or blind,' Noble yelled. 'They're still coming straight at us!'

'And those yachts behind them could make a sudden alteration of course rather tricky, Number One,' Hailey said, straining his eyes.

'Two of the tankers are turning to port, sir,' shouted a lookout, his voice trembling slightly.

'Yes, and the other two are turning to starboard,' Hailey cried alarmingly. 'And if they continue on that course one of them will pass dangerously close to us. Pipe, "Close all Red doors and openings. Assume Weapon State Monty. Stop both engines.'

The pipe sent a feeling close to panic running through the ship. Battle bags containing anti-flash gear, life jackets, an emergency supply of 'nutty' (sweets and chocolate) and a drink were carried by everyone including officers when at sea. Life jackets were hurriedly donned.

Sadie Thompson entered the girls' mess in time to hear Jilly Howard shout. 'What the hell's happening?' She cried, looking wild-eyed at the PO. 'Are we sinking or summat?'

'No we're not,' answered Thompson, looking sternly at four other girls who were off duty. 'Just put on your life jackets and keep calm.'

'Keep calm, you say,' cried Kate Harrison, her voice raised to fever pitch. Her period still hadn't started and she was feeling overwrought with worry. 'Surely we must be in some danger or else . . .'

Thompson immediately interrupted her. 'Pipe down, Harrison,' she snapped angrily, 'and do as I say. This is probably just a precautionary measure.'

In the seamen's and stokers' messes everyone reacted with relative calm. Like the Weapons Electrical ratings' mess aft, a well-scrubbed wooden table rested in the middle, secured to the deck. Most of the port bulkhead was occupied by a forty inch plastic television set under which was a small cabinet containing a DVD and discs. Strips of neon from a low slung deck head provided a clear, all round lighting. Wooden chairs occupied most of the space and at the far end a narrow passage lined with two tier bunks and lockers led into the heads.

'Don't forget your Barclay card, lads,' cried Peter Walker, as he donned his life jacket.

'Bugger that,' shouted a stoker, opening his locker, 'I'm gunna put my cash in a French letter.'

'At least you've found some use for them at last,' added Pete Price, grinning while placing a photograph of his wife in his packet.

Down below in the engine room, Bosley glanced apprehensively at Williams. Even though the bulkheads were made of reinforced steel they both new if they sprung a leak or suddenly caved in either here or in the boiler room, nobody would stand much of chance of survival.

Meanwhile, Hailey and those on the bridge watched anxiously as both tankers, looming larger by the second, gradually approached on either side of the stationary frigate.

'Christ almighty!' screamed Shirley Mannering, who along with the lookout was on the port wing staring anxiously through their binoculars. 'They're about a mile away and coming right at us.'

Everyone watched with bated breath as the tankers converged on them. Noble was on the starboard wing, his knuckles white as he gripped the guardrail.

'Bloody hell, sir' gasped the starboard lookout, 'the buggers must be fuckin' blind.'

Feeling his heart pounding against his chest, Hailey, shouted 'Start engines, increase revolutions two thirds.' Then with a thin line of sweat trickling down the side of his face, he glanced alarmingly at Noble and said, 'With a bit of luck we'll pass down the middle of them.'

Both officers were well aware that *Dawlish* carried a mass of explosive material. A collision might cause this to detonate. The thought sent a shudder of fear running through them.

By this time, the huge tankers were within fifty yards of the frigate. Like massive seagoing monsters, they passed fifty yards either side of *Dawlish*, each sending a gigantic tidal wave towards the frigate. Luckily, *Dawlish* was moving too fast and managed to avoid colliding with them. In a matter of seconds the tankers drove past them sending a massive white bow wave curling in the air and leaving a line of frothy sea in her wake.

'Send them a radio signal, Pilot,' snapped Hailey, glancing at the ashen face of Lieutenant Gooding, 'and say, "intend reporting you to the admiralty for dangerous procedures at sea. Suggest you take a refresher course in the laws appertaining to the rules of sea lanes".'

'Very good, sir,' Gooding answered nervously licking his lips, 'I've made a note of their port of registration and pennant numbers.'

With audible sighs of relief Hailey and Mannering watched as the tankers gradually disappeared.

'The yachts have dispersed, sir,' reported the lookouts, who like everyone else was glad to see the last of the tankers.

'Thank God for small mercies,' said Hailey. 'I was hoping to launch the helicopter, but that will have to wait,' he added glancing up at the sky which was clouding over. 'Revert to Cruising stations.'

'Excuse me, sir,' said Mannering, trying in vain not to blush, 'but do you mind if I go below and change my underclothes.'

'Of course not,' Hailey answered with a grin. 'I'm sure a few of us,' he added, looking around at the pale faces surrounding him, 'will have to do the same.' He then turned to Noble and with a sigh of relief, said, 'Let's return to Portsmouth, Number One. I think we've had enough excitement for one day.'

CHAPTER TEN

Dawlish arrived in Portsmouth at 2200, and tied up alongside Gunners Wharf. Half an hour later, what was once a clear blue sky suddenly became a mass of angry looking altostratus clouds. Then, without warning, the heavens opened up. Walls of torrential rain slanted down peppering the upper deck with miniature volcanic eruptions.

Hailey had just ordered all engines stopped, when Logistics Officer, Mary Milton, a tall, fair-haired twenty three year-old Lieutenant, arrived on the bridge.

'Lorries will arrive tomorrow morning at 0900, sir,' she said handing Hailey a signal. 'They'll be carrying boxes of frozen foodstuff, bread, vegetables, beer, and tinned fruit. Ammunition and medical stores will arrive the next day at 0800.'

'Thank you,' Hailey replied, accepting the signal. Turning to Noble, he went on, 'Better put on Daily Orders Number One, "All hands off duty will be required fall in on the quarterdeck 0845 tomorrow to store ship.".'

The rain continued throughout the night and by the morning the cobbled stones on the quayside glistened like black coals. On the fo'c'sle, puddles of rainwater formed on the green painted non-slip steel deck. Shortly after 0900, three Leyland lorrys, driven by civilians, arrived and parked alongside the ship's flight deck. Under the watchful eyes of Harry Tate and Lieutenant Milton, a working party formed a chain leading from the wharf up a metal gangway to the ship. Each rating wore oilskins, leather gloves and caps with the chinstrap secured against the strong cold breeze blowing downriver.

'Standby to unload the first lorry and look lively about it,' shouted Milton.

A rating undid the canvas awning covering the back of each lorry and unloading began. As each box was passed down, Milton, holding a clip board, checked each one against her itinerary.

'I don't know about you, Shady,' muttered Bud Abbott to Shady Lane, 'but heaving boxes of tinned tomatoes and fruit is no job for a sailor.'

'Ah, stop fuckin' moanin' will yer,' Shady replied, wiping drops of rain from his face with back of his hand. 'Just think, if you drop one on your foot you could get a few day in hospital.'

'And just think of all those needles in your bum,' chimed in Jilly Howard who was standing behind Shady. Her nose was running and as she spoke she felt cold drops of rainwater running down the back of her neck. 'Personally,' she mumbled dispassionately, 'I'd settle for a nice warm cuppa tea.'

Kate Harrison was standing at the bottom of the gangway passing hefty wooden boxes up to the rating in front of her. Her arms were beginning to ache and she felt slightly dizzy. Behind Kate stood Lottie Jones.

'Thank goodness we don't have to do this often,' Lottie moaned, puffing wildly. 'And be careful, love,' she added, handing a large box to Kate, 'this bugger's very heavy.'

Kate hardly heard her. She took hold of the box and was about to pass it up to the outstretched arms of a rating when suddenly, her foot slipped on the bottom of the gangway. She immediately dropped the box and fell sideways onto the cobbled ground and struck her head on a large, rusty ring bolt. The last sensation she felt was a sharp pain cutting through her head, then oblivion.

All work immediately stopped as ratings surrounded Kate's inert figure lying on the ground.

'Kate! Kate! Are you all right?' cried Lottie, kneeling beside her friend.

There was no response to her cries. It was then she noticed a trickle of blood running down the left side of Kate's ashen face. 'Someone call the doc,' she yelled 'and bring a duvet or something to cover her.

Smyth arrived holding his medical valise. Behind came Dean and Susan Hughes.

'All right you lot,' shouted Chief GI Digger Barnes, pushing his way through the onlookers, 'give the doc some room.'

He was joined by Noble and Midshipman Parker-Smith.

'What's happened?' asked Noble, looking anxiously at Kate's inert figure. 'Is she badly hurt, Doc?'

'I'm not sure,' Smyth replied. Then shooting a quick inquisitive glance at Lottie he asked, 'How did she fall?'

As best she could, Lottie explained what had taken place, her voice trembling slightly.

Using a small torch, the doctor opened each of Kate's eyes and examined each pupil. To his consternation he saw the right one was well dilated. Gently removing her cap he saw a large egg-like swelling above Kate's left temple.

'Better call an ambulance, sir,' he said glancing warily at Noble. 'We'd better get her to hospital as soon as possible.'

Parker-Smith hurried up the gangway pushing past a rating carrying some bedding.

'Thank goodness the rain has stopped, sir,' said Hughes placing a pillow under Kate's head and covering her with the duvet and tucking it around her.

A few minutes later the naval ambulance arrived. Two male medical assistants opened the rear door, lowered a metal ramp and rolled out a small cot on wheels. With the help of Hughes and Dean, Kate was gently placed on the cot which was retracted inside the ambulance. One of the MAs placed small plastic tube in each of Kate's nostrils and slowly turned on an oxygen cylinder.

'I'll go with her,' said Smyth climbing inside. 'You'd better come with me as well, Hughes, if she wakes up it'll do her good to see a friendly face.'

'Do you think she'll be all right, sir?' Hughes asked, concern etched on her pale face.

'Hard to say,' Smyth replied checking Kate's pulse and finding it faint and slow, 'it depends on the severity of the fracture.' He asked Hughes to remove one of Kate's shoes and socks. Using the blunt end of a biro he gave an upward stroke from the base of her foot and noticed the toes curling upwards. Hughes' experience during her training on the A and E in Derriford

Hospital, Plymouth told her that this was known as Babinski's reflex, and the downward movement of Kate's toes indicated a possible fractured skull.

'Not good, is it, sir?' Hughes asked, furrowing her brow.

'I'm afraid not,' Smyth replied, slowly shaking his head.

The journey to Queen Alexandra's Hospital seemed to take ages but in fact took less than fifteen minutes. Situated in Cosham, a small suburb few miles outside Portsmouth, the hospital consisted of several large red-bricked modern five-storey buildings. On the left of a wide tarmacked road leading to the main entrance above which was the name of the hospital embossed in the stonework. Away to the left was a crammed car park and a bus terminus. The road continued around the back of one building to the A and E Department.

No sooner had the ambulance driver backed onto the entrance to the A and E, than two white- coated orderlies appeared pushing a trolley. The ambulance driver opened the back door and lowered a metal ramp allowing the two MAs to slide the cot onto the trolley. A tall Asian doctor arrived with part of a black stethoscope hanging from the side pocket of his white coat.

'Doctor Mukherjee,' he said, introducing himself to Smyth. 'I take it this is the head injury we were told to expect. How is she?' he added looking down at Kate as she was wheeled through the doors into the main examining section.

'Not good,' Smyth answered warily. 'Positive Babinski and her right pupil is dilated.'

'Better take her straight to X-ray then,' said Doctor Mukherjee.

The immediate A and E area was a hive of quiet efficient activity. On one side nurses sat busily working at computers. Other staff, some pushing blood pressure apparatus or carrying trays containing an assortment of bottles and syringes hurried by. Orderlies were pushing cots with patients ranging from elderly men and women huddled under thin, but warm linen sheets, to some in plastic splints or heavily bandaged limbs, on their way to be examined in one of the many curtained off bays. It was a typical of the many A and E departments in hospitals throughout the country.

The X-ray department was down a long hallway. With the help of Hughes, a female technician removed Kate's oilskin.

'Left and right parietal and frontal, please,' the doctor said as a technician manoeuvred the X-ray apparatus into position over Kate's head. A few minutes later, the technician and the two doctors went into a darkened room. The technician pressed a series of buttons on a computer and four medium-sized black and white pictures appeared on a screen.

'Mm . . .' Doctor Mukherjee muttered thoughtfully as he pointed to one of the films, 'there appears to be a small fracture of the right parietal bone.'

'Yes, I can see it,' replied Smyth. 'It's just above her right ear.'

'Of course it'll have to be confirmed by the head radiologist, but the fracture is quite clear,' said Doctor Mukherjee as they left the dark room. Looking at the two orderlies, he said. 'Take her to room fourteen on ward eleven. I'll write her up for quarter hourly blood pressure, temperature, pulse, respiration and oxygen levels. Do we have any of her details? '

'Maybe I can help,' interjected Hughes, 'her name is Kate Harrison. She's a Communications Technician, twenty years old and lives with her parents in Bridlington.'

'Thank you, nurse,' replied Doctor Mukherjee, writing down the details on a pad.

'Perhaps you could FAX more information when you return to your ship,' the doctor added, looking at Smyth.

'Of course,' answered Smyth. 'I'll have clothes and toilet gear sent and the ship will inform her parents.'

'Thank you,' said Doctor Mukherjee, giving Smyth a thankful smile. As two male orderlies wheeled Kate away, he added, 'There doesn't appear to be anything else for you to do, so you may as well return to your ship. I'm sure we can provide you with transport. Thank you for everything.'

'It is us who should thank you,' Smyth replied graciously as they shook hands.

Upon returning to *Dawlish*, Hughes immediately made her way to the girls' mess. The time was shortly after 1200. A few girls were sitting down sipping cans of beer. Others were having their dinner. Everyone stopped what they were doing and looked up as Hughes entered.

'How is she?' they asked almost in unison, anxious expressions on their faces.

While Hughes was telling them what had happened, Smyth was also informing, the captain and First Lieutenant the severity of Kate's injury.

'I'd better telephone her parents,' Hailey said, 'I'm sure they'll want to come and see her, and you'd better make a pipe, Number One, the crew will want to know how she is. But be discrete, just say she has a head injury.'

Peter Walker was on the quarterdeck putting a group of marines through a series of calisthenics. They wore blue shorts, matching sweat-stained vests and well-scrubbed white pumps.

'Come on you rough tough boot necks,' shouted Walker. 'Ten more push-ups then a dozen curls and I might give you a breather.'

'Miserable bugger,' muttered a tall, muscular marine, drops of perspiration falling from his gleaming brow.

'I heard that, Lofty,' cried Walker, smiling ruefully at the culprit. 'Ten extra push-ups if you don't . . .' at that moment the voice of the first lieutenant came over the tannoy informing everyone about Kate.

Walker immediately stopped the exercises and listened.

'Try not to worry, Clubs,' remarked Butch Cassidy, a small, pugnacious-looking sergeant with a body like a weight-lifter. Like everyone else, he knew about Walker's relationship with Kate. Placing a consoling hand on Walker's shoulder, he added, 'She's in good hands and I bet she'll be back on board in no time. Just you wait and see.'

'I hope you're right, Sarge,' Walker replied, anxiously biting his lip, 'I really do.'

No sooner had Smyth and Hughes left the hospital, than nurses in cabin fourteen began removing Kate's clothing.

'My God,' exclaimed one of them as she took off Kate's trousers. 'She must have been haemorrhaging, her underclothes are soaked with blood...'

CHAPTER ELEVEN

'If you're doing nothing would you like to come ashore for a few drinks tomorrow?' asked Diana.   Her question was directed at Ashir. The time was 1100 on Friday 26 July. They were in the Ops Room and had just finished an exercise

Diana's invitation caught Ashir unawares. He had removed his head set and stared blankly at her.

'Who, me?' he replied, raising his eyebrows in surprise.

It had been just over a week since they met and began working next to one another. At first he was reluctant to ask her for advice. However, his confidence grew after Murphy gave him a 'well done' after he reported sighting the tankers and yachts.

Each morning Diana's confident manner and pleasant demeanour enabled Ash to relax and adjust to his surroundings. He even detected a faint aroma of perfume; something he knew was forbidden by regulations. Not that anyone in the Ops Room seemed to mind. In fact it made a pleasant change from smelling the alcoholic fumes of the previous night's run ashore. The close proximity of their seats meant that on several occasions their knees would touch. When this happened, Ash glanced quickly at Diana, who didn't appear to feel anything.

However, as time passed Ashir became more and more aware of Diana's attractive presence.

When this happened, he reminded himself he was here to do Allah's bidding and not to be distracted by the obvious charms and beauty of a girl. Now, hearing her ask him out for a drink left him tongue-tied.

'Yes, you,' said Diana, peering at him while removing her headset. 'Who did you think I meant? And don't look so worried,' she added, grinning and shaking her head slightly, 'the day after tomorrow is Saturday and it's my birthday. We're having a bit of a knees up at Jimmy's Bar in Southsea. Some of the girls and lads will be there. All right?'

My goodness, he really does look surprised, thought Diana looking at Ashir's face. She was loathed to admit it, even to the girls in her mess, but from the first moment they were introduced, she felt herself drawn to him.

'How's Omar Sharif getting on?' Jilly Howard asked her one evening. 'Has he err . . .?'

'No, he hasn't,' Diana angrily replied. 'And even if he did, I wouldn't tell you.'

'Temper, temper,' chimed in Susan Hughes. 'He can make a pass at me anytime.'

With an air of resignation, Jilly Howard said, 'Give him, time, Di, he will . . . '

'If he doesn't, he must be gay.' said Susan.

Now, sitting next to Ashir she quickly dismissed Jilly's crude remark. He seemed unlike the other members of the crew, in that he appeared extra shy and reserved. But when he looked at her with his large, intelligent brown eyes, she felt a strange tingle run through her.

'Of course, if you're too busy. . . ' Diana said, nonchalantly shrugging her shoulders and allowing her voice to trail off.

'No, no,' Ashir quickly replied, 'it's just that I didn't know it was your . . . birthday.'

'Good,' replied Diana, placing her headset on the desk. 'We'll meet on the wharf at 1900 and catch a taxi outside the dockyard.'

At supper that evening in the mess, Ashir mentioned Diana's birthday to some of the lads.

'I think she fancies you, Ash,' said Shady Lane stuffing a piece of fish in his mouth. 'Us lot,' he added, looking around at Dutch Holland and Pete Price, 'were asked by one of Di's friends. At least you got a personal invite.'

'Diana is the best looking girl in the ship,' said Shady Lane, opening a can of beer. 'A few of the officers have tried their luck with her, but she turned them down, you lucky bugger.'

That night Ashir lay in his bunk thinking about what Shady had said. Despite his strong religious beliefs, he had to admit he was attracted to Diana. However, as he always did whenever he had carnal thoughts, he said a silent prayer to Allah asking his mind to be purged of such sordid meanderings. This did not prevent him waking up at night with an erection, and having what he had heard his messmates call a 'wet dream.'

On Saturday afternoon after secure, Ashir, Shady Lane, Pete Price and Dutch Holland went ashore to a jeweller's in town. Earlier, Dutch had met Lottie and it was decided the lads would buy Diana a silver bracelet with her name engraved on the inside.

'And the girls and myself,' gushed Lottie, 'will buy some silver charms for the bracelet, and order a bouquet of roses from all of us to be delivered to Jimmy's Bar at twenty-hundred'

'Good idea, Lot,' replied Dutch, 'I can't wait to see you and the girls in mini-skirts.'

'Don't you fellows ever think about anything except sex?' Lottie asked, tossing her head back and laughing.

'Not if we can help it,' said Dutch, giving her a lecherous grin.

Shortly before 1930, Ashir and the lads went ashore. It was still daylight and high above a pale sun darted in and out of a cluster of grey clouds. With exception of Ashir, who wore a plain brown sports coat, white, open-neck shirt, grey slacks and shoes, the others wore dark, zip-up leather jackets, colourful shirts, trainers and jeans.

A few minutes later the girls appeared on the flight deck.

'Christ almighty!' Exclaimed Duty PO Dusty Miller, sniffing the warm, evening air, 'this ship smells like a Jippo knocking shop.'

'Of course, you'd know all about that, wouldn't you,' Diana remarked, giving Miller a disarming look.

'I don't care,' cried Duty QM Bud Abbott, admiring the girls. 'You lot look fab in civvies, I could almost fancy you myself.'

'Chance would be a fine thing,' remarked Jane Wootton who looked very sexy in a tight yellow sweater and short, button-down skirt. 'But I'd rather be shot than poisoned.'

Looking up from the wharf, Shady Lane gave Ash a nudge in the ribs and said, 'That green mini dress Di's wearing clings to her like a second skin.'

Ashir didn't reply, he was too engrossed staring at Diana balancing precariously on a pair of black high-heeled shoes as she carefully made her way down the gangway.

'Yeah,' chimed in Dutch Holland, 'and if that scarlet skirt Jilly Howard has on is any shorter she'd be had up for indecent exposure.'

'I'll say,' Shady answered, giving Dutch a lecherous glance, 'and you can see her tits bouncing under that tight yellow sweater. What I wouldn't give to get my laughing gear around them.'

'Play your cards right and you never know,' answered Pete Price with a sly grin.

Behind Diana came Emily Jackson wearing a short pink skirt, and white blouse. Behind her, dressed in a smart cream sweater and pencil blue skirt came Jane Wootton. Cook Polly West, followed on, demurely holding onto the hems of her short, flowing pale green dress. Behind Polly was the , slightly overweight figure of Lottie Jones, whose long blonde hair stood out against her shiny black blouse.

'I hope it doesn't soddin' rain,' Polly cried, pulling down her short tartan skirt. 'Me hairs still wet and I'll catch me death.'

'That's not all she'll catch,' muttered Bud Abbott, perversely grabbing his crutch.

'I hope you lot have your mobiles, as per standing orders,' shouted Dusty Miller, as the girls arrived on the wharf, adding, 'and don't be adrift.'

Lottie Jones was last to leave the ship. As she stepped onto the gangway, Bud Abbott smiled benignly at her. 'Hey, Lottie,' he said taking out a small object wrapped in foil, 'would you like a sweet?'

'That's generous of you,' Lottie replied, holding out her hand, 'I don't mind if I . . . you dirty bugger,' she cried looking at the 'sweet. 'It's bloody condom!' At which point, she threw it at his face, and trying her best not to laugh, turned on her high heels and walked away.

'Perhaps you should have kept it, Lot,' Diana remarked grinning salaciously at Lottie. 'You never know your luck.'

'Too true, love,' Lottie replied, giving Diana an all-knowing look. 'That's why I've got a few in my shoulder bag.'

Standing nearby, Gooding, his telescope neatly tucked under his left arm, simply shook his head and diplomatically walked away.

Two taxis waited near the bottom of the gangway. After more ribald comments from both parties, the lads watched as the girls, flashing plenty of thigh, climbed into the first. The lads clambered into the one behind.

Paraphrasing words from many a gangster movie, Dutch Holland tapped on the driver's window and, pointing at the taxi in front, cried, 'follow that car and step on the gas.'

With a look of disdain, the driver, an elderly, grey-haired man, rolled his eyes up and turned on the ignition.

CHAPTER TWELVE

Jimmy's Bar was situated on the main stretch of busy road opposite South Parade Pier. Two narrow flights of stone steps led to the entrance. A sign in glittering red neon above the door proclaimed its name. The pub was a popular watering hole with both service personnel and locals, mainly due to its extended licensing hours and rather loud rock group.

Inside, the atmosphere was warm and slightly damp. The time was just after 2000, and with the exception of Betty, a small buxom blonde barmaid, the place was empty. Tables and chairs made of light yellow Scandinavian pine, surrounded a small circular dance area, which like the rest of the room was covered in well-worn brown linoleum. The low-slung oak- beamed ceiling and white-washed walls dotted with posters of rock bands, gave the place a lively Bohemian appearance.

On a narrow platform at the back of the dance floor, three, young unshaven musicians wearing traditional jeans, torn at the knees and off-white T-shirts, were lazily preparing for the evening's entertainment. One of them was bending down ensuring the leads from his electric guitar were firmly plugged into the wall socket near the stage. Another, sent sharp, eerie sounds into the air as he tuned his guitar, while the third member, sat behind a set of drums staring idly into space.

Jimmy, a large, portly, round-faced man, was stood behind a well-stocked bar. He wore a spotless white apron and the neon lighting made his bald head shine like a new laid egg. As Diana and the rest of the crowd entered, his large, humorous blue eyes, set below a pair of bushy grey eyebrows, broke into a wide, toothy smile.

'Come in lads and lassies,' he cried, 'I do believe it's a certain young lady's birthday, which one is it?' he added, looking at the girls.

'Her,' they cried in unison, pointing at Diana.

'Then this is for you,' said Jimmy, producing a bouquet of a dozen roses wrapped in pink floral tissue paper. Grinning like a Cheshire cat, he walked around the bar and handed the flowers to Diana, who, blushing profusely, gave him a chaste kiss on the cheek and thanked him.

'They're gorgeous,' Diana said, smelling the flowers, 'what a wonderful surprise, thank you all,' she added glancing approvingly at everyone.

'Speaking of surprises,' said Dutch Holland, taking out a small silver box tied in a bow with a pink ribbon, 'this is from all of us, happy birthday, Di,' he added handing it to her.

Passing the flowers to Lottie, Diana, her hands trembling with excitement, untied the ribbon and opened the lid of the box.

'Oh, thank you all,' she cried, gently removing the shiny silver bracelet, 'and it's got the charms I love so much,' she added as her eyes filled with tears. She immediately placed the bracelet on her left wrist, admired it, and with her voice cracking with emotion, went on, 'thank you all again. It's really lovely . . . Her voice was suddenly drowned out by everyone singing 'Happy Birthday.'

Betty, the buxom barmaid, appeared carrying a large tray of drinks. Jimmy stood next to her.

'Come on, you lot,' he said, beaming as usual, 'these are on the house. Beer for the lads, vodka cocktails for the girls, and I suggest you put two tables together to accommodate you all afore the rush.'

Amidst raucous laughter, everyone did as Jimmy suggested. Quick as a flash Diana took a chair next to Ashir. The girls followed suit and sat by the lads. The twanging of the electric guitar and thump of the drums heralded the start of the music as the group attempted to play *A Hard Day's Night.*

Gradually, the place began to fill up with girls in colourful summer dresses. By comparison their companions all appeared to look the same - faded jeans, leather jackets and an assortment of shirts and sweaters.

'You look so different in a dress, Di,' Ashir remarked shyly as he took a sip of beer. 'I hardly recognised you.'

'I hope you approve,' Diana coyly replied, 'in fact,' she added, giving Ashir a radiant smile while squeezing his thigh, 'I think you look better in civvies than in uniform.'

Ashir felt his face redden and hurriedly took another swallow of beer. Diana removed her hand but pressed her knee against his. 'Come on,' she said, downing her drink, 'let's have dance before the mob arrive.'

'I'm afraid I can't . . . Ashir stuttered as Diana grabbed his hand and pulled him up.

'Of course you can,' said Diana, 'it's dead easy. Just follow me.'

For a few moments Ashir stood and watched Diana seductively gyrate her hips to the rhythmic beat of the music. With every movement, the silky green dress she wore clung to her, exaggerating every curve of her body. Ashir felt his pulse quicken and was about to sit down when Diana grabbed his arm.

'Oh, no you don't,' she cried, 'just move your feet and keep in time with the music.'

But try as he might, Ashir failed to do as Diana suggested. Suddenly the beat of the music changed and the tempo slowed down.

'Now just relax, Ash,' Diana said, looking up into Ashir's eyes and gently pulling him close to her. 'Move your feet slightly and keep in time with the music.'

The sudden softness of Diana's body sent an unexpected thrill running through him. The intoxicating smell of her perfume almost made him dizzy. Her hand felt warm and smooth as they began to shuffle to the rhythmic twang of the guitars, he began to relax.

'There now, 'said Diana, giving Ashir's hand a confident squeeze, 'you're doing fine.'

Diana leant her head against his chest and pressed herself against him. His immediate reaction was to feel his penis becoming erect. Diana was only too aware of the bulge pressing against her and felt excited. Overcome with embarrassment Ashir tried to move slightly away from her. Diana's reaction was to pull Ashir even closer and nuzzle her head against his chest.

'Just keep moving slow like that, Ash,' she muttered, 'and don't worry, it feels lovely.'

In the meantime, Dutch and the others were also dancing, moving in close proximity to one another.

'Nowt like a good old smooch,' said Dutch, pulling Lottie close to him while sliding his hand into her bottom.

'And just you mind where you putting your filthy paws,' Lottie replied, smiling coyly as she reached behind and tugged his hand up around her waist.

By 2100 the place was fairly full. Jimmy and Betty were kept busy serving drinks. The noise made by the band was so loud that people had to shout to hear themselves speak. Nobody noticed as four very tall, heavily-built lads came in, and pushed their way to the bar and ordered pints of larger. They were unshaven and casually dressed. The tallest of the group stood well over six feet with a mop of untidy ginger hair, a squashed, boxers nose and a jagged scar running down the left side of his pale, fleshy face.

'There's a lot of fanny here tonight, eh, Tosher,' said one of them, a stocky lad with a bad case of acne.

'Yer, not wrong there, mate,' Tosher cautiously replied, focussing his beady brown eyes on Diana, 'and I've just seen the best lookin' bint in the place.'

Noticing the direction Tosher was staring, a third member, a tall, thin-faced lad with fair, curly hair, said, 'Ah, you've no chance with her, Tel, she's well and truly taken for.' As he spoke he displayed a set of uneven yellow teeth.

'And she's with a Paki,' added the fourth member of the quartet, a hefty looking fellow with a crew-cut and a pot belly.

At that moment the group struck up their version of a latest pop song.

'Not for long, just watch me,' grunted Tosher. Downing the dregs of his lager he put the glass on the bar. With a conceited shrug of his shoulders, he walked up to the table Ashir and were Diana were sharing with the others.

'How about a dance, gorgeous,' said Tosher, taking hold of Diana's arm and attempting to pull her up off her chair.

'No, thank you,' Diana cried glaring up at him, 'And take your hands away, you're hurting me,' she shouted angrily, trying unsuccessfully to wrench her arm away from Tosher's tight gasp.

'You heard her,' said Ashir, staring defiantly up at Tosher. 'She doesn't want to dance so remove your hand.'

'And who the hell are you?' growled Tosher. 'You're nowt but a fuckin' Paki.'

Suddenly the atmosphere around the table changed from joviality to stony silence. The band, sensing trouble, stopped playing. Betty gathered several empty glasses and quickly moved behind the bar.

'That's enough, you lot,' shouted Jimmy who was standing nearby. 'It's the girl's birthday so leave her alone.'

'Get stuffed,' was Tosher's contemptuous reply.

'Anyway,' Diana ventured, feeling her mouth go dry. 'His parents are from Pakistan. He was born in London and he's in the navy like the rest of us.'

Plucking up courage, Lottie glared up at Tosher and stuttered, 'y . . . es, now why don't you piss off and leave us alone.'

Tosher's pale face slowly turned crimson. 'So lover boy here, is a bloody Muslim, eh!' he exclaimed.

'Our 'Arry was in killed in Iraq last year by one of yer Al Qaeda bastards.' His face wrinkling into an ugly sneer as he spoke. He turned towards his three pals and with a sarcastic grin, said, 'It seems the navy is taking any sod these days, especially fuckin' jihadists.'

Up till now, Ashir had done his best to control his temper, even though he knew Tosher had unknowingly told the truth about him. But allowing the remarks to go unchallenged would look bad, especially in front of his messmates. Ashir immediately stood up, and although he was over six feet tall, he found himself looking up into Tosher's beady dark brown eyes.

Sensing danger, Pete Price, shot a warring glance at Shady Lane and Dutch Holland and glared defiantly at Tosher's three pals.

'Look here, lads, let's have no trouble,' pleaded Jimmy, 'or you'll force me to call the police.'

Ignoring Jimmy's warning, Ashir and Tosher stared defiantly at one another like two boxers at a weigh-in.

'And just what,' Tosher snarled, stabbing Ashir in the chest with a finger, 'd'you think you're gunna do, Paki?'

'You were told before,' Ashir answered, angrily gritting his teeth, 'I was born in London.'

'So what,' Tosher replied glibly, 'you wogs are all the fuckin' same.'

'Please Ash,' cried Diana, noticing Ashir's clenched fists, 'sit down. The sod's not worth it. You'll only end up in trouble.'

'Yeah, you 'eard the bitch,' said Tosher, 'sit down.' He then gave Ashir a hefty thump in the chest. Ashir lost his balance and fell onto the floor. Cries from the girls echoed around as glasses and tables crashed onto the floor. Beer and other drinks spilt over onto everyone's clothes. Girls, sitting with their boyfriends at other tables screamed.

Pete Price and the other two made a move to help Ashir but were immediately confronted by Tosher's burly friends.

'I wouldn't if were you,' growled one of them, as and the other two slowly took out ribbed brass knuckledusters from their pockets and slipped them on their fingers. 'That is if yer know what's good fer yer,' he added with a wicked glint in his eyes

Ashir, glowering at Tosher, attempted to get up. With an ugly grimace on his face, Tosher placed his boot on Ashir's chest and pushed him back. 'Stay where you are, you black bastard,' he grunted, 'I'm not finished with you yet.'

Tosher put a hand inside his brown leather jacket and drew out what appeared to be a piece of metal. With a quick movement of his finger, he pressed a small button and a three-inch steel blade with a gleaming sharp serrated edge shot up.

With a look of horror, Ashir stared at the knife and tried to wriggle free. But Tosher removed his foot and straddled himself across Ashir's chest pinning him down with a knee on each shoulder.

'*My God, he's got a knife!*' Diana screamed, dropping her bouquet on the floor.

Jimmy, who was standing close to Tosher, nervously licked his lips and shouted, 'that's enough. Put that knife away or I'll call the police.'

'If anyone so much as reaches for a mobile, I'll slit the bugger's throat,' cried Tosher, placing the knife near to Ashir's jugular vein.

Jimmy and Ashir's three oppos glanced warily at one another and backed away.

'Go on,' yelled one of Tosher's gang, 'cut him up. Remember what they did to your 'Arry.'

'*For Chrissake, no, no!*' screamed Diana, dropping her bouquet on the floor. '*Don't do it, you cowardly bastard.*''

'Yes, that's what you are, a bloody coward,' shouted Jane Wootton, 'let him stand up and fight fair.'

'Just like the jihadist did to me brother, eh?' cried Tosher, his eyes ablaze and focused on Ashir.

'They cut the poor sod's head off, but that's nowt compared to what I'm gunna do to you, you cunt.'

Once again, Ashir, wide-eyed with fear, made a massive effort to break free by pushing his body upwards and move his legs. But it was no use. Tosher was too strong and heavy. With his face clouded with hate, he grabbed Ashir's hair and jerked his head backwards.

'Now it's your turn, you Moslim bastard,' growled Tosher as he raised the knife.

'*Please, I beg you, no*!' Ashir shouted as Tosher was about to strike.

At that moment Ashir saw the pugnacious face of Sergeant Butch Cassidy appear over Tosher's shoulder.

In one quick movement, Butch placed a muscular arm surround Toshers neck head, jerked it back and held it in a firm hold. At the same time he reached down and with a quick movement twisted the knife from Tosher's hand and dropped it on the floor.

Standing behind Butch were three other marines, all of whom wore standard leather jackets of various colours and denim jeans. They immediately moved in front of Tosher's pals, who seeing the defiant expressions on the marines' faces, glanced warily at one another and shuffled backwards.

Meanwhile, Tosher, his face red with anger, reached up and tried to grab Butch's hand.

'*I'll kill you for this, you fuckin' bastard!*' he yelled, '*let me go.*'

'Bollocks,' said Butch grinning wildly. Taking hold of Tosher's hand, bent it backwards and, with Tosher screaming in pain, pulled him off Ashir. Straightaway, everyone crowded around Ashir and helped him to his feet.

'Thanks a million, Butch,' gasped Ashir, beads of sweat running down the sides of his face. 'That mad bugger,' he added, staring frantically at Tosher, 'was going slit my throat'

By this time Butch had bent Tosher half in two with his arms pinioned painfully high behind his back.

'And I fuckin' will,' cried Tosher, his face contorted in pain, 'if this bastard lets go of me.'

'Ah, shut up,' Butch replied, giving Tosher's hands a quick twist. Looking up at the Diana, Butch grinned and said, 'Just thought we'd drop in to wish you all the best, love.'

'Thank God, you and your pals did,' Diana replied, shaking with relief. 'A few seconds later he'd have killed Ash.'

Just as Diana finished speaking, the pub door opened and in came three burly policemen. The tallest was a sergeant, a dark-haired, well-built man.

Unknown to everyone, Betty who despite being petrified, had stealthily lowered herself behind the bar, and with trembling hands, took out her mobile and dialled 999.

'Now what's going on here?' the sergeant said in a stern voice, watching Butch restraining Tosher. 'And who's the proprietor?'

'I am,' said Jimmy, 'and if it hadn't been for that man,' he pointed to Butch, 'and his mates, the man who's being held down would have probably killed that lad,' he added, nodding towards Ashir. 'And this,' he added, picking up the knife and handing it to the sergeant, 'is what he was gunna do it with.'

'Thanks very much,' said the sergeant, wrapping the knife in a handkerchief and putting it in his pocket. 'And who are you?' he asked staring at Dutch who still had Tosher's hand behind his back. Butch quickly told the sergeant where he and his three mates were from and what they had done.

'Well done to you,' the sergeant replied. Then with more than a touch of pride, added, 'I did my twelve in Forty Commando before joining the force. I'll report all this to your CO, I'm sure he'll be pleased.'

Staring quizzically at Tosher's sweaty face, then at his mates, he exclaimed, 'I know you, don't I? You and your pals have just come out of Pentonville after doing two years for GBH, your photos was in the Portsmouth News.'

'So what if we 'ave?' growled Tosher, looking up from his bent position, 'these bastards started it.'

'I bet,' grinned the sergeant. Glancing at the other policemen, he went on, 'Better cuff them and dump them in the van outside. A night in the cells will do them the world of good. And you sir,' he added looking at Jimmy, 'can come to Southsea nick tomorrow and make a statement.'

The policemen quickly placed handcuffs around the wrists of Tosher and his mates. Loudly protesting their innocence and yelling obscenities, they were marched out of the pub.

With a sigh of relief, Diana put her arms around Ashir and said, 'How are you feeling, Ash. You still look a little shaken?'

'I'm all right,' Ashir replied, wiping sweat from his brow with the back of his hand, 'but thank goodness for the bootnecks. I think I owe Butch and his oppos a few pints.'

With tears in her eyes, she threw her arms around Ashir. 'Oh, Ash,' she cried, 'I don't know what I'd have done if that brute had killed you.' She paused and gazing up into his eyes, went on, 'you see, I think I'm falling in love with you.'

Ashir was only too aware of what she said, but didn't quite know what to say. Instead he smiled weakly and using a finger wiped away a tear that was running down her cheek. At that moment, Betty arrived and began to mop up pools of lager and spilt vodka martinis while the rest picked up the chairs.

'I don't know about you lot,' said Lottie, picking up the bouquet of roses off the floor and handing them to Diana. 'But I could do with a good drink.'

.

CHAPTER THIRTEEN

The shrill sound of the bosun's pipe over the tannoy woke Hailey up. The time was 0630 on Sunday 28 July. A few seconds later the smiling face of Flannigan came into the cabin holding a steaming hot mug of tea.

'Top o' the mornin', sir,' he said, placing the mug on a table near Hailey's bunk. 'The weather's gloomy and the wind's bloody cold.'

'Thank you for those few cheerful words,' Hailey replied. Stretching his arms above his head and yawning. 'Two lightly boiled eggs, toast, marmalade and coffee, please and don't forget *The Times*.'

An hour later, wearing his number one uniform, he left his cabin. The time was 0750, which meant that morning colours would be in ten minutes time. This is a historical ritual carried out, morning and evening on ships whenever they are in port.

Hailey left his cabin and walked up two flights of steel ladders onto the port side of the ship and made his way aft to the flight deck. As he did so, the 'bloody cold wind,' as Flannigan had so colloquially put it, whipped against his face.

Waiting for him was the First Lieutenant, Lieutenant Gooding, Jock Forbes and Bud Abbott. All three snapped to attention and saluted. At the stern of the ship, Signalman Scott stood ready with a folded White Ensign. Meanwhile, at the bow, another signalman, colloquially known as a 'bunting tosser,' was standing in order to hoist the Union Jack.

'Good morning, gentlemen, stand at ease,' Hailey said, rubbing his hands together while glancing warily up at the grey, cloudy sky, 'a slight chilly, eh?'

'Indeed, sir,' Noble answered, 'it looks like being a miserable day.'

Not half as miserable as I feel, thought Bud Abbott, stifling a yawn.

At exactly 0755, the shrill whistle of the bosun's pipe pierced the morning stillness. This was the signal for a rating amidships to raise a green and yellow pennant, known as the 'prep flag' to the top of the main mast.

'Five minutes to colours, sir' AB Jack Frost reported, watching from the port wing.

Four minutes later the prep flag was lowered.

'One minute to colours, sir,' Frost cried, at which time Hailey and Gooding and Jock Forbes came smartly to attention.

The prep flag was lowered prompting Frost to report, 'colours, sir.'

'Make it so,' Gooding, sharply replied.

At the corner of the flight deck, a rating struck the ship's bell eight times. Gooding then gave the order, 'Pipe the still.' One long, even call on the bosun's pipe followed this, and the White Ensign on the stern and the Union Jack on the bow, were hoisted simultaneously, as all the officers saluted.

The 'carry on' was then piped and at the last note the officers brought down their salute. The reverse of this procedure occurred every evening in port.

'Thank Gawd for that,' Bud Abbott muttered to himself, who, having had the morning watch, was looking forward to having a 'make and mend.' (An afternoon off duty ostensibly to repair clothing.)

As soon as the colours party had been dismissed, Hailey turned to Noble, and in a concerned voice, said, 'What's the latest on Harrison's condition, Number One?' It's been almost a week since she was injured.'

With a heavy sigh, Noble answered, 'I'm sorry to say, the doc tells me the poor girl is still unconscious. Her divisional officer, Lieutenant Mannering, the Doc and Leading PTI Walker are the only ones from the ship allowed to see her. Her mess-mates wanted to visit her, but the doc told them it would be a waste of time. Her parents are staying at a local hotel and go to the hospital every day. The doc and Leading PTI Walker are going to see her again this afternoon.'

Hailey glanced furtively at Noble, and replied, 'Thank you, Number One. Please keep me informed.'

Smyth and Walker left the ship at 1300. Waiting on the wharf was the ship's tilly, ordered by the doctor. Both men wore civilian clothes–the surgeon in a dark blue blazer white shirt and tie and grey slack, Walker casually dressed in a zip-up brown bomber jacket, fawn sweater and cream coloured Chinos.

The journey to Queen Alexandra's Hospital took about twenty minutes. This was their second visit during the week and they were familiar with the routine.

Both men made their way down a corridor and took the lift to the second floor. A pair of wing doors led into a long passage-way. The walls were a pale green with wooden bars on one side for patient support. Nurses in white, yellow and blue uniforms busied themselves in the open ward units on the right. Sitting behind a desk cluttered with patient's folders sat Sister Davies, the same nurse they had met on their previous visits. Upon seeing them, she looked up and with a polite smile, said, 'Good afternoon gentlemen, I take it you've come to see Kate again?'

'Yes, how is she, Sister?' Smyth asked.

'Still the same, I'm afraid, although her vital signs remain good,' replied the sister.

'Well, at least that's something,' replied Smyth.

'She's still in room eleven, her parents are with her,' the sister added standing up and walking around her desk, 'I'll come with you.'

So far, Walker hadn't spoken. But as they stopped at a glass panelled door, he glanced nervously at the sister and asked, 'err . . . know I asked this before but how long d'you think she'll be unconscious?'

'It's hard to say,' said the sister, 'perhaps your own doctor,' she added glancing at Smyth, 'could answer that better than me.'

'I'm afraid I can't help you,' Smyth replied, 'as I told you on our last visit, it depends the severity of her injury and any complications that may arise because of them.'

Despite having seen her on a previous visit, the sight of seeing Kate still lying in bed, pale-faced with her eyes closed, made Walker feel crestfallen. Except for the steady movement of her chest under a sheet, she lay quite sill. Her shoulders clad in a floral pink night were barely visible and a cotton hairnet keeping a dressing in place covered most of her head. On an oblong plastic screen above her bed a series of electronic waves recorded her heartbeat, pulse and oxygen levels. These, plus her blood pressure and temperature, taken every half hour, were shown on a chart hanging on the end of her bed. Kate was being nasally fed through a narrow brown rubber tube attached to a bottle of milky substance that disappeared up one of her nostrils.

From the right side of the bed, a saline and glucose drip hung from a bottle clipped onto a metal stand. Attached to the end of the tube, a metal cannula was inserted into a vein on the dorsum of her right hand.

The blinds on the window were drawn allowing the dull after noon light into the room painted in a relaxing pale green. A line of coloured 'Get Well' cards rested on a shelf below the window alongside a bunch of red roses.

Kate's parents were sat at her bedside. Both looked around, their faces tired and drawn as the sister, together with Smyth and Walker, entered the room.

'I do hope we're not disturbing you,' the sister said, 'but the doctor and Kate's boyfriend are here.'

'That's quite all right,' Hilda answered sighing as she spoke. With one hand she quickly pushed back a strand of fair hair from her face. The other grasped Kate's hand, gently squeezing hoping desperately to elicit some sign of recognition. 'We were too upset to speak much the last time we met, so it's nice to meet you both again,' Hilda added, reaching up and shaking the doctor's and Walker's hands. 'Please thank your captain for the lovely letter explaining what had happened. It was very considerate of him, wasn't it Henry?'

Henry, raised a faint smile and replied dryly, 'Yes, dear, I suppose it was.'

'How long have you known Kate?' her mother asked Walker.

'Err . . . for about six months,' he answered, staring forlornly at Kate, wishing she would open her eyes and smile at him.

'And is it serious?' Hilda asked, giving Kate's hand another gentle squeeze.

'Yes,' replied Walker, feeling his face redden. 'I was hoping to . . .'

'I know what you were hoping to do,' Henry gruffly interrupted him, 'you sailors are all alike. I used to be one and . . . '

'Not now, Henry,' said Hilda tersely, 'there's a time and place for everything.' She then looked up at Smyth. 'We've been told she could wake up at any moment. What do you think, Doctor?' she asked, anxiously biting her lower lip.

'It's possible,' Smyth replied, not wishing to raise her hopes. 'I spoke to the neurosurgeon when I came here on Wednesday. He told me we'll all have to be patient.'

'And pray to the Almighty,' Hilda replied, doing her best not to cry.

'Indeed,' said Smyth.

Realising there was nothing much to be gained by remaining, Smyth and Walker said goodbye to Kate's parents and, with a concerned glance at Kate, left the room.

Twenty minutes later they arrived back on board the ship. Smyth immediately made his way to Hailey's cabin and reported Kate's condition.

'What do really think her chances of recovery are, Doc?' Hailey asked.

'I'm not sure, sir,' Smyth replied with a worried frown, 'we'll just have to wait and see.'

CHAPTER FOURTEEN

No sooner had Smyth left than a knock came at Hailey's door. 'Come,' grunted Hailey. The door opened and Noble came in.

'Ah, Number One, come in and sit down,' said Hailey. 'What's the problem?' He added, looking at the concerned expression on Noble's face. 'You look a little perplexed.'

Noble removed his cap and sat down.

'Well, sir,' Noble replied apprehensively, 'I've just had a call from Cynthia,' he paused momentarily, then went on. 'She's returned from modelling and is here in Portsmouth, she's even booked a room at the Queen's Hotel in Southsea.'

Hailey sat back in his chair and folded his arms. 'Now, don't tell me,' he said, his face breaking into a smug grin, 'you want permission to leave the ship . . . say, for twenty-four hours. Am I right?'

'Err . . . yes, sir,' Noble replied shuffling his feet nervously.

'Permission granted,' said Hailey, leaning forward. 'Now, don't just stand there, away with you and tell the officer of the day where you'll be, and give the lovely Cynthia my best wishes.'

'Thank you, sir,' Noble replied and hurried away.

Feeling elated, Noble left and quickly made his way down a flight of steel ladders to his cabin. On his way he used his mobile phone to contact Cynthia.

'Hello darling, how lovely to hear you,' she said, 'I see you got my message, then?'

'Yes, I did,' Noble replied, listening to the soft mellow voice her remembered so well. 'I'll be with you in less than an hour,' he paused slightly, he added, 'God, I've missed you so.'

'Me too, my love,' she cooed seductively, 'come quickly. I can't wait to see you.'

As he put the phone into his pocket he almost bumped into Bob Henderson.

'My goodness, Ray,' Henderson remarked as Noble brushed passed him, 'what's the rush? Have you been caught short, or something?'

'Sorry, Bob,' Noble replied, slightly breathless, 'Cynthia's in Pompey. I'm meeting her in Southsea.'

Like the other officers, Henderson was aware of Noble's relationship with Cynthia.

With a salacious expression on his handsome, leathery features, Henderson said, 'you lucky blighter. Here,' he added, taking out a set of car keys from his jacket pocket and handing them to Noble. 'You'd better take the car I have rented. It's the green MG on the wharf, next to the ship's tilly, and give her my regards.'

'Thanks, Bob,' Noble replied, accepting the car keys, 'I'll do that.'

Twenty minutes later Noble, dressed in a smartly-tailored grey, pinstriped suit, cream coloured shirt dark blue naval tie and shiny black shoes, arrived on the fight deck. In his left hand he carried a small canvas grip containing a clean shirt, toilet gear and a large box of Belgium chocolates courtesy of Barney Watts, the NAAFI manager. The time was shortly after 1400. Bounding down the gangway, he hardly noticed the dull clouds or felt the chilly wind.

'On a promise, sir,' remarked Duty Chief Harry Tate. 'A dicky bird told me you're meeting your lady friend,' he added grinning like a Cheshire Cat.

Bloody hell, thought Noble, ignoring the chief's cheeky remark, is nothing sacred on board this ship?

Henderson's green MG was parked on the wharf close to the foot of the gangway next to the ship's tilly. Noble unlocked the small door, threw his grip on the back seat and climbed in. He switched on the engine and drove off. The last time he and Cynthia had been together was four months ago. They had spent a short weekend at the Savoy, eating, drinking and making passionate love. The thought of holding her in his arms again and smelling the intoxicating perfume she always wore sent a thrill of wanton excitement running through his body.

He drove through the dockyard passing HMS *Victory,* Nelson's famous flagship, which had never been decommissioned and was still a member of the fleet. After leaving the dockyard he emerged onto The Hard, a stretch of busy road facing Portsmouth's, modern shopping complex dominated by the Spinnaker.

Leaving the United Services Sports Ground and Southsea Common in his wake, Noble reached Southsea promenade. On the right, the placid green waters of the Solent shone in the late afternoon sunlight. On the opposite side was a series of hotels, boarding houses, clubs and pubs.

The Queen's Hotel, a large, four-storey red-bricked Victorian building stood almost opposite Southsea Pier. On either side of a gravelled pathway was a partially full car park. He switched off the engine and in one quick movement, grabbed his holdall and vaulted over the door onto the ground.

On either side of the entrance stood an elaborately carved Doric column above which was a double archway. With a newly found spring in his step and listening to his heart beating a cadence in his chest, he sprang up the three flights of steps, then pushed the swing doors open and went inside.

The atmosphere was intimate, warm with hint of Victorian charm. Noble hardly noticed the floor of the foyer covered in black and white square tiles, the wallpaper embossed in a tasteful floral pattern and the glossy green leaves of the potted plants. Instead he hurried passed couples sitting on plush brown leather sofas and armchairs, and made for the reception desk

'Lieutenant Commander Noble,' he said breathing heavily while glancing at a tall, attractive brunette. 'I believe a Miss Maclean . . .'

But the receptionist quickly interrupted him. 'Your lady friend checked in earlier today, sir,' she said, while doing her best to disguise a coy smile. 'She's in room twenty-one on the third floor,' she added unhooking a small iron key off a board and handing it to him. 'The lift is in the corner next to the staircase or you can use the door close by.'

Noble accepted the key and, with a grateful smile thanked her. Ignoring the lift, he walked quickly to the door and taking the steps two at a time soon arrived at the third floor. Room twenty-one was last on the right at the bottom of a corridor. Feeling his mouth suddenly go dry, he nervously knocked on

Cynthia was standing, barefooted, in the middle of an elegantly furnished room. The short-sleeved pale green chiffon night dress she wore clung seductively to her like a second skin outlining her slightly rounded stomach and nipple-pointed breast. The evening light from the bay window she stood in front of shone through her nightwear, showing the dark contours of her long, shapely legs and firm thighs. A faint, satisfied smile played around her red lips. She had purposely practised standing in this pose, wondering what his reaction would be.

The desire and excited expression on his face told her the plan had worked perfectly.

'Oh, darling' she cried, her midnight blue eyes sparkling while stretching out her arms, 'come here. I've missed you so.'

For a few seconds, Noble stood transfixed, taking in her translucent beauty. His eyes then gazed admiringly at her lovely, impeccably made-up face and her soft blonde hair tumbling around her shoulders like a waterfall.

Noble dropped his holdall and in a matter of seconds they were kissing so hard they could feel each other's teeth through the softness of their lips. The intoxicating aroma of Chanel No.5, together with the touch of Cynthia's warm, naked body made him tremble with desire.

'My God, you look lovely,' Noble muttered as he slid his hand down the silky smoothness of her night dress onto her smooth, round buttocks.

'Oh, darling,' gasped Cynthia, feeling his erection pushing hard against her stomach. 'You don't have to tell me, I can feel . . .' she didn't have time to finish. In one quick movement Noble picked her up in his arms and carried her across the room, gently laid her onto the king-size bed and kissed her again. Breaking free she reached up and almost tore off his tie, then gasped. 'For God's sake, darling take off your bloody clothes and make love to me.'

In a matter of second his once immaculate grey suit was a wrinkled mess on the floor. The rest of his clothes quickly followed. Then with undue haste he rolled on top of her. Feeling the hardness of his penis throbbing against her stomach, Cynthia, her heart racing like a train, entwined her legs around his waist and like an animal in pain, cried out, 'Do it quickly, darling before I go crazy.'

Borne out of mutual frustration, passion and lust, the first time was embarrassingly quick. They climaxed together, he moaning out loud, she with her finger nails digging into his back.

'I'm sorry,' Noble muttered, feeling beads of warm perspiration running down the sides of his face. 'It's just . . . '

'Forget it, my love,' Cynthia mumbled, feeling his penis still erect against her thigh. 'That was wonderful. And anyway,' she added, 'it's only nine o'clock,' she said glancing at her small silver Rolex, 'and we have all night.'

Noble ran a hand down the side of her face and was about to kiss her when he heard a buzzing noise coming from his jacket lying on the floor.

'Now what,' groaned Noble, stretching down and fumbling in his pocket for his mobile phone.

'Yes,' he grunted, placing the phone to his ear and sitting back in bed.

Cynthia looked at his face and suddenly felt a sense of foreboding. She sat up and began gently stroking the marks she had made on his back. She also noticed his erection had abruptly turned into a pale curly worm. A second later she heard him give an audible sigh, and say, 'I understand, sir. I'll be along as soon as I can, say half an hour.' He paused then rolling his eyes, added. 'Yes, sir. I'll give Cynthia your, err . . . regards, as you put it.'

'Don't tell me you have to go back to your ship?' Cynthia cried, removing her hand from his back and glaring at him.

'Yes,' Noble sullenly replied. 'That was the captain. Something's happened and all the crew who are ashore are being recalled.'

'Well, I'll be damned,' Cynthia replied, her face a picture, a mixture of frustration and disbelief. 'I travel thousands of miles to see you, and now this. To think, I could be whooping it up at some party in Mayfair or attending a premiere on the arm of a handsome male model.'

'I really am sorry, darling,' Noble said, turning around and kissing her on lips. 'It must be something serious for the old man to phone me personally.'

'But you don't have to go straightaway, do you, my love?' She cooed, pressing her warm, pointed breasts seductively against his chest while running her hand along his thigh. 'You did say half an hour. . .'

'Or maybe a little more,' Noble muttered pulling her close to him. He was about to kiss then gave her a quizzical look and said, 'I thought you once told me those male models were all gay?'

'Oh do shut up,' she mumbled grasping his buttocks. 'We're wasting valuable time.'

CHAPTER FIFTEEN

Shortly after Noble left to see Cynthia, Hailey was sipping a cup of coffee while reading *The Sunday Times*. The current situation in Syria between President Assad's government and rebels was deteriorating. Hailey agreed with the decision of parliament not to send arms to the insurgents in case they fell into the hands of the powerful Muslim Brotherhood.

However, his eyes focused a report describing an attack by Taliban gunboats on the Shell oil tanker SS *Millhouse*, in the Strait of Hormuz. He was well aware that this area was of vital strategic importance for the safe conduct of tankers carrying oil to every corner of the globe. Fortunately the combined firepower the tanker's international escorts, HMS *Doncaster* and warships from Norway and Denmark managed to beat the gunboats off. Luckily, no service personnel were injured.

Hailey put down the paper, and opened '*Culture*', the section that dealt with the arts. He was about to close it and finish his drink when a shock ran through him. Above the page about forthcoming movies, in bold capitals it read; ANNABEL SUTHERLAND AND RUSSEL CROWE TO STAR IN A WARNER BROTHERS' BLOCKBUSTER. Underneath it went on: 'This is a big budget film about the crusades. It is hoped the film can be shot on location somewhere in the Middle East, depending on the political position'. The article went on to give a potted history of Annabel's background, however, it failed to mention their marriage and subsequent divorce.

The effect of seeing Annabel's name in print and reading about her sent a wave of nostalgic pain running through him. He still kept a framed photograph of her in the bottom drawer of his desk. With a wistful sigh, he admitted he was still in love with her. Had it really been three years, four months and two days since their divorce he asked himself? The hurt was still there, but it was too late now. They were still worlds apart.

Hailey spent the rest of the afternoon reading through the signal log and an assortment of requests, interrupted by 'stand easy' being piped, and Flannigan coming into his cabin bringing coffee.

After tea he worked his way through more paperwork, then along with the Liz Hall, he took a stroll around the upper deck. A stiff, chilly afternoon breeze blew downriver and in the sky, an anaemic sun occasionally poked through the masses of cirrocumulus white clouds. The only signs of life on board the ship was the dull throb of the generator, and a few ratings of the duty watch lazily mopping the flight deck. Jake Whitton and Buck Taylor stood nearby with bored expressions on their faces.

'Not many ashore then, Liz?' Hailey asked as they walked along the port side of the ship.

'Just seven who live locally, sir,' Liz replied, then with a smile, added. 'The rest are still sleeping off their hangovers.'

How right she was.

In the after mess deck, Ashir was lying in his top bunk listening to the angry rumblings coming from his stomach. It was late afternoon and many of those off duty were still turned in.

'Gosh, I feel awful,' he muttered dolefully to Dutch Holland who was in the bunk below. 'What time did you and the girls get back?' he added as a wave of nausea swept over him.

'Never you mind,' Dutch answered after yawning, 'all I can say is that the beds in the Jolly Roger need new springs.'

'And judging by the noise we heard in the next room,' moaned Shady Lane from the top bunk across from Ashir, 'they need new mattresses as well.'

The door opened and Pete Price came in. 'Anyone for a nice greasy sarnie?' he shouted gleefully.

The answer came in the shape of boot hurled at him from someone's bunk.

In the girls' mess, Diana was in bed feeling nauseous. Wearing a tiny red thong and brassier, she gingerly got up and staggered to the heads in time to vomit into a toilet pan. Just then, Lottie, looking pale and sickly came in.

'Bloody hell!' Lottie exclaimed staring hard at Diana. 'You look how I feel. Come on, birthday girl,' she added, placing a helping hand around

Diana's hunched shoulders. 'Spalsh your face with cold water, and when I've had a pee, I'll help you back to your kip.'

'H . . . how did I get back on board?' mumbled Diana, steadying herself against the edge of the sink. 'I don't remember a thing.'

'Ash brought you back,' she replied. 'He and the duty PO helped you down to the door of the mess. One of the girls put you to bed.'

'Thanks Lottie,' Diana answered meekly, 'did you and the others go to the Jolly Roger?

'Of course,' Lottie replied, a salacious grin on her face.

'I hope you used those johnnies you took ashore,' said Diana warily.

'Might have done,' Lottie answered nonchalantly shrugging her shoulders, 'I can't remember.'

After 'secure' at 1600, he and Gooding, who had taken over from Liz Hall, and was now OOD, spent an hour or so checking the charts for the Persian Gulf and the Gulf of Aden.

'Why those particular areas, sir?' Gooding asked jokingly, 'do you know something we don't?'

'Not really, Pilot,' Hailey replied, stroking his chin, 'just a precautionary measure.'

The remainder of the evening was taken up with more paperwork. Hailey had a shower and then enjoyed a mug of coffee Flannigan had waiting for him.

'Will you be having dinner on board, sir?' Flannigan enquired, 'I believe it's bubble and squeak and jam roly-poly.'

'Sounds fine,' said Hailey, drying his hair with a towel, 'nineteen hundred, all right?'

Hailey settled down in an armchair and tried to read the rest of his newspaper. Shortly afterwards he dozed off and was woken up by the ringing of the telephone on his desk. With a tired yawn he reached across, picked up the receiver and as surprised to hear the crusty voice of Captain Storey.

'Good evening, sir,' Hailey said, suddenly sitting upright, 'as it's Sunday I thought you might be still on the golf course.'

'Firstly,' grunted the captain. 'It's not a good evening so I'll come straight to the point.' He paused, and Hailey heard the muffled sound of the captain puffing on his pipe. 'The *Doncaster*, one of the escorts in the Persian Gulf has been involved in a collision with some uncharted rocks and has been badly damaged. No fatalities but several minor injuries. A Polish frigate, the *Gadansk*, has towed her into Bahrain. She's now in dry dock and God knows how long she'll be out of commission. This means the escorts for the tankers are one warship short.' He paused slightly to take a breath then went on, 'Now, my boy,' the captain added, taking another puff of his pipe. 'There is something else you should know. It'll be on the nine o'clock, news so I might as well tell you now. An Islamic militant group have stolen three Mirage Delta wing fighters from Tripoli airport. As you know after the assassination of Colonel Gaddafi two years ago, Al Qaeda have controlled parts of the airport. It is thought that the Masked Men Brigade, an Islamic organisation, have captured the fighters.'

'My God!' exclaimed Hailey. 'Do we know where they've been flown to?'

'Somewhere in Syria, I think,' the captain answered cautiously. 'But nobody's sure.'

Hailey furrowed his brow and pursed his lips, then said. 'If that is true, sir, they could be within striking distance of the Gulf.'

'That's right,' replied the captain, 'and the blighters have thirty millimetre cannons and Exocet missiles, one each wing that can be deadly at three hundred yards. Luckily, we have an allied air base in Bahrain, and the aircraft carrier, USS *Coral Sea*, is in the area.'

'I'm sure the long range radar system and our Sea Wolf missiles can deal with them if we're attacked,' Hailey answered confidently.

'Maybe so,' the captain replied cautiously, 'but remember, the Sea Wolfs only have a maximum range of ten kilometres.' The captain paused then took a deep breath, then went on, 'There us something else you should know. A French destroyer, the *La Gallant*, exploded and sank off the coast of Libya two weeks ago. MOD thinks it was a flat mine so called because of its shape. It contained an explosive called Trysin and floats just below the surface. Consequently, it's hard to detect by radar. The damn things appear to, be laid down from a dhow or skip. The boffins don't know too much about it but it is very powerful. However, I'm told they are rather expensive for Al Qaeda to manufacture in bulk, so it's unlikely you'll come across them. Nevertheless you'd be wise to let your officers know about it.'

'Indeed I will, sir,' Hailey replied, furrowing his brow, 'were there any survivors from the French destroyer?'

'Luckily,' Storey replied, 'most of the crew got away and were picked up by an American frigate. Now, my boy, how soon can you put to sea?'

'Tomorrow morning at the earliest sir,' Hailey confidently replied. 'Several of the crew living locally can be recalled and the others are on board nursing hangovers I imagine.'

'Splendid,' the captain answered taking a deep breath. 'You are to sail for Bahrain and report to Fleet Commander Vice Admiral Phillip Jones, at the UK Component Command. He will give you further instructions. I will send you all this in a confidential fax. Any questions?'

'Yes, sir,' Hailey replied, nervously licking his lips. 'I've been reading in the papers that there is an increased gunboat activity in the Gulf area.'

'Indeed there is,' the Storey said, 'and as you may know, NATO has agreed for a twenty-mile no- go area around the Yemen. This was done hoping the Yemeni ruler would stop turning a blind eye to the pirates operating from that area.'

'And has it?' Hailey asked.

'I'm afraid not,' Storey replied, 'but nevertheless, try not to enter the no go zone as it might cause an international incident, but the admiral will fill you in on all that. Good luck, my boy and Godspeed.'

CHAPTER SIXTEEN

It was shortly after 2215 when Noble drove through the dockyard gates, parked the MG, switched off the engine, locked the door and hurried on board. The White Ensign on the stern flapped wildly in the stiff north westerly breeze and high above the moon's white orb flitted in between clusters of grey clouds scudding across the sky.

Gooding was standing on the top of the gangway as Noble stepped onto the fight deck. Close by stood Jack Whitton, and Pete Price.

'What the devil's happening, Paul?' Noble asked, slightly out of breath while acknowledging the salutes of all three.

'You've probably been too preoccupied to have heard the nine o'clock news,' Gooding replied with a suggestive grin. After telling Noble about the jet fighters being hijacked and the accident involving HMS *Doncaster*, he gave Noble an all-knowing look and added, 'So a pound to a penny it's something to do with that.'

'You're probably right,' answered Noble. 'Anything else I should know?'

'The captain has told the crew that the ship is under sailing orders and hands will be required for leaving harbour at 0800 and he would announce more details when we were at sea.'

'All very hush-hush, then,' said Noble, raising his eyebrows

'So it seems,' Gooding remarked, a puzzled expression on his face. 'The engineer officer and chief stoker have been ordered to flash up the engines.' Almost as an afterthought, he added, 'Oh, and the officers are to muster in the wardroom at twenty-three hundred.'

Standing a few yards away, Whitton and Price overheard what was being said and glanced warily at one another.

'This won't go down too well with the lads,' Whitton whispered to Price

'Aye, you're right there, PO,' Price quietly replied, 'especially with those who are RA.'

(RA meant personnel who lived locally and were 'rationed ashore.')

On his way to the captain's cabin, Noble stopped halfway along a passage way and decided to phone Cynthia. He took out his mobile phone and pressed in her number.

'I was hoping you would phone, darling,' Cynthia answered, doing her best to stifle a yawn. 'What's happening?

'Err . . . sorry darling,' Noble replied hesitatingly. 'We sail in the morning. At the moment I'm not sure where to or for how long.'

'Oh my God,' Cynthia cried, 'don't tell me. I watched the ten o'clock news on the television. It's something to with that frigate and the jet fighters being captured by Al Qaeda, isn't it?'

'You probably right, darling,' Noble replied, 'but I'm . . .'

Cynthia abruptly interrupted him. 'It seems we're fated not to be together,' she said, trying her best not to cry. 'You've not long come back from the West Indies, and now this.'

Noble sighed wearily then repeated, 'I'm sorry, but that's the navy for you . . .'

'The damned navy,' she cried angrily. 'I'm sick and tired of the bloody navy,' and switched of her phone. He tried to contact her again but she didn't answer. Oh well, he thought, to himself, I can't say I blame her for being pissed off, and put his phone in his pocket.

Noble arrived outside the captain's cabin and knocked on the door. Hailey was sitting behind his desk reading a document. As Noble came in he looked up.

'Ah, Number One,' he said, raising his eyebrows, 'sorry to drag you away from the lovely Cynthia, but do sit down and I'll tell you why I did so.'

'Thank you, sir,' Noble replied lowering himself into an armchair and crossing his legs. 'I missed the news on the radio, but Paul has filled me in.'

'Bad business all round,' Hailey said, 'as you've heard the ship is under sailing orders and I've ordered Norman and his stokers to stand by. It'll take about four hours for the engines to be ready, then another thirty minutes or so before we can sail.'

'The situation really does sound serious, sir,' Noble replied, frowning as he spoke. 'Luckily all the crew are on board.'

'Yes, it is,' Hailey answered, nodding in agreement. At that moment a knock came at the door and Gooding came in.

'Twenty-two fifty-five, sir,' said Gooding, removing his cap. 'All officers mustered in the wardroom.'

'Thank you, Pilot,' Hailey replied standing up, 'the First Lieutenant and I will be there presently.'

At precisely 2300 Hailey and Noble entered the crowded wardroom. As they did so those officers who was seated stood up. Having watched the drama unfold on the ten o'clock news they had a firm idea of the implications it had for *Dawlish* and waited anxiously to hear what Hailey had to say.

Hailey immediately sensed the tension in the air as he felt the eyes of the men and women he knew so well peering apprehensively at him.

'Good evening, everyone,' said Hailey, 'do sit down. There's coffee on the sideboard, so do help yourselves.'

Hailey stood with both thumbs protruding from his jacket pockets. Noble waited slightly behind him.

'I'll come straight to the point,' said Hailey. 'I'm sure you have all heard the news about the situation in the Gulf. As you all know, *Dawlish* has been maintained at high readiness for such an emergency. Well tomorrow morning we are to sail for the Persian Gulf and become part of the Armilla Patrol.' He paused momentarily as Noble handed him a cup of coffee. After taking a sip, he looked inquisitively around at his audience and said, 'Any questions.'

Several officers immediately indicted by a slight raising of their hand.

'Yes, what is it Martin?' Hailey asked, looking enquiringly at his supply officer.

'Will we be taking on stores, sir?' Rogers asked, pensively stroking the bristles on his chin. 'By the time we reach Bahrain, the chief cook tells me we will have used nearly twenty thousand eggs and a tons of beans, and that's just for breakfast.'

Hailey gave a short, throaty laugh. 'I'm glad to hear the crew have hearty appetites, Martin,' Hailey answered, 'But I expect to RAS with RFA *Wave Ruler* but as yet a rendezvous has not been arranged. Rest assured I'll let you and everyone else know when it has.' (RAS means Replenishment at Sea.)

'What about fuel, sir?' asked Bosley. 'As you know, we use forty-five tons a day.'

'Quite so, Norman,' Hailey answered after taking a sip of coffee. 'We'll take more fuel on when we meet *Wave Ruler.*'

'How long do you expect us to be away, sir? Asked Henderson who was sitting on a settee next to Liz Hall.

'Your guess is as good as mine, Bob,' Hailey replied flatly. '*Dawlish* will be part of Operation Oracle, which is the UK's contribution to the war on terror.'

'How many other ships are involved besides ourselves, sir?' asked Gooding, his pale blue eyes wide-eyed with concentrated interest.

'Good question, Pilot,' said Hailey, finishing his coffee and placing the cup on a nearby table. 'As far as I know, there are seven of our ships plus a Polish and a French frigate, as well as RFAs *Fort Austin, Cardigan Bay* and *Diligence.* But the main priority of all of them is the safety of the oil tankers and vessels carrying nuclear waste.'

'What's the range of these Delta Mirage fighters, sir,' Shirley Mannering asked nervously as. 'Are they likely to attack the shipping in the Gulf?'

'That's a contingency we will have to be prepared for,' Hailey replied with a firm glint in his eyes, 'but I'm confident we'll be able to deal with them should it become necessary.

Somersby raised his hand. 'Excuse me, sir, 'he said in a crisp north country accent. 'I read in the papers that piracy is still a major problem? As you know my Royals made several helicopter landing on ships when we were in the Caribbean.'

'And a damn good job you and your team did, John,' replied Hailey with a wry smile. 'Piracy in the Gulf of Aden, Persia and Somalia have reached unprecedented levels during the last ten years. In 2012 seventy-five ships reported attacks as well as twenty-eight hijackings.' Hailey paused for a few seconds then with a grave expression on his face, went on. 'Remember, ladies and gentlemen, that seventy-two percent of oil supplies flow through the Gulf and Middle East, so anti-terrorism and anti-piracy will be high on our agenda. So I expect your men will be required again.'

'Excuse me, sir,' Midshipman Dunlop, ventured nervously raising his hand while his pale features slowly turned red. 'I hear that Somalia is a haven for terrorists and pirates. Is err . . . that right, sir?'

'I'm glad to see our young officers are up to date on international affairs,' Hailey replied adding with a smile. 'You hear right, my boy, this makes catching the blighters difficult as the local population give them shelter in return for protection from unfriendly tribes. Although we must be aware of the dangers posed by pirates, our main concern will be the Persian Gulf area. Now,' he went on looking at the tired faces staring at him, there is something else you should know.' For the next five minutes he told them about Al Qaeda's flat mines.

'If my team can't pick them up on radar, sir,' said Henderson gravely, 'how the blazes are we to find them?'

'Report anything, big or small, Bob,' Hailey answered calmly, 'but so far none have been found in the Gulf.' Hailey gave a quick, inquisitive scan at the faces in front of him, and said, 'Now ladies and gentlemen, if there's no more questions . . .'

'I have one sir,' offered Milton, blushing slightly.

'Yes, Mary,' Hailey said, 'what is it?'

'I'm sorry to say, sir,' she went on, slightly embarrassed, 'but we may be needing more toilet rolls before we reach Bahrain.'

Her words brought forth a peel of laughter from the other officers.

'Thank you,' Hailey replied supressing a smile, 'send a signal to Gib requesting some. If those jet fighters the Islamists stole, attack us, we may need them.' When the resultant laughter had died down, he added, 'Now if there's no more questions, II suggest we turn in. We're in for a busy day tomorrow.'

As the officers left the room, Henderson turned to Liz, 'Pity we're sailing so soon,' he said delicately whispering in her ear, 'I was going to ask you to have dinner with me.'

'Where you indeed,' Liz answered glancing up at his handsome features, 'and you a happily married man.'

'Well,' Henderson muttered almost incoherently, 'let us just say married. Anyway, would you have accepted my offer?'

'I might, and then I might not,' Liz replied giving him a coquettish smile, and walked ahead of him towards her cabin.

CHAPTER SEVENTEEN

Thanks to Jack Whitton and Pete Price, the news that the ship would soon be sailing spread around the ship like wildfire.

In the senior ratings mess it was greeted with typical equanimity.

Harry Tate grinned at Wally Hardman, who was married and lived in Gosport.

'Well mate,' Wally said taking a good gulp of beer, 'that'll put paid to you and the other RA lads getting a bit for a while.'

Harry shook his head and with a grateful sigh, replied. 'I could do with a rest. I'm sure that b bloody woman of mine's become a nympho.'

'Lucky you,' chimed in Jock Forbes, 'my missus is as frigid as ice.'

With a loud guffaw Harry downed a small glass of whisky and cried, 'maybe the fact that she's had five kids might have summat to do with it.'

'Oh well,' muttered Jock climbing into his bunk, 'perhaps those swarthy birds with big tits in Bahrain will do a turn.'

'In your dreams,' chimed in Wally, 'I was in Bahrain on a minesweeper two years ago. The local women are all Muslims so you've got no chance, mate.'

The girls had also watched the ten o'clock news on the BBC.

'I wonder if that's anything to do with us sailing tomorrow,' yawned Jilly Howard slipping into her nightgown and climbing into her bunk.

'I don't care,' said Susan, who, like Lottie in the bunk above was also turned in. 'This is my first ship and I'm dying to go to sea.'

'Don't forget to take some of your sea-sick tablets, love,' muttered Laura Griffiths as she started to undress. 'You'll need them when we hit a drop of roughers.'

'Personally I'll be glad to get to sea, again,' chimed Fiona Green, 'being alongside the wharf is boring and there's not much to do in Pompey'.

In the bunk below Laura, Diana had her eyes closed thinking of Ashir. The realisation that she was in love with him worried her. After all he was a Muslim, and she a catholic. Her instinct told her he was more than fond of her. She could see it in his eyes when he looked at her. Furthermore she knew the Koran forbade an intimate relationship between a Muslim and a Christian girl. It was a very frustrating situation.

At that moment Sadie Thompson came into the mess. She wore a white towelling dressing gown and pink, fluffy slippers. 'Pipe down, you lot,' she said switching off the lights, 'and get some sleep. You're in for a busy day tomorrow.'

Nobody was asleep in the ratings' mess. The lights were on and several men in their bunks, reading and wondering when they would see their wives and girl-friends again.

'How long do you think we'll be away for this time?' said Pete Price poking his head over the side of his bunk and glancing down at Dixie Dean.

'How the fuck should I know, you dozy bugger,' Dixie replied, engrossed in reading *Fifty Shades of Grey,* 'anyway,' he added impatiently, 'don't bother me, the bird in this book is just about to get tied up and shagged.'

'After you with the book,' cried Dutch Holland from across the mess.

'Fuckin' pervert,' grunted Shady Lane as he climbed up into his bunk. 'But put me on the list. I'll force myself to read it.'

Walker heard the news of what was happening with a heavy heart. From his bottom bunk he stared at the sagging mattress directly above him worrying about Kate. Earlier, he had met Smyth on the flight deck. The doctor told him that Kate had been moved to the intensive care ward.

'Does that mean she's getting worse, sir?' he had asked Smyth.

'Err … not really,' Smyth hesitatingly replied, 'it's just so she can receive more expert treatment.'

However, the tone of the doctor's voice and the pained expression on his face was not convincing. Walker closed his eyes knowing sleep wold be impossible.

Ashir, who slept below Shady Lane, hardly heard what his mess mates were saying, his thoughts were elsewhere. Tomorrow, he told himself, he would leave England never to return. He consoled himself by remembering the teachings in the Koran that said families, after they died would be united in Paradise. Allah had given him a task to do. This involved not only the death of himself, but also Diana, the woman who had stirred emotions that were completely alien to him and his religious beliefs. His thoughts turned to his mess mates; men who, despite being infidels, he had grown to trust and even liked. Then there was Butch Cassidy, who had saved his life that night in Southsea. After he had undressed he had opened his locker and reached under a set of shirts and gingerly felt the package of Trysin, the explosive that would send him, Diana and the rest of the crew to their deaths. Now, as he slipped into bed, he began to doubt himself. He closed his eyes and silently prayed to Allah to give him strength and the courage to do his bidding.

CHAPTER EIGHTEEN

Shortly before 0800 on Monday 5 August, preparations were made in readiness for *Dawlish* to leave harbour. All hatchways were closed and the crew were at Enhanced Cruising Stations, this is the normal peacetime passage state defined as the third degree readiness for battle. Clusters of grey, altostratus clouds, racing d across the sky promised rain and a harsh north westerly wind blew down river.

On either side of the fight deck a line of ratings and royal marines were fallen in for leaving harbour. This was a ritual ceremony dated back to Nelson's time. When in those days, entering or leaving port it demonstrated that the guns were not manned and that the ship was friendly.

Using a loud hailer Noble ordered duty ratings to release the fore and after breast ropes. This was followed by the removal of the after and fore breast springs. (These so-called 'springs' are used to prevent the ship moving back or forward). Lastly the head rope and stern rope are unshackled. With this last drill completed, the ship rolled gently as she moved away from the wharf.

Standing near the binnacle Hailey nodded to Gooding, and in a quiet, calm voice said, 'set he lever at thirty, Pilot, half ahead both engines.'

Almost immediately the whine of the two Rolls Royce Spey gas turbine engines, delivering 123,190Kw (31,100shp), burst into action. From the stern the dark green waters began churning into a mass of foamy turbulence. The frigate trembled slightly then began moving forward. A few minutes later, gaining speed, the ship cruised past Semaphore Towers. Close by, moored alongside the wharf were two frigates. On the starboard wing of each of them an officer stood to attention saluting.

'Attention on the upper deck, face the port,' came the strident tones of duty Dutch Holland, over the tannoy.

Hailey and Noble moved to the port wing, stood to attention and saluted

The tall dark haired figure of Lieutenant Martin came onto the bridge holding a signal pad. 'Message from Admiral Fearnley, sir, it reads, "*Good luck and Godspeed.*"'

'Reply,' said Hailey, 'say, "'*Thank you, sir, God Save the Queen*"'

After passing the frigates Hailey glanced at Dutch Holland and ordered, 'Pipe the 'carry on, QM.' This allowed those fallen in on the upper deck to relax and return to their duties.

Even though it was shortly after 0800, a small gathering of wives and girl-friends had congregated on The Hard. (Situated near the end of the harbour the Hard was once a slipway built in the 19th century by rolling clay until it was hard, hence the name.)

Breaking with protocol, Hailey said, 'Make a pipe, Number One, and tell those on the upper deck to give them a wave.'

Using his binoculars, Noble made out the tiny image of Cynthia's face and shoulders looking out of the window of Queen's Hotel, smiling as she waved her hand, no doubt, wondering as he was, when they would next meet

Dawlish made her way past Fort Blockhouse and entered the choppy waters of The Solent. On the starboard bow, the dark outline of the Isle of Wight could be seen partially shrouded by the early morning grey mist.

'Looks like rain, Number One,' Hailey remarked, glancing warily at the sky while easing himself into his high-backed chair, 'alter course ten degrees to starboard. Is there anything on the radar?

'WEO tells me there is four container ships coming up the channel, two miles apart, sir.' Noble replied, 'and behind them are two more, otherwise, nothing else at the moment.'

Shortly after 0900 *Dawlish* cruised past The Needles, a row of thee distinctive craggy pillars of chalk rising out of the sea on the western extremity of the Isle of Wight. In the days of sail and before radar, these were a navigation hazard. At this point the ship encountered the high rolling seas of the English Channel. Without warning, the sky suddenly darkened accompanied by the booming sound of thunder. This was quickly followed by jagged flashes of forked lightning. Each ear-splitting clap lit up the heavens. Then, with the blink of an eye, the flash disappeared leaving the sky a rumbling mass of darkness. Adding to nature's cacophony, walls of rain began belting down, obscuring the view from the bridge. The bitterly cold westerly wind increased, whipping the sea into a cauldron of angry white horses. The ship began to roll, dip and dive sending foamy bow waves exploding high over the fo'c'sle.

'Fall out special sea duty men,' Hailey said, watching the rain splatter against the outside of the three inch thick Plexigras windows, 'assume Cruising Stations, and pipe all hands keep clear of the upper deck. '

The sickbay, situated aft on number two deck was fairly big. Strips of neon from a in a low slung white deck head provided a clear lighting and the sharp smell of antiseptic permeated the warm, comfortable atmosphere. The deck was covered in brown linoleum kept pristine by daily polishing. Close by secured to the deck was a glass medicine cabinet. Next to this was a tall oaken chest with drawers and cupboards containing medicines and drugs. Snug against one bulkhead was a desk on which rested a computer used for recording case histories and consultations with specialists in the Queen Alexandra's Hospital. Two bunks which could be partitioned off should anyone be admitted occupied on side. A stainless steel sink with elbow taps lay next to closed door leading into a bathroom, heads and shower. The time was 1000. 'Stand Easy' had just been piped and Dixie Dean was standing next to the glass topped treatment table. At regular intervals a rating would knock on the door and come in. On one such occasion, the tall figure of Able Seaman Baker entered, the pallor of his face resembling the pale green bulkheads. Like those before him he was obviously suffering from the dreaded mal de mere.

'Never mind, Baggsy,' Dixie remarked, handing him two small pink tablets, 'remember Nelson was always seasick whenever the *Victory* left harbour,' then with a sly grin added,, 'by the way, would you like a greasy bacon sandwich I brought from the galley a few minutes ago ?'

'Fuck off, you miserable pox doctors clerk,' muttered Baker accepting the tablets then slamming the door as he left.

Among the sea sick suffers was Susan Hughes who had retreated to the sanctuary of her mess and was now lying on her bunk.

'I did warn you, love, 'said Laura Griffiths, noticing Susan's greenish pallor. Along with Lottie Jones and Jilly Howard, Laura had come into the mess for a mug of tea. 'But don't worry,' she added, giving Susan a commiserating smile. 'We were all the same when we first went to sea.'

'Is it always like this?' Susan moaned, using a handkerchief to wipe the sweat from her brow.

'Wait till we reach the Bay of Biscay,' chimed Jilly, grabbing hold of the table in a vain attempt to avoid spilling her tea onto the carpet. 'Then it really cuts up rough. Doesn't it girls?

Susan didn't wait for them to answer. With a sudden cry, she clutched her stomach, slid quickly from her bunk and with the help of Laura staggered to the heads.

Down in the operations room, the tactical nerve centre of the ship, P WO (Pronounced 'Pea-woh), Bob Henderson stood next is assistants Lieutenant Tug Wilson and Spud Murphy.

'Keep a careful watch on those container ships,' Henderson said, studying the tiny blips on his radar screen, showing the presence of all shipping in the English Channel within a radius of ninety miles. 'We don't want a recurrence of the fiasco that happened during sea trials.'

Henderson smiled inwardly. Gone were the days of the gunnery officer giving firing instructions from the director platform above the bridge, in modern warships this was done using the automatic weapons systems Now, on modern warships everything was computerised . . . everything except dealing with the irrational behaviour of the sea, and that was dealt with by good old fashioned seamanship.

Ashir and Diana formed part of a six man team manning their respective screens. The atmosphere was pleasantly warm and the only sounds were the gentle whine of the engines and the buzz of the generators. Situated directly under the bridge everyone in the Ops Room felt every movement as the ship coursed its way through the rough sea. Ashir was no exception. Each sway and dip of the ship increased the pressure rising in his stomach.

'How are you feeling?' enquired Diana, shooting Ashir a pensive glance. The orange glow from his radar screen on his swarthy skin hid the effects of the weather on him. 'Not feeling seasick or anything. If you are, tell Chief Murphy, he'll understand. After all, this is your first ship.'

Diana's remarks, although conciliatory, seemed to increase Ashir's nausea. He mumbled thanks then with a glance at Murphy, unhooked his earpiece and left the room. A few minutes later he was heaving his heart out in the heads.

Normally during fine weather visibility from the bridge was roughly ten nautical miles. (One nautical male equals 1.151 land miles). However walls of rain slanting against the windows restricted this to roughly four miles.

'What's our speed, Number One?' Hailey asked, clasping both sides of his high-backed chair.

'Twenty knots, sir,' Noble replied, 'and the nearest vessel is two miles to port,' he added bending slightly and staring through the compass repeater.

'Too close for comfort in this weather,' Hailey, said warily, 'set the lever at ten degrees to starboard and increase speed to twenty-two knots.' Glancing pensively at Gooding, he added, 'how long is this weather expected to last, Pilot?'

'About twenty-four hours, sir,' Gooding replied, scratching his chin while looking the barometer, 'and at the speed we're going, we ought to sight the Rock in three days.'

'Thank you, Pilot.' Hailey answered. Then glancing at Noble he went on, 'ask the flight commander and the marine officer to come to the bridge, please Number One.'

Five minutes later Commander Jerry Ashcroft and John Somersby, arrived. Both officers were bareheaded. Ashcroft wore is uniform trousers with his white shirt and tie visible over his dark blue jersey. Somersby was dressed in khaki. The creases in his trousers were knife-edged and on each shoulder of his jersey the Royal Marine insignia was clearly evident.

'Good morning, gentlemen, such as it is,' said Hailey. Before the officers had time to reply, Hailey went on. 'I won't keep you long. I'm told we should expect better weather tomorrow. If this is so, I'd like to launch the helo and practice landing marines on the port bridge wing. We haven't practiced this since we returned from the West Indies and I want us to be ready in case it's needed. Any questions?'

'No, sir,' both officers replied.

'Right, answered Hailey dismissively, 'then I suggest you both go and have a nice warm cup of coffee in the wardroom.'

CHAPTER NINETEEN

Just as Gooding predicted, next morning was dull and overcast but the rain had stopped. The cold north westerly wind remained strong and high above a pale yellow sun flitted in between clusters of dark grey clouds. Hailey came onto the bridge at exactly 0800, closely followed by the First Lieutenant.

'Good morning,' Hailey said, glancing at Shirley Mannering, who had just taken over the morning watch from Gooding. 'What's our position and speed?'

'Latitude, fifty degrees north, longitude ten, speed twenty knots, sir,' Mannering replied, lowering her binoculars.

'Thank you,' Hailey answered as he eased himself into his high chair. 'Thank goodness the rain has stopped, Number One,' he said giving Noble an approving smile, 'here's hoping it stays like this.''

Hailey wasn't the only one glad that the weather had abated. At 0730, Susan Hughes, looking slightly better than yesterday, entered the mess. However, the sharp smell of fried bacon and eggs attacked her taste buds and nearly made her turn around and head for her bunk.

'Well, now that you've found your sea legs, Sue,' said Lottie Jones, 'how about a nice fried egg sarnie?'

'You know what you can do with that,' Susan responded acidly, 'and don't spare the tomato sauce.'

'Never mind, Sue,' chimed in Diana, 'you weren't the only one to suffer. Ash, the poor thing became green and had to be turned in.'

'Pity you couldn't have joined him and stroked his fevered brow,' said Jilly Howard with a hint of jealousy.

'Or stroked something else,' Jean Rochester grinned salaciously. Jean was a tall, statuesque brunette with emerald green eyes. She was Kate Harrison's replacement and had joined the ship the day prior to sailing.

116

'Meow, meow, saucers of milk all round,' Diana replied, pulling a face at Jean, 'anyway I met him earlier in the passage way and he's fully recovered,'

'And raring to go, no doubt. Here,' Jean added filling mug of tea from a large aluminium urn and handing it to Susan.

'Cheers, Jeanie,' Susan said accepting the mug, 'but don't you girls think of anything else but sex?' 'Not with all those gorgeous boot necks flashing their muscles,' Lottie replied with a mischievous grin.

Shortly after 0900 Hailey sent for Ashcroft and Somersby. A few minutes later both officers came onto the bridge.

'Good morning, gentlemen,' Hailey said, looking at the pensive expressions on their faces. 'As you can see,' he added, giving a reassuring glance out of the bridge window, 'the weather has improved sufficiently to launch the Lynx and also to give the royals a bit of PVV practice.'(Potential Violating Vessel).

'When sir?' Ashcroft asked.

'Thirteen hundred, 'replied Hailey, 'I'll reduce speed as the wind is still quite strong. How are your Royals, John?' Hailey added raising his eyebrows and looking at Somersby.

'Raring to go as usual, sir, grinned Somersby.

'Good,' Hailey flatly replied. 'Landing on bridge wing may prove a challenge in this wind, but I'm sure your lads will manage it.'

'I'm sure we will, sir,' Somersby replied warily, listening to the high wind beating against the bridge windows.

At 1200, the tall figure of Flight Engineer Hector Pascoe, stood outside the hangar. The blue overalls he wore was slightly oil-stained as were those worn by the six maintenance ratings lined up before him. Earlier, they had enjoyed an early dinner of chicken and chips and roly-poly jam pudding.

'Right then, my 'andsomes,' Pascoe grunted in his sharp West Country accent, 'let's get the old Bug out. The flight commander wants a take-off at thirteen hundred.'

'It's still blowing a bastard,' chimed Able Seaman Dolly Gray. As if to confirm this a sudden gust of wind attacked his mop of dark, curly hair, making him look as if he'd had an electric shock.

'Ours is not reason why,' replied Pascoe, 'so just get on with it.'

A few minutes later the tannoy clicked into action. This was quickly followed by strident voice of the duty QM.

'D'you hear there. The helicopter will be launched at thirteen hundred. Hands keep clear of the flight deck.'

Noble also shared Gray's concern about the strength of the wind.

'Are you sure it's wise to launch the helo, sir,' queried Noble, 'the WEO tells me it's bowing a force five gale.

Perched on his high chair, Hailey gave Noble an all-knowing glance. 'You may have forgotten, Number One,' he said somewhat smugly, 'but the Lynx differs from its army counterpart in that it can operate safely on a pitching and rolling flight deck. This is because it's fitted with a mechanical harpoon that hooks that engages with a trellised grid on the flight deck. The mechanism locks the helo onto the flight deck allowing it to swivel into the wind for take-off and land safely, even in a heavy sea.'

'I'm well aware of that, sir,' Noble answered feeling as if he were being lectured to. 'If you remember, I did the helo course at Lee-on-Solent. I just thought it prudent to mention what could be a dicey business.

'Thank you for your concern, Number One,' Hailey replied tersely, 'but I can assure you there's nothing to worry about. '

'You hope,' Noble muttered under his breath as he turned away.

A few minutes after 1230 the metal door on the hanger was raised. Pushed by the maintenance crew the Lynx emerged, its rotor blades folded like a butterfly emerging fresh from its chrysalis. Powered by two Rolls Royce Gem 60 engines that drive the four-bladed rigid -rotor system, the aircraft can climb at a normal rate of over 2100 feet per minute and cruise at 125 knots even when fully loaded with nine passengers. On patrol in the Gulf or other vital areas, the Lynx can carry a contingent of Royal Marine Commandos who can be lowered onto the deck of any vessel suspected of carrying, drugs, arms or explosive devices. This, plus being armed with four Sea Skua anti-ship missiles and two anti-submarine torpedoes make the Lynx is a formidable weapon.

'Spreading rotors,' shouted Pascoe to one of the crew.

'Pin out,' cried another rating, making sure the main body was free of the hangar.

'All ready,' called Pascoe, he then added, 'align rotors.'

In the hangar the tall figure of Lieutenant Mike Roberts, the flight observer, was joined by Ashcroft and Harry Thomas, the Duty flight deck officer.

'Everything all set, Mike?' Ashcroft asked, watching the crew at work.

'Yes, sir,' Roberts replied, adjusting the strap on his helmet. 'All we need now are the Royals,' he added.

A few seconds later Ashcroft was joined by Somersby. Behind him, six marines led by Butch Cassidy, filed out of the hangar and lined up close to the helicopter. All seven wore their green berets firmly clamped on their heads, flak jackets over their green fatigues and carried a small arms rifle. (Type 556SA80, a standard weapon for all forces.) Except for a 9mm Browning strapped to his side in a leather holster, Somersby was similarly dressed. Nearby stood Able Seaman Buck Taylor. In his left hand he carried a coil of a thick, green wool and nylon rope.

'Right, now listen you lot,' Cassidy said, staring at the marines. As he spoke a gust of wind hit him and the group knocking them slightly back. 'You've all done a drop several times on the decks of ships. But this time you'll land on the port wing of the bridge deck. Savy?' he paused momentarily allowing this information to sink in. 'So be extra careful. I don't want any fuck ups, understand?'

'I say sarge,' chimed in Knocker White, 'Won't it be a bit dicey dropping in this wind?'

'Yours is not to reason why, Knocker,' Cassidy relied curtly. 'Now shut up while I tell you the drop order. Pedlar Palmer, then Spider, Yorkie, Taffy, Jock and lastly Knocker. I will then drop followed by the lieutenant. Any questions?'

Knocker was about to speak, but caught Cassidy's steely eyed gaze and changed his mind.

On the bridge Hailey glanced impatiently at Noble, and said, 'better phone Jerry Ashcroft,
Number One, and ask when the helo will be ready to take off.'

Just as Hailey finished speaking, the bridge intercom buzzed and was unhooked by Gooding.

'Flight deck reports helo will take off in fifteen minutes, sir,' Gooding reported, and replaced the intercom.

'Reduce speed to fifteen knots, Number One,' Hailey said, giving Noble a disarming look.

On the flight deck Ashcroft put on a set of orange gloves and climbed into the helicopters cockpit and began checking his instruments. Mike Roberts quickly followed him and belted himself in.

'Right, sergeant,' Somersby said, nodding approvingly at Cassidy, 'let's get on board.'

Cassidy snapped to attention and gave a smart salute. 'Sir,' he gruffly replied, then turned to his fellow marines and shouted, 'Ok you lot, get a move on.'

One by one the marines climbed into the Lynx through the side door of the fuselage and sat opposite one another. Taylor slammed the door closed, then gave a thumbs up to Somersby.

'All correct, sir, ready when you are, sir,' Somersby said to Ashcroft, who immediately nodded in acknowledgement. Using his left hand, Ashcroft moved the 'collective', a lever that would start the ascent of the helo. Immediately, the four rotor blades began to turn, slowly at first then increasing into a roaring blur of circular motion. Ashcroft gradually eased the collective up and adjusted the trim. Below, the flight deck team grimaced and moved away from the powerful downward draught created by the rotors. Almost straight away the Lynx moved upwards, hovering momentarily, then leaning gently to one side before surging gracefully upwards towards the open sea, climbing steadily.

At about 1000 feet and two miles away, Ashcroft turned his head and glanced below at the battle-grey shape of *Dawlish* cruising through the heavy, rolling sea.

'The old girl looks like one of those models I made when I was a boy, doesn't she Mike?' making his voice head over the smooth buzzing sound of the engines.

With a wry smile, Roberts glanced at Ashcroft and said, 'yes she does, sir, only the ones I made always sank in the bath.'

Ashcroft didn't reply. Glancing down quickly he imagined the faint smell of diesel oil, mansion polish permeating throughout the ship, and food being prepared in the galley for tonight's dinner; Bob Henderson in the darkened Ops room overseeing his radar team; the doctor giving some poor bugger an injection; Liz Hall pouring over her computer and Shirley Mannering shouting out compass bearings to Jock Forbes.

'Turning for home,' shouted Ashcroft easing the collective to port.

From a window on the bridge, Hailey peered upwards at the tiny black speck approaching the ship.

'Landing on the port wing of the bridge could prove tricky in this wind, don't you think, sir?' Noble remarked again, giving Hailey a wary glance.

'As I told you before, Number One,' Hailey replied, slightly irritated at having to repeat himself, 'the helo is more than capable of doing t. Besides, they need more practice dropping onto restricted areas. The flight deck and fo'c'sle have become too easy. So stop worrying.'

On board the Lynx, Taylor shackled the nylon rope to an eyepiece on the bulkhead and gave a thumbs up to Cassidy.

'Everyone take your positions,' shouted Cassidy.

Pedlar Palmer was the first to drop. He moved forward, and holding onto a side strap, sat at the open door with his legs dangling outside. As he did so, he winced as a gust of a gust of wind hit him full in the face. Like those behind him, he wore a pair of heavy duty black suede gloves that prevented burns and enabled him to grasp the rope firmly.

Ashcroft eased the Lynx across *Dawlish*'s bow fifty feet below, casting a pale grey shadow that glided eerily across the fo'c'sle, the 4.5 Vickers gun and the Sea Wolf missile silo. Roberts gave a quick, glance downwards, noticing the flattening of the sea caused by the downward thrust of the rotor blades.

'Rope gone,' yelled Taylor, heaving the line out of the door.

Palmer nervously moistened his lips as he watched the rope straighten into a rod as it hit the deck. Using his leather gloves, grasped the rope and quickly descended onto the swaying deck. The next three marines quickly followed on. Knocker White, who was fifth in line, then began his descent. Half-way down, he felt a sudden jerk and came to an abrupt halt. He quickly looked over his shoulder and saw the shoulder strap of his rifle caught on the corner of the bridge wing. In vain, he swayed from side to side in an attempt to loosen the strap. At that moment a gust of wind almost forced him to loosen his grip on the rope.

Feeling his heart beating a cadence in his chest, he looked up and saw the face of Cassidy peering down from the open door of the Lynx.

'For fuck's sake, Sarge,' he yelled frantically, 'do summat, me rifle strap is snagged up.'

'I can see that, you dumb bugger,' Cassidy shouted, 'just hold tight, if you let go you'll probably fall in the drink.'

'Thanks a lot, Sarge,' Knocker shouted, his eyes bulging with fear and beads of sweat running down his pale face. 'Don't bloody worry, I'll fuckin' hold on.'

On board the Lynx, Somersby gave Ashcroft a worried look while explaining Knocker's predicament. 'Perhaps if you swayed the chopper a little, it might loosen the strap, sir,' Somersby shouted to Ashcroft.

Ashcroft shook his head. 'It might also force him to let go and in this wind, God knows where he'll end up,' he yelled, glancing over his shoulder, 'and if I landed the chopper, the downward thrust of the rotors could throw him against the bridge and injure him.'

Cassidy, gripping hold of the edge of the door overheard Ashcroft shouting. Then, looking down at Knocker clinging desperately onto the rope for dear life, he had an idea. He took off his gloves, unhitched his rifle then undid his flak jacket and dropped them on the floor.

'What are you doing, Sergeant?' shouted Somersby, feeling the Lynx jolt as the wind battered against the fuselage.

'I'm gunna go down and try and loosen the strap, sir,' Cassidy replied. 'This fuckin' wind is getting stronger and we'll have to do summat.'

'Well be damn careful,' warned Somersby, clutching hold of an overhead hand grip, 'and don't try anything foolish.'

'No problem, sir,' cried Cassidy taking hold of the rope. 'I've done more dangerous things on the battle training course at Lympstone.' He then looked down and yelled. 'Hold tight mate, I'm comin' down.'

'Well, for fuck's sake, be quick,' shouted Knocker, 'my arms are gettin' numb.'

Adjusting his green beret firmly on his head, Cassidy reached out for the rope. Until now he had never held the rope without using gloves and was surprised to feel how smooth and slippery it felt. Feeling it sway slightly, he slowly lowered himself until the soles of his leather boots were a few feet above Knocker's head.

'The straps are caught behind me, Sarge,' Knocker cried frantically, 'that's why I couldn't undo them.'

'I can see that,' yelled Cassidy, looking at the straps of Knocker's weapon twisted around the corner of the bridge roof. Feeling his heart beat a cadence in his chest, Cassidy placed both ankles around the rope to strengthen his position. With one hand he gripped the rope and using the other, he reached across and was about to unravel the strap when, to his horror, he felt his free hand slip slightly. The situation suddenly became even more precarious when yet another strong gust of wind rocked both the Lynx and the two men hanging onto the rope.

'*For Chrissake, Sarge, hurry up!*' Bawled Knocker, his voice barely audible in the wind. '*I can hardly feel my arms!*'

With beads of sweat running down the sides of his face, Cassidy tightened his grip on the rope, clenched his teeth and reached across and touched the straps. To his dismay, he found that the constant movement of the rope had tightened the straps. By now his fingers were numb with cold. He was only too aware that if he fell he would end up in the water and as the ship passed, he'd probably be caught by the propellers. He took a deep breath and after two attempts finally managed to unhitch the strap and grip the rope with his hand.

Hailey and everyone on the bridge looked up and saw the stationary figure of Knocker grimly
hanging on to the rope. They also noticed the reason for this.

'What do you think Ashcroft will do, sir? Noble asked, giving Hailey a worried glance.

'I'm not sure,' Hailey replied, 'but he'll have to do something bloody quick, the poor beggar can't stay there much longer.'

'Especially in this wind,' Noble added ironically.

At that moment they saw Cassidy appear.

'My God,' gasped Gooding, 'that takes some guts, better him than me.'

With bated breath they watched anxiously as Cassidy managed to free Knocker's rifle strap. A relieved expression immediately spread across Knocker's sweaty face as he disappeared from view quickly followed by

Cassidy. As Knocker slid to the deck in to the arms of his comrades, he didn't hear the cries of relief coming from Hailey and the others on the ridge.

Using his hands, Cassidy carefully followed Knocker down.

'Thanks Sarge,' gasped Knocker, breathing heavily while leaning and grasping a stanchion, 'but I did tell yer this fuckin' wind was too strong, didn't I?'

'Piss off and get below,' Cassidy replied curtly, 'that's a couple of cans of beer you owe me and be more bloody careful in future.'

A few seconds later, Ashcroft moved the collective upwards. Straightaway, the Lynx rose and banked to port. Ten minutes later, he landed the aircraft safely on the flight deck.

Noble glanced at Hailey who was now a very relieved man. 'What was that you said about having nothing to worry about, sir?' He asked, a smug expression written all over his heavily tanned face.

With a mischievous glint in his eyes, Hailey eased himself off his chair and replied, 'I hope you realise, Number One, that keelhauling for insubordination is still on the naval punishment statute book, now kindly increase speed to twenty knots. If you want me I'll be in my cabin,' and he slowly walked away.

CHAPTER TWENTY

During the night *Dawlish* entered the Bay of Biscay. The clear glow from the full moon, hovering among the fluffy white, altocumulus clouds, turned the dark sea into an undulating mass of silver. The time was 0200. The ship was in darkness. In the background, the constant hum of the air conditioning system and the monotonous throb of the engines was barely audible over the somnolent hiss coming from the frothy tide race passing down each side of hull.

The ship's company were at Cruising Stations. On the bridge Sub Lieutenant Morris, his carroty hair, covered by a navy blue beret, was sat comfortably on the captain's chair.

'The Bay seems unusually calm for this time of year, doesn't it Peter?' His question was directed to Midshipman Dudley-Small, who was using his sextant to obtain a fix. He could have easily asked the duty communications rating to consult his computer in the Ops, but use of the sextant was mandatory if he was to obtain his watch ticket. The breeze blowing from the east was cold and he, like Morris and Jake Whitton, wore duffel coats.

'Yes it is, sir,' Small replied, holding his instrument in his left hand, while using the other to adjust an aperture. 'The sea was so rough the last time I was sea sick until we reached Gib.'

'And, all being well,' said Whitton, stifling a yawn, 'that should be the day after tomorrow.'

Shortly after 0400 on Sunday 11 August, Nick Carter, one of four ratings on duty in the Ops Room, peered at his rectangular yellow screen and stifling a yawn, glanced across at Spud Murphy and reported. 'Coastline of Spain about a hundred miles on our port bow, Chief.'

'Cheers, Nick,' Murphy replied, 'I'll let the bridge know. With a bit of luck we'll arrive in Gib sometime on Monday.'

Morris received Murphy's report with a tired sigh. Even though his six-hour watch was up at 0600, he would still be required for day duty.

'Make a note in the log,' he said to Dudley-Small, while casually, watching a grey line of white appearing on the eastern horizon. 'And see if you can rustle PO Whitton and myself a nice warm mug of tea.'

In the engine room PO Dai Evans, was busy logging the level of oil pressure gauges. Four other stokers were keeping their eyes on temperature and diesel consumption dials. Everyone wore black, non-slip boots and overalls, washed so often the original dark blue had lost their original colour, and was now pale grey. Even though the atmosphere was pleasantly warm, beads of sweat ran down the sides of their faces.

Suddenly, Evans pricked up his ears, stopped what he was doing and listened.

'Did you hear it, Jacko?' he said to one of the stokers, 'that buzzing noise sounds like it's coming from the port diesel engine '

Everyone stood still and listened.

'And the diesel has fallen slightly, PO,' said another stoker, tapping the gauges glass covering.

'Bloody hell, boyo,' snapped Evans, nervously dabbing his brow with an off-white handkerchief, 'don't tell me we've got a problem with that bugger again.'

'I thought the dockyard had fixed it in Pompey,' replied Jacko, stroking the bristles on his chin.

'Indeed to goodness, didn't all of us,' Evans dolefully answered, 'I think I'd better wake the chief and the boss,' he added, unhooking the telephone from the bulkhead.

'I don't think he'll be too pleased, eh, PO?' muttered Jacko, taking a long swig of water from a bottle.

'Nor will the boss,' another stoker added, referring to Bosley.

Five minutes later, the bulky figure of Chief Engineer Bungy Williams came down the steel ladder, bleary eyed and yawning. Behind him came Bosley. The pink pyjamas poking under his white overalls, looking incongruously out of place, attracted a few raised eye brows.

'What's the problem, PO?' Bosley asked stifling a yawn.

'I can hear an odd buzzing noise coming from the port engine, sir,' replied Evans, 'can you hear it?'

Bosley stared at Evans, cocked his head to one side and listened. 'Yes, you're right, isn't he Chief?' said the officer, darkly furrowing his brow while giving Williams a look of concern.

'Yes, he is,' replied Williams, 'and it does sound like it's coming from the diesel engine.' Looking warily at Bosley, he tactfully added. 'Hadn't you better inform the captain, sir?'

'Yes,' replied Bosley, 'and someone wake up Lieutenant Vellacott and ask him to come down.'

The loud blare of the voiced pipe above his bunk woke Hailey up. He immediately reached up and unhooked the receiver.

'Captain,' he muttered, switching on his bedside light. The time by his wristwatch read 0415.

For a few minutes Hailey listened intently as Bosley explained the reason for disturbing him.

'I see, thank you, Norman,' Hailey replied, then, for a few seconds listened to the engines, 'yes, I can hear it. Do you it might be the same problem as before?'

'Yes, sir, it sounds like the turbocharger and brush alternator are at fault again.'

'Damn and blast!' Hailey exclaimed, throwing off his duvet, 'I thought the dockyard people in Pompey had dealt with that. Better inform the First Lieutenant and reduce speed to fifteen knots. I'll come up presently.'

Five minutes later, wearing a blue beret and a duffle coat over his night clothing Hailey arrived on the bridge. Noble, dressed similarly followed on behind.

'How soon long will it take to fix it, Norman?' Hailey muttered, blinking to allow his eyes to become accustomed to the dim blue lighting.

'I'd say about two days, sir,' Bosley replied cautiously. 'But it must be done in harbour. What d'you think, Dicky?' he added, looking speculatively at Vellacott.

After pursing his lips, Vellacott answered cagily, 'only if we worked around the clock, sir.'

'Very well,' Hailey replied. With a weary sigh he looked at Noble and went on. 'Send a signal to the harbour master at Gib, Number One,' say, "have a problem with port engine. Will remain Gib forty eight hours approx. Can only make fifteen knots max. Request berthing instructions. ETA now Monday 12", repeat the signal to MOD and Bahrain and announce the change of plans to the crew at 0630.'

Needless to say, the news of a run ashore in Gibraltar was greeted warmly.

'Pity we're not on the way home, eh, Pete,' quipped Shady Lane, glancing up from his 'herrings in'. (Herrings in tomato sauce.) Lane, and the others were in the mess having breakfast. 'Gib's a great place for buying rabbits.' (Rabbits was a naval nickname for presents.)

'Yeah, you're right there, mate,' Pete Price answered, mopping up his plate with a piece of bread, 'and the booze is duty free as well.'

'Bugger the rabbits,' chimed in Bud Abbott, opening a can of beer and taking a deep gulp, 'I'm gunna go up the Rock and take a few photies of them apes to send to me mum. Last time we were here, I was on duty.'

'If I were you, Bud,' said Dutch Holland, spreading jam on a piece of toast, 'I'd take a selfie and send that. I bet your mum wouldn't know the difference.'

'Maybe we could ask the girls to come with us for a run ashore,' said Shady, giving Ashir an all- knowing smile. 'I'm sure Di wouldn't mind.'

'I, err . . . don't know,' Ashir warily replied, 'after that night out in Pompey, she might not be keen.'

'Go away,' cried Bud Abbott, grinning like a Cheshire cat, 'she and the others will jump at the chance. We could meet at Jury's Bar on Main Street. If you remember, Pete, we had a great run ashore last year on the way to the West Indies.'

'Any news about Kate, Clubs?' asked Baggsy Baker.

Everyone stopped talking and looked expectantly at Peter Walker.

'Nothing, as yet,' he answered soberly, 'the last I heard she had been moved into the intensive care ward.'

In the senior ratings' mess, Harry Tate's weather-beaten features broke into a warm smile.

'Bloody great,' he said, downing the dregs of his mug of tea, 'I might be able to get in some fishing.'

'Personally, I'm gunna catch up on some sleep,' said Jock Forbes. 'I've lost count of the times I've been to Gib.'

'I think we'd better make the most of it,' Dusty Miller guardedly remarked. 'God only knows when we'll get another run ashore.'

Everyone in the wardroom had finished breakfast and were standing around having a last cup of coffee before going on duty.

Liz Hall put her empty cup on a nearby and was about to leave when Bob Henderson approached her, his handsome face wreathed in smiles.

'Before you go, Liz,' he said casually, 'as it looks like we'll be in Gib for a few days, I wondered if you'd given any thought to having dinner with me?' He paused, then added, 'as I recall, the Rock Hotel restaurant has the finest fresh fish in Gib.'

For a few seconds, Liz pursed her lips, then with a slight air of caution, replied, 'all right, but on one condition.'

'And what might that be?' Henderson asked, smiling slightly.

'That I'm back on board by twenty-three thirty,' she answered, 'you see I'm on duty at zero six hundred.'

'Of course,' Henderson replied, nodding slightly, 'you have my word.'

'Oh, and another thing,' Liz said, glancing furtively around, 'I'd prefer to leave the ship on my own and meet you ashore. I'm familiar with Gib having been here on holiday before joining up.'

'Fair enough,' Henderson replied. 'Meet me outside Ragged Step Gates at nineteen thirty. Is that all right?'

'Yes,' Liz replied guardedly, 'but remember what I said.'

'You have my word,' Henderson answered flatly. 'I'll have a taxi waiting, all innocent and above board,' he added with a smile and slight nod of his head.

'Right,' Liz answered, 'and in the meantime, when we meet in the wardroom or anywhere else, behave normally. I don't want anyone getting ideas. Understand?'

'Perfectly,' Henderson said, silently breathing a sigh of relief, 'and I quite agree with you.'

Shortly after 0900, Hailey was in his cabin sitting at his desk glancing through a signal log when a knock came at his door.

'Come,' he grunted, closing the log and taking sip from his half-filled cup of coffee.

The door opened and in came Liz Hall. In her left hand she held a small sheet of paper.

'Good morning, Liz,' Hailey said, noticing the worried expression on her face. 'What have you got for me this morning, you seem a little upset.'

'Morning, sir,' she quietly replied. 'This fax has just arrived,' she added, passing him the paper. 'It's from the Queen Alexandra's Hospital, in Portsmouth. It's about Kate Harrison.'

'Thank you,' Hailey said, giving Liz a guarded look. He reclined back in his chair and read the contents in the message. 'Please be good enough,' he added, furrowing his brow, 'to ask the doctor and Leading PTI Walker to come and see me.'

CHAPTER TWENTY-ONE

'You say Kate's regained consciousness but can't remember anything, sir!' Exclaimed Walker, shaking his head in disbelief.

'I'm afraid that's what the medical report says, my boy,' Hailey answered guardedly, looking up from his desk.

Feeling the blood drain from his face, Walker muttered. 'You mean she can't even remember her name or her mum and dad or what happened to her, sir?'

'It's called post-traumatic amnesia,' said Smyth, glancing at Walker while nervously shuffling his feet.

'What . . . what exactly does that mean, sir? Walker asked anxiously.

'It means the injury she sustained has affected the memory centre of her brain,' Smyth replied

'How long will that last, then, sir?'

'It's hard to say,' Smyth replied. 'Recovery could take days, weeks or even months.'

A dejected expression spread across Walker's face. 'I . . . I see, sir,' he muttered, looking first at Smyth then at Hailey. 'I have phoned her parents twice, but got no answer. They don't have mobiles and I expect they're at the hospital. So I suppose I'll just have to wait?'

'It looks like we'll all have to,' Hailey said. 'I'm sorry, but rest assured, we'll keep you informed. If you have any problems, don't hesitate to see the doctor or the First Lieutenant. Please carry on.'

Looking somewhat disconsolate, Walker said, 'Thank you, sir,' then left the cabin.

'Poor chap,' Hailey remarked, glancing at the fax, 'the quicker she recovers, the better we'll all feel.'

With the coast of Spain a distant thin line away to port, *Dawlish,* cruising at fifteen knots, continued towards Gibraltar. A few cotton wool clouds drifted lazily in an otherwise clear, cerulean sky, and a warm breeze blew from the east.

'When was the last time we had small arms practice, Number One?' The time was1030, Hailey was sitting in his chair on the bridge watching a group of marines on the fo'c'sle stripping down a general purpose machine gun. Others busied themselves cleaning and oiling a mini gun.

'About four months ago, sir,' Noble replied, stroking his chin. 'While we were in the Caribbean.'

'I see,' Hailey ponderously replied. 'Then I think we should do it again. Just to be on the safe side. Inform the Chief GI, Somersby and the Pee-woh. All hands off duty to muster on the flight deck at fourteen hundred. The marines can use the fo'c'sle.'

'Very good, sir,' Noble said with a sly grin, 'that should liven things up a bit.'

The order to practise small arms firing was greeted with equanimity

'If I wanted to shoot a fuckin' rifle,' Bud Abbott moaned, 'I'd 'ave joined the army.'

Hands to dinner had just been piped and Bud and several other ratings were in the mess

'Personally, I like it,' said Pete Price, taking a sip of tea from an enamel mug. 'Makes me feel like John Wayne. What about you, Ash?'

'I don't care one way or the other,' Ashir replied, about to tuck into his cottage pie. 'If we have to use them, then, so be it,' he added, saying a silent prayer to Allah to beg forgiveness.

As expected, the girls hated the thought of firing weapons.

'I don't know about you lot,' said Lottie Jones, 'but I joined up to see the world not shoot some poor bugger's head off.'

'If a big hairy terrorist came at you, Lot,' chimed Jilly Howard, 'and you had to kill him or be killed, you'd soon change your mind.'

'Ha! No she wouldn't,' cried Emily Jackson, 'she'd just flash her tits at him and run away.'

Two hours later, the sporadic sound of gunfire echoed around the ship. All ratings off duty lined the port and starboard side of the ship's waste.

'Fuckin' ship sounds like Dodge City,' quipped Buck Taylor, slipping his noise protectors over his head.

'Yer right there, Buck, my son,' said Swampy Marsh, frowning while sniffing the acrid smell of cordite hovering in the warm air, 'I wouldn't mind but this buggering about is spoiling my make and mend.' (An Afternoon off duty, ostensibly to repair clothing, but usually took to his bunk or, in harbour, sent ashore.)

At a nodded signal from Digger Barnes, a man came forward onto the flight deck.

'This is a standard DS thirty millimetre weapon,' the Chief said to each rating. 'It is used for inshore attack and for defence. As you can see it's mounted on a tripod and it pointing seawards. Keep it that way. Stand with your legs firmly apart, hold the but tightly against your shoulder, look down the sight and gently squeeze the trigger. Give four short bursts and stop. Then place on the safety catch and carry on.'

One by one each rating took it in turn to fire four rounds. Last in line were the girls.

'Don't let the size of it frighten you,' Barnes said to Jane Wootton. 'Just relax, get comfortable, spread your legs then gently squeeze the trigger.'

Jane nervously did as she was told, and was about to fire, when Barnes shouted, 'Open your legs wider, girl. It'll give yer more balance.'

'She should find that easy to do,' grinned Emily Jackson, 'after all the hectic nights she's had with Dutch Holland.'

On the fo'c'sle, the marines were firing short bursts from the general purpose BAR machine gun into the sea. This is an automatic, air-cooled, gas- operated weapon modelled on the WW2 Browning rifle.

Watching tiny spurts of water erupt some distance away, Butch Cassidy shouted, 'When yer finished, make sure the barrels are clear, remember those little buggers fire between two hundred and six hundred rounds a minute.'

'No kiddin' Sarge,' grunted Knocker White, glancing up from his prone position, 'we have fired the buggers before, you now.'

'Yeah, just like you'd done a deck landing before,' snapped Cassidy, 'now make sure you strip and oil the bugger properly.'

At 1930, the pipe, 'clear up mess decks and flats for rounds. Men under punishment muster outside the Master-at-Arm's office,' echoed around the ship. Hailey was in his cabin relaxing in his armchair, reading an old copy of *The Times*. With the exception of the sound of Flannigan preparing his supper and the soporific humming of the air conditioning, everything was quiet. A gentle knock at the door made him look up from his newspaper.

'Yes, come in,' he said, adopting an upright pose.

The door opened and in came Liz Hall.

'Good evening, Liz,' Hailey said, giving her a cheerful smile. 'What have you for me?' He added, looking at the signal she held in her left hand.

'Another fax from MOD, marked top secret, sir,' she guardedly replied. 'Sounds rather important.'

'Thank you,' he said, accepting the piece of paper. A few seconds later, he looked up, a frown on his brow and a worried expression in his eyes. 'Kindly ask the First Lieutenant to see me immediately. It seems Gibraltar is expecting an attack from Al Qaeda and is on a Red Alert '

CHAPTER TWENTY-TWO

Hailey vacated his armchair and sat behind his desk as Noble knocked on the door and came in

'Better read this, Number One,' Hailey said, handing Noble the message.

After doing so, Noble looked up, 'Good Lord, sir,' he muttered, 'maybe it was just as well we had small arms practice, any further information?'

With a weary sigh, Hailey sat back and folded his arms. 'None, so far,' he replied, 'what time do we arrive in Gib tomorrow?'

'Zero nine hundred, sir,' Noble answered, glancing pensively at the signal again before placing it on Hailey's desk.

'Right,' Hailey replied, standing up, 'all officers to muster in the wardroom immediately.'

Ten minutes later, with the exception of Shirley Mannering, who was OOW, all officers were in the wardroom. The atmosphere was subdued and the conversation muted. As Hailey entered, those who were sat down stood up. The rest stood to attention. Noble took a position slightly behind his captain.

'Stand easy, everyone,' said Hailey, noticing the anxious expressions on their faces. 'Do sit down and smoke if you want to.' He paused, then, took out the fax from his pocket and in a grave voice continued, 'before going on, I will read you the message I have received from MOD. "*To all ships in the Mediterranean, info, the harbour master and naval squadron stationed in Gibraltar. Information received from MI6, warns of a threatened suicide attack on shipping in Gibraltar by Al Qaeda. No date or time is specified. Accordingly, Gibraltar had been put on Red Alert. It is expected that oil tankers will be the targets. In the event of an attack, blasts on the harbour siren will be made. All personnel shore are to report back to their ship. Further information will follow when known."*

As Hailey finished reading the message, he felt the tension rise and saw the anxious expression on the faces in front of him.

'I don't have to tell you,' Hailey added, gravely, 'that such an attack, if successful, would cause worldwide economic chaos.' He paused, allowing the implications of the message to register. Several officers swapped guarded glances and spoke in muffled tones. Hailey, furrowing his brow, looked around, then asked, 'any questions?'

Henderson, raised a finger. 'What naval forces do they have in Gib, sir?'

Hailey gave a despondent sigh. 'Not much, I'm afraid, Bob, two fast patrol craft armed with fifty calibre Brownings and three rigid-hauled inflatable boats.'

'Good Lord!' Henderson exclaimed, who like several other officers, looked visibly shaken. 'The Brownings are excellent machine guns but there's not much to stop a determined enemy, eh, sir?'

'Quite,' Hailey soberly replied.

'And I bet Al Qaeda know just how poorly defended the port is,' Gooding added.

'Anyway, sir,' Liz Hall added cautiously, 'the message did say, it was a *threatened* attack, so let's not too carried away.'

'Nevertheless, Liz,' Hailey replied, raising his eye brows, 'we must be prepared. When we enter Gib, all hands must carry battle-bags and everyone closed up at Weapons State Monty, is that clear?'

A series of nodded heads and a murmur of 'yes, sir,' followed this.

'Right,' Hailey said, shuffling his feet, 'any more questions?'

'I have one, sir,' said Noble, 'will the crew have normal leave?'

'Yes,' Hailey answered, 'but they must all carry mobiles, or be in company of those who have one.'

Shortly after 0700 on Monday 12 August, Europa Point, the southern tip of Gibraltar, with its lighthouse, painted red and white, hove into view. After passing Cape Spartel, a rocky prominence off the coast of Tangier, the massive jaw of the Rock, jutting out against the pale blue sky, could be seen.

'No matter how often you see that gigantic monolith,' Noble remarked, staring out of the bridge windows, 'it never fails to impress, eh, sir?'

'I agree, Number One,' Hailey replied, using his binoculars to study the Rock's topography. Ignoring the rocky terrain sweeping down to the dozens of white topped buildings, hotels and houses, he went on, 'It's a pity the guns of those batteries situated around the top are obsolete, they could be more than useful against Al Qaeda.'

'What do you think the chances are of an attack, sir?' Noble enquired tentatively.

'I don't know,' Hailey, gravely replied, observing a cluster of antennae, rising from the Rock's highest prominence, 'but at least they have the most sophisticated radar station in the Med.' Lowering his binoculars, he added, 'Better put all this on Daily Orders and stress the Red Alert is only a warning.'

'There seems to be a lot of shipping despite the Red Alert, Number One,' remarked Hailey scanning the harbour with his binoculars.

'Maybe they haven't been informed of it yet, sir,' Noble replied.

'I very much doubt that,' Hailey murmured, lowering his binoculars.

'Perhaps, sir,' Noble went on, 'but if I were their captains, I'd get out of Gib as soon as possible. But I expect many of the tourists may not have seen the Rock and have paid good money for the visit and would complain if they had to leave.'

'I agree,' Hailey said, shaking his head. 'I suppose commerce must go on no matter what.'

Four rusty tankers, two with the yellow Shell logo on their red funnels, lay at anchor, their Plimsoll line barely visible indicated they were topped up with oil. Two others, low in the water with black smoke circling from their funnels, were about to leave. Two liners, their pristine white hulls and funnels shining in the morning sun, had dropped anchor, awaiting motor boats to take tourists ashore. And looking somewhat incongruous amongst this armada of commerce, two large, expensive cabin cruisers, the toys of the rich and famous, had dropped anchor in the middle of the harbour. The backdrop to this colourful spectacle was provided by the rolling, green hills of Spain partially shrouded in morning mist, and the busy port of Algeciras a few miles across the bay.

By 0930, *Dawlish* was secured alongside Ragged Steps Wharf. Bosley and his team of mechanics immediately descended into the warm atmosphere of the engine room.

'Looks like we'll have to strip her down, sir,' Williams said, staring forlornly at the huge cylinder that housed the two GEC electric motors and Paxman Valenta brush alternators.

'Better check on the electric system as well, Chief,' Bosley replied, wiping the beads of sweat from his brow with a handkerchief.

'And as you know, Chief,' added Vellacott, 'it's the motors that supply the electricity to the Rolls Royce Spey engines.'

'And if there's anything wrong with them,' Williams replied, shaking his head warily, 'we may be here for more than two days.'

Meanwhile, Hailey was in his cabin talking to Commander Paul Jeffries, the commanding officer of the local naval forces, a tall, heavily tanned man with a boxer's square jaw and intelligent brown eyes.

'As you are the only British warship in port,' he said, crossing his legs and relaxing back in his armchair, 'I thought I'd better come and inform you that I intend to use one of my patrol boats to keep a watch some five miles to the east. The other one can patrol some distance behind in the harbour.'

'What about your inflatable craft?' Hailey asked as Flannigan appeared with two cups of coffee.

'They'd be too slow to attack a fast moving motor boat, but the patrol boats have Browning four point five inch machine guns mounted on their bows and should be more than capable of dealing with any intruders,' Jeffries replied confidently before taking a sip of his coffee. 'What about your ship, how long do you think you'll be here?'

With a weary sigh, Hailey replied, 'That depends on how long it'll take the engineers to repair the engines.'

'Here's hoping it won't take long, then,' Jeffries said, finishing his drink and standing up. 'Nice to have met you,' he added as they shook hands. 'If you can, come to the mess and have dinner.'

'Thank you,' replied Hailey, 'I'll keep that in mind.'

The time was 1200. 'Secure. Hands to dinner. Mail is now ready for collection,' was piped over the tannoy. Although many of the crew were able to communicate with home using their mobile phones, some still preferred the written word.

'My missus wants me to increase her allotment,' cried Swampy Marsh, after reading a letter. 'She says the springs on our bed have gone and she wants a new one.'

'How old is the bed?' asked Dutch tearing back the metal tab on his can of beer and taking a good gulp, while giving Bud Abbott a sly wink.

'We only bought it when we moved,' replied Swampy, shaking his head in disbelief. 'Sometimes I think she's havin' it away with the milkman.'

'What makes you think that, Swampy?' asked Shady Lane, grinning like a Cheshire cat.

'It's the same one we had in Manchester before we moved to Portsmouth six months ago.'

Just then Pete Price came into the mess. 'I've spoken to Di and the girls,' he said, pouring himself a mug of tea from a large aluminium tea pot. 'She and the others are off duty and they'll meet us at Jury's Bar at twenty hundred.'

'I bet that fuckin' siren will sound just as I'm gettin' me leg over with Lottie,' said Shady Lane.

'What about you and Di, Ash?' chimed Pete Price, a salacious grin on his face, 'Isn't it about time you and her . . .' He added, reinforcing his question by bending his arm at right angles.

Ashir nonchalantly shrugged his shoulders, took a sip of beer from his can and replied, 'err . . . maybe.'

Walker was sat with a worried expression on his face on his bunk reading a letter. Dutch and the others stopped talking and watched him.

'Any news about Kate?' Dutch finally asked hopefully.

Walker took a deep breath and looked up. 'Not really,' he said, 'this letter is from her mum. She says Kate still can't remember anything, but the doctors say she could regain her memory anytime.'

'Well,' muttered Bud Abbott, 'that's summat, at least.'

Standing outside the senior ratings' mess, Williams took off his shoes and went inside. His face and overalls were smeared with oil and his socks had holes in them.

'Och, how's it going, Bungy?' asked Jock Forbes, holding a small glass of Bells whisky, 'yer look like one o' them black and white minstrels that used to be on telly.'

'Aye, and you look as if you could do with a drink, Bungy,' Bogey Knight said, handing the chief his whiskey, 'get this down yer, it's on me.' 'Bogey' as he was nicknamed, was a tall, broad-shoulder man with small intelligent grey eyes and well-groomed dark brown hair.

'What's the latest on the engines?' asked Digger Barnes.

After taking a good sip of whiskey, Williams wiped his mouth with the back of his hand, and said, 'Luckily the electronic system is OK. But the problem is the brushes. We'll have to take them out and repair them. The boss has told the old man. With a bit of luck we should have it fixed by tomorrow at the earliest.'

Later that day, Liz met Shirley Mannering outside her cabin and told her about her tryst with Henderson.

'As I told you before, love,' Shirley said, 'be bloody careful. And don't forget to ask him about his wife,' she paused, shook her head then went on, 'I've a feeling there's something wrong there.'

'Perhaps,' Liz muttered cautiously. 'Anyway, Shirl, what do think I should wear?'

'Nothing too short,' replied Shirley, 'if you flash those lovely legs at him, he's bound to get the wrong idea.'

'Oh no,' answered Liz, shaking her head, 'he did say everything was innocent and above board.'

'Nonsense,' cried Shirley. 'That man's as innocent as a tarantula.'

CHAPTER TWENTY-THREE

At precisely 1730, a pipe came over the tannoy. 'Leave, leave to the first part of port and second of starboard from eighteen hundred to zero six hundred. Liberty men and women are reminded to carry mobile phones or be in the company of anyone who has one,'

In the after seamen's mess, Dutch Holland, Pete Price, Shady Lane, Ashir and several other ratings, were ready to go ashore. With exception of Ashir and Shady, who wore sports coats, open necked shirts and slacks, the rest wore the customary leather jackets and trainers.

'You're sure the girls know where Jury's Bar is, Dutch?' Shady asked while looking in the mirror while combing his hair.

'Yeah,' replied Dutch, zipping up his jacket, 'I told Di yesterday to tell the girls it's down Main Street on the left. If I remember, there's a bloody big sign outside.'

In the girl's quarters the overpowering smell of perfume, talcum powder and make-up hovered in the warm atmosphere.

'Do you think this is too short?' Lottie asked Diana, turning and twisting slightly while looking in the long mirror at her tartan, button-down skirt.

'Not really, love,' Diana replied, giving Jane Wootton, who was standing close by, a sly wink, 'providing you don't bend down.'

'Thanks you very much,' Lottie answered with a smirk, 'if that tight checked skirt and sweater you're wearing doesn't give Ash a hard on, nothing will.'

'I wish I had a figure like yours, Di,' remarked Jilly Howard, checking herself in the mirror, 'if I did I wouldn't bother with a bra, do you think this pink blouse makes me look like a tart?'

'If the Dutch cap fits, wear it,' Diana replied cheekily.

'Personally,' chimed in Jane Wootton, coyly pulling down her red sweater over her black jeans, 'I'm not wearing a bra, it's too warm.'

'It's a just as well, Jane,' Emily Jackson added, struggling into her black pencil skirt, then straightening her white sweater, 'because I bet you've got no knickers on either.'

'Let's see, now,' said Lottie Jones, opening her shoulder bag, 'make-up, perfume, money, hanky . . .'

'Don't forget the French letters, Lot,' added Jane, grinning like a Cheshire cat, 'you never know your luck.'

'Chance would be a fine thing,' Lottie replied, zipping up her bag, then shouting, 'Come on you lot or the lads will have drunk the place dry.'

A few minutes later they arrived on the flight deck.

'Now, don't be adrift,' warned Duty PO Dusty Miller, watching the girls carefully make their way down the metal gangway. 'Remember leave expires at zero six hundred.'

The time was 2000 with darkness about to fall. A balmy breeze blew from the east and high above, a full, moon beamed down from a cloudless sky.

'We'll bear that in mind, PO,' Lottie Jones shouted over her shoulder as she and the others carefully made their way along the cobble-stoned wharf towards Ragged Staff Gates. Built in 1786, this was once a defensive wall surrounding the town.

A few other ratings, including Harry Tate and Jack Whitton joined Diana and the girls.

'Do you know where Jury's Bar is, Chief?' asked Jilly Howard, lighting a cigarette.

'Turn left at the end of this road into Main Street, and it's on your left, you can't miss it,' Tate replied. 'Jack and I are off to see if the dancing girls are still around like they were in my granddads days.'

'Ha!' laughed Jane Wootton, 'I shouldn't bother if I were you, they're probably all pensioned off by now.'

Main Street was a bustle of tourists seeking duty free bargains in the many shops on either side of the busy thoroughfare. Nevertheless, the girls soon found the bar with its large sign proclaiming its name in bold red lettering and the words, 'UK WINES AND SPIRITS SOLD HERE.'

'Come on girls,' cried Diana, pushing open the wooden swing doors, 'the first round of vodka is on me.'

The bar was small, poorly lit, stuffy and slightly claustrophobic. A few tourists wearing summer clothes occupied a narrow bar, behind which a stocky, swarthy, stout man in an off-white apron served drinks. A few young couples gyrated on the tiny concrete dance floor to loud music provided by a DJ situated in a small alcove at the end of the room. Coloured posters of pop singers decorated the whitewashed walls and two tubes of flickering neon on the low ceiling bathed the place in a dull yellow glow

'My God,' cried Emily Jackson, squinting her eyes at Diana, 'are you sure this is the place, it looks more like a bloody dungeon than a bar.'

'Oh shut up, Jacko,' Diana replied. 'Grab a table and ask the girls what they want to drink.'

Just then the doors opened and in came Pete Price and the others.

'Hello, girls,' shouted Shady Lane, seeing Diana making her way to the bar, 'looks like we're in time. Pints of Red Eye all round, Di.' (Red Eye was blackcurrant juice laced with vodka.)

As they did in Southsea, they joined two tables next to one another.

'Makes it cosy, like,' said Dutch Holland, putting his arm around Lottie Jones's waist.

'If you can't afford the goods, don't touch them,' Lottie replied with a smirk, 'unless you promise to buy me a double vodka.'

'You're on, Lot,' Dutch, answered, giving Lottie a bear hug.

Diana arrived with a tray containing pints of Red Eye. She then sat down next to Ashir and said, 'Aren't you going to take sip of your drink Ash?'

'Err . . . yes,' he replied hesitatingly, 'but I'm gunna take it steady. You know what happened last time,' he added taking a small sip.

During the next two hours the place gradually filled up with tourists. The dance floor became jam packed by couples, moving robotically to the blare of disco music. Just before 2200, Harry Tate and Jack Whitton almost fell into the bar. Behind him stood Butch Cassidy and two marines. All five wore silly, alcoholic induced expressions and looked worse for wear.

'Hi, Chief,' Jane Wootton shouted, 'did you find any dancing girls?'

'Naw,' Spud slurred, 'my granddad must have been pissed in 1943, they're all ugly like you lot.'

'Charming, I must say,' Jane cried. Grabbing him by the arm she dragged him onto the crowded floor, she added, 'Just for that you'll have to dance with me then buy all the girls a drink.'

Making their way to the bar, Butch and the marines roared with laughter as Jane just managed to rescue Tate before he fell over.

'No sign of Al Qaeda then, or the sirens then, Butch,' bellowed Dutch Holland, whose arms were firmly entwined around Lottie Jones who, with her eyes closed was snuggled up to his chest. 'Not that we'd hear anything in here with this noise.'

'Negative,' Butch yelled, 'if yer ask me it's a storm in a tea cup.'

'Yer probably right,' Dutch replied, allowing his hands to slide down onto Lottie's warm backside.

Suddenly, the music slowed down. The neon lights dimmed and became a dull, foggy blue. This appeared to be the signal for some of the couples to kiss one another as progress around the floor almost came to a standstill.

'You're getting quite good,' Diana shouted to Ash, pressing herself against his groin.

'How can you tell?' Ash asked, sensing himself becoming aroused, 'we're hardly moving.'

'I know,' Diana replied, feeling his erection pressing against her through his trousers, 'and that's how I like it,' she added with a salacious smile. 'You know, Ash,' she went on, gazing coyly at him, 'we don't have to go back on board tonight. We could stay at a hotel. I love you and want you so much.'

Her suggestion caught Ash off guard.

'I . . . I'm not sure,' he muttered, feeling his erection subside.

'Oh, come on, Ash,' Diana cried, pushing herself harder against him, 'this could be our last chance before we return home.'

Ashir didn't reply. With a sly grin, he realised when he carried out the task allotted to him by Allah, none of them would ever see their homes again.

CHAPTER TWENTY-FOUR

Liz Hall left the ship at 1910. As she stepped ashore, the faint aroma of spices, blowing on the eastern breeze assailed her nostrils. Under a short, lightweight fawn cashmere jacket she wore a white, open necked blouse buttoned low enough display a small, diamond shaped pendant. As suggested by Shirley Mannering, her pleated, dark brown skirt reached below her knees; sheer tights covered her legs and her feet were encased in a pair of comfortable black brogues.

To her annoyance, a gust of wind ruffled her short chestnut hair, washed and set the previous night. She brushed back a few strands, and ignoring the grinning glances and muted remarks from a few ratings, continued on her way.

Two yellow taxis, full of ratings bound for the town centre, passed her as she made her way along Queensway, a narrow road surrounding the dockyard. Having been to Gibraltar before on holiday, she soon recognised the two large archways of Ragged Steps Gates.

True to his word, Henderson was waiting next to a taxi near one of the arches. She immediately saw him, smiled and waved, noticing how smart he looked in his dark blue, double-breasted blazer, white shirt, naval tie and grey slacks. The sight of his six foot plus frame and handsome features increased her pulse rate. It also reminded her to heed Shirley's advice to enquire about his wife.

'Right on time, Liz.' he said, flashing her a welcoming smile. 'And your carriage awaits, ma'am,' he added, detecting an intoxicating smell of Chanel No 5. Then bowing gallantly, he opened the passenger door.

'Thank you, kind sir,' Liz replied, her hazel eyes flashing a grateful smile as she climbed into the back seat.

'You know where to go, driver,' Henderson said as he sat next to her. 'And don't spare the horses.'

With a startled look on his face, the driver exclaimed, 'Horses, sir, what horses?'

Liz and Henderson looked at one another and burst out laughing.

The taxi turned into Ragged Steps Road, passing the Trafalgar cemetery (the name is a misnomer as it only contains two graves from the famous battle) and turned into Europa Road and arrived at the hotel.

The magnificent stuccoed, five storey hotel looked like an outcrop of the rocky, sloping terrain. Palm trees, silhouetted against the fading light, surrounded a garden, whose well-kept beds of multi-coloured geraniums and wisteria filled the evening air with a sweet smelling aroma.

The driver stopped at a paved forecourt, near where a few taxis awaited customers. A wide, gravelled path lead up to an arched entrance, over which a large sign, painted in bold black lettering, proclaimed the name of the hotel.

Henderson, thanked the taxi driver and paid him, adding a generous tip.

Walking up the three flights of stone steps leading to the revolving doors, Henderson, glanced casually upwards, and said, 'I bet each of those room must have a lovely view of the town and harbour.'

'And so do the windows on the terrace,' Liz curtly replied, 'so don't get any ideas.

Giving a playful laugh, he replied, 'As if I would,' he then held open one of the two highly polished oaken doors, allowing Liz to enter the hotel.

A welcoming smile from a pretty, dark-haired receptionist standing behind a long, oak desk, greeted them as they came in.

'Good evening,' Henderson said, smiling, 'I have reserved a table in the restaurant.'

'Very good, sir,' replied the receptionist, 'as you can see it is at the end of the foyer.'

The atmosphere was comfortably warm and welcoming. Ornately framed oil paintings of local scenes covered the walls embossed in plush burgundy. And on the floor of foyer, large square white ties glistened under an opulent, crystal chandelier. In a corner, next to a lift, a stairway with shiny balustrades, led to the floors above.

French windows overlooked a wide terrace dotted with couples sitting at tables protected by multi-coloured umbrella shades.

'This really is lovely,' Liz remarked looking around, 'I especially think the embossed burgundy tapestries are beautiful.'

'I'm glad you like it,' Henderson answered, 'in days gone by, it was frequented by Winston Churchill and movie stars such as Errol Flynn.'

'Now, I really am impressed,' Liz gushed, 'my grandmother thought Errol Flynn was the most sexiest movie star in Hollywood. Personally, I prefer Brad Pitt.'

A tall waiter, dressed immaculately in a black tie and tails, showed them to a table and held a chair for Liz to sit down. She then took off her jacket and with a smile, handed it to the waiter. A warm breeze from a nearby open French window caressed their faces as they sat down.

'Would you care to order, sir?' the waiter asked, bowing politely while handing Henderson a leather-bound menu.

'This was your idea, Bob,' she said, with a wry grin, 'so if you don't mind, surprise me, I'm sure I'll enjoy whatever you choose.'

'Righto,' Henderson replied, 'now, let me see,' he added, carefully studying the menu. After a few minutes, he gave Liz a guarded smile, then beckoned the waiter near and whispered his order to him.

The meal was sumptuous; watercress with comfit ocean trout and poached quail's eggs, washed down with a bottle of chilled Chablis; followed by pan-fried fillet of sea Bass, fennel, green olives and lemon vinaigrette, ending with gateaux, a selectin of cheeses, coffee and brandy.

'Mm . . , that was delicious,' Liz said, dabbing her mouth with a linen serviette. But it isn't going to do my figure any good,' she added, taking a deep breath and relaxing back in her chair. 'But I don't care.'

'Just enjoy it, and let me worry about your figure,' replied Henderson, topping up her glass and grinning.

'Oh, Bob, that was absolutely fantastic,' Liz gasped, 'thank you, but I suspect, very expensive.'

'Not at all,' Henderson replied, reaching across and placing his hand over hers. 'It was worth every penny, especially as you're here to share it with me.'

'Nevertheless, thank you again,' Liz said gently squeezing his hand and withdrawing it.

Shortly afterwards, Henderson suggested a walk onto the terrace. 'Like Errol Flynn did in the movies,' he said, with a twinkle in his eyes.

Henderson paid the bill with his credit card, thanked the waiter while discreetly placing a ten pound tip in his hand.

As they stood up and walked towards the open French windows, the waiter slipped her coat over her shoulders. She thanked him and feeling Henderson's warm hand in hers, went onto the terrace and stood near the stone balustrade overlooking the town and harbour.

The time was shortly before 2230. From somewhere inside the hotel the nostalgic strains of *Moon River,* being played on a piano filtered through the evening air.

'My goodness, Bob,' she exclaimed, 'you were right about the view, it really is breath-taking. Everything including all the ships in the harbour are lit up like Christmas trees.'

'Yes, and there's dear old *Dawlish*,' Henderson said, indicating with his free hand. 'The duty watch have done a good job rigging those lights.'

For a few seconds, they stood in silence admiring the scene below. It was then, Liz decided to ask Henderson about his wife and family.

'Err . . . if you don't mind me asking, Bob,' she said hesitatingly, 'how long have you been married?'

Henderson gave a weary sigh and quietly replied, 'I was wondering when you would ask me that,' he paused, removed his hand from hers and placed his on the rounded edge of the balustrade, then went on, 'Caroline and I have been married for fourteen years. We have two children, Simon who's twelve and Amanda who is ten. At the moment both of them are away in private schools. '

'A boy and a girl, eh, sounds idyllic,' Liz thoughtfully replied.

'Yes, the children are wonderful, but . . .' He broke off and stared at the ground, a deep frown etched on his face.

'But what . . .?' Liz tentatively asked.

'Caroline and I don't love each other,' he replied, staring blankly into the night. He took a deep breath, and in a strained voice, continued, 'we haven't done so for some time.'

'I . . . I don't understand,' Liz said, nervously licking her lips, 'how . . .'

'Two years ago, December the tenth, to be exact,' he said, glancing down at the floor, 'we were in Regent Street shopping for presents. It was early evening and the stores were ablaze with lights. The street was festooned with the usual glittering reindeers, and . . .' he paused and took another deep, then went on, 'we arrived outside Hamley's toy shop when she stopped, looked up at me and out of the blue, told me she didn't love me anymore.'

'Good Lord,' Liz muttered, 'just like that. You must have been mortified.'

'Not really,' Henderson replied softly, 'because she also said that she knew I didn't love her, and she was right.'

'I'm sorry, Bob, but I still don't understand. Had she met someone else, fourteen years is a long time . . .'

'No, we'd both been faithful. There was no third party involved. What with being away at sea quite regularly, we simply drifted apart emotionally. Even today, the navy has the highest divorce rate of all the three services.'

'Are you, err . . . getting divorced, then?' Liz asked, feeling somewhat embarrassed for interloping into his private life.

'No, you see Caroline and her family are staunch Catholics and wouldn't agree to such a thing.'

'What about the children?' Liz asked. 'Are they aware of anything?'

'No,' he answered, shaking his head slightly, 'you see, we decided to stay together for their sake. We have a flat in Holland Park, London, separate bedrooms and put on a brave face when I'm on leave, but otherwise go our separate ways, no questions asked.'

'Is your wife seeing anyone now?'

Henderson casually shrugged his shoulders and said, 'Maybe, I don't really care.'

'And you?' Liz asked cautiously, 'are you involved with . . .?'

'No,' he immediately replied. 'I'm not.'

'So why me, then?' Liz asked, giving him a questioning look.

Liz immediately regretted asking him such a stupid question. She was perfectly aware she was attractive to men. At university she had had a few casual affairs, and had even tried to use her obvious charms to gain favour with her tutors. On board *Dawlish,* one or two officers had made a pass at her, but she was only too aware of the golden 'no touch' rule. Besides, she had her career to consider and wasn't going to jeopardise it for a meaningless affair. So, why, she asked herself, had she accepted Henderson's invitation. As she looked up into his soft brown eyes, she knew the answer; it was a long time since she'd been with a man, and, after all, he was very attractive. So why not?

He took hold of her hand, and noticing how the reflection from the moonlight made her eyes shine, was about to reply when suddenly, the sound of an explosion coming some distance down the Straits, interrupted him.

'Good Lord, Bob!' Liz exclaimed, 'what on earth was that?'

'I'm not sure,' Henderson replied cautiously, 'but I've got a good idea.'

People hurried out from the restaurant onto the terrace, chattering excitedly and gazing away to the bright crimson glow in the sky.

Even though the Red Alert warning had been spread via the radio and signal to all ships, many tourists were not aware of the danger.

'Maybe there's been a collision,' someone said.

'Or a fire on board one of the tankers,' another offered.

At that moment, the wail of a siren told those better informed what was happening.

'Fire be buggered,' yelled a man dressed in an evening suit, 'that's the Red Alert siren. The harbour is being attacked by terrorists.'

His words immediately produced a few gasps from the onlookers as all eyes were concentrated on the orange glow hovering in the sky.

'I say, old girl, I think we'd better stay at the hotel till morning,' an elderly grey-haired man, said to a plump woman wearing a white evening gown. 'If those damn terrorists are attacking the ships, we're safer here.'

However, several people, overhearing his advice, ignored him and made a mad dash for their cars.

'Come on, Liz,' said Henderson, taking hold of her arm, 'we'd better get back on board. If we hurry we can catch a taxi before they're all taken.'

Liz and Henderson joined the crowd hurrying down the steps towards the car park. Suddenly, the harbour and the town was lit up by massive eruption, bigger and louder than the one earlier. The ground shook as a vivid coruscation of bright red and yellow flames accompanied by palls of black smoke poured upwards. An ominous warm heat wave fanned the faces of everyone as they hurried down the steps leading to car park.

'*Great Scott!*' Henderson yelled, noticing the frightened expression etched on Liz's pale face. 'It looks like one of the tankers has been attacked.'

CHAPTER TWENTY-FIVE

Pockets of burning oil leaking from the stricken tanker spread over the harbour as more explosions leapt into the sky. The noise was deafening as the reflection of the conflagration turned the water surrounding the vessel into a lake of angry flames. The sharp, acrid smell of smoke permeated the evening air smarting eyes and nostrils of the people pouring out of the hotel.

Breathless and perspiring, Liz and Henderson arrived at the car park and managed to find a taxi.

'Ragged Steps Wharf, driver,' said Henderson as he and Liz climbed into the back seat.

'Sorry, sir,' replied the driver, 'what with this red alert and those explosions, I want to get home as quickly as possible, but I'll take you to as far as Ragged Steps Gates.'

'That's all right,' Henderson quickly replied, 'and please hurry.'

On the way down Europa Road they passed crowds of people, taxis and cars hurrying from the town centre. They soon arrived at Ragged Staff Gates. Across the harbour the flames from the tanker continued erupt into the air like Roman candles. An ugly black cloud of smoke hung over the harbour, blotting out the coast of Spain.

No sooner had they climbed out of the taxi than they met many of the ship's company hurrying towards *Dawlish*. Among them was Shady Lane and the other lads. Lottie and the girls, puffing and panting, followed on, doing their best to keep up with them. Diana, walked behind, clutching Ashir's hand as if her life depended on it. Like the rest of the girls, her face was a mixture of fear and apprehension. The sight of Henderson and Liz together caused a few ominous glances from the group.

'I wonder if he's giving her one,' Shady said to Bud Abbott.

'If he's not, he must be gay,' Bud replied, breathing heavily. 'She's bloody gorgeous.'

'Can't you buggers think about anything but sex?' Said Jilly Howard who was walking behind Shady and Bud.

'To be perfectly, honest, Jill, no,' was Bud's curt reply.

'Do you think it is a terrorist arrack, Ash?' asked Diana. Her voice coming in short bursts as she strained to keep up with him.

'Probably,' Ashir replied, giving her a comforting smile, 'but don't worry, you'll soon be back on board the ship, safe and sound.'

'Do you think we'll put to sea, sir?' gasped Lottie Jones, hurrying alongside Henderson and Liz.

'I'm not sure, Jones,' Henderson replied, not wanting commit himself. 'We'll have to wait and see.'

'Are you all right, ma'am,' Jilly Howard asked Liz. 'You look a little shaken.'

Realising that she and Henderson had been seen together, Liz felt her face redden. 'Aren't we all,' she replied meekly.

'Looks pretty grim, eh, sir?' Shady Lane said to Henderson. 'The crew on that tanker couldn't have stood a chance, the poor buggers,' he added gulping for air. 'Us lot left the pub as soon as we heard the siren, didn't we Dutch?'

'Aye, and after that second big bang, it were bloody pandemonium,' shouted Pete Price, 'people in the street poured out of the pubs and shops, shouting and screaming.'

'They probably thought the town itself was next,' Bud Abbott cried, sweat running down his face.

'You're right there, Bud,' Dutch Holland gasped, 'especially when the building shook.'

By the time everyone arrived at the ship it was 2230. The orange glow from the flames and smoke illuminated every vessel in the harbour, including *Dawlish.*

'Pity we weren't able to stay at that hotel, wasn't it?' Diana whispered, to Ashir as they made their way up the gangway.

'Err . . . yes, it was, 'Ashir quietly replied, offering a silent prayer of thanks to Allah.

153

An hour earlier, Hailey had been in his cabin sitting at his desk checking the ship's log. Shortly before 2100 the pipe, 'stand by for evening rounds, men under punishment muster outside the Master-at-Arms office,' echoed around the ship. It was then Hailey heard the first explosion. He immediately rushed from his cabin and arrived on the flight deck and saw the sky aglow, several miles down the Straits. Then he heard the mournful wail of the siren coming from somewhere further along the dockyard.

'Call out the duty watch,' Hailey snapped, looking at Gooding, who was OOD, 'make sure all compartments are secure.'

'Aye, aye, sir,' Gooding replied, passing on the order to Jock Forbes.

Spider Webb, the duty QM, overheard Hailey's order. He was about to unhook the tannoy voice-pipe when the tanker, which was lying at anchor in the middle of the harbour, suddenly erupted into gigantic ball of orange flames and bellowing black smoke. He, like Hailey, Gooding and Webb instinctively shielded their faces as a warm blast of air wafted over their faces. This was followed by a shock wave causing the ship to rock slightly.

'Christ almighty!' Hailey cried, 'How many are ashore?'

As he spoke he could clearly see Gooding's face reflected in the harsh light from the tanker's billowing flames.

'Everyone except the duty watch, sir,' Gooding replied, 'I expect they'll hear the siren and get back on board as soon as possible.'

'Right, I want everyone to carry battle bags, and send the QM to the engine room and ask Bosley and Somersby to come to my cabin.'

A few minutes later Hailey looked up from his desk as Bosley, as he entered the cabin. His ruddy complexion was streaked with sweat. He was slightly out of breath and the dark smudges under his tired grey eyes told its own story.

Behind him stood Somersby, looking alarmed and worried.

'Come in gentlemen, and sit down.'

Both officers sat down on a settee opposite the captain's desk.

Hailey sat forward, his brow creased in a worried frown. 'I'm sure you're aware that Al Qaeda has attacked shipping in the harbour, so I'll come straight to the point,' looking sternly at Bosley, he went on, 'When will the engines be ready, Norman?'

'Dicky and his team have almost completed repairing the turbocharger, sir,' Bosley replied, stifling a yawn, 'but the bush alternator will take quite a while to fix.' He paused, and with a tired effort took a deep breath, 'If we work through the night, I'd say we'll ready to go to sea around midday.'

'Good,' Hailey replied. As he spoke, Flannigan, who had been listening at the galley door, came in with a tray of coffee.

'To be sure, I thought, you'd all like a drink,' he said passing the cups around.

'Thank you Flannigan,' Hailey said, 'I see you didn't go ashore, then.'

'Just as bloody well, sir,' Flannigan tersely replied, 'what with all that bloody noise, a man couldn't have a quiet beer or two.' He then retreated into the galley and closed the door.

'Now, John,' Hailey said, after taking a sip of coffee, 'I want armed sentries placed around the upper deck. I don't want to take any chances. We're sitting ducks here, remember what happened to the USS *Cole*.'

'Yes, I do, sir,' Somersby replied, confidently. 'It was attacked in Aden harbour by Al Qaeda suicide speed boats. Eleven of her crew were killed. Sometime in October, 2000 I think.'

'Correct, John,' Hailey answered soberly, 'and you'd better mount a BAR machine gun either side of the bridge. Any questions?'

'Do we know where the speed boats came from, sir?' Somersby asked, as he finished his coffee.

'I don't know,' Hailey replied, 'you're guess is as good as mine, but they must have been from somewhere fairly near. I want to sail as soon as possible.'

'What about the engines, sir?' Bosley asked anxiously, 'when we've repaired them, wouldn't it be wise to test them before we sail?'

'No time, Norman,' Hailey answered with a wry smile, 'Call it on the job training. We'll find out soon enough when we're at sea, If that is all,' he added standing up, 'please carry on, gentlemen, I'm sure you've got plenty to do.'

Twenty minutes later the duty QM's loud voice stating rounds was over, came over the tannoy. Five minutes later, a sharp knock came at Hailey's door.

'Come,' he grunted, sitting back in his chair, a worried expression etched on his face.

Gooding entered, pale-faced and sweating. 'Signal from the harbour master, sir,' he said, handing Hailey a small piece of white paper.

Hailey looked up at Gooding and with an irritable wave of his hand, he curtly replied, 'then read it man.'

'Err . . . yes, sir,' Gooding said, nervously. Then, clearing his throat, he went on.

"Signal from harbourmaster, Gibraltar, info MOD and C in C Mediterranean. Suicide attack on Shell tanker, SS Python, 2100, by two Al Qaeda motor boats. One boat blown up by local naval forces. The second rammed SS Python. No survivors from tanker or motor boat. It is thought the attack was launched from a mother ship detected by radar somewhere off the coast of Algiers. All ships in the area have been alerted." That's it, sir,' Gooding said, looking up and handing the signal to Hailey.

'My God, Paul!' Hailey exclaimed, furrowing his brow, 'I hate to think how we would have coped if there had been more than two attackers . . .'

'I shouldn't worry, sir,' Gooding answered confidently, 'Bob Henderson and his team would have dealt with them.'

Hailey pursed lips, nodded his head and replied, 'I'm sure you're right.'

'By the way, sir,' Gooding went on, 'all hands are on board safe and sound.'

'Thank goodness for that,' sighed Hailey, easing himself slowly up from his chair. 'Please carry on, I'll be up top shortly and will make a pipe to the ship's company.'

The sight that met Hailey as he arrived on the flight deck made him gasp with astonishment. The spot where the tanker had once lay peacefully at anchor, was like a scene from Dante's Inferno. From within the bubbling mass of smoke and explosions, jets of burning oil shot upwards, turning the night sky into a flickering shroud of daylight. A small armada of fire tenders, their red and white superstructures clearly visible, were beaten back by the scorching heat as they inched forward attempting to pour streams of white foam curling into the stricken vessel.

Hailey was joined by Gooding and Jock Forbes, their faces a sweaty red caused by the fierce glow coming from the raging fire.

'What a bloody shambles, eh,' Hailey gasped. He then unhooked the voice pipe and cleared his throat. For the next five minutes he explained what had happened, adding, 'I hope to get under way some time tomorrow. Special sea duty men only will be required. Everyone to carry battle bags in case of emergencies. That is all.'

CHAPTER TWENTY-SIX

The time was shortly after 0815on Tuesday 13 August. Colours had just finished. A clear, pale blue sky and a balmy, easterly wind promised another fine day. Across the harbour the tanker continued to bellow clouds of dense black smoke. Hailey, Noble, Gooding and Forbes stood on the flight deck watching the efforts of a large group of fire tenders continuing to spray the tanker with foam.

'God only knows how long it'll take them to put the fire out,' Hailey muttered to no one in particular.

'It makes you wonder what might have happened if there'd been more than two suicide boats,' Gooding added solemnly.

'Yes, indeed, sir,' said Noble, 'you can hardly see the tanker for that bloody smoke.'

'Poor beggars,' Hailey muttered, then walking away, added quietly, 'I'll be in my cabin if you need me, Number One.'

Overnight there had been very little wind and a pall of bubbling black smoke now ascended and hung in the air like the aftermath of a nuclear explosion. Ships, including liners and luxury cabin cruisers were coated with dingy black soot. Blobs of viscous oil floated on the once blue waters of the harbour threatening the wild-life, and coagulating against the yachts and dinghies moored in the nearby Rosia Bay.

No sooner had Hailey entered his cabin and sat down behind his deck than Flannigan came in.

'Nasty business, to be sure, sir,' he said, placing a steaming hot mug of coffee on Hailey's leather- bound blotter. 'And that smoke gets everywhere. The sooner we get to sea, the better, that's what I say, sir.'

'I agree with you,' Hailey sighed wearily. 'Thank you for the coffee. It's just what I needed.'

Hailey blew across the top of the mug and was about to take a sip of his drink when a shark knock came at his door.

'Come.' He grunted, he then carefully took a sip of coffee before placing it on his desk.

The door opened and in came Bosley. His once pristine white overalls were streaked with oil and his face looked tired and drawn.

'Come in, Norman, you look all in, do sit down, Hailey said, 'would you like some coffee?'

Pre-empting Hailey's question, Flannigan appeared holding another mug of scalding hot coffee and handed it to Bosley, who gave him a grateful smile.

'Better not spoil the covers on your chair,' Bosley replied, blinking his tired, bloodshot eyes, 'as you can see I'm a bit mucky.'

'To blazes with that, man,' Hailey cried, 'sit down and bring me up to date.'

'Good news, I'm happy to say, sir,' Bosley said before taking a sip of coffee. 'Despite those damn explosions, we managed to repair the engines, even though we had to work all night.'

'Bloody marvellous, Norman,' cried Hailey, slapping his desk with the palm of a hand. 'How soon do you think we can sail?'

Stifling a yawn, Bosley replied, 'At least three hours, sir. It'll take that long to flash everything up.'

'Let's see,' Hailey muttered, glancing at his wristwatch. 'It's a little after zero nine hundred, would fourteen hundred, be all right?'

'Yes, sir,' Bosley answered, finishing his drink then placing the empty mug on Hailey's desk. 'But I still think you should test the engines first.'

'Don't worry, Norman,' Hailey replied, giving Bosley a reassuring smile, 'if anything untoward happens, I'll take full responsibility for your precious engines. Now, when you leave, ask the First Lieutenant to see me. And give the chief and his lads a red recommend on their service papers. They and you have done a fine job.' (A red recommend is a report written on their service documents.)

A few minutes after Bosley left the cabin Noble knocked on the door and came in, his heavily tanned face wreathed in smiles.

159

'Norman told me the good news, sir,' Noble, taking his cap off. 'When are we sailing?'

'Fourteen hundred, Number One. I want the ship's company closed up at Defence stations.' Hailey answered, standing up and placing both sets of fingers on his desk. 'Special seaman only will be needed. I'll address the ship's company during stand easy. And you had better notify Bahrain, MOD and the harbour master.'

'Very good, sir,' Noble replied, 'I'm sure everyone will be glad to put to sea again.'

Meanwhile, in the for'd seamen's mess everyone listened as Hailey finished his speech.

'Thank fuck for that, Shady,' muttered Bud Abbott, 'the sooner we leave, the sooner we get rid of that stink of oil.'

'Never mind, Bud, my old gash bucket,' Shady replied taking a deep gulp of beer from his can, 'By the way, have you ever been to Port Said?'

'No,' Bud replied, 'what's it like?'

'You'll find out,' Shady answered, 'they don't call it the arse-hole of the world for nowt.'

'You're right there, Shady,' chimed in Baggsy Baker, 'it's as if everyone in the port has farted at once.'

'It can't be any worse than the smell Dutch Holland makes after a night on the beer,' Bud answered. 'He makes more noise than Vesuvius erupting.'

At 1330, the slight vibration of the engines and the churning of the two massive brass propellers could be felt as the ship prepared to sail. Special Sea Duty men fell in on the fo'c'sle and flight deck. At precisely 1400, Hailey gave the order to cast off for'd and aft springs.

'Set the lever at five degrees to starboard, Coxswain, 'Hailey said calmly, feeling the deck sway gently. 'Half head both engines.'

'Aye, aye, sir,' snapped Forbes.

Dawlish gradually moved away from the wharf and slowly turned right and nosed her way into the harbour.

'God knows how long that tanker will burn, sir,' Noble remarked, watching the fire tenders still at work.

'Indeed,' muttered Hailey, 'but it looks as if the tide is beginning to take away the oil into the open sea.'

'And provide a danger to the wild-life around the Spanish coast, no doubt,' added, Shirley Mannering.

'Well,' said Gooding, 'thank goodness, it's not our problem, eh sir?'

'Quite so, Pilot,' Hailey said, anxiously listening to the almost silent purr of the engines, 'we have enough to worry about.'

By 1000 the ship had cleared the harbour and was cruising steadily into the Mediterranean. The waters were now a deep blue but the pall of black smoke could still be seen a few miles behind them silhouetted against the bright cerulean sky.

Throughout the ship everyone continued their duties as normal. In the engine room Bosley, Vellacott and Bungy Williams and his stokers were keeping a watchful eye on the various gauges and dials.

'So far so good, sir,' said Williams, using a piece of cotton waste to mop beads of sweat from his brow.

'Yes,' Bosley muttered warily, 'but let's see what happens later on when we increase speed.'

On the flight deck and fo'c'sle, work parties were busy using buckets of detergent and squeegees to clear away the remnants of oil stains..

'These battle bags are a soddin' nuisance,' muttered Sandy Powell, to Dinga Bell, as he swished the deck with foamy water.

'I dunno,' said Dinga, pausing to lean on the handle of his squeegee, 'I always keep a few cans of beer and some nutty in mine, just in case . . .'

'I'll have to remember that,' said Jean Rochester, feeling a few drops of warm sweat run down the sides of her face.

'I suppose you keep knitting in yours,' chimed in Bud Abbott giving her a wide grin.

Jean was about to say something obscene, when the sharp voice of Harry Tate interrupted her. 'Pack it in there, you lot,' he shouted, 'or you can carry on during stand easy.'

In the Ops Room everyone was close up, peering at their orange radar screens.

'Quite a lot of traffic approaching, sir, about ten miles away to port.' Diana reported, glancing up at Henderson.

'And three more, five miles behind them,' cried Ashir.

'Yes, I can see them,' Henderson replied, studying the black dots on his screen. Remembering that the Al Qaeda speedboats might have been launched from a ship, he cautiously replied, 'monitor their progress. Report if any of them stops or comes close to us.'

'Stand easy' was piped and a rating appeared with a tray mugs of steaming hot tea. Diana accepted one and loosened her mouth piece, and took a sip. Ashir did the same.

'I keep on thinking of all those poor buggers on board that tanker, Ash,' she said, his face barely visible under the dim blue lighting, 'They couldn't have stood a chance. What a terrible way to die.

'Yes, I agree,' Ashir answered, doing his best to sound sincere, but inwardly giving thanks to Allah for the death of the infidels. 'It must have been awful for them,' he added, looking into the softness of Diana's soft blue eyes. At that moment, he felt a slight pang of sorrow knowing that a similar fate awaited her and everyone on board *Dawlish*. He quickly looked away and said a silent prayer to Allah for forgiveness, and to give him courage to carry out the task he had been allotted.

CHAPTER TWENTY-SEVEN

'Increase speed to twenty-two knots, Number One,' Hailey said, 'I want to try and make up for lost time.'

The time was 1600, the duty watch had fallen out and those off watch were in their messes enjoying a mug of tea.

Below in the boiler and engine rooms, Bosley, received the order to increase speed.

'At least we're only less than a fifty miles from Gib in case anything does goes wrong, sir,' Williams remarked, giving Bosley an anxious look.

'That's if we don't break down and have to be towed back,' Bosley replied sullenly.

As the ship gathered speed nobody spoke. During the next two hours the tension was palpable and showed on each face. All eyes became focused on a set of the engine gauges and dials. Everyone listened intently to the gentle throbbing of the engines silently praying for their steady, almost inaudible, rhythmic beat to continue unabated.

'Sounds fine, sir,' said Williams, giving Bosley a guarded glance while flicking a bead of perspiration from the side of his face.

Bosley was about to speak but was interrupted by the ringing of the engine room telephone. He moved across to the bulkhead and unhooked the receiver.

'Bosley,' he said, feeling his throat suddenly go dry. After a few seconds he went on, 'no problems so far, sir, yes, I'll keep you informed,' and replaced the receiver.

Suddenly the tension evaporated.

'I don't know about you lot,' said Williams looking around at the relaxed expressions on the faces of the stokers and engineers, 'but I could do with a nice mug of tea.'

During the next three days. *Dawlish* passed several ships, some merchant vessels, others commercial liners sailing westwards. Hailey challenged each one and after being identified, allowed to carry on. The ship's company were now wearing white tropical rig known as 1BWs.

The time was 1400 on Friday 16 August. The sky was a dazzling blue and the sun a ball of yellow heat.

On the port side of the flight deck, several off duty ratings were lying on towels, striped to the waist. As smoking wasn't permitted below decks, it was allowed in this area. The girls enjoyed a similar arrangement further for'd in a space on the upper deck behind the bridge structure. Officers used the port and starboard wing decks either side of the bridge. However, as very few of the crew smoked so this wasn't a problem.

Hailey was sat on his high chair feeling a trickle of sweat run down his back. Even though the air conditioning was fully on, the atmosphere inside the enclosed bridge was uncomfortably hot.

'What's our position, Pilot?' Hailey asked, stretching his arms above his head and yawning.

'As you know, sir,' Gooding replied, 'we passed Sicily and Malta during the night. We're now two hundred miles off the coast of Libya. Latitude twenty degrees north, longitude fifteen east, sir.'

'And the temperature?'

'It's just over eighty degrees Fahrenheit outside, sir, and the water is ten degrees below that, I pity those poor bloody booties,' he added, watching a group of marines, clad only in shorts and pumps, glistening with sweat being through a series of calisthenics by Butch Cassidy.

'Yes,' Hailey answered, 'perhaps it's time to give the crew a quick dip, but inform Bob Henderson I'd like the Ops Room manned. And tell Norman not to shut down the engines completely, just as a precautionary measure.'

'Against what, may I ask, sir?' Noble replied, giving Hailey a quick, searching glance.

'Pirates and speed boat attacks,' Hailey answered warily, 'and God knows what else. Fourteen thirty all right, Number One?'

'Yes, indeed, sir,' Noble replied, 'I expect that'll cool everyone off. I'll spread the good news,' he added, reaching for the bridge intercom.

'This is the First Lieutenant speaking,' he said, dabbing his brow with a handkerchief. 'Hands to bath will be piped at fourteen thirty. The ship will stop for a half an hour allowing those off duty to have quick swim. A lifeboat and crew will be launched to stand by in case of emergencies. The ship's siren will sound recall. That is all.'

'Bloody marvellous,' cried Swampy Marsh, to nobody in particular. 'Just wait until the girls see my hairy chest, they'll probably faint.'

'Aye, they will that,' replied Pete Price, a wide grin spreading across his face, 'they'll faint with shock. I've see you in the shower, you look like a bloody gorilla.'

'Anyway, Swampy,' chimed in Bud Abbott, giving Shady Lane a sly wink, 'I shouldn't worry, the sight of you half-naked will keep the sharks away.'

'Sharks?' Swampy exclaimed, his hand poised in mid-air holding a fork full of mince, 'they don't have sharks in the Med . . . do they?'

'Of course they do,' Shady replied, nodding his head. 'An oppo of mine on board the *Reclaim* got his leg bitten off by one last year.'

'Fuck that for a skylark,' Swampy answered emphatically. 'I think I'll stay on board and have a wank.'

In the girls' mess, some were listening to a CD recording of Blondie's gravelly voice singing, *Take My Heart*.

'I bet the water is warm in enough to go skinny dipping,' said Lottie Jones, 'just like we did in the Caribbean.'

'Yes, but we were on the beach and it was pitch dark,' Jilly Howard remarked, 'try that and the lads will have heart attacks.'

Right on cue Sadie Thompson came into the mess. Her oversize figure threatened to burst out of her tight white shorts and shirt and her florid, sunburnt complexion shone light a ripe apple.

'Now, I don't have to remind you girls,' she said, staring sternly around at the girls, 'that bikinis and skimpy bathing wear are forbidden. One piece bathing suits only are to be worn. And,' she paused as her rubicund features broke into a weak smile, 'make sure you don't have any unseemly hairs sticking out from embarrassing places, we don't want to get the men excited, do we?'

'What will you be wearing, PO?' Diana asked, doing her best not to laugh.

'I don't believe in mixed bathing,' she replied haughtily, then turned sharply and left the mess.

At 1425, the ship came to a gentle stop, rolled slightly and lost way. Harry Tate, and the duty watch had secured a nylon scrambling net over the port side of the flight light deck. A lifeboat manned by Jack Whitton and a crew of four was secured alongside the ship.

The flight deck was crowded with ratings feeling the sudden sway of the deck and the warm breeze on their faces and bodies.

'Bugger me, Ash!' Shady Lane exploded, staring at some of the girls, 'Jilly Howard looks bloody great in that red swimsuit, doesn't she?'

Ashir didn't reply. He was too engrossed smiling at Diana, whose pale green swimming costume clung to her full figure like a second skin.

She returned his smile and admired his dark, handsome features and well-muscled swarthy body. With a regretful sigh, she said, 'What a pity we couldn't have stayed in that hotel in Gib.'

At that moment the tannoy crackled into action.

'This is the First Lieutenant speaking. Hands to bath may commence.'

This was a bizarre naval tradition that temporarily transformed the warship into diving platform. Ratings and officers stepped onto the edge and peered apprehensively into the crystal clear blue water twenty feet below. Then, one by one, some diving head first, others holding their noses, they braced themselves and leapt over the side.

Among the officers were Midshipmen Damian Parker-Smith and Peter Dunlop.

Coughing and spluttering, they both surfaced almost together. The water was warm but the unexpected swell of the sea made them and the other swimmers, rise and fall as if being pushed by some unseen hand.

'My God, Duners,' gasped Parker-Smith, treading water and moving his hands, 'doesn't the ship look huge from down here?'

Dunlop didn't reply. He was too busy blinking and coughing while doing his best to stay afloat.

Hailey and Noble were leaning on the port wing of the bridge watching the swimmers.

'They remind me of a lot of kids splashing about in the sea off Brighton, don't they, sir?' Noble remarked, feeling his shirt stick to his back.

'Yes, they do, 'Hailey replied, grinning. 'Why don't you pop down and have a quick dip?'

Noble was about to reply when the sound of Ops Room intercom made them both turn around. Jock Forbes immediately unhooked the handset.

'Bridge,' he said, licking a bead of sweat from his upper lip. A few seconds later he added. 'Right, thank you,' and replaced the handset. 'Radar reports unidentified aircraft approaching at ten thousand feet sixty miles away on port beam, sir.'

Straightaway Hailey, Noble and Forbes, using their high-powered binoculars peered away to the left.

'I can just about see its Delta wings, sir,' Noble shouted, 'they look like French Mirages.'

In a flash, Hailey remembered Al Qaeda had captured three Mirages from the airport in Triploi. He also remembered they carried three Exocet missies on each wing. Suddenly he felt a surge of panic run through him. At the speed the fighter was travelling he estimated it would pass over the ship in roughly fifteen minutes.

'Do you think it could be . . . ?' Noble cried, recalling what had happened in Tripoli.

'I sincerely hope not, if it is we're sitting ducks,' Hailey replied, doing his best to stay calm. 'Pipe hands to Weapons State Monty. I'm not taking any chances.'

'Shall I sound the siren and recall the swimmers?'

'No,' Hailey answered, feeling his mouth suddenly go dry. 'If the ship is attacked, they're safer in the water. Some will have heard the pipe so use the loudhailer and tell them this purely a precautionary measure and to keep clear of the ship.'

Hailey was right.

Over the spluttering and coughing many, including Somersby and his marines heard the pipe.

'W . . . what do yer think is happening, sir,' gasped Tosher White, frantically treading water. It was a question etched on the wet faces of the other marines swimming nearby.

'I don't know,' gasped Somersby as a small wave slashed against his face. 'Just do as the pipe says.'

A group of ratings, male and female, some on their backs, rising and falling with movement of the sea, others going through a series of strokes also heard the tannoy.

'Swim clear of the fuckin' ship,' Bud Abbott cried, gagging as he swallowed a mouthful of salty water. 'Are you sure there's no sharks around here?'

'Keep a level head, Bud,' gasped Shady, floating on his back and feeling the warm sun on his face, 'if you feel something bite yer leg, you'll soon know.'

'Bugger this,' spluttered Bud, 'I'm making for the lifeboat, sharks or no fuckin' sharks.'

The girl's reaction was more sanguine.

'It's probably a bloody exercise,' cried Jilly Howard, fighting against the strength of the waves while trying to master her breast-stoke.

'I don't mind what it is,' gasped Lottie Jones, 'anyway, I've just had a pee, so don't swallow any water.'

On the bridge, the Ops phone rang and was answered by Forbes.

'The Pee-woh reports all Sea Wolf missiles are locked onto the fighter, sir, but the radio operator reports difficulty in contacting the pilot. He says the frequency seems jammed.'

Knowing the maximum effective range of the missiles was 10 km, Hailey replied, 'Very good, Chief, tell him to keep trying and tell the Pee-woh to stand by.'

With mounting trepidation, everyone hurried onto the port wing of the bridge. With straining necks and binoculars firmly clamped to their eyes, they anxiously watched as the fighter gradually drew closer, its silver fuselage glinting in the hot, afternoon sun. In a matter of seconds the aircraft was upon them, roaring as it streaked over the ship, the red, white and blue roundels on the underside of its bat-like delta wings showing its French origin. In a blink of an eye the fighter soared into the sky then banked to the left.

'Good Lord, sir,' yelled Gooding, 'I do believe the blighter is turning to come at us again.'

Hailey felt his heart beating hard against his chest wall. In a matter of seconds he and the rest of the crew would know if the fighter was friendly or not. But, he asked himself, should he take the risk and shoot it down. If he did so and his assumption was wrong, it would mean a court martial and a probable dismissal from the service. He only had seconds to decide what to do. Lowering his binoculars, Hailey grabbed hold the Ops Room phone. Henderson's sharp voice immediately came on the line.

'Stand by to assume Weapons State Golf, Bob,' Hailey said feeling his pulse quicken.

'My God, sir,' Henderson cried, knowing this meant preparing the missiles for firing, 'are you sure? What if . . .'

Gooding shouting, 'He's waggling his wings, sir,' made Hailey look up into the sky. As he did so the fighter swooped low and moved both wings in a gesture as if saluting the ship, then streaked up into the sky and quickly vanished over the horizon.

'Belay that last order, Bob,' Hailey gasped, his face wet with perspiration and his shirt clinging to him like a second skin. 'Our friend has gone home.' He turned to Noble, and feeling as if a heavy weight had suddenly been lifted from his shoulders, took a deep breath and said, 'revert to Cruising Stations, Number One and sound the siren, then let's get under way.'

CHAPTER TWENTY-EIGHT

The time was 0600 on Saturday, 17 August. High above in the pale blue sky the last of the stars were quickly disappearing, as if snuffed out by an unknown hand. In the blink of an eye the yellow orb of the sun continued to rise from the eastern horizon allowing her cousin, the moon, to retreat into the heavens, the stars faded away and a new day was born.

By 0800, Port Said hove into view roughly ten miles away covered in a misty heat haze. A dozen or so cranes around the dockyard, looking like dark predators, poked into the sky. The funnels and part of the superstructures of shipping berthed in the port could also be seen along with minarets of varying sizes plus a line of white topped buildings.

On the fo'c'sle Shady Lane and Bud Abbott were busy wiping down the metal deck.

'Jesus!' exclaimed Bud Abbott, grimacing while leaning in the handle of his squeegee, 'what the fuck is that smell?'

Shady threw is head back and gave a loud guffaw. 'I told you Port Said was the arsehole of the world, didn't I?'

'What causes that?' Bud asked, 'it's the worst pong I've ever smelt.'

'Bad sanitation,' Shady replied tersely, 'not to mention dead bodies and animals.'

'And look at the water,' Bud added, staring over the side of the ship, 'it's turned a shitty green. Why is that I wonder?'

'Summat to do with the sand, I think,' Shady said, wiping his brow with an off-white handkerchief, 'or else everyone pissing in the sea. Now get on with cleaning before PO Whitton arrives.'

At precisely 0900 *Dawlish* entered Ports Said's main harbour, dominated on the right by the Custom House, a tall, white four storey building, its three golden domes gleaming in the early morning sunshine.

Despite the air conditioning, the shirts on everyone on the bridge were stuck to them like second skins.

'I see the temperature is thirty degrees centigrade, Number One,' Hailey remarked glancing at the ship's temperature gauge, while wiping his neck with a handkerchief.

'Or, if you prefer it, sir,' Noble replied, 'eighty-six degrees Fahrenheit.'

'And I expect it'll become worse as we go down the canal and reach Aden,' added Shirley Mannering feeling trickles of warm sweat run down between her buttocks.

'Send a signal to Port Authority, Number One, say, "*request pratique before proceeding*".

(Pratique is medical clearance requested by all warships entering the canal.)

Five minutes later, Pincher Martin arrived on the bridge holding a piece of white paper.

'Signal from Port Authority, sir,' said, 'it reads, "*pratique granted. Take position behind SS Beymoth and proceed into canal at 1200*".'

'Thank you, Chief,' Hailey said, 'reply, "*Many thanks, will comply*".'

'*Beymoth,* that's the big cargo ship in the middle of the harbour behind the container, sir,' remarked Noble, using his binoculars to scan the harbour.

'Yes, I can see that, Number One,' Hailey replied. 'We'll move a hundred yards to her rear and stop. Slow ahead both engines, set lever to four degrees to port, please Pilot.'

Dawlish slowly eased behind the large cargo vessel; her tall funnel, lying in front of her high bridge was painted bright red. This was in sharp contrast to the dingy black colour of her numerous derricks, cranes and superstructure. She was lying low in the water showing clearly that her holds were full. *Hamburg,* her port of origin was painted in white on her rusting stern and a German red, black and yellow flag hung loosely from her mainmast.

'Stop both engines,' Hailey ordered, licking a bead of sweat from his upper lip.

Almost imperceptibly *Dawlish* came to a stop, rolling slightly as she lost way.

'Here come the bum boats, sir,' shouted Bud Abbott. 'They're coming alongside the flight deck.'

Hailey and Noble grinned at one another, and along with Gooding and Jock Forbes went onto the port wing deck. Straightaway a hot, off-shore wind attacked their faces.

The sight that met their eyes was colourful and noisy. Flocks of squawking pigeons circled above the ship, like hungry vultures in search of food. A small fleet of gaudily painted motor boats heavily laden with everything from bubble pipes, to ladies underwear was just about twenty feet below each side of flight deck. From each boat swarthy, black bearded Arabs, wearing off- white disdashas and baggy trousers, stood up shouting excitedly and waving their goods in the air.

'Dirty pictures of my sister, Jack,' cried a tall, pockmarked Arab, brandishing a handful of photographs, 'Only one English pound or a hundred piasters.'

Another Arab, holding a model of a camel in one hand and a fistful of small, green covered booklets in the other, was yelling, 'Good books to read in your hammocks, only fifty euros each, camels half price.'

After heated bargaining, several ratings including girls were bent over the side and dropped their money down into eager hands and who then threw them various, so-called souvenirs. Among the items sought after were some of the small green-backed paper booklets.

'What kind of books are they, Shady?' Lottie Jones asked Shady Lane, winking slyly at Jilly Howard and Jane Wootton. The girls were not naïve. They had been long enough in the service to have heard about the pornographic booklets, known colloquially as 'Jippo AFOs' (Admiralty Fleet Orders), but were attempting to embarrass Shady.

'Oh, nowt that you'd be interested in, Lot,' Shady replied innocently.

'Let's see then,' Lottie said, quickly snatching a booklet out of his hand.

'Hey, give it back to me, you miserable sod,' Shady yelled, attempting in vain to retrieve the booklet.

With a girlish cry, Lottie stepped back and opened the booklet. Jilly and Jane peered over Lottie's shoulder and together read the first page.

With mock indignation etched in her eyes, Lottie cried, 'Oh my God, this is pure unadulterated filth, you ought to be ashamed of yourself, Lane,' and threw the booklet back at him.

As the girls turned away, Jilly gave Shady a salacious grin and said, 'When you've read it pass it on to me and the girls.'

Shortly after 1200 the screws of *Beymoth* churned up the muddy waters of the harbour as the ship slowly moved forward.

'Half ahead both engines, Number One,' Hailey ordered, then looking sideways at Jock Forbes, added, 'and keep a regulation two hundred yards from her stern. I'd hate to collide with the big bugger.'

By late evening, *Dawlish* and the convoy of shipping had passed down the canal and entered the Gulf of Suez. At what seemed the blink of an eye, day had suddenly turned into night. On the left some fifty yards away, the sweeping sands of the Sinai desert glowed deep bronze under the bright, yellow sickle moon. On the opposite side of the canal, a long stretch of rugged mountains disappeared into the eerie wilderness of the Eastern Desert.

Hailey and Noble moved onto the port wing to admire the scene. As they did so a warm, stiff wind greeted them.

'That wind is called the Khamseen, Number One,' Hailey remarked, 'It comes all the way from North Africa, similar to the Sirocco.'

'I only hope it doesn't cause a sandstorm, sir,' Noble replied, shielding his eyes from the tiny pickles of sand attacking his face.

'Don't tempt providence,' Hailey guardedly replied, who, feeling the effects of the wind on his face, turned and retreated into the sanctuary of the bridge.

CHAPTER TWENTY-NINE

After a brief stop in the Bitter Lakes, *Dawlish* entered dark blue waters of the Red Sea on Sunday 18 August at 0600. By this time the SS *Beymoth* and several other vessels had gradually dispersed and were fading away in the distance.

The time was 1300. Hailey was in his cabin sitting behind his desk. Noble was sat opposite him sipping a cup of coffee.

'In four days we will have passed through the Red Sea and be off the off the coast of Yemen and be near Aden,' Hailey remarked, folding his arms across his chest.

'A rather dangerous neck of the woods, eh, sir,' Noble remarked, finishing his drink and placing the cup and saucer on a nearby table.

'Quite so,' Hailey guardedly replied. 'Yemen is a hot bed of Al Qaeda terrorist and pirates. Sometimes the buggers take a pot-shot at ships, especially warships, so everyone is to keep clear of the upper deck, understood?'

'Yes, sir,' Noble stoically replied, 'I'll have it put on Daily Orders.'

On the flight deck, Shady Lane, Dutch Holland and Swampy Marsh were lying on towels, stripped to the waist basking in the hot sun.

'Remember what the doc said' muttered Shady Lane, putting on a pair of sunglasses, 'only fifteen minutes or else we'll all turn red like ripe plums.'

'Maybe that's why they call it the Red Sea,' Swampy Marsh grunted, rubbing lotion on his hairy chest.

'What about the Black Sea, the Yellow Sea and the White Sea?' Dutch Holland mumbled lazily. 'How d'yer account for them?'

'Easy,' Swampy quickly replied, 'it's because the people what live near them are that colour.'

'What a load of bollocks,' grunted Shady Lane, 'I suppose everyone that lives near the Dead Sea are corpses.'

'How the fuck do I know,' Swampy replied and angrily turned over onto his stomach.

Ashir and Diana were on the upper deck below the bridge. Both were still in their whites having just come off duty and were stood with their hands resting on the guard rail. For a few minutes neither spoke. It was as if they were hypnotised by the warm wind wafting gently caressing their faces, and glittering blue waters stretched out as far as they could see.

Finally, sensing Ashir's usual shyness, Diana spoke. 'Tell me, Ash, is the Koran a thick book like the bible?'

'I think so,' Ashir answered somewhat taken aback by the question. 'The Koran consists of six thousand, six hundred and sixty-six verses, so, yes, it is as thick as the bible.'

'And have you read every verse?' Diana asked, still looking at him.

'Some, but not all of them,' he replied, 'the secondary school I went to was mixed religion. My parents made me read some verses at home, but I've forgotten,' he added, hoping his lies sounded convincing.

'I read in a newspaper the Koran was a book of tolerance and that Muhammed welcomed all religions and cultures to Mecca. Is that right?'

'Muhammed,' Ashir hesitatingly replied, stopping himself from adding the traditional, 'peace be upon him,' 'was a man of great wisdom.'

'If he was so wise, why does Al Qaeda murder innocent men and women in his name?' Diana asked, shaking her head. 'It doesn't make sense, does it?'

Foolish, ignorant woman, he thought, how was she to know that all non-believers are infidels and must die.

'No, no it doesn't,' Ashir muttered before gritting his teeth to hide his self-condemnation. 'Now I think I'll go below, it's getting too hot for me here,' he added quickly before Diana asked any more difficult questions.

The six hundred miles journey through the Red Sea took four days. In order to keep the crew on their toes, Hailey ordered a series of evolutions. These included, man overboard, fire and flood exercises.

'Better pipe 'abandon ship', Number One,' Hailey said, 'just to be on the safe side.'

'Shall we go to Emergency Stations first, sir?' Noble asked, 'just to practise a head count.'

'No,' Hailey replied, stroking his chin, 'If we have to leave the ship, we may not have much time. Let's see how long it might take to launch the inflatables and lifeboats.'

Much to Hailey's surprise everyone, including the officers, remembered their stations. Even Noble, who, when the pipe was made, immediately collected the ship's secret codes, and placed them in a water-proof bag.

'Well done, Number One,' said Hailey, 'that only took ten minutes.'

'Thank you, sir,' Noble replied, 'but if you recall, we did the abandon ship drill a few times last commission in the Caribbean.'

On Thursday, 22 August, *Dawlish* entered the Gulf of Aden without incident. The time was shortly before 1200. Far away on the port side the rugged coastline of Yemen quivered in the heat haze. What little wind there was seemed to envelope everyone in a hot, sweaty cocoon. It was so warm that sun bathing was banned; even Somersby ordered Cassidy to suspend the usual morning exercises.

'Fair enough, sir,' said Cassidy standing facing Somersby in the officer's cabin. 'I'll hold a weapon inspection in their mess, then they can do a few dozen press-ups,' he added with a mischievous grin, 'that'll keep 'em busy.'

After dinner several rating were sat around in the mess, sipping cans of beer while watching a recording of *Downton Abbey*.

'I can't make up my mind who's doing what to who in this bloody programme,' muttered Lofty Day, taking a good gulp of beer.

'Personally,' said Bud Abbott, 'I think that Michelle Docherty is essence.'

'Too skinny fer me,' added Shady Lane. 'I like 'em with a bit of meat on 'em.'

'Like Lottie Jones, eh, Shady?' Dutch Holland replied with a salacious grin.

At that moment Pete Walker came into the mess, his bronzed face wreathed in smiles.

'Kate's got her memory back,' he cried excitedly, 'the First Lieutenant just sent for me. The hospital sent him an e mail saying she's gunna be all right.'

Everyone stopped what they were doing and looked at him and grinned.

'That's great news, Clubs,' shouted Darby Allen, 'and it calls for a celebration. All spare cans of beer on the table, lads.'

No sooner had he spoken than a loud buzzing sound came from the pocket in Walkers short. He immediately took out his Nokia and pressed the text button. 'It's from her!' he exclaimed, feeling his hand shake. Then, after glancing nervously around he, read out the message. "Memory back. Going home 2morrow. Where R U? Miss U, you. I Love U. Kate. XXXX."

'It's a pity the reception is not too good here,' said Bud Abbott, who, like Shady Lane had stood up and was looking over Walker's shoulder at the text. 'I think you'd better reply straightaway.'

Feeling his finger trembling slightly, Walker texted, "Fab news. In the Red C. Miss and love U 2. Will U marry me? XXXX."

The next five minutes seemed like an hour as everyone holding cans of beer waited impatiently for Kate's reply. Suddenly, Walker's mobile phone came alive.

To everyone's relief the message read, "Yes, yes, anytime any place. I love U."

A loud cheer rang around the mess. Hands slapped Walker on the shoulder.

'Come on, mate,' said Swampy Marsh, 'see that beer off. There's plenty more where that came from.'

Shortly afterwards, Noble announced the news of Kate's full recovery over the tannoy. Needless to say this was greeted with hugs and cheers in the girls' mess.

'Right girls,' cried Lottie Jones, excitedly jumping up and down, 'I just happen to have a small bottle of gin in in my locker. Somebody get the plastic cups from beside the water tank.'

Things were a lot calmer on the bridge. The time was 1400. Hailey was relaxed in his customary seat sipping a cool glass of water, compliments of Flannigan. Julian Morris busied himself making a note of the ship's position from the navigation computer and Jack Whitton was staring up at the clear blue sky, wishing he was with his wife, Hilda, and two children on the beach at Brighton.

Suddenly, the buzzing of the Ops Room intercom interrupted the tranquillity of the scene. Hailey reached across and unhooked the receiver.

'Yes, captain,' Hailey said, while pushing himself upright.

'Pee-woh, here, sir,' came the strident voice of Bob Henderson, 'urgent May Day message from the *Beymoth,* sir. It reads, "*Three unidentified craft sighted on radar fifty miles on port bow. They don't reply to our request for identification. Could be pirates. Request assistance.*"

'We have the three objects on our radar, sir,' Henderson went on, '*Beymoth* is just over a eighty miles directly ahead of us, sir.'

'Thank you, Bob,' Hailey said. Glancing at Gooding, he went on, 'How far are we from the coast of Yemen?'

After a quick look at his screen, Gooding replied, 'a hundred miles on our port beam, sir.'

'Thank you, Pilot,' Hailey replied. He then continued talking to Henderson, 'keep me in formed of the three craft's progress please Bob, and reply to *Beymoth*, "*will come immediately.*" Better inform Bahrain. Are there any warships in the area?'

'*Montrose* and the French frigate *Royale,* are in the Strait of Hormuz escorting a Dutch ship probably carrying nuclear waste to Dar es Salaam, sir,' Noble replied.

Hailey looked at the anxious expressions on the faces of Noble and the others, 'Increase speed to twenty-eight knots, Number One,' he said calmly. 'It looks like we're in for a bit of excitement.'

CHAPTER THIRTY

The Ops Room was suddenly a hive of concentrated activity. Ashir, Diana and the five other radar operators peered at their respective screen, each reporting the position of *Beymoth* and the three unidentified craft. These movements were then plotted on a large pale yellow screen by Spud Murphy and Henderson, who then passed on the information to the bridge.

'How soon do you think we'll sight *Beymoth*, Pilot?' Hailey asked Gooding.

The chart room was a small extension in the back of the bridge. Using a pair of dividers on his chart, Gooding carefully replied, 'At the speed both ships are making, we should sight her in three hours, sir.'

Hailey pursed his lips, slid off his chair and walked to the port side of the bridge and stared pensively out to sea.

'Let's see now, that'll be about seventeen hundred' he mused, glancing at his wristwatch. 'As the crow flies, Bahrain is over two thousand miles away, too far away for any aircraft to reach *Beymoth.*'

Hailey gave Noble a searching look, 'That means it's up to us, Number One,' he said gravely. 'Tell Norman I want every ounce of speed he can give me I'll take full responsibility for any engine damage. Now kindly unhook the bridge intercom and pass it to me.'

During the next five minutes, Hailey explained to the ship's company over the tannoy what was happening, ending with, 'as soon as the *Beymoth* is sighted, the ship will go to Weapons State Monty. That is all.' He looked at Noble and added, 'Tell Somersby I want a BAR machine gun mounted on either side of the bridge and ask Jerry Ashcroft to come and see me.'

Shortly after the captain's address to the crew, Ashcroft arrived. An all-knowing expression was written on his heavily tanned features.

'Don't tell me, let me guess, sir,' he said, grinning at Hailey, 'you want the Bug at full readiness.'

179

'That's right, Jerry,' Hailey replied, 'at fifteen hundred I want you to take off and identify those three boats then report their position. My guess is that if they are pirates, the sight of the helo will deter them, knowing that a warship is close.' He paused and slowly stroked his chin, 'but their mother ship cannot be too far away. Follow the blighters and see if you can find her. Understood?'

'Yes, sir, I do, but . . .' Ashcroft hesitatingly replied.

'What is it, man, is something wrong?'

'No, sir,' Ashcroft replied, 'it's just that . . . these blighters aren't stupid. If they do turn around and see the Bug following them, do you really think they'll lead us to the mother ship, especially as they'll know a warship must be close?'

'Mm . . . You have a point, Jerry,' Hailey replied, 'but it's a risk I'll have to take. The mother ship can't be all that far away and if we pick her up on radar, you can deal with the boats as you think fit, but don't get too close to them, remember they may be armed. And tell Leading Seaman Lee to video everything as much as possible.'

The corners of Ashcroft's dark blue eyes creased into a wicked smile. 'What shall I do if the buggers open fire on the Bug, sir?'

'Defend yourself, of course, old boy,' Hailey replied smiling warily.

'Very good, sir,' Ashcroft said, with a rakish smile, then left the bridge. He hurried away and informed Flight Deck Officer Harry Thomas what was happening.

In the marines' mess deck, Somersby was briefing the Butch Cassidy and his team.

'We may have to board the vessel,' he explained, staring at them, 'so be on your toes. Smithy, you and Chalky will man a BAR machine gun on both wings outside the bridge. Any questions?'

'Yes, sir,' said Cassidy, 'if we do have board her and meet any resistance shall we retaliate?'

'I'm sure you'll know what to do, Sergeant,' Somersby replied, with a wry smile. 'Have your men ready by fourteen thirty.'

After Somersby had gone, Knocker White turned to Pedlar Palmer, and with a wicked grin on his face, took out his Fairbairn-Sykes Commando knife, (named after the two men who invented it during WW2), and said, 'Maybe I'll be able to use this little beauty at last.'

'Bloodthirsty bugger,' Spider Webb said, adding, 'personally, I'd prefer to shoot the bastards up the arse and be done with it.'

In the seamans', mess Dutch Holland glanced apprehensively at Bud Abbott and said, 'don't forget to put a few cans of beer and some nutty in your battle bag, mate.'

'If those bastards manage to ram us,' Bud replied, nervously licking his lips, 'fat lot of use they'll be.'

'Too true, Bud,' Shady Lane added, 'remember what happened to that tanker in Gib.'

'Looks like your lads are in for some target practice, eh, Digger?' Said the portly figure of Wally Hardman who was standing outside the main galley wiping his hands on his pristine white apron. His remark was aimed at Digger Barnes as he hurried along the passageway.

'Don't worry about that, Wally,' Barnes shouted over his shoulder, 'just make sure you've got plenty of corned dog sarnies ready in case we're closed up for some time,' and disappeared down a hatchway leading to the 4.5 gun bay.

'All hands keep clear of the flight deck. Helo is about to be launched,' came the gravelled voice of the duty QM over the tannoy.

At precisely 1430, Hector Pascoe and his team of mechanics pushed the Lynx out of the hangar onto the flight deck.

Somersby and the marines, their green berets firmly clamped on their heads and wearing full action kit, and life belts, climbed on board the Lynx, each clutching a small arms rifle. Leading Seaman Tansey Lee, his small video camera case slung over his shoulder followed on. He immediately slid open the door on the fuselage shut and locked it.

By this time Ashcroft and Mike Roberts were in the cockpit. Thomas then gave the 'take off' signal by whirling a hand in the air. Ashcroft immediately acknowledged with a thumbs up, then moved the collective upwards.

The rotors sprang into action and in a matter of minutes the Lynx was airborne, leaving behind Dicky and his team quickly moving away to avoid the helo's strong downdraft.

Everyone on the bridge watched anxiously as the Lynx quickly ascended, quickly becoming a black dot high above the clear blue sky. Hailey and the others then focused their high-powered binoculars towards the horizon, hoping to see *Beymoth*'s masthead.

The Lynx was now some five thousand feet above sea level.

'*Beymoth* is just over seventy miles ahead of us, skipper,' Mike Roberts shouted, peering at the large pale green radar screen in front of him.

'Any sign of the three bogeys?' cried Ashcroft.

'Not as yet,' Roberts replied. A few seconds later he saw blips appear on the screen. 'Yes, there they are,' he cried excitedly, 'about forty miles away. They must have turned as they're now directly in front of the ship.'

'Thanks, Mike,' Ashcroft replied, and immediately reported the information to Hailey, on board *Dawlish.*

'Thank you. Message received,' said Hailey over the radio. 'Approach with caution.'

'Wilko, out,' replied Ashcroft.

In the darkened Ops Room, Ashir, noticed three black blips appear on his screen.

He marked it with a reference number, then pressed the scan-change button.

This immediately increased the range of the radar map from fifteen to ninety-six miles..

'Three unidentified objects, zero four, one hundred, decimal six, sir,' he shouted.

'Thank you,' Henderson replied, 'well spotted. The Lynx has them also.'

Hailey left his chair and unhooked the bridge intercom. 'This is the captain speaking,' he said gravely, 'we are about to go to the aid of the cargo vessel. Three craft thought to be Al Qaeda have been sighted. The Lynx is investigating and may force them to turn back. If they don't we might have to engage them. Therefore we will go Weapons State Golf. The foc'sle, for'd and after launcher decks are out of bounds. No smoking at all on the upper deck. Remember, this is not a practice drill so be prepared.' Glancing apprehensively at Noble he added, 'Pipe WSG, please, Number One.'

Well drilled and anxious, within minutes everyone was closed up at their respective stations.

In the constantly darkened, windowless Ops Room, the tactical nerve centre of the ship, Henderson ordered the ship to assume Weapon State Golf. This was the order to arm the weapons with live ammunition and to load the air defence missiles all of which were fully automated and under Henderson's control. He felt a sudden surge of excitement and looked around at everyone busily staring at their pale green screens. This, he told himself, was his world. A world in which dedication and training had made him feel confident to face the dangerous situation the ship was about to encounter.

In the after seamen's mess, Bud Abbott and some other ratings were struggling into their anti-flash gear.

'Fuck me,' Bud Abbott shouted hurrying after Dutch Holland, Shady Lane and Swampy Marsh out of the mess. 'I guess this is the real thing.'

'Not half, mate,' Dutch cried, as he and the rest, wearing anti-flash hoods, gloves and battle-bags opened a hatch and climbed down into the belly of the ship and unlocked the magazine.

It was here that a whole range of ammunition ranging from high velocity bullets for the BARs, armour-piercing and tracer shells for the DS3Omm automated guns, the four Sea Skua anti-ship missiles, the two anti-submarine torpedoes and the thirty-two canisters for the Sea Wolf missiles, were stored.

All that was missing was the ammunition for the Harpoon Launchers which were kept constantly in their pods.

On either side of the ship, (WEO) Lieutenant Ray Greenacre and his team of engineers, having brought up the Sea Wolf rockets up from the magazines on lifts and carefully placed them on trolleys and wheeled them to the launchers.

'Bloody hell, Jacko,' remarked Scouse Kennedy, to his oppo, Geordie Jackson, 'I like the way those the body and fins on them fuckin' rockets are painted white with shiny red noses, they look like bloody great fireworks.'

Jacko gave a loud guffaw, the said, 'If one of them goes off you'll soon know the difference. Every one weighs one hundred and eighty pounds and each warhead carries high explosives. That bit you can see at the end is the booster engine to increase its range, so handle the bastards with loving care.'

At that moment Greenacre stepped forward and armed the missiles by connecting them individually to their electrical circuits. He then unhooked a telephone from the bulkhead and after nervously clearing his throat, spoke to Henderson in the Ops Room.

'All missies and weapons systems are now at a state of readiness sir,' he said gravely.

Henderson promptly reported this to Hailey

'Thank you, Ray,' Hailey replied, adding cautiously, 'I certainly hope we won't need them.'

Meanwhile, under the watchful eye of Digger Barnes, the ratings, sweating profusely in the gun bay's hot, clammy atmosphere, lowered the shells onto a series of hoists.

'These bloody prodjees get heavier every time we do this,' grunted Bud Abbott, placing a shell on the feed ring. He then lowered it onto another a hoist, which was taken automatically into the gun.

'Anyway, if what the captain says and we have to fire them,' said Swampy Marsh passing Bud another shell, 'we won't have to put the buggers back in the racks.' (Each shell weighed 46lbs (21kg).)

At the same time the first aid team consisting of NAAFI manager Barney Watts, Laura Griffiths, Logistics Assistant Joe Woods, and Officer's Stewards Jock Glenister and Jack Munro, reported to the sick bay. Dixie Dean then informed the bridge that the medical party were closed up.

'Sounds serious, doesn't it sir?' Watts nervously asked Smyth.

'Yes, it does,' the doctor gravely replied, 'so we'd better be prepared for some real casualties.'

'Oh, my God!' Watts painfully exclaimed, 'I hope not, I hate the sight of blood.'

Dean and Susan Hughes looked at one another and burst out laughing.

Everyone on the bridge listened intently as the voice of Ashcroft came over the bridge radio.

'In contact with *Beymoth,*' he said, despite the intermittent crackling, Ashcroft's voice was loud and clear. 'She has all fire hoses outboard ready to repel any boarders. Have reduced height to five thousand feet. Craft in sight, they appear to be twenty feet wooden skips with an outboard motor. Each craft is manned by seven men and are armed with what looks like Kalashnikov rifles. All three are flying the black Al Qaeda flag on the stern and have a machine gun mounted on their bows. Request instructions. Over.'

Hailey frowned then picked up the radio intercom. 'Gain more height and keep out of range. Circle and report. Over.'

A few minutes later, Ashcroft voice spoke again.

'Skips have sighted the helo and have fanned out. Crews are waving their rifles in the air. They do not appear to be turning back. Over.'

'Thank you, Jerry,' Hailey replied, continue to circle and keep a safe distance. Over and out.' Hailey then unhooked the bridge intercom. 'This is the captain,' he said, doing his best to sound calm. 'The Lynx has sighted the container and the three craft and is investigating. I will keep you informed.'

Throughout the ship tension rose as everyone anxiously waited, wondering what would happen.

On each bridge wing Marines Smith and White ensured the mountings on their BAR were secure and the ammunition boxes were full. Both had seen action in Afghanistan and were in relatively calm. Stokers glanced apprehensively at one another, knowing they would stand little chance of survival if a rocket hit them in the engine room. The faces of the gunnery ratings in the stuffy, claustrophobic gun bay appeared tense. The cooks occupied themselves by nervously making sandwiches, while the stewards, chattered nosily, hoping they wouldn't be called upon as stretcher bearers while making sure all loose furniture and fittings in the wardroom were secure.

Shortly before 1640, everyone else on the bridge sighted the black stern of *Beymoth,* her masts and yardarms silhouetted against the darkening sky.

'I can just make out the wash of the craft, sir,' Gooding shouted. 'There' one about a hundred yards either side of *Beymoth.* I expect the third one is somewhere in front.'

'She's got all her water hoses out, sir,' Noble said, then added, 'and the Lynx is circling high above them.'

'Thank you, gentlemen,' Hailey said, 'I can see . . .' the strident voice of Ashcroft Interrupted him. 'One of the skips has moved ahead of the ship', he said, 'the other two are creeping closer to her. Some of the blighters are carrying ladders. Request instructions.'

Hailey knew his duty was to defend the cargo ship against the attack by Al Qaeda. He took a deep breath. This would be the first time in his career that he had to order men, albeit, very dangerous ones, to be killed. He swallowed nervously, then said, 'we are now within range of the skips, but I can't use the Sea Wolfs as the skips are too close to *Beymoth* and could be damaged. I therefore order you to sink one of them, then hopefully, the other two will turn turtle and lead us to the mother ship. Over.'

'Very good, sir,' Ashcrfoft shouted, 'I have already armed the Sea Skuas and have the skips on my sight monitor. Over and out.'

He glanced apprehensively at Roberts and yelled, 'tell John and the marines to hold tight as I intend to go in close and zap one of the boats.'

'My God, sir,' Roberts shouted, a startled expression on his tanned face. 'Not too close. The buggers are armed.'

Ashcroft raised the collective and adjusted the flight control lever. The Lynx slowly banked and descended towards the skip some fifty yards in front of *Beymoth*.

'The bastards have elevated their machine gun and are firing at us, sir,' Roberts yelled. With his heart pounding like an express train he adjusted the cross-sights until they were in the centre of the block dot on his pale green attack panel.

'Yes, I can see that, Mike,' Ashcroft replied. Looking down he could see spurts of flame coming from a machine gun. With the exception of the Arab manning the outboard motor, the rest were aiming their rifles at the helicopter.

On board the Lynx, the steady growl of the engines muffled the sound of the bullets. With beads of sweat trickling down the sides of his face, Ashcroft clenched his teeth then shouted to Roberts, '*Fire at will!*'

By this time *Dawlish* was only ten miles away from *Beymoth*. From the bridge, Hailey and the others couldn't see the skip in front of her, but they watched anxiously as a narrow jet of what looked like white steam left the Lynx and zoomed downwards. This was immediately followed by a loud explosion and a swirling column of dense black smoke and flames, rising into the sky. Suddenly, the wind was full of sparks carrying pieces of wood and debris. A pool of flaming oil surrounded the area where the boat once was. At the same time the Lynx banked and quickly regained height, apparently undamaged.

The sound of ecstatic cheering almost drowned Ashcroft's voice coming over the radio.

'Pipe down,' Hailey yelled and moved close to the radio receiver. 'Say again, Jerry,' he said, glancing at the excited expressions on the faces of those around him. 'Reception bad.'

'One bogey down,' came Ashcroft's calm voice, 'bits of wooden wreckage and bodies floating everywhere. There doesn't appear to be any survivors. Request instructions. Over.'

'Excuse me, sir,' said Noble, taping Hailey on the shoulder, 'the other two skips are turning around.'

Hailey acknowledged Noble with a quick nod of his head. 'Captain to Lynx. Take out another skip. We have the last one on radar and will follow. Well done, over and out.'

'Wilko,' Ashcroft replied confidently. 'It will be a pleasure.'

Hailey and those on the bridge watched as the Lynx turned, increased speed, and descended. Another jet of white, bubbling white steam suddenly emerged from the Lynx's side armament and exploded on the skip two hundred yards on the port side of *Beymoth*. Another loud explosion followed as the craft disintegrated into a dense mass of billowing black smoke and orange flames.

'Second boat down, out,' Ashcroft said over the radio.

'Return to the ship,' Hailey replied, 'and damn good work, all of you.'

In the Ops Room everyone cheered as the black dot representing one of the skips disappeared off their screens.

'I wonder if they've got enough virgins to go round in Paradise, eh, Ash?' Quipped Spud Murphy grinning at Ashir.

'Why ask me?' Ash replied pushing back his head-set, 'I don't bother with all that religious nonsense,' he replied, offering a silent prayer of forgiveness to Allah.

'I don't know about Paradise,' said Taff Jones, 'but in Cardiff where I come from they'd be hard pressed to find one.'

'Do you mind,' Diana replied indignantly, 'I come from Cardiff.'

Jones grinned salaciously and was about to make an appropriate reply, when Henderson interrupted him.

'Pipe down,' he snapped, 'and concentrate on the remaining boat and any shipping in the vicinity.'

CHAPTER THIRTY-ONE

The Lynx touched down on board *Dawlish*'s flight deck at 1800. Harry Thomas and everyone else applauded and cheered as the fuselage door slid open and he crew climbed out.

'Glad to see you're all in one piece,' said Thomas, giving Ashcroft, Roberts and Somersby a welcoming grin while shaking their hands, 'large Horse's Necks in the wardroom when you're ready and double issue of beer to the marines and Leading Seaman Lee.'

'Thanks, Harry,' Ashcroft replied, removing his helmet and wiping his sweaty brow with the back of his hand. 'They'll be more than welcome, I can assure you.'

'Later on, I expect the old man will want to see you for a de-briefing,' said Thomas, 'but right now he's too busy hoping to find the skips mother ship.'

Hailey had left the bridge and was in the Ops Room having a heated debate with Henderson.

'Do you think it wise, sir,' Henderson said, his plummy accent emphasising his words, 'to chase after the mother ship. She could have put into any one of the small ports along the coast of Yemen. And remember, there's a twenty mile no go area around the Yemeni coast and our main task is to get to Bahrain as quickly as possible.'

'Thank you, Bob,' Hailey replied impatiently. Then, taking Henderson by the arm and moving out of earshot of the staff, added, 'but I don't need you to remind me about our mission or the no go area. That bastard could have been the one responsible for providing the speed boat that blew up the tanker in Gib.'

'Maybe so, sir,' replied Henderson, 'but have you informed MOD or Bahrain about the attack?'

'I'll be doing that after I have de-briefed Jerry and Mike,' Hailey curtly replied.

'Then wouldn't it be prudent to wait and hear what they have to say, sir, I mean . . .'

Hailey was becoming irritated by Henderson's attitude but realised his PWO had a point and quickly cut him off, 'Yes, yes,' he replied, 'if it will make you happy, I'll do just that.'

Ten minutes later Ashcroft and Roberts, still wearing their flight kit, were in Hailey's cabin sitting in front of him. Both had cups of coffee resting on a nearby table. Liz Hall sat in a corner, pad in hand taking notes.

'Did Lee manage to video everything especially pictures of that black flag they were flying and the men firing at you?' Hailey asked taking a sip from his cup.

'Yes, sir,' Ashcroft replied, 'he told me he managed to get most of the action videoing through the Lynx's window, if we'd been any closer they might have hit us.'

For the next fifteen minutes Ashcroft and Roberts gave their version of events.

'I made sure everything was taped in case there's an enquiry, sir,' Ashcroft added, finishing his second cup of coffee.

'Splendid, you have all done very well,' Ashcroft said, easing himself up from behind his desk. 'And more importantly, no one was hurt. Please carry on,' he added with a satisfied smile, 'I do believe your presence is required in the wardroom.'

After the two officers had left, Hailey sat down behind his desk and began dictating a report of the day's proceedings including the ship's position, to Liz, ending with, '*permission to alter course and search and destroy the mother ship.*' When he had finished, he sat back, gave a weary sigh and said, 'Thank you, Liz, please email this to MOD, Bahrain, and the harbour master in Gibraltar and let me know the minute a reply is received.

Liz closed her pad and stood up, 'Very good, sir,' she said, smiled pleasantly and left the cabin.

Hailey was on the bridge sitting in his chair sitting in his chair. Using his binoculars Hailey scanned the coast of Yemen, barely visible some fifty miles away. At that moment Liz Hall arrived. 'Email from MOD, sir,' she said handing him the message.

'Thank you, Liz,' Hailey said, lowering his binoculars. He accepted the message and quickly read its contents.

Henderson's voice suddenly came over the bridge radio.

'Skip thirty miles away, turning ten degrees to port. A bigger vessel which is probably the mother ship is about five miles in front. Both are making for the coast.'

'Thank you, Bob,' Hailey replied, smiling smugly at the message from MOD granting permission to proceed and investigate but not to infringe the twenty mile limit. He then glanced at Noble, and said, 'alter course fifteen degrees to port, increase revolutions one third.' He then lent forward and unhooked the bridge inter com.

'This is the captain speaking.' His voice was calm and controlled. 'The Lynx has sunk two of the speed boats.' He paused sensing a cheer echoing around the ship. He then went on to describe what Henderson told him, adding, 'I am sure the larger vessel is the mother ship. I intend to follow and sink both of them Everyone to remain alert. That is all.'

'Ops Room, sir,' came Henderson's voice over the radio, 'the blighters might be making for Al Ghaydah, a port some forty miles away on the coast of Yemen. '

'Thank you, Bob,' Hailey replied, 'I think you're right,' he paused, 'this is where rogue shipping firms are sending arms and explosives for Al Qaeda. If the skip and mother ship reach port, we won't be able to touch them. I'd use the Lynx but it would take too long to get her air born.'

'Very well, sir,' Henderson replied, then as if reading Hailey's mind, he added cautiously, 'I have both vessels on my screen and as I reported earlier, WEO reports the Harpoons are armed and ready.'

'That's very reassuring, Bob,' Hailey said, nervously clearing his throat, 'let me know if the skip reaches the ship.'

'Darken ship, Number One,' Hailey said, glancing apprehensively at Noble. 'If it is the mother ship and she doesn't see us, we may be able to nail her with the Harpoons.'

'And if it isn't the mother ship, sir?' Noble replied, raising both eyebrows.

With a worried sigh, Hailey replied, 'That's a risk I'll have to take.'

The time was now 2030. Everyone was still closed up at Weapons State Golf. The cooks had passed around mounds of corn beef sandwiches and mugs of steaming hot tea to crew. In the Ops Room everyone was enjoying a mug of tea and a sarnie, when Henderson staring at his large radar screen, suddenly cried through the inter-com, 'Bridge. The skip appears to be going alongside the ship. I have them both vectored on my attack monitor.'

'How far away from the port are they?' Hailey asked, nervously biting his lip.

'Ten miles, sir', Henderson answered, 'and at the speed they're moving you won't have much time before they cross into the safety zone.'

Hailey swore inwardly and angrily banged the side of his chair with a hand. Now, he really was faced difficult decision. What if the ship wasn't allied to Al Qaeda and he sunk her. A court martial? Certainly a court of enquiry and few red faces in MOD, not to mention running any chances he might have for promotion. But if he was right . . .

'How far are they from the port, now? He asked Henderson, feeling his heartrate increase.

'Five miles and closing fast,' Henderson replied. Like everyone in the Ops Room he was sweating profusely as the tension rose.

'Won't the captain warn the ship before firing on it?' Ashir asked.

'He may not have time,' said Spud Murphy, lowering his voice, 'and if he did, I bet the old man'll give 'em the same warning the buggers gave to those tanker lads in GIb.'

Darkness had fallen two hours ago. The bridge was bathed in pale blue lighting an hour ago. All eyes were focussed on Hailey who glanced apprehensively at the bridge clock. The time was almost 2100 and the large hand on the clock seemed to move quicker than usual.

Suddenly, Hailey realised he was about to make the most momentous decision of his life. He unhooked the Ops phone.

'Pee-woh,' answered Henderson.

'Stand by to fire the Harpoons, Bob,' Hailey said calmly. 'I intend to try and sink the pair of them.''

'Very good, sir,' Henderson replied as if it was a routine exercise.

High above in the night sky the clear crescent moon bathed *Dawlish* and the surrounding sea in a pale yellow light. A few minutes earlier Hailey had spoken over the tannoy informing the crew what was about to happen. A mixed feeling of disquiet and apprehension quickly spread throughout the ship. This would be the first time the missiles were to be fired in earnest.

'I'm going to the Ops Room, Number One,' Hailey said to Noble, 'so make sure Lee videos everything.'

In the Ops Room the team of operators were concentrating on their computers. As Hailey entered Henderson glanced up. In the centre of his large radar screen two thin black lines crossed the two blips representing the skip and mother ship.

'Target data processed by the computers, sir, targets locked on,' Henderson said confidently. 'Harpoon systems ready.'

'Thank you, Bob,' Hailey replied, blinking several times to accustom his eyes to the dimness of the room.

In the magazine under the Harpoon silos Nobby Clark glanced guardedly at his oppo, Pete Jackson.

'Bloody hell, Jacko,' he muttered, 'just to think the missiles will be killing people. Not very nice, eh?'

'Yeah,' Jacko cautiously replied. 'I know they're terrorists, but all the same it gives me a funny feeling.'

'Just remember,' said WEO Greenslade wiping beads of sweat from his brow with a handkerchief, 'the buggers wouldn't think twice before ramming us if they could, so spare your sympathy for the poor sods that were killed in Gib.'

On the bridge, everyone watched nervously through the windows looking onto the fo'c'sle at the tops of the eight missile launchers each containing a single GWS-26 Sea Wolf in four rows of two. Behind these lay the deadly harpoon launchers poised upwards primed and ready. Noble glanced apprehensively at Gooding aware that they were about to witness an event that would result in death and destruction to some fellow human beings, albeit ones who would do the same to them if they could.

'Not the same feeling as a practice shoot, eh, sir,' Gooding remarked, feeling his throat suddenly go dry.

'It ought to be,' Noble replied, staring at the moon glow dancing on the tops of the missile canisters and turret of the 4.5 gun. 'We've gone through the drill often enough.'

In the Ops Room, Diana looked at Ashir, noticing the tension in his eyes and lines of sweat running down the sides of his swarthy features.

'Are you all right, Ash?' she asked, loosening her head set. 'You look worried.'

'I'm all right,' he answered, 'just a little tired, that's all.' Of course he was lying, knowing that any second some of his fellow Al Qaeda followers would shortly be in Paradise. His thoughts were immediately interrupted by hearing Hailey's calm clear voice.

'Fire two Harpoon missiles, Bob,' then, muttering anxiously to himself, added, 'and to hell with the consequences.'

A few seconds later, the Ops Room shook slightly as they felt the missiles leave their respective canisters. Noble and everyone on the bridge instinctively shielded their eyes as the jagged jets of yellow flames poured angrily from the missile exhausts. In an instant the fo'c'sle looked like a small version of a launching platform at Cape Canaveral, as the deadly missiles, belching red flames shot out of their cannisters and streaked high into the night sky leaving behind a trail of curling white smoke.

Everyone on the bridge watched in awe as the two Harpoon missiles arced upwards heading towards the port of Al Ghaydah, and almost imperceptibly, began their descent onto their targets. At the same time, in the Ops Room Henderson, stared at his screen tracking the missiles.

'Any second now, Ash,' cried Diana, excitedly touching Ashir on his shoulder, 'the buggers will never know what hit them.'

Ashir could hardly bare to look at his screen knowing what was about to happen. He merely smiled weakly and carefully averted his eyes.

A loud cheer erupted around the room as the computer and radar operators saw two black dots vanish from their screens. Henderson simply reacted with a satisfied smile. Diana immediately pushed her head set to one side. 'The bastards have been blown away, Ash, great eh?' She cried excitedly and slapped Ashir on his back.

'Yeah,' Ashir replied, doing his best to sound enthusiastic, 'now maybe we can all get some sleep.'

'Well, you might sound more cheerful,' Diana said, giving him a searching look. 'Are you sure you're all right?'

'Yes, thanks, Di,' he answered dryly, 'nothing to worry about.'

Everyone on the bridge listened as a loud explosion was quickly followed by a pall of yellow and red flames shooting into the air lighting up the night sky.

'Well, one things for sure, sir,' Noble remarked sarcastically, 'the blighter's not carrying a cargo of bananas.'

'I couldn't agree more, Number One.' Hailey who was sitting on his high chair, a satisfied smirk etched on his weather beaten features, 'I only hope Lee managed to catch it on film,' then added, 'starboard ten, revolutions one third. Revert to Cruising Stations, let's get back on course for Bahrain. If you want me, I'll be in my cabin composing an email for MOD and the Lords of the Admiralty.

CHAPTER THIRTY-TWO

'*Would you believe it!*' exclaimed Hailey staring angrily at the email he had just received from the MOD. He was sitting behind his desk. Noble, sipping a cup of coffee, was sat facing him. The time was just after 'Stand Easy', on Sunday 25 August. 'The Yemeni president, Aba Rabbuh Mansur Hadi, has lodged an official complaint to Cameron, saying the ship we blew up was carrying a cargo of timber and dried fruit despite the video evidence I presented. It also says the prime minister wishes the whole episode to be kept quiet from the media until he comes to some agreement with Hadi. And wants me to order the crew not to mention what happened when they text home.'

Noble had just taken a good gulp of coffee and almost choked. 'My God,' he spluttered, placing the cup on the saucer, 'the man must be either stupid or blind. The video of the skips firing on the Lynx and threatening *Beymoth,* plus the type of the explosion when the Harpoons hit the ship must have proved beyond doubt the ship was involved.'

Hailey placed both hands down on his desk. 'I agree,' he replied with a tired sigh, then added, 'but to his credit, after consultation with the MOD, Cameron has refused to apologise to Hadi.'

'Now what?' Noble asked, finishing his coffee.

Hailey gave a quick, nonchalant shrug of his shoulders and said, 'we'll have to wait and see, but I expect it'll blow over. According to the BBC news, Hadi has his hands full repressing a revolt by his generals.'

In the wardroom, Liz Hall and Shirley Mannering were standing enjoying a cup of coffee along with a few other officers. After the worrying events of the past three days the atmosphere was one of relaxed relief.

'I don't suppose you've seen much of lover boy, have you, Liz?' Shirley asked with a touch of sarcasm. Earlier Liz had told Shirley of her dinner with Henderson in Gibraltar and the quick retreat to the ship following the explosions in the harbour.

'No need to be like that,' Liz replied, finishing her drink and placing the cup and saucer on a table. 'As I said, he behaved like a perfect . . . '

'Speak of the devil,' Shirley interrupted, watching the tall figure of Henderson enter the wardroom, 'and he's just come in. Anyway, I'm off, duty calls,' she said, handing her empty cup and saucer to a steward, 'so don't do anything I wouldn't do,' she added with a saucy smile.

No sooner had Shirley left than Sub Lieutenant Morris moved away from Parker-Smith, with whom he was sharing a joke, and joined Liz.

'And how are things in the captain's office?' Morris enquired, flashing her a smile while staring lecherously at the bulge in Liz's white shirt. 'Back to normal now, I trust?'

'Yes, thank goodness,' Liz replied. During action stations she had been closed up in the stuffy communications office, and was more than glad to breathe some fresh air. As she spoke, she gave a quick, cautious glance at Henderson who was standing next to Noble, sipping a cup of coffee. He turned, offered an excuse to Noble and moved slowly towards by her, coffee cup and saucer in hand. His uniform looked as if he had slept in it and his thick, dark wiry hair, tinged with grey, appeared slightly dishevelled.

'I bet our bit of action shook you up, eh, Liz?' he said, staring into her soft hazel eyes while taking a sip of his drink.

'Yes, I was somewhat,' Liz replied, looking up and seeing the dark smudges under his bloodshot brown eyes. 'I'm sure you've been kept busy. You look all in.'

'I am a bit,' he said, supressing a yawn, 'but never too tired to talk to you. If I may say so, you look as beautiful as ever.'

'Don't start,' Liz hastily replied, glancing furtively around. 'This is neither the time nor the place.'

'Fair enough,' he answered flatly, giving Liz a sly smile. 'My cabin, half an hour?'

'Shush,' she whispered, feeling her face redden. 'You're going to get us both in hot water.'

'Actually,' he said, after finishing his drink, 'I could do with a nice warm shower, care to join me?' He added, grinning like a Cheshire Cat.

197

'Oh, you're incorrigible,' she said glaring angrily at him, then with a shake of her head, turned and left the room hoping nobody noticed her flushed face. However, the serious note in his voice suggested he really meant what he said. On the way to her cabin, the thought his warm, soapy hands running over her body sent a tingle of excitement running down her spine, but of course, she told herself, this was completely out of the question. . . on board the ship.

Below in the Ops Room, Ashir sighed as he removed his headset, 'I don't know about you, Di,' he said slowly easing himself up from his chair and stretching his arms above his head, 'but I feel as if I've been closed up in here for days.'

The time was 1200. Ashir and Diana had finished their six-hour duty and had just been relieved by two radar operators.

With a weary sigh, Diana replied, 'Yes, I know what you mean, Ash,' she said standing up and taking off her headset. 'I could do with a good hot shower and a few cans of beer.'

After leaving the Ops Room, they walked up a set of steel stairs and through a hatchway onto the port side of the upper deck. For a few minutes, they stood their hands resting on the guard rail, blinking to accustom their eyes to the bright sunlight.

'Mm . . .' that sun feels lovely,' gasped Diana, her face upturned to the sky. With her eyes still closed, she gave an envious sigh and added, 'Just think, Ash, there are people who pay good money for a voyage like this.'

'Yes,' Ashir replied, thinking how beautiful she looked, her eyes now open, staring down into the clear, undulating blueness of the sea, 'but they don't have to put up with being cooped up at action stations for all hours.'

'Just imagine, Ash,' Diana said, grasping the guard rail tightly with both hands, 'you and I on a cruise somewhere in the Mediterranean. Away from Al Qaeda, the trouble in the Ukraine and Syria and these other terrorists called Isis.' She released a hand from the guard rail, turned and with a look of anger in her eyes said, 'why do they do it, Ash, why do they slaughter people like that?'

Ashir took a deep breath and swallowed hard. 'It's just the way they are, I suppose,' he answered tamely, noticing the pained expression in her eyes.

His thoughts were suddenly interrupted by a female voice saying, 'Aye, aye, what's going on here, then?'

Ashir looked to his left and with an inward sigh of relief saw Lottie Jones standing a few yards away, a suspicious expression etched in her soft blue eyes.

'If you must know,' Diana replied, glaring angrily across at her friend, 'we're just having quiet talk, do you mind?'

'Suit yourselves,' Lottie answered, 'but don't get too close, remember the 'no touch' rule,' then giving them a sly, coquettish smile, she turned and climbed down a steel ladder and vanished through a hatchway.

Hailey was in his cabin studying a list of routine signals when Flannigan appeared holding a mug of steaming hot coffee and a plate of beef sandwiches.

'As you seemed to have missed lunch, sir,' he said, placing them on the captain's desk, 'to be sure, I thought you'd be a wee bit peckish.'

'Thank you, Flannigan,' Hailey replied, yawning slightly while sitting back in his chair, 'that'll do nicely.'

Flannigan smiled benignly and returned to the side galley. Hailey was about to pick up the mug when a sharp knock came at the door.

'Come,' grunted Hailey, blowing across the top of the mug before taking a sip.

Gooding entered holding a signal.

With a weary sigh, Hailey looked at him, placed his mug on the desk and said, 'what is it now, Pilot, more trouble?'

'Not really, sir,' Gooding replied, 'it's a signal from *Wave Ruler,* she's suggesting a RAS at latitude fifty degrees north, sixty degrees east on 28 August.'

'Mm, in three days, eh? Hailey mused, 'Norman informs me we're in need of ten tons of oil, and the supply officer requires more bread, fresh meat, eggs and coffee,' with a cheeky grin he added, ' better check with Mary Milton to see if she wants to order more toilet paper.'

'And don't forget the gin, sir,' Gooding added with a light hearted smile.

'Right,' replied Hailey, 'reply and request those items, and add, "*Looking forward to seeing you .Many thanks".*' And ask Number One to have it promulgated on tomorrows Daily Orders.'

The news of the forthcoming RAS was welcomed by the ship's company, especially by those ratings in the after seamen's mess.

'Thank fuck for that,' remarked Pete Walker. Morning 'Stand Easy' had been piped and he and several others were enjoying a mug of tea. 'The canteen manager tells me we're running short of beer, so the *Wave Ruler's* more than welcome.'

'Not to mention nutty,' Bud Abbott chimed in. Glancing over his mug at Dixie Dean, he added, 'how about French Letters, doc, are we running short?'

('Nutty' is a colloquial term for sweets and chocolate.)

'No,' Dixie replied, 'but I'll have to order more needles as the ones I'm gunna use on you lot for your yellow fever boosters are blunt.'

'I wish someone would explain to me what a RAS is,' Ashir asked, taking a sip of tea, 'this is my first ship and I don't know what you're talking about.'

'It's one of the most dangerous operations at sea,' Shady Lane replied. He put his mug down on the table, and said, '*Wave Ruler* and us' he added, placing both hands near one another, 'come close enough for the tanker to pass an oil line across our ship and for a while us and *Wave Ruler* will be sort of attached to one another. Stores are passed by jackstay. Both ships must be kept at the same distance from one each other. If the sea is rough, that requires expert ship handling, or else there can be a right fuck up. You see,' he added, picking up his mug and taking a good gulp of tea, 'the main danger is if the two ships collide, simple, eh?'

'You mean us and the tanker will be really closes to one another?' Ashir asked, raising his eyes.

'That's right,' replied Shady, 'and that's what makes it a tricky business.'

'Thanks, Shady,' said Ashir, finishing his drink, 'it does sound rather dangerous.'

Suddenly an idea flashed through Ashir's mind. Praise be to Allah, he thought, this is the perfect opportunity to carry out his mission.

CHAPTER THIRTY-THREE

Wednesday 28 August was like any other day; a cerulean, cloudless sky with the dark blue sea stretching around the ship as far as the eye could see. The time was 0600. But as was common in the Arabian Sea, for no apparent reason the wind suddenly increased from a balmy breeze to a force eight gale, and by 1000, the ocean was a mass of angry white horses. Despite the modern stabilising mechanism, *Dawlish* began to roll and dip slightly as huge foamy bow waves curled wildly over the fo'c'sle.

'I thought it was too good to be true,' grunted Hailey, squirming uncomfortably in his high chair. 'A rough sea, just what we need for the RAS, eh, Number One?'

'Yes indeed, sir,' Noble replied, frowning in agreement. He was about to continue speaking when Henderson's voice came over the Ops Room intercom.

'A large blip fifty miles on our starboard bow, sir,' he said, 'it's probably the *Wave Ruler*.'

'Thank you, Bob,' Hailey replied, 'trust her to be on time. We should sight her in a few hours.' Glancing at Gooding, he added, 'better send her a signal, say, *"have you on radar, will rendezvous as arranged".'*

A few minutes later the reply from *Wave Ruler* arrived. *"Welcome. Sorry about the weather. Please take position on port side".'*

He turned and looked at Shirley Mannering. In her right hand she held an intercom that was attached to a headset that had made a mess of her short brown hair.

'I'd like you to take charge of the RAS, Shirley,' Hailey said, 'if you're to pass your watch-keeping ticket, you'll have to do this in all kinds of weather. How do feel about it?'

'Err . . . fine with me, sir,' Shirley replied, doing her best to sound confident. 'As you say, it's important if I'm to get my ticket.' However, deep down, she was suddenly filled with trepidation. Conning a RAS was a nerve-racking business at the best of times, but in a rough, high running sea it could be treacherous.

By 1200, Hailey, Noble and Gooding sighted *Wave Ruler's* wash roughly ten miles away. The wind increased sending the dark clouds scudding angrily across the dark grey sky.

'All right, Shirley,' Hailey said, 'you can take it from here.'

'Two cables and closing, ma'am,' Jock Forbes reported, giving Shirley a confident wink.

Wave Ruler's rounded stern, tall mast and cranes in front of the bridge were clearly visible a few miles away. Everything was painted a dull grey except the whiteness of her squat funnel.

'Roger, Steady on course two- four- one. Set lever at forty,' Shirley replied, bending down to look through the prismatic eyepiece of the ship's compass to establish *Wave Ruler's* exact position. My God, she thought, I'm coming in too close and quickly ordered, 'Steer two three five, Chief,' knowing full well her error had been noticed by Hailey.

Dawlish was now lying immediately astern of the large supply ship.

'Port five,' Shirley ordered, feeling her mouth go dry.

Gradually *Dawlish* moved up until both vessels were virtually side by side doing fourteen knots. Shirley glanced apprehensively at Hailey who she knew was watching her every move. She also knew the importance of keeping the bows pointing slightly away from each other as the hydraulics of both ships running so close and at the same speed could cause suction, and a slight steering error might result in a collision or the fuel lines parting.

'Half a cable, ma'am,' said Forbes.

'Thank you, Chief, set lever at forty,' Shirley replied, then glancing confidently at Hailey, said, 'ship is ready to RAS. Permission to inform *Wave Ruler* by hoisting Flag Romeo for close up.'

'Granted,' Hailey replied, watching the huge vessel with its high bridge and long superstructure move closer to the much smaller frigate.

By this time *Wave Ruler* was one hundred and fifty feet away, slightly forward of *Dawlish,* on the port side.

With mounting trepidation Shirley felt the heavy sea buffeting *Dawlish,* while looking down at the turbulent sea racing angrily between the two ships. It was then she realised *Dawlish* was too far behind the tanker. She was aware that everyone, Hailey included, was watching her. Beads of nervous perspiration ran down the sides of her face.

'Set lever at eighty, steer two three-six,' she snapped. She hoped this would move he frigate forward a final few yards so that hoses could be hoisted across for refuelling. With an inward sigh of relief *Dawlish* immediately surged forward, accelerating to the twenty-two knots needed to push through *Wave Ruler*'s pressure waves to a position she thought appropriate to start replenishing.

Feeling her pulse racing she ordered, 'Easy, steer at two- three- five.' She now had to judge the moment to call for a speed reduction or else *Dawlish* would overshoot the tanker.

'Set lever twenty, Chief,' she snapped. 'Steady at six knots.'

Dawlish slowed down and settled. The manoeuvre was now compete.

Suddenly she felt a warm hand on her shoulder. She turned and saw Hailey smiling at her.

'Well done, Shirley,' he said, 'I couldn't have handled it better myself.'

'Thank you, sir,' she replied, feeling the tension drain from her body.

The two vessels were now 30 yards apart. On *Dawlish*'s port side, the RAS crew under the eagle eyes of Harry Tate, were in place. Steadying themselves against the heavy roll of the ship, two marines, one on the flight deck another on the fo'c'sle, fired two bright projectiles across into the waiting hands of men on *Wave Ruler*. Attached to each length of nylon twine was a hemp rope which in turn hauled over a load bearing wire.

Wave Ruler's captain, wearing a headset, was in radio contact with Hailey and Shirley Mannering, leant over the starboard side of the bridge and using a loudhailer, shouted, 'Secure the oil hoses to the cable.'

A group of sailors on *Wave Ruler* immediately carried out her order.

Dawlish's RAS team, feeling icy beads pf spray attack their faces, begin to haul the heavy duty hose across from the tanker.

'Bloody hell,' cried Baggsy Baker, feeling the ship roll heavily as high waves batter the bulkhead, 'if this bleedin' weather gets any worse we might be pulled over the side'

'Save yer breath,' Tate yelled, his voice barely audible over the whine of the wind, 'and haul away.'

At the end of the hose was a metal probe. Two ratings on board Dawlish took hold of the probe   and fitted it into a large steel, device shaped like a bell.

A stoker immediately connected the bell to a pipeline leading into the fuel tanks in the bowels of the ship.

With a satisfied grin on his weather-beaten face, Tate waved to *Wave Ruler*'s captain confirming this has been done. The tanker's captain then ordered a red flag to be hoisted and pumping oil began.

In the diesel generator room, Bungy Williams, his eyes focused on the fuel flow gauges, glanced cautiously at Bosley. 'Oil flowing into for'd tanks, sir, should be full in twenty minutes.'

'Thank you, Chief,' Bosley replied, watching the arms on the dials quiver as the oil flowed.

Meanwhile, in the Ops Room, Ashir was becoming more and more anxious as the minutes ticked by. His anxiety was increased by Henderson announcing that the RAS should be over soon.

Cursing his luck at being on duty, he silently prayed to Allah for him to find a way to do his bidding. Suddenly, as if his prayers had been answered, he had an idea.

'You're very quiet today, Ash,' Diana remarked, pushing her headset aside, 'everything all right?'

Knowing she knew he had a history of seasickness, Ashir grimaced slightly and placed a hand over his stomach. 'Not really, Di,' he replied, 'I'm afraid I'm not feeling too well. The roll of the ship an' all.'

'What's the matter?' asked Spud Murphy who, standing nearby, saw Ashir's hand rub his stomach.

'It's Ash, Chief, Diana said, glancing up at Murphy, 'I think he's feeling seasick.'

'Better go a get a pill from the sickbay then, Ash,' said Murphy, bending down and looking at Ashir's radar screen. 'The RAS should be over in ten minutes or so.'

'Thank you, Chief,' Ashir replied, grimacing sullenly. This was the chance he had prayed for. He removed his headset and stood up. Looking down at Diana, he felt slight pang of regret run through him realising this was the last time he would gaze upon her beautiful face. He quickly dismissed the thought from his mind, after all, he told himself, there were forty virgins awaiting his pleasure in Paradise.

'I . . . I'll see you later, Di,' he said half-heartedly. He then gave her a quick smile, turned and left the room.

Making his way along the main passage way, Ashir had to grasp a stanchion in order to steady himself as the ship began to roll badly. Swaying from side to side he finally reached his mess. Luckily the place was empty. He went down the narrow passage leading to the bunks and metal lockers. He paused momentarily and took out a small silver yale key.

The deadly Trysin and detonators were safely stowed away under a layer of shirts in a top drawer. It would only take a few seconds to time a detonator and insert it into the explosive's soft substance. Two minutes would be enough for him to say a prayer to Allah, before the infidels in both ships would be blown to hell. His parents, he told himself, would be so proud when they heard he had succeeded in carrying out his mission.

His hand trembled as he inserted the key into the small aperture in his locker. As he turned the key, he felt his heart beating a cadence in his chest and beads of cold sweat ran down the sides of his face. What would it be like being blown up, he asked himself opening a drawer, would it be over so quickly he wouldn't feel anything? However, he hoped Allah would protect him from any pain. He was about to find out.

At the same time that Ashir was about to open his locker, the weather suddenly deteriorated yet again. Ugly black clouds, low and foreboding, blanketed the sky. The wind increased to howling pitch.

'My God!' shouted Hailey as he and the others watched in horror as, without any visual, warning, a freak tidal wave suddenly appeared and crashed over the bows of the two vessels causing them to yaw dangerously.

What happened next seemed to take ages but was over very quickly. The ship pitched upwards, as an angry mass of black water curled over the fo'c' sle.

Hailey, Shirley Mannering, Noble and the others watched anxiously as the hose, still spewing oil, dropped into the tumultuous waves and was hauled desperately on board *Wave Ruler*'s crew.

'Set lever at sixty,' Shirley cried as she and those on the bridge felt the ship yaw as the black, oil-stained waters of the tidal wave swept between the two vessels. She then grabbed the ship's tannoy and shouted, 'D'yer hear there. Hold on to anything at hand. The ship is about to heel to starboard'

Straightaway, the computerised steering mechanism in the bowels of the ship responded. At the same time, *Wave Ruler*, blasting her siren, peeled away to starboard, as the gap between the two ships widened. In matter of seconds, *Dawlish* pulled away and regained an even keel. However, in the process, a few personnel injured themselves.

'Well done, Mannering,' Hailey said, smiling at Shirley, 'you coped very well with that emergency.'

'Thank you, sir,' she replied, wiping the sweat from her brow with a handkerchief.

'It's a pity there wasn't a mention of surprise tidal waves in my manual.'

'Quite so,' Hailey replied, using his binoculars to see the dark superstructure of *Wave Ruler* moving quickly away.

In the sick bay, Susan had just finished attending to two female cook who had burnt arms. 'Come back in the morning,' she said, 'and keep the dressings as dry as possible.'

'Fat chance of that, working in the galley Sue,' said one of them as they left.

'I realise that,' replied Sue,' but tell the chief cook to put you on light duties.'

'You haven't broken anything,' Smyth said as he strapped up a stoker's ribs, 'but they'll be very painful for a time.'

As he spoke, the door opened and in came Bud Abbott and Shady Lane. Both of them were supporting Ashir who had a shell dressing tied firmly around his head.

'Better sit down before you fall down,' Dixie said, helping Ashir into a chair. 'What happened?'

'We found him in the mess, didn't we, Bud?' Shady said, wiping his brow with the back of his hand.

'That's right,' Bud replied, catching his breath, 'he'd cut his head and was lying on the deck unconscious. His locker was open and so was one of the drawers.'

Even in his semi-conscious state Ashir overheard what Shady said, and inwardly panicked, wondering if they had found the Trysin. However, he was relieved to hear Shady say he had closed both the drawer and locker.

'You should have sent for us, and not moved him,' interrupted Smyth, who had dismissed the stoker after telling him to rest in his mess for the next few days. You'd better lay him on the table,' he said to Dixie, 'and let me take a look at him.

'Thank you for your help,' he added glancing at Shady and Bud, 'but you can carry on.'

Under Ashir's blood-stained shell dressing as a five inch laceration above his left eyebrow.

'You're very lucky,' said Smyth, gently dabbing the injury with a piece of gauze, 'if it had been a few inches lower you could have lost your eye.'

After giving Ashir a thorough examination, Smyth stood back and said, 'You've definitely got a severe concussion and the cut needs stitching. I'm going to keep you in here for a few days go make sure everything is all right.'

A sharp knock came at the door, and in came Diana, her hair hung loosely around her neck was and her face was sweaty and flushed.

'Is it all right to come in, sir?' She asked looking anxiously at Smyth.

'Yes,' he answered, 'but don't stay too long.'

'My God' she exclaimed seeing Ashir lying on the examination table. His dark complexion was slightly paler than normal. His eyes were closed and a blood soaked piece of gauze covered a wound on the left side of his forehead.

'Wha . . . what happened? She cried glancing apprehensively at Susan, then at Ashir

'Two of his mates found him unconscious in his mess and brought him here,' Hughes replied.

Ashir opened his eyes and looked up at Diana.

'How are you, Ash?' Diana asked, taking hold of his hand. 'What were you doing in your mess, I thought you were going to the sickbay for some seasick tablets.'

Suddenly, Ashir had to think quickly. The throbbing ache over his left eye didn't help. He glanced painfully at Diana and murmured, 'I was, but thought I had some of them in my locker from before.'

'But how did you hurt your head?' Diana asked, gently squeezing his hand.

Ashir's mouth felt like sandpaper and he felt slightly sick. 'I had just opened my locker,' he muttered, 'when the ship rolled badly. That was when I must have lost my balance and fell down,' he paused and ran his tongue across his lips, then added, 'The next thing I remembered was seeing Shady and Bud looking down at me.'

'I'm afraid you'll have to leave, now, Di,' interrupted Susan. 'The doctor has to put a few stitches in him. And he'll have to be kept here for a while.'

Diana felt warm tears well up in her eyes, then, looking anxiously at the blood-soaked piece of gauze over Ashir's injury, she squeezed his hand again and said, 'Take care love, I'll come and see you when I can.'

That evening after supper, Bud Abbott, holding a small package in his hand, and Shady Lane knocked on the sick bay door and waited. A few seconds later Dixie opened the door.

'Is it all right to see Ash?' Shady asked, 'we won't stay long, Bud's got summat for him. Haven't you, mate,' he added glancing at his oppo.

'Yeah,' Bud replied, showing Dixie the package.

'OK,' Dixie replied, 'but just for a few minutes.'

Bud and Shady entered and saw Ashir lying in his cot with his head heavily bandaged. His eyes were closed but he immediately recognised the voices of his two messmates. He opened his eyes and saw Shady and Bud looking down at him.

'How are you feeling, mate?' Shady asked forcing a smile. 'That was some fall you had.'

'Not bad,' Ashir replied, pushing himself up on is elbows, 'but my head's aching a bit.'

'I'm not surprised,' said Shady, 'by the way, Bud found a package on the deck by your locker, didn't you, Bud?'

Suddenly, Ashir felt his stomach contract with fear. To his horror he saw that Bud was holding the deadly parcel of Trysin.

'Yeah and it certainly is heavy,' Bud replied, 'what's in it, bullion?' he added with a silly grin.

'No,' Ashir replied, feeling his heartrate quicken, 'It's just pipe tobacco for my father. I bought it in Gib.'

'Better have it, then' said Bud, nonchalantly tossing the package onto Ashir's bedding. 'Best not to let the Joss know,' he added jokingly,' or he'll have you up fer smuggling.' (Joss is short for Jossman, a nickname for the Master-at-Arms as he was allowed to carry a joss-stick.)

'Yes,' Ashir answered doing his best not to sound nervous, 'thanks a lot, that's can of beer I owe you both.'

'By the way, Di sends her, err . . . love,' Shady said with all-knowing grin, 'I met her as she was on her way to the Ops Room.'

'Times up, lads,' Dixie said, 'the MO will be here to check on Ash shortly.

'OK,' Shady replied, then looking at Ashir, asked, 'is there anything you want?'

'No, thanks,' Ashir replied, doing his best to smile while slowly pushing the parcel under his duvet, 'thanks for coming, I'll see you in the mess.'

Two days later Ashir was discharged from the sickbay.

'What about the stitches, sir?' Ashir asked carefully touching the Elastoplast dressing over his left eyebrow.

'Don't worry about them,' replied Smyth, smiling, 'the sutures I used are called 'vicryl rapide' and are self-absorbent, they'll disappear in about a week or so. You've had a lucky escape, my boy, so be careful.'

Luck had nothing to do with it, Ashir thought as he left the sick bay, it was Allah's wish. With a determined gleam in his eyes, he thought, next time I shall make sure you and the crew won't be so fortunate.

CHAPTER THIRTY-FOUR

Thursday 29 August dawned calm and clear. The foul weather that had persisted over the past two days had abated leaving the warm sun beating down from a clear, deep blue sky. Hailey was sat on his chair looking through a bridge window at a group of sailors on the fo'c'sle. All of them, including Betty Morgan, a buxom blonde, wore blue shorts, shirts and sandals and were busy moping away layers of salt off the deck, a legacy after the freak storm.

'It's a pity all of us couldn't strip off to the waist,' said a rating, leering at Betty, who had undone the four top buttons of her shirt. 'This heat is killing me.'

'And so will I if you don't shut up, you sex maniac,' Betty replied.

Of course, Hailey couldn't hear what they said. He could only guess it was something rude, and joined Noble and the others laughing as Betty flicked water over the rating.

'What's our position, Pilot?' he asked, without moving his head.

'Two hundred miles off Ras al-Hadd, that's a small port on the Southern tip of Oman, sir,' Gooding replied from the pilothouse. 'And, at the speed we're doing, we should enter the Gulf of Oman tomorrow morning.'

Hailey smiled and said, 'Thank you, Pilot, and for the geography lesson.'

Since leaving the carnage of the Al Qaeda attack in Gibraltar just over two weeks ago, the crew had been closed up at action stations for days, but were now at Cruising Stations. Now, they could relax, send and receive news from home.

'All I need is one of those gorgeous marines to rub oil into my back,' muttered Lottie Jones, wriggling her hips suggestively. She and Diana were lying face down feeling the heat of the metal deck penetrate the thick material of the towels underneath them.

Both girls were using the private sunbathing area on the upper deck situated in between the bridge and the funnel mounting. The straps of their costumes lay loose displaying a pair of lilly-white shoulders.

'Personally,' Diana mumbled, feeling a line of warm sweat run down her face, 'I'd prefer to feel Ash's lovely big hands all over me.'

Lottie turned over and took out her phone. 'Pull down your cossie and flash your boobs and I'll take a photo of you,' she said, giggling like a schoolgirl. 'You can give it to Ash as a souvenir.'

'That's not all I'd like to give him,' Diana sighed wearily. She was about to do as Lottie asked, when Sadie Thompson appeared, hands on hips, wearing full whites despite the searing warmth of the sun.

'Right, you two, time's up,' she said, in her sharp Yorkshire accent. 'You look like a pair of hussies, lying their half-naked. Cover yourselves up and get below.'

Giving a reluctant sigh, the girls eased themselves up and picked up their shoulder bags. With the towels draped demurely over their shoulders they made their down a steel ladder along the passage way, past the admiring glances and wolf whistles from some of the crew.

On the flight deck, several ratings, including Ashir, wearing swimming trunks and sandals were lying on towels against the closed hangar shutter. Ashir was sat, up holding his phone. Next to him, Pete Price lay on his towel watching him.

'Better not let Di see you texting,' said Pete, wiping sweat from his brow with an off-white handkerchief, 'she'll think you're sending a message to some bint at home.'

'I doubt it,' Ashir replied, smiling weakly. 'I'm texting my parents.' He then punched in the pre-arranged text saying, 'I am keeping well. Love Ashir.' He then switched off his mobile, yawned, and lay down on his stomach. He was becoming progressively frustrated. For the umpteenth time, he wondered how he could carry out his mission. It had all seemed so easy listening to his father before the ship left Portsmouth. But whenever he decided to do the deed, there was always someone off duty either in the mess or in one of the bunks making it impossible for him to undo the wrappings on the Trysin without attracting attention. Somehow he must succeed. Perhaps, he told himself, feeling a line of sweat trickle down his back, when the ship arrived in Bahrain there might be another opportunity to carry out Allah's wishes.

With a weary sigh, he took a deep breath, closed his eyes and listened to banter of his shipmates.

'It's a pity I can't tell my mum and dad about sinking that Al Qaeda ship,' said Pete Price, 'they'd be made up.'

'I agree,' muttered Bud Abbott, 'I was hoping we'd get a medal or summat.'

'That miserable bugger, Cameron hasn't even allowed it to be mentioned on the telly,' added Dutch Holland, 'a shame really,' he added, giving a lazy yawn, 'my missus would have told everyone at the bingo I was a hero.'

'Wonderful things, those new Samsungs,' mumbled Shady who was studying the naked girls in his dog-eared copy of *Men Only*. 'I can remember my granddad saying how much they looked forward to receiving letters from home. He served on board a destroyer in the Far East and they had to wait up to three weeks before the mail arrived.'

'Not any more, mate,' Walker replied, 'here,' he added, showing the photograph of Kate posing in her garden wearing a pair of skimpy white shorts and a see through pink blouse, ' better than all your porno photies, eh?'

'I hope my missus doesn't send me one of her,' Shady said, looking enviously at the photograph of Kate. 'When I was on leave before we sailed, she'd put on so much weight she couldn't get into her clobber.'

'It's all right for you fish heads,' chimed in Knocker White, one of three Royal Marines lying nearby. 'That party I met in Pompey has sent me a text of a black American soldier she met, an' he's asked her to marry him.' (Fishhead is Army/ RAF slang for anyone in the Royal Navy. 'Party' is a colloquial term for girls.)

'Well, you know what they say about the black lads, Knocker,' said a marine, then with lecherous grin, added, 'and having seen you in the shower, I'm not surprised. If your dick was any smaller, you'd be a eunuch.'

Shortly after supper, Betty Morgan made her way aft to the officer's cabins. She wore white shorts and shirt and her normally humorous blue eyes were red with crying. Ignoring Jilly Howard and Jane Wootton, who were in a queue outside the NAFFI, she walked down a flight of steel stairs and along a narrow passage way, then stopped outside the cabin door marked, S. MANNERING, Lieutenant Commander. Using a tear-stained handkerchief, Betty dabbed her eyes, took a deep breath and knocked on the cabin door.

'Come in,' came a female voice from inside.

Betty nervously opened the door. As she entered Shirley looked up from the letter she was writing on the small table of her fold-up bureau. She was the divisional officer to all the girls and was always on hand to give advice or listen to their problems.

'Morgan,' Shirley said, noticing the strained appearance on Betty's round features, 'do come on. What is it, is something wrong?'

'It's my mum, ma'am,' Betty said, doing her best not to cry. 'My dad phoned me up and told me she's in hospital with cancer of the lung. He . . . he sounded very upset and asked when I'd be home.' She paused and took out her phone. 'I've recorded what he said in case you wanted to hear it.'

'Never mind that,' Shirley replied, standing up, 'I believe you. You'd better come with me,' she added, putting on her blue beret. 'We'll go and see the captain, I'm sure he'll be able to help you.'

Hailey was on the bridge sitting comfortably in his chair feeling the gentle movement as the ship dipped gracefully in and out of the sea. The time was 1900. Darkness had fallen and he was watching the lines of phosphorescence from the bow flash down either side of the ship.

Mickey Finn manned the console and nearby stood Sub Lieutenant Morris.

Hailey's reverie was interrupted when Mannering and Morgan arrived on the bridge.

'Sorry to bother you, sir,' Shirley said, 'but there's something urgent you should know about.'

'Indeed,' Hailey replied, glancing first at her, then at Betty, 'and what might that be?'

Shirley quickly told him about Betty's phone call about her mother.

213

'My goodness, Morgan,' he said, frowning while pushing himself into a more upright position. 'I'm very sorry to hear that. Where do you live?'

'Manchester, sir,' Betty answered wearily.

'Right,' Hailey said, glancing at Morris, 'how far away are we from Bahrain?'

'Just over six hundred miles, sir.'

'And Abu Dhabi?'

'Four hundred, sir,'

'Thank you, Morris,' Hailey replied, 'please ask Lieutenant Ashcroft to come to the bridge.'

A few minutes later Ashchroft arrived. Without any formal greeting Hailey immediately explained Betty's problem.

'I had hoped to fly Morgan to Bahrain where she could catch a flight to UK,' he said, glancing furtively at Ashcroft, 'but am I correct in knowing the maximum range of the Lynx is just over three hundred and fifty miles?'

'Yes, sir,' Ashcroft replied, 'but I've never flown the Lynx that far, so I can't be certain.'

Hailey suddenly realised he was faced with a dilemma. It would be two days until *Dawlish* was close enough to fly Morgan in the Lynx to Bahrain. He could risk sending her to Abu Dhabi where she may or may not be able to catch a flight to UK, in which case she could be stranded.

'Damn and blast,' Hailey cried, thumping one arm of his chair with his hand.

'I'm sorry, young lady,' he added, looking at Morgan's red-rimmed eyes and anxious expression, 'but we'll have to wait by which time it might be too . . .' He abruptly stopped talking realising the implications of what he was about to say.

Just then the Ops Room telephone next to the console rang.

Hailey unhooked it. 'Bridge, captain,' he snapped impatiently.

'Pee-woh, here, sir, we've just picked up on radar what looks like an aircraft carrier and a destroyer escort, fifty miles on our port bow.'

Hailey looked across at Pincher Martin who had overheard what was said, 'Contact the vessels on VHF, please, Chief.'

'Aye, aye, sir,' Pincher retorted and turned the dials of his wireless set. '*Warship, warship,*' he said smartly, speaking down his mouthpiece. '*This *is Royal Navy frigate Dawlish, nine zero, calling you on channel ten. Please identify yourself, over.'*

Shortly afterwards, Pincher listened on his earphones, then turning to Hailey, said, 'It's the US aircraft carrier, *Coral Sea*, sir, accompanied by a destroyer, the USS *Spruance*.'

Suddenly an Idea flashed through Hailey's mind. He gave Morgan a confident smile, and said, 'don't look so downhearted, maybe our American friends can help us.' Then, looking hopefully at Pincher, went on, 'ask if I can speak to her captain, 'say it's most urgent.'

'*Warship Coral Sea,*' Pincher said down, '*My captain urgently wishes to speak to your commanding officer. Over.'*

A few minutes later, Pincher listened again, then, said, 'One second, sir, I'll pass you over to our captain. It's the carrier's CO,' he said, removing his headset and passing it over to Hailey.

'Commander John Hailey, here, sir,' he said, feeling his throat suddenly go dry. 'Sorry to bother you, but I have an emergency on board.'

'Captain Larry Costello,' replied a deep resonant voice with a distinct Southern accent. 'No bother at all, how can I help, anything for the Royal Navy.'

While smiling confidently at Morgan, he quickly explained the problem, adding, 'If I send her over in the Lynx, I was hoping you could fly her to Bahrain so she could catch a flight to UK.'

'Sure thing, Commander,' Costello confidently replied, 'as you may know we have an air base at Muharraq and it's very close to Bahrain International Airport. How soon can you send her over?'

'Thank you, sir,' Hailey answered, 'I'll contact you again in a few minutes.' He removed the headset Pincher had given him and looked at Noble. 'Pipe for Ashcroft to come to the bridge right away, please, Number One.'

In less than two minutes Ashcroft arrived.

'You sent for me, sir,' he said, feeling somewhat perplexed at being summoned so quickly.

Yes,' Hailey replied. He smiled reassuringly at Morgan then gave Ashcroft a quick resume' of her predicament, adding sternly. 'How soon can you get the Lynx in the air?'

'Let's see,' Ashcroft murmured, glancing at his wristwatch, 'the time is almost twenty-hundred,' he paused momentarily, then confidently replied, 'twenty-forty-five, sir.'

'Splendid, Jerry,' Hailey answered, 'please carry on. You haven't much time.'

Hailey replaced the headset, and called up the carrier and identified himself. He immediately recognised Costello's drawl. 'How is everything, Commander? No problems I hope. Over.'

'No, sir,' Hailey replied. 'The Lynx will leave *Dawlish* at approximately twenty forty-five.'

'That's fine,' Costello said, 'I'll have the deck lights switched on and a jet ready for take-off. The trip will take roughly twenty minutes. I'll signal Muharraq to have transport waiting to take your gal to the airport. My exec tells me there is a Boeing 707 leaving at midnight that arrives at Heathrow at zero four hundred, Over.'

'Many thanks for your excellent co-operation, Captain,' Hailey replied. Knowing American Warships were 'dry', he added, 'I'll send over a few bottles of our finest wardroom scotch. Over and out.'

'Sure sounds fine,' Costello drawled, 'I only hope she arrives home safe and sound to see her mother. Over and out.'

Hailey removed his headset and passed it to Chief Martin. 'Right young lady,' he said, 'the Americans are going to help you.'

A look of relief immediately came over Morgan's pale face. 'Gosh, sir,' she cried, 'I can't thank you enough.'

Hailey quickly told her what was about to happen.

'But sir,' Morgan cried, now wide-eyed with excitement. 'I've never flown in a plane before, never mind a helicopter.'

'Well, there's a first time for everything,' Hailey jokingly replied, 'besides,' he added, 'it'll be a fine tale to tell your mother when you get home, won't it Mannering?' He said, glancing at Shirley who was standing nearby, smiling.

With a sigh of relief, Mannering replied, 'Indeed it will, sir.'

'Now listen carefully,' Hailey said to Megan, using a fatherly tone of voice, 'make sure you have your ID and passport. Change into civilian clothing. Pack your uniform and warm clothing. It gets cold in England, even in August. Lieutenant Mannering will obtain leave pass and a return flight pass from Bahrain to Heathrow and arrange for you to draw a month's pay.' He paused for a few seconds to allow his words to sink in, then continued. 'Lieutenant Mannering will give you her mobile number in case you need anything. Now, have you got all that?'

'Err . . . yes, sir,' Morgan replied, trembling slightly with excitement.

'Right, carry on and be quick about it,' Hailey cautioned, 'the Lynx takes off in just over half an hour.'

As soon as Morgan and Shirley left the bridge, Hailey ordered the QM to set the lever to ten and increase revolutions one third. 'The nearer we are to the carrier the better,' he added impatiently. 'And pipe, 'the Lynx will be taking off shortly, hands keep clear of the flight desk.'

Just before 2045, with the good wishes and kisses from both male and female shipmates, fresh in her mind, Morgan passed her suitcase plus a small canvas bag containing three bottles of Bells whiskey up to Mike Roberts, who then helped her into the Lynx.

Five minutes later, Ashcroft eased the lever up slightly and the helicopter was airborne.

High above in the dark, cloudless sky, shafts of light from a bright, crescent moon and a mass of twinkling stars turned the tranquil sea into an, undulating carpet of silver.

By now the aircraft carrier was roughly ten miles away, her angle deck lights reflecting onto her island, bridge and squat funnel. Hailey, Noble and the others on duty, watched as the black, spidery shape of the Lynx headed towards the carrier. Hailey also noticed the silver fuselage of an F/A-18 Super Hornet fighter waiting to be catapulted from the after end of the angle deck.

Five minutes later, the Lynx landed safely close to the fighter. Shortly afterwards the Lynx took off and, banking slightly, headed for *Dawlish.* Almost at the same time, the attention of everyone on the bridge was directed to the silver fighter, tiny sparks coming from the each jet exhaust on her delta wings, streaking off the carrier, turning to the left before disappearing high into the night sky.

CHAPTER THIRTY-FIVE

During the night *Dawlish* passed through the Gulf of Oman and entered the Strait of Hormuz, the name of which was derived from the 17th century Kingdom of Ormus, who once ruled the island.

To the north lay Iran and the Zagros Mountains, their jagged peaks swathed in early morning mist, sweeping down to the red-sanded, hilly coastline. On the southern side, the rolling yellow desert of the United Arab Emirates stretched as far as the eye could see, disappearing into the pale blue hue on the southern horizon.

Time was 0800. As usual, the sky was an eye-smarting blue and with each passing second the heat from the sun became stronger. Hailey was sitting in his customary chair, sipping a mug of coffee, courtesy of PO Flannigan. A mile in front of *Dawlish* were several oil tankers bound for the oil fields of Bahrain, Kuwait and Saudi Arabia.

'Make sure we keep a steady course,' Hailey said to John O'Grady, 'as you know ships entering the Strait keep to the left, and those leaving use the right lane.'

'Yes, sir,' O'Grady replied, carefully checking the compass repeater, 'after all, the Strait is only twenty-one miles wide at its narrowest point.'

Using his binoculars, Hailey studied the stern of the tanker ahead of *Dawlish*, noticing how high she was out of the water, then continued, 'Tankers from all over the world transport two millions barrels of oil through here every day as well as vessels taking nuclear waste to Europe and the UK for safe storage. If this area was blocked all hell would be let loose.' Lowering his binoculars Hailey added, 'as I remember in 1988, an Iranian mine badly damaged an American destroyer, the USS *Samuel B. Roberts,*'

'Good grief, sir,' O'Grady answered, giving Hailey an inquisitive stare. 'What happened?'

'The Americans retaliated and sank an Iranian frigate, a gunboat and six small speedboats,' Hailey replied with a satisfied smile.

'Maybe that's why the *Westminster, Somerset, St Albans* and that French frigate *La Notte-Picquet* were sent here a few years later,' O'Grady answered, pursing his lips.

'And last year the navy's latest acquisition to the fleet, HMS *Daring,* did a stint here before returning home, now it's our turn,' Hailey added sternly, 'and we must be on our toes. It's a dangerous part of the world.'

By 1000 the temperature was 30 degrees Fahrenheit in the shade.

In the main galley, Fiona Green, was standing near a large vat of sizzling fat using the handle of a large metal basket to move chips around. The white vest and shorts she wore under her apron clung to her plump body like sticking plaster.

'Bloody hell,' she said to Wally Hardman who was standing nearby admiring the clear outline of her black brassiere under her vest, 'I bet it's cooler than this in the engine room and boiler rooms'

'Ah, stop moanin' will yer,' Wally replied, 'and give those chips a good stir.'

Fiona was wrong. The temperature gauges in the gas turbine room read fifteen degrees Fahrenheit. The overalls of the stokers were unbuttoned to the waist revealing sweat stained hairy chests that appeared incongruously pale compared with their tanned faces.

'I don't know about you, sir,' remarked Bungy Williams, gently tapping a pressure gauge, 'but I'll be glad when we reach Bahrain. A few pints of Tiger-Tops in American base will go down a treat.'

Norman Bosely was noting the level of a temperature gauge. Since coming on watch at 0700, he had felt bouts of hot and cold flushes. His breakfast had consisted of two cups of coffee and a slice of dry toast. He was now slightly paler than usual and he had dark rings around his eyes.

Earlier, at breakfast Tug Wilson glanced worryingly at Bosley and said. 'You look a little peaky this morning, Norman, 'are you all right, old boy?'

'Just a little queasy,' Bosley replied, dabbing his mouth with a napkin, 'didn't sleep to well last night. Nothing to worry about.'

However, half an hour later, Bosley was about to speak to Williams' remark when he suddenly felt a sharp, excruciating pain in his chest. Beads of perspiration poured down his face, and his pulse rate increased.

'I think I'd better sit down somewhere, Chief,' Bosely muttered almost incoherently. One hand clutched his chest and using the other one, he steadied himself by placing it on Williams shoulder, 'I feel a bit off colour,' he muttered. He had difficulty breathing and his legs felt like jelly. It was a similar feeling he had some years ago when he broke his leg playing rugby. At that time the doctor said he was suffering from shock.

'My God,' gasped Bosley, 'the pain in my chest it . . . It's,' he didn't finish. Instead he grimaced and collapsed against Williams.

'Bloody hell, sir!' he exclaimed, and felt Bosley's hand grabbing the front of his overalls. He reacted quickly and put his arms around Bosley and supported him. 'Just sit down on the grating and take it easy,' he added, watching Bosley's face become distorted with pain.

Two of the stokers stopped what they were doing and came over and helped Williams to lower Bosley onto the warm steel grating.

Feeling his mouth and throat suddenly become dry, Bosley muttered, 'I . . . I'd like some water.'

'Someone call the doctor,' Williams shouted, glancing anxiously at another stoker, 'tell him the engineer has a pain in his chest and feels sick, and be quick about it.'

A stoker did as Williams ordered while another one, standing nearby, quickly removed his overalls and made a makeshift pillow for Bosley's head.

'Easy does it, sir,' the chief said, unzipping the front of Bosley's pristine, white overalls, revealing a cream coloured vest saturated with sweat. 'The doc'll be here soon,' Williams added, in a consoling tone, 'he'll have you right as rain in no time.'

A stoker arrived carrying a mug of water and handed it Williams, who gently lifted Bosley's head. 'Just take few sips, sir,' said Williams, 'don't gulp it.'

Smyth arrived and immediately knelt down next to Bosley. 'What happened, Noman?' he asked, placing a finger on Bosley's wrist and finding his pulse rate very slow and weak.

'I . . . suddenly felt a terrible pain in my chest,' Bosley muttered in between gasping for breath.

'Do you have pain anywhere else?' asked Smyth, noticing Bosley's difficulty in breathing.

Grimacing slightly Bosley replied, 'Yes, down my left arm, but that's gone now.'

Realising Bosley was in shock, Smyth gave Williams a guarded look and said, 'Have you got anything to raise his legs?' (Shock occurs in injury and causes the blood to leave the brain and upper extremities and pool in the lower part of the body resulting in faintness and sweating. Raising the legs helps to reverse this.)

'A soluble aspirin, Dean,' he said, glancing up at Dixie, who was stood nearby holding a medical valise and a small green rectangular box called a defibrillator. This was a device that could send an electric current to stimulate the heart until a normal beat is obtained, and a plastic bag containing four soft square-shaped brown pads. Dean opened the valise and passed it to Smyth. Smyth quickly removed a small bottle of white pills, shook two out onto is hand and bending down, said to Bosley, 'Open your mouth, sir and let these dissolve.'

A stoker produced a large bundle of overalls and handed them to Dean who tucked them underneath Bosley's legs. Dean then opened an oblong box and took out a small oxygen cylinder with black and grey and markings. Attached to this was a coiled length of plastic tubing and a mask with ear attachments. Without waiting for the doctor's orders, he switched on the oxygen, looked at the dial and tested the flow. Satisfied this was correct, he said placed the mask over Bosley's nose and said. 'Don't be alarmed, sir, just breath slowly an try and relax. I'm just going to loosen your overalls so the MO can check you out.'

By this time, Smyth had taken out a small portable blood pressure apparatus. This consisted of an inflatable cuff and a small mercury unit called a manometer. He placed the cuff around Bosley's upper arm and switched it on. The reading on the unit showed when the blood was returning to normal. This was called the Systolic pressure. In a healthy heart this was usually 120mm of mercury. The pitch of the blood disappearing is known as the Diastolic pressure and is normally 80 mm of mercury. This is recorded as 120/80. With a frown Smyth noted both pressures were dangerously high.

Using his stethoscope Smyth listened to Bosley's chest and lungs and found them clear. He then concentrated on listening to the rapid beating of Bosley's heart.

'Have you ever had anything like this before, Norman?' Smyth asked, while checking Bosley's pulse again. 'Any family history of heart problems?'

Bosley was still having difficulty breathing and felt the tightness in his chest becoming worse.

'Yes,' he gasped, 'my father died of a heart attack and my grandmother had problems as well.' He paused and nervously licked his dry lips. 'It . . . it's my heart, isn't it Doc?' he muttered weakly. 'I knew it as soon as I felt the pain in my chest.'

Smyth took out a small red bottle. He quickly unscrewed the top revealing a spray 'Open your mouth, Norman, I'm going to spray this under your tongue. It will help to slow down your heart beat.' (This is called a GTN spray and contains Glyceryl Trinitrate. It is sprayed under the tongue where a good blood supply enables the substance to reach the body quickly.)

Bosley opened his mouth and Smyth carried out the procedure, then said, 'I'll repeat it again in five minutes if the pain continues and your heat rate remains the same.'

However, after five minutes Bosley's pulse became weak. His BP had dropped slightly and his lips became dark blue, sure signs that his body needed more oxygen. His eye were closed and his breathing under the oxygen mask was laboured.

'*Norman! Norman! Open your eyes,*' shouted Smyth, a hint of desperation in his voice, but got no response. 'Quick, Dean, use the defibrillator,' he cried.

Dixie immediately opened the plastic bag and took out two self-adhesive electrode pads. Attached to each electrode was a wire lead and small plug. Feeling his hands shake slightly, Dixie plugged the leads into a socket in the defibrillator.

Smyth placed one pad above Bosley's left nipple and the other below the right side under his breast.

'Switch on, Dean,' Smyth said and moved slightly away from his patient. Bosley lay quiet, unaware that an electric current was being passed into his heart.

Within a few minutes, Bosley's pulse rate increased and his BP level was reduced. His lips gradually regained their natural colour and his breathing became easier.

Using his stethoscope, Smyth listened to Bosley's heart, glanced up at Dean and gave a satisfactory nod.

At that moment, Bosley opened his eyes, blinked and stared wildly at the pads and wires attached to his chest. 'Wh . . . what happened, Doc?' He managed to say.

'Now don't be alarmed, Norman,' said Smyth, giving him a comforting smile, 'you've had a slight heart attack, but we've got you stabilised now, so lie back, try and relax and have a drink of water.' Smyth stood up. 'We're going to keep you here for a while, then get you to the sick bay. Meanwhile, I'd better inform the captain,' he said handing Dean his stethoscope, 'check his BP, pulse and breathing, give him sips of water and keep him on oxygen.' He looked gravely at Bungy Williams and went on, 'sorry about this chief,' he said, 'but I can't move him yet.'

'I understand, Doc,' the chief replied, mopping his brow with an off white handkerchief, 'don't worry, we'll keep an eye on him.'

Bosley closed his eyes and felt the coolness of the oxygen permeating through his lungs. A philosophical thought suddenly occurred to him. He forced a smile. If he were to die, what better place than here, surrounded by his precious dials, gauges and pipes not to mention his beloved Paxman Valenta diesel generators.

CHAPTER THIRTY-SIX

Except for the somnolent hiss of the air conditioning and faint hum of the ship's engines all was quiet on the bridge. The time was 1130. Midshipman Dunlop was standing on the starboard wing holding a sextant in readiness to take a midday fix, its brass and silver fixtures occasionally glinting like a small heliograph under the scorching sun.

'That must be Bandar Abbas,' remarked Hailey sitting on his chair. Using his binoculars, he was studying the outline of an uneven line of red and yellow building some ten miles on the ship's starboard beam.

'Yes, sir,' replied Julian Morris. 'It's the main base of the Iranian navy in this area.'

Just then Smyth arrived and quickly told Hailey about Bosley.

'What's the nearest port besides Bandar Abbas, Sub?'

'Abu Dhabi, sir,' Morris replied, 'about two hundred miles away. As I recall, there's a large military hospital on the outskirts of the city.'

'Let's see,' Hailey muttered, thoughtfully stroking his chin, 'we could be there in less than two days. Can Norman be moved?

'Not at the moment sir,' Smyth cautiously replied. 'I'll have to keep him in the gas turbine room until he's recovered sufficiently to be moved.'

'And how long will that take?'

'I'm no sure, sir,' Smyth answered guardedly, 'but when we do move him to the sickbay the next twenty-four hours will be critical. His condition would have to be carefully monitored, so I would say at least three days.'

'Is he well enough to be taken by helicopter to Abu Dhabi?' Hailey asked.

'I'm afraid not,' Smyth answered, shaking his head, 'the movement might raise his blood pressure and . . .'

'Mm . . .' Muttered Hailey, 'that rules that out then,' Hailey answered flatly. He paused momentarily to gather his thoughts, then went on, 'If I

224

increase speed to twenty-eight knots, we should arrive in Bahrain in three days. Will he be well enough by then to be moved ashore?'

'I'm not sure, sir,' Smyth replied, moping his brow with a handkerchief.

'Right, then,' Hailey said, taking a deep breath. 'Please keep me informed. Meanwhile I'll signal Bahrain giving our ETA Wednesday approx. 0800, requesting berthing instructions to have a doctor and ambulance waiting for us.'

'Thank you, sir,' replied Smyth and hurried back to the gas turbine room. On his way he met Vellacott, his pristine white overall splattered with spots of black oil. Behind him stood Chief Stoker Patrick Flynn.

'The chief stoker and I have been in the auxiliary machinery room, Doc,' he said, wiping beads of sweat from his brow with a handkerchief, 'and just heard about Norman, how is he Doc, can I see him?'

'Yes, of course,' Smyth replied, 'but he's still rather poorly.' With Vellacott following on behind, he hurried to the gas turbine room

The pads were still attached to Bosely's chest and is eyes were closed. Dean was using a piece of gauze to dab lines of perspiration tricking down the sides of Bosley's ashen face. 'His BP is a hundred and forty over forty and his forty and his pulse is stronger.'

Bosley opened his eyes and gave Smyth a weak smile.

'How are you feeling, old boy?' Smyth asked, 'how is the pain in your chest?'

'Not too bad, Doc,' Bosley answered, running his tongue along his dry lips, 'much easier than it was.' He noticed Vellacott standing close by and with a faint smiled muttered, 'Look after my engines, won't you Dicky?'

'Don't you worry,' Vellacott replied bending down and giving Bosley's hand a comforting squeeze, 'we all know how fond you are of them.'

'Good man,' Bosley muttered.

'I think we can see about moving you to the sickbay,' Smyth said, glancing at the Vellacott, he added, 'Phone the bridge and have ask the captain to pipe for the first aid party to report here and to bring a Neil Robertson stretcher and a blanket.'

The officer went to the bulkhead, unhooked a phone and spoke to Hailey. A few seconds later this was followed by the duty QM's loud voice over the tannoy relaying Smyth's orders.

Shortly after the pipe was made, Susan Hughes clambered down a set of steel stairs onto the metal grating clutching a pink blanket.

'My goodness, sir,' she said, staring at Bosley's inert figure lying on the grating, 'what's happened?'

'He's not feeling too good,' Hailey replied, tapping his chest, 'I'll tell you more later.'

Behind Hughes came Jock Glenister, Jack Munro and Barney Watts, puffing and panting. The last to arrive was Joe Woods carrying a Neil Robertson stretcher. This consisted of laminated bamboo slats strengthening a tough, outer duck canvas casing, buckled straps, a thick manila guide rope, a head support and two side rope handles.

Named after its inventor, a naval officer, in 1912, the stretcher has since been invaluable to mountain rescue teams and the armed forces.

'We're going to put you on a stretcher and take you to the sick bay, Norman,' Smyth said, removing his plastic gloves and checking Bosley's pulse. Finding it dull and rapid, he frowned and added, 'It'll be a bit uncomfortable, but don't worry, we'll get you there safe and sound. How are you feeling?'

'Better than before, the pain in my chest is a lot easier,' Bosley murmured, running his tongue across his dry lips, 'but I could do with another drink.'

'Can Williams and Flynn I be of any help, Doc?' Vellacott asked.

'No thank, but I think you'd better remain here,' Smyth replied, 'you'll all be needed down here if the ship goes any faster.'

Dean supported Bosley's head allowing him to take a few sips of water from a cup. He removed the pads from Bosley's chest and detached the wires from the defibrillator. He then unhooked his oxygen mask and removed the crumpled pile of overalls from under Susan's feet.

Meanwhile, Susan spread the blanket in the stretcher and made sure the straps were loose.

'I'll take the head rope, Sue,' Dean said, 'if you'll bring the defibrillator and oxygen and follow on with the doctor.'

Two of the team knelt down either side of Bosley and gripped the rope handles.

'Good luck, sir,' said Williams, giving Bosley's hand a comforting squeeze, 'the Doc'll soon fix you up. '

The four first aiders lifted up the stretcher and moved to the foot of the stairway, which was just wide enough to allow each man to stand sideways. With Dixie pulling on the head rope the others managed to half slide then carry the stretcher upwards until they reached the next steel platform.

'Only another deck to go, sir,' Dean said looking at Bosley's anxious pale face, and gave him a confident smile.

They repeated the exercise and five minutes later reached the main passageway and breathing heavily, lay the stretcher down on the deck.

'All right, Norman,' Smyth asked, checking Bosley's pulse and finding it rapid and full. 'Are you feeling any pain, Norman?'

'Just a dull ache in my chest,' Bosley muttered, 'otherwise all right.'

'Good man,' the doctor replied and nodded again to Dixie. 'Let's get him to the sickbay.'

Shortly afterwards, after attracting concerned looks from members of the crew in the passageway, they arrived at the sickbay and managed to carry the stretcher inside and lay it on the deck. Dean and Susan immediately released the straps from around Bosley.

'Thank goodness for that,' gasped Bosley, grimacing slightly while taking a deep breath. 'Do you think I could have a drink?'

While Dean's help, Bosley took hold of a glass of water and took a good gulp and with a contented sigh rested his head on the back of the stretcher.

'Thank you, gentlemen, you may go,' Smyth said, smiling at the first aid team, 'we'll take it from here.'

'Just give us a shout if yer need anything, beer or nutty,' Barney Watts replied, wiping hid sweaty brow with a handkerchief.

After wishing Bosley well they left.

Dean and Susan removed Bosley's overalls, socks and shoes leaving only his vest and underpants. With the help of Smyth, they lifted Bosley into the bottom bunk and covered him with a white duvet.

Smyth checked Bosley's pulse and BP and wasn't surprised to find them both raised.

'The pain seems to be worse,' muttered Bosley, 'all that moving I suppose.'

'Yes,' Smyth replied, frowning, 'I expect so.' He opened his medical valise and took out a small bottle, a syringe and two needles, all encased in sterile plastic holders.

'I'm going to give you an injection of morphine to ease the pain,' he said, slipping on a pair of plastic gloves.

He bent down and after wiping the top of the bottle with a cotton wool swab, and withdrawing morphine in to the syringe, he changed the needle. Using a fresh swab, he cleaned an area on Bosley's upper arm and gave him the injection. 'I'm also going to give you a Plavix tablet. Then you must try and rest. ' (Plavix is given to prevent blood clotting.) He stood up, looked guardedly at Dean and Susan, and went on, 'Half hourly TPR and BP, and we'd better go eight-hourly watches until we reach Bahrain. Now,' he added, taking a deep breath, 'I must go and see the captain.'

CHAPTER THIRTY-SEVEN

'Message from Vice Admiral Jones, UK Component Command, Bahrain, sir,' Noble said accepting a signal form from a communications rating, 'it reads, "*Secure at number three berth, long jetty. Ambulance and doctor to meet*",'

'Thank you, Number One,' Hailey replied, 'reply accordingly and you'd better make a signal to that Shell tanker in front of us, and repeat it to the other three ahead of us, say, "*intend passing you. Sick man on board*", I'm sure they'll understand. '

'It'll be too bad if they don't, sir,' Noble replied with a grin, and passed Hailey's order to the Communications Room.

The time was 1330. Hailey watched as *Dawlish* heeled slightly to port and overtook the Shell tanker a hundred yards in front. 'I know we're breaking the sea lane rules, Number One,' he said crisply to Noble, 'but to hell with it.'

The news of Bosley's heart attack quickly spread around the ship. On his way to see Hailey several of the crew, including Williams and Flynn, enquired about Bosley.

'Tell 'im, all the best from the stokers, sir,' said Flynn.

'Aye, and if he needs anything, let us know,' Williams added, a look of concern etched in his eyes.

Smyth arrived on the bridge, sweating and slightly out of breath.

'How is our man, Doc?' Hailey asked, an anxious air in his voice, 'any improvement?'

'At least the pain in his chest has eased slightly,' Smyth answered, frowning slightly and pursing his lips, 'but he's far from out of the woods yet. The next twenty-four hours will be critical.'

'I hate to say this, Doc,' said Noble who was standing close to Hailey. 'But could he die?'

Smyth immediately gave a Noble dark look. 'Not if I can bloody-well help it, sir,' he gruffly replied, then turned away and left.

'I think you upset our sawbones, Number One,' said Hailey, grinning at Noble.

'I didn't really mean to,' Noble answered. 'Nevertheless, Norman will no doubt have to leave the ship, and that'll mean we only have Dicky Vellacott , Williams and Flynn.'

'Good point, Number One,' Hailey said, scratching his chin, 'it'll take God knows how long for a relief to arrive from UK, but I've got great confidence in them, especially Vellacott, he's been on the ship for two years and knows every nut and bolt below.'

Throughout the evening, *Dawlish* continued cutting through the sea at twenty-eight knots. The time was 2000. Ashir and Diana had just come off duty and were on the port side standing near the guard rail.

'Isn't it beautiful,' Diana said, staring up into the inky blackness of the night sky and feeling the warm breeze caress her face. 'Look at all those stars, Ash, they seem so near, and that lovely moon makes the sea shine so,' she paused and gave a relaxed sigh, then added, 'it reminds me of a scene from one of those old TV movies.'

Ashir gave a short laugh. 'You've been watching *Casablanca* too many times,' he said feeling the warmth of her thigh pressing against his.

'Anyway, we'll be in Bahrain in two days,' she replied, 'and from what I hear The capital Manama is quite close, and,' she paused, and lowering her voice to a whisper, went on, 'they have quite a few nice hotels . . .' Diana's voice trailed away, but Ashir was well aware of her message.

'Do they,' was Ashir's non-committal reply. Since his accident he had been racking his brain how to complete his mission. At one point he had decided creep into the heads during the night, armed with the Trysin, sit on the toilet, set the detonator and blow up the ship. The time was 0345. He was about to do climb out of his bunk when he felt someone shake his arm. It was Dutch Holland reminding him he had the morning watch in the Ops Room. He hardly heard Diana suggest a run ashore in Manama, thinking even if he completed his task in Bahrain, the objective of mass slaughter would fail as most of the crew would no doubt have overnight leave and would be ashore.

Diana tugging at his arm and saying, 'What do you think, Ash,' abruptly interrupted his thoughts.

'Oh, err . . . yes, all right,' he answered almost incoherently.

In the wardroom, dinner was over and Henderson was sitting in an armchair holding a cup and saucer. On the far side of the room sat Liz Hall and Shirley Mannering. In front of them two empty cups of coffee and saucers rested on a small table.

'He's hardly taken his eyes off you, Liz,' Shirley said, guardedly, while glancing away from her friend.

'I know,' Liz replied, 'I can feel his eyes boring into me,' she added, turning her head to one side and pretending not to notice him.

'Has he asked you out when we get to Bahrain?'

'Not yet,' Liz answered, keeping her eyes averted, 'but I expect he will. He's been here before and probably knows plenty of restaurants.'

'And what would you say if he did?' Shirley asked, sitting back on her chair giving Henderson a casual glance.

'I'd agree,' Liz replied toying with her empty cup. 'After all, in Gib he behaved like a perfect gentleman.'

'Good heavens,' Shirley replied with a short, throaty laugh, 'considering what was happening at the time, he didn't have much choice.' Liz didn't reply. Instead she sat looking at the deck and biting her lip.

For a few seconds, Shirley studied the faraway look in Liz's eyes. Then, glancing furtively around, she whispered, 'Good Lord, you're in love with him.'

'Well, what if I am,' Liz answered with troublesome sigh.

'Be bloody careful, Liz,' Shirley warned, 'he's married and much older . . .'

'Dammit,' Liz cried, 'don't you think I don't know that.' Then in a sudden fit of pique, she grabbed her shoulder bag and made her way outside onto the starboard side of the upper deck. Doing her best to control her frustration, she gripped the steel guard rail wire and stared blankly into the darkness. Suddenly, from behind her, the voice of Henderson interrupted her reverie.

'What's the matter, Liz?' she heard him say. 'You looked upset when you left the mess. Was it something Shirley said?'

Liz felt his warm hand on her shoulder and turned around. 'In a way, yes,' she replied, 'but,' she added taking a deep breath,' I'm all right, now.'

He tightened his grip on her shoulder and even though he knew he was already breaking the 'no touch' rule, he was tempted to take Liz in his arms and kiss her. 'Good,' he answered, removing his hand and moving alongside her. 'For a moment you had me worried.'

'Why would you worry about me?' Liz asked looking longingly into his eyes.

Henderson gently touched her on the cheek, feeling its warm smoothness and quietly replied, 'you know quite well why.'

Liz didn't reply. For a few seconds they stood in silence. Finally, Liz, despite the sudden dryness in her throat, said, 'I think I'd better leave before . . .'

Henderson abruptly interrupted her. 'Yes,' he stuttered, 'I understand. I . . . I have a mound of paper work to catch up on,' and quickly turned, opened a bulkhead door and left.

While Henderson was making his way to his cabin, Dean was quietly opening the sickbay door and entering. This was where he normally slept and was easily available in case of emergencies. The time was just after 2100. Since securing at 1600, he had been in his mess, watching a rerun of *Game of Thrones* on TV. He was now taking over the watch from Susan Hughes.

Except for the dim light from an angle-poised lamp shrouded by a small towel, the room was in darkness. Bosley lay in the bottom cot with his pale features turned to one side. One arm with the BP cuff attached to allow a reading to be done without disturbing him, lay outside the white duvet, which was barely moving due to the shallowness of his laboured breathing.

Susan Hughes, was sat on a swivel chair close to Bosley's cot. A stethoscope hung loosely around her neck and a cream-coloured medical chart attached to a clip board rested on her lap. Close by the cot was a small oxygen cylinder, plastic tubing with a mask attached, a square green box containing the de-fibrillator and a BP monitor.

She looked up as Dixie came in.

'How is he?' he asked, looking at Bosley's ashen features.

'His pulse is weak and slow and his BP is raised,' Susan replied, handing Dean the clip board.

'Hmm . . . I see,' Dixie replied, carefully studying the chart, he then noticed how tired and drawn Susan's face was.

'Cheers, Sue,' he said, 'I think you'd better go and get some rest. You look knackered.'

'Thanks, Dixie,' she replied, standing and yawning. 'If you need anything,' she added, handing Dean the stethoscope from around her neck, 'don't hesitate to call me.'

'Now that you mention it,' Dean said, with a salacious leer, 'there is one thing you could do . . .'

'In your dreams,' she snapped, giving him contemptuous stare. She picked up her bag and slipped it over her shoulder. Then, turned, opened the door and quietly left.

No sooner had the door closed then Dean immediately went to work and noted that Bosley's pulse was alarmingly weak and his BP was 170 over 90. Just as he was recording this on the chart, he heard Bosley give a muted moan followed by a throaty cough. Dean waited anxiously to see if Bosley would open his eyes, but they remained closed. It was then that he noticed there was no movement of the duvet covering Bosley's chest. Straight away, Dean felt for Bosley's radial and neck pulse and was alarmed to find neither.

Dean instinctively knew he was faced with an emergency and time was at a premium. Straight away he whipped back the duvet and picked up the defibrillator and in a matter of seconds had the pads in place on Bosley's bare chest and carefully turned up the electric current. He then quickly placed the rubber mask over his nose and mouth and gently switched on the oxygen. But was alarmed to see the BP monitor wasn't registering anything and Bosley had stopped breathing.

At that moment, the door opened an in came Smyth carrying his medical valise.

'Thank Christ! It's you, sir!' Dean exclaimed, staring frantically at Smyth, keeping a finger on Bosley's carotid artery, 'I can't find his pulse and he's not breathing. I've used the defibrillator but it's hasn't had any effect.'

In a flash, Smyth quickly saw the monitor wasn't registering and knew what he had to do. The procedure he was about to perform was dangerous and almost obsolete in modern medicine. But he had no other option. He was alone, hundreds of miles from land and didn't have time to use the ship to shore phone to call for advice. 'Keep using the defibrillator, and keep the oxygen on full,' he said, feeling his own heart pounding like sledgehammer.

He immediately opened his valise and, after what seemed an eternity, took out a small bottle of adrenaline, a narrow gauge needle and a syringe, both in plastic covering. He broke the open both the needle and syringe then hastily took off the top of the bottle. Keeping the bottle and syringe at eye level, he withdrew one millilitre of fluid into the barrel of the syringe. He knelt down and using the fingers of one hand he quickly found the fourth intercostal space in between the left side of Bosley's ribs. Then slowly and carefully, inserted the needle, silently praying it would enter the heart's ventricular chamber and not a coronary artery.

He gently withdrew the needle, and with beads of sweat running down his face, kept his finger on Bosley's jugular pulse while peering anxiously at the defibrillator's monitor.

'Please God, please,' he heard Dean, mutter. A few seconds later the monitor came alive. Numbers began to flicker on the face the dial.

'He's coming round, sir,' cried Dean, 'and he's breathing!'

With an enormous sigh of relief the doctor felt Bosley's pulse, weak at first then gradually quickening.

Bosley opened his eyes and with a faint smile, looked at Smyth. 'How am I doing, Doc?' he quietly uttered, then closed his eyes.

Wiping his brow with the back of his hand, Smyth glanced at Dean, and said, 'Looks like your prayer was answered.'

Just as Smyth stopped talking, the door opened and Hailey came in. 'My God, Doc, you have been busy,' he said, seeing Bosley's bare chest with the pads attached to the defibrillator. 'How is he?'

With an effort Smyth stood and grimaced due to the stiffness in his knees. He moved away from the cot. 'He's had a bit of a nasty turn, sir,' he said, touching the left side of his chest, 'but he seems to have recovered.'

'Good,' Hailey replied. 'Is there anything you want?'

With a forlorn smile, Smyth replied, 'An increase in speed would help.'

'Sorry, Doc, we're going flat out as it is,' Hailey answered, raising his eyebrows, then with smile, added. 'Thank goodness we arrive in Bahrain tomorrow.'

CHAPTER THIRTY-EIGHT

As dawn broke on Wednesday 4 September, *Dawlish* was off the southern coast of Bahrain. The time was 0600. As if by magic the myriad of twinkling stars and yellow crescent moon gradually faded. The great yellow orb of the sun appeared over the hitherto invisible horizon bathing the sea into a patina of pale gold, and in matter of seconds the blackness of night changed into a shimmering dawn.

Sub Lieutenant Morris was on the bridge using his binoculars to the landscape ten miles away on the port beam.

'According to the travel brochures,' he said, adjusting the lens slightly, 'Bahrain is an archipelago consisting of thirty-seven islands close to the shore of the Arabian Peninsula. And,' he paused then went on, 'it is supposed to be the land of shady palm groves full of bright coloured birds, fruit and flowers, but all I can see is a low lying sandy coastline and coral reefs.'

'The temperature outside will rise to forty degrees Fahrenheit,' chimed In Midshipman Dunlop, 'and a hots south-westerly wind that will make life decidedly uncomfortable.'

'You seem well informed, Dunners,' said Morris, 'don't tell me they taught you that at Greenwich?'

'No, sir,' Dunlop replied smugly, 'I got a first in geography at Oxford.'

'Then what's the name of the king, smartarse?'

'Hamad Bib Isa-al-khalifa,' Dunlop answered with a grin, 'anything else, sir?'

Morris rolled up is eyes and shook his head. 'Just belt up and find me a mug of coffee,' he said dismissively.

As he spoke the duty QM sitting at the console, took hold of the ship's tannoy and in strident tones, shouted, 'D'yer hear there. Hands to breakfast. Duty Watch fall in on the flight deck at zero, eight hundred.'

Shortly before 0745, Hailey and Noble came onto the bridge followed by Gooding. 'What's our ETA, in Bahrain, Pilot?'

'We should arrive at Mina Salman at ten hundred, sir,' Gooding replied, having checked his chart before coming on duty. Mina Salman is a busy port near Manama. It houses both the Royal Navy and American bases.

'Thank you,' Hailey replied, then glancing pensively at his wristwatch, he said, 'I'll address the ship's company at zero eight-thirty.'

Below in the ratings' bathroom, several men had finished taking a shower and were busy shaving. The sound of the toilets flushing added to the ribald conversation.

'A few of the lads are thinking of going on a banyan,' said Shady, who was standing next to Ashir. 'I was here on the *Reclaim* two years ago,' he added, rinsing foam from his face, 'and if I remember rightly, there's a fabulous beach a few miles along the coast from where we are called Tubli Bay.'

'Sounds great,' cried Bud Abbott, admiring his shaven face in a mirror, 'all that sea, sand and "you know what", just like in that movie, *From Here to Maternity.'*

'We could hire a few taxis same as we did in Pompey,' said Shady, drying his face on a towel. 'I've asked a few of the girls and they're keen on the idea. How about it, Ash? I expect Di will be going.'

'Mm . . . OK,' Ashir answered, running an electric the razor down the side of his face, 'when will this be?'

'In a couple of days,' Shady replied, then with an inquisitive frown, added, 'I wonder if they allow skinny dipping.' (A Banyan is a picnic usually involving more beer drinking than eating food).

In the girls' mess, most of them had completed their ablutions and were dressing.

'Any idea where we'll be going on this banyan, Shady is on about, Lot?' asked Polly West, buttoning up her shirt over her ample bosom.

'Not really,' Lottie replied, 'but I read somewhere that the Garden of Eden is supposed to be somewhere in Bahrain.'

'How romantic,' said Diana, 'I wonder if Ash knows anything about it?'

'Anyway,' chimed in Jane Wootton, 'it wasn't the apple that Eve tempted Adam with, that started all this sex business,' she said with a mischievous smile on her face, 'it was the pair on the ground.'

'I don't understand,' Lottie replied, with a puzzled expression on her chubby face. 'Do you mean the pear that you eat, or what?'

'No, you daft bugger,' Jane answered, shaking her head in disbelief, 'I mean pair, meaning a man and a woman shagging.'

'Oh, I see,' Lottie answered vacantly, zipping up her shorts.

At exactly 0800, the pipe, 'Hands turn too. Duty watch fall in on the fight deck,' echoed round the ship. Hailey was sat on his chair watching two Shell tankers some three hundred yards away escorted by a French frigate. Both tankers were so low in the water that their Plimsoll lines were barely visible. Noble stood nearby sipping a mug of coffee. Hailey was about to speak when Pincher Martin arrived.

'This just came in from the Admiralty, sir,' he said handing Hailey a signal.

'Thank you, chief,' Hailey replied, 'nothing serious, I hope?'

'Could be, sir,' Martin answered guardedly.

After reading the signal, Hailey frowned and shook his head. He then unhooked the Ops Room intercom. Henderson's plummy voice came on the line.

'Oh, Bob, would you please come to the bridge,' Hailey asked, doing his best to disguise his concern.

A few minutes later, Henderson arrived slightly out of breath. 'Good morning, sir,' he said, using a wrinkled handkerchief to wipe beads of sweat from his brow, 'is there a problem,' he added, cautiously noticing the signal in Hailey's hand.

'I'm afraid so, Bob,' Hailey replied, wearily, 'this has just arrived from the Admiralty. It says, you are to report to Admiral Oscar Hewitt, Commanding Officer, Brooklyn Navy Yard, New York to act as adviser on the new tactical destroyer that they are building.'

'What!' Henderson exclaimed, his face a picture of disbelief, 'why me, sir? Surely there are Pee-wohs who are just as capable as me ashore?'

'Apparently the Americans were very impressed by your handling of the attack on the Al Qaeda ship last week,' Hailey answered.

'My God.' Henderson muttered, shaking his head, 'When do I leave, sir?'

'In two days' time, on Saturday the 7th, Hailey replied, 'transport will be on the jetty at zero nine hundred. You're booked on the midday BA flight from Bahrain to Heathrow. You are to have fourteen days leave. Then you are to take an American Airways flight from Heathrow at twelve hundred on the twenty-second of September to Washington where you'll be met by the British Naval attache and taken to your quarters, which, knowing the Americans, will be quite salubrious, and be at the admiral's office at zero nine hundred 0900 on the twenty-third. This will all be confirmed to you by email.'

'What about my wife and children?' Henderson asked.

'There is no mention of them in the signal,' Hailey replied, glancing at the white form. 'But I'm sure their passage can be arranged as well.' Hailey paused momentarily, then, with a weary sigh, added, 'I realise this is a bit of a pier head jump, old boy. I'm really sorry to see you leave, but as I'm sure you can appreciate, it's out of my hands.'(A pier head jump is a draft naval parlance for appointment that has to be taken at short notice.)

'Yes, sir,' Henderson soberly replied. 'I understand.'

'Right then,' Hailey said, 'you'd better go speak to Tug Wilson, then pack what you'll need; the bulk of your things will be sent by air to your new address.'

'Very good, sir,' Henderson replied, then giving a forlorn glance around, he said, 'but I'm going to miss the old ship.'

'And I can assure you, old boy,' Hailey answered soberly. 'The ship will miss you.'

The first person Henderson thought of as he made his way to the Ops Room was Liz. Shortly after hands secured at 1600, he went to her cabin and feeling very nervous, gently knocked on the door.

'Whoever it is, please wait,' he heard her say. A few minutes later she said, 'come in.' Liz looked up as Henderson entered. Even though she had applied make-up, he could see that her eyes were red with crying. He was about to speak but she quickly interrupted him. 'I . . . I know,' she muttered, fighting back a tear, 'I saw a copy of the signal after all I am his secretary.'

Henderson stood looking at her, not knowing what to say. He hadn't told her that he had fallen in love with her, and this wasn't the time to say so.

'I . . . I'm not leaving the ship till the day after tomorrow, perhaps we could . . .'

Liz stood up and feeling tears well up in her eyes, said, 'no Bob, it would be no good. Let's just,' she didn't finish. Instead their arms went around each other as they kissed he felt the wetness of her tears on his face. 'I love you,' she sobbed as they parted, 'but I think we both knew it wouldn't work out.'

Feeling a lump in his throat, Henderson managed to say, 'You know I love . . .'

'Don't speak,' she cried, placing a warm finger over his lips, 'just . . . just go.'

With a pained expression in his eyes, Henderson let his arms slowly fall from around Liz's waist, turned then he opened the door and left.

A few minutes later a knock came at Liz's door. 'It's me, Liz,' said Shirley, 'can I come in?'

'Yes,' Liz replied, doing her best to stop crying.

Shirley came and immediately noticed Liz's mascara had run and her eyes were puffy. Shirley drew up a chair and next to Liz. 'What happened, love?' Shirley asked, placing a comforting arm around Liz's shoulders.

Dabbing her eyes with handkerchief, Liz managed to tell Shirley about Henderson's new appointment.

'You won't thank me at present,' Shirley said, giving Liz a gentle hug, 'but it is probably for the best. A similar thing happened to me a few years ago. I met an army officer and fell in love with him. However, he, like Henderson, was married. When he was posted abroad I was heartbroken,' Shirley paused and sighed, then continued, 'But as time passed I got over it. You will too.'

'Thanks, Shirl,' Liz muttered, 'I hope you're right.'

'Of course I am,' Shirley answered, giving her friend's hand a tender squeeze. 'Remember you're a very attractive woman and one day, you'll meet the right man. Now, dry your eyes, put on some make-up and we'll go to the mess and have cup of coffee.'

At 0900, Hailey unhooked the bridge intercom. After clearing his throat he began, 'This is the captain speaking.' His voice was clear and concise. 'As you know tomorrow we arrive in Bahrain. There are certain important rules to be observed. The population are Muslims. The King, government and police are Sunnis and are in the minority. The rest are Shi'ites. This often leads to local conflict. If this happens, keep well away and don't under any circumstances get involved.' He paused momentarily to allow the importance of this to sink in, then continued, 'The exchange rate is one point eight pounds to the Dinar. Also dress must be conservative - no short skirts, low-cut blouses, tongue rings and nude bathing. Tropical routine will be adopted and hands will secure at twelve hundred. All night leave will be granted from thirteen hundred. That is all.'

In the seamen's mess, Bud Abbott grinned at Shady Lane and said, 'Well, that puts paid to your skinny dipping, mate.'

Giving a quick nonchalant shrug of his shoulders, Shady replied, 'We'll just have to see, won't we.'

Henderson spent the remainder of the day either in the Ops Room or in his office compiling reports and handing over his department to Tug Wilson. Feeling somewhat cowardly, he purposely avoided seeing Liz by having a very late dinner. But that night, he lay awake wondering what might have been if things had been different.

At 0700 the next morning, special sea duty men were called and the ship's company fell in for entering harbour. From the bridge everyone watched as Mina Salman hove into view. Cranes, looking like gigantic praying mantises and bulky warehouses dominated the pale blue skyline. Beyond the long-jetty the buildings of the Royal Naval base could be seen. Further inland the larger structures of American Naval headquarters was evident and in the distance the city of Manama with its tall minarets bathed in the hazy morning sunshine.

'My goodness, Number One,' Hailey said, as *Dawlish* slowly approached the starboard side of the jetty, 'The frigate tied up at the end of the jetty is the type 25 frigate, HMS *Duncan*, and there's only two liners and few mine sweepers in harbour.'

'Yes, sir,' Noble replied, 'but it's a much busier port than I imagined. Notice all those cargo ships and container vessels alongside the wharf away to our left?'

In the sickbay Dixie, Susan and Smyth gently lifted Bosley from his cot into the Neil Robertson stretcher and tucked a duvet around him. Barney Watts and the first-aid team stood by ready when needed.

'I'm sorry about this, Norman,' said Smyth, observing a slight colour in Bosley's cheeks, 'but it's the only way we can get you onto the flight deck.' He paused and smiled, then added, 'However, don't worry, you won't be in it very long, I expect there's an ambulance on the jetty to take you to the base sick quarters and a nice comfortable bed.'

By 0900, hands fallen for entering harbour had been dismissed and *Dawlish* was secured to number three berth on Long Jetty. A surgeon lieutenant and an LMA waited on the jetty next to a dark blue ambulance with the letters RN painted boldly in white on its side.

Under the eagle eyes of Harry Tate, the duty watch secured the metal gangway to the port side of the flight deck. Immediately this was done the officer and LMA stepped on board *Dawlish*, whose salute was returned by Hailey, O'Grady and Whitton.

'Commander Hailey, Doc,' Hailey said, shaking the officer's hand.

'Surgeon Lieutenant McBride, sir,' the doctor replied as they shook hands. 'I believe you have a sick officer?'

Just then Smyth and the first-aid team arrived carrying Bosley, firmly strapped into the Neil Robertson stretcher, and gently laid it down on the deck. Dixie, holding a brown canvas bag containing Bosley's dressing gown and toilet gear, shook hands and said a brief hello to the LMA. Susan stood close by the stretcher holding the oxygen cylinder and tubing.

Hailey introduced the doctors to one another. Smyth gave a quick resume of Bosley's condition to McBride. 'I've written the details of his treatment in this report,' Smyth said, handing McBride a buff envelope.

'How are you feeling, sir? McBride asked, smiling pleasantly.

'Not too bad, Doc,' Bosley muttered wearily.

'Right, then,' said McBride, checking Bosley's pulse and finding it rapid and weak. 'We're going to take you into the ambulance then put you on a stretcher. It's only a short drive to the sick quarters, so try and relax.'

By this time Bungy Williams and Patrick Flynn, Dicky Vellacott and several stokers plus many of the ship's company were crowded on the flight deck quietly watching events.

'Good luck from all of us, sir,' Vellacott said, taking hold of Bosley's hand and gently shaking it. 'And get well soon.'

'Godspeed, old boy,' Hailey added, 'we'll all miss you.'

Dixie and the first aid team lifted the stretcher and carefully made their way down the gangway. Suddenly, a spontaneous chorus of '*For He's a Jolly Good Fellow*' broke out from the crew. The back doors of the ambulance opened and as Bosley was lifted inside he slowly raised a hand In acknowledgement. Dixie, carrying the Neil Robertson stretcher followed by the first-aiders came on board the ship. The ambulance drove off and the singing died down. Hailey turned around to leave and was met by Liz Hall.

'Message from Fleet Commander's office, sir,' Liz said. 'Admiral Jones will expect you at eleven hundred. A car will pick you up at 1045.'

'Thank you, Liz,' Hailey replied, glancing at his wristwatch. 'That gives me time to have a cup of coffee and change into my number ones.'

CHAPTER THIRTY-NINE

The time was 1040. Hailey was stood on the fight deck holding a briefcase and watched as a black Mercedes arrived at the foot of the gangway. The driver, got out and opened a passenger door. After returning the salutes of the OOD and duty PO, Hailey hurried down the gangway. He quickly returned the driver's salute and climbed into the back seat into the welcome coolness of the vehicle's air conditioning.

The jetty led directly into the naval base. After passing lines of small brick houses, the car continued down a wide tarmacked road flanked by official looking buildings, these, the driver told Hailey, were transit quarters for crews of ships in dry dock.

The headquarters of the UK Component Command was a large, three-storey white building with wide windows and various sized antennae poking up from a flat roof and a White Ensign hung lazily from a tall flagpole. A wrought iron balcony in the rear overlooked a full-size football pitch. The entrance, gained via a narrow concrete path, consisted of a stout, brown oaken door, above which was a red sign proclaiming the building's name. In of the door stood a rating in whites holding a rifle across his chest.

The driver stopped the Mercedes at the end of the path then got out and opened the passenger door.

'Thank you,' Hailey, said as he climbed out of the car. 'I'm not sure how long I'll be,' he added, returning the rating's salute, 'but I think you'd better wait.'

'That's all right, sir,' the driver replied with a pleasant smile. 'I'm on duty all day, so there's no hurry.' Ignoring the rating's flippant comment, Hailey picked up his briefcase and made his way up the path to the entrance. The time by his wrist watch read 1055.

After acknowledging the guard presenting arms, he opened the door and went inside and was immediately met the buzzing of the air conditioning and the pungent smell of mansion polish. The entrance hall was quite spacious with a corridor way leading off from the right. At one end two desks manned by petty officers sat at computers. Shiny brown linoleum covered the floor. Strips of neon attached to a low slung, cream-coloured ceiling could, when necessary, provide adequate lighting. The walls were papered in pale green and above a nearby staircase hung an imposing portrait of Bahrain's monarch, King Hamad Bab isa-al-Khalifa, wearing a pristine white Ghutrah, (traditional Arab headgear.)

Hailey was met by a stout, red-faced chief petty officer.

'Can I help you, sir?' he asked staring at Hailey with a pair of bloodshot brown eyes. He spoke with a sharp Scouse accent and Hailey detected a faint smell of whisky in his breath.

'Yes, thank you, Chief,' Hailey replied, coughing discreetly while taking off cap, 'I have an appointment with the admiral.'

'Right, sir,' the Chief replied curtly, 'down the corridor and his office is s the second door on yer left.'

Hailey glanced nervously at his wristwatch. After all, it wasn't every day he was summoned to meet an admiral. He thanked the Chief and quickly walked down the corridor and stopped outside a door marked 'UK Component Command.' He knocked, went inside and was met by a petty officer standing next to bulky green filing cabinet, in what was a large room containing rows of box files, a computer and printer. In one corner, a coffee percolator and cups lay on a small tale. Two wooden chairs faced a desk cluttered with folders, a black telephone and an assortment of office material. A few feet away from the desk was a door with Vice Admiral Phillip Jones's name painted neatly in bright gold lettering on a an oaken plaque.

Once again Hailey looked at his watch then introduced himself.

'Don't worry, sir, you're bang on time, sir,' said the PO, drawing open a file. 'Just knock and go straight n. He's expecting you.'

As Hailey entered the room he felt his shoes sink comfortably into the pile of the dark blue carpet. Unlike the anteroom, the admiral's office was impressively furnished. Vice Admiral Phillips was a tall, forty-five year old man, whose sturdy physique suggested a youthful indulgence in a variety of sporting activities. He was sat behind a wide, mahogany desk topped in dark green leather, studying a batch of reports. Several strands of grey hair lay carefully plastered a bald scalp, which, like his face was heavily tanned. Over the left pocket of his white cotton shirt was a thin row of medal ribbons and on each shoulder rested the insignia of his rank, a gold epaulette with crossed silver swords and two small silver stars.   On the wall behind his desk was an ornately framed coloured photograph of Queen Elizabeth and the Duke of Edinburgh. As Hailey entered the office the admiral's sharp dark blue eyes wrinkled into a warm smile.

'Ah Commander Hailey,' he said, pushing his six foot fame up and offering his hand, 'do come in and take a seat. Coffee?' his voice was deep and resonant with a slight touch of the West Country.

'Thank you, sir,' Hailey replied politely as he removed his cap.

The admiral's grip, as they shook hands was warm and firm. Feeling somewhat nervous, Hailey placed his briefcase by the side of the armchair and sat down.

The admiral took his seat and relaxed back in his chair. 'Your report about you run-in with Al Qaeda was very interesting,' he said with a wry smile. 'It proves beyond doubt that the terrorists have a firm footing in the Yemen.   However,' he added, folding his bronze forearms across his stomach, 'the most important thing was you had no casualties other than your engineer's heart attack.

'Indeed, sir,' Hailey answered calmly, 'thanks to the expert treatment of Surgeon Lieutenant Smyth and his staff, Lieutenant Commander Bosley came through his ordeal, but it was a close-run thing.'

'Yes, so you mentioned in your report,' said the admiral. 'Coffee?'

'Not at the moment, thank you, sir, perhaps later,' Hailey politely replied.

'Now,' said the admiral, unfolding his arms and sitting forward. 'I'm aware that you've had a long and sometimes dangerous journey from the UK, and I know your crew need a rest, but I'm sorry to tell you that you'll be going back to sea sooner than you expected.'

Hailey uncrossed his legs and with a surprised look in his eyes, sat forward. 'Why is that, sir? He asked, hesitatingly.

'In six days' time two Shell oil tankers and a French cargo ship full of nuclear waste will leave Kuwait for Dar es Salaam. By Friday the thirteenth, the ships will be thirty miles off the southern tip of Bahrain. *Dawlish* is to meet them at zero nine hundred and escort them through the Strait of Hormuz.' The admiral paused and took a deep breath and with a smile, continued, 'on Monday the sixteenth, you will be met by an American destroyer, the USS *Spruance* and the aircraft carrier *Coral Sea*. Both warships are bound for the States but will escort the tankers to the UK. *Dawlish* will then return to Bahrain.'

Hardly daring to question the admiral, Hailey nervously cleared his throat then replied, 'May I ask why *Dawlish*, sir, what has happened to the *Doncaster?*'

'She is still in dry dock following her collision a few weeks ago,' said the admiral, 'and *Duncan,* the frigate you saw when you entered harbour, has engine trouble and won't be ready to sail for at least a week.'

'And that leaves *Dawlish*,' Hailey replied with a slight sigh.

'However to soften the blow, so to speak,' said the admiral, 'I'd like you and your officers to attend a cocktail party tomorrow. It'll be held upstairs in my private quarters. Twenty hundred, rig 1BWs. I've invited a few nurses and some people you might find interesting. (IBWs are tropical white suits button up the front epaulets of rank on each shoulder.)

'That's very kind of you, sir, and if you don't mind,' Hailey answered, running his tongue along his dry lips, 'I think I'll have that coffee, now.'

The news that *Dawlish* would be sailing in a week was met with a mixed reaction.

After lunch in the wardroom, O'Grady glanced casually at Harry Thomas, shrugged his shoulders slightly and said, 'After what we've been through another week at sea won't seem too bad.'

Holding a cup of coffee in one hand Thomas grinned like a Cheshire cat and said, 'And just think of all that duty free booze we're going to have tonight, courtesy of the admiral.'

In the senior ratings' mess the feelings between the old timers were similarly sanguine. 'At least we should have a fairly long spell in harbour when we return,' Hector Pascoe remarked to Jock Forbes.

'You hope,' came Jock's dubious reply.

However, the marines seemed quite happy to go to sea.

'Thank fuck we'll be spared that desert route march Lieutenant Somersby mentioned this morning,' Knocker White said to his oppo Lofty Day.

'Oh, I dunno,' grinned Lofty, who looked up from polishing his boots, 'at least it'd be a change from being cooped up on board here.'

'I was hoping to buy a few rabbits for me missus,' said Buck Taylor who was in the seamen's mess sitting down downing the dregs from his can of beer.

'Good idea,' Shady Lane answered, 'I've seen her. She's so ugly I'd buy her one of those, what do they call 'em, Niqabs isn't it, that'll cover her face.' With a grin, he ducked as Buck threw his empty can at him.

Up for'd, Jean Rochester and some of the girls were hoping to go and ashore and explore the local Casaba and market stalls.

'I shouldn't bother if I were you, love, 'Lottie Jones replied with a mischievous gleam in her eyes. 'You'll only end up in the harem of some big fat greasy sheik.'

'Anyway,' Diana added with an air of conceit, 'some of us are going on a banyan with Shady and the lads.'

Just then Sadie Thompson entered the mess and overheard Diana speaking. 'And remember what the captain said about nude bathing,' she warned, placing her hands on her sturdy hips and glaring around.

'Bloody spoil-sport,' muttered Lottie, and left the mess.

That evening, while the officers were throwing a farewell party for Henderson, Shirley Mannering and Liz were sitting at the cocktail bar in the most luxurious hotel in Bahrain being entertained by two good-looking American naval lieutenants.

CHAPTER FORTY

Shortly after secure the next day, Ashir was sitting in the mess. Like several ratings, he was texting home. By now Prime Minister Cameron had lifted the ban about *Dawlish*'s encounter with Al Qaeda and news of her escapade was on the television and in the newspapers. And although the ship had suffered no casualties, their messages were simply to confirm they were safe. Ashir was aware that his parents would be anxious to know when he could complete his mission. He had decided to try to carry out Allah's wishes when the ship put to sea in a week's time. To reassure them, he sent a coded message, saying, 'Alllah be praised. Arrived Bahrain. Will be at sea soon then all will be well. Your loving son, Ashir.'

Half an hour later, Shady Lane came into the mess carrying two boxes containing the beer issue.

'Come on, you lot who are going on the banyan,' he said, beaming broadly, 'an American sailor on the jetty gave me the phone number of a taxi firm. Two taxis will pick us up at nineteen hundred. By then it should be a bit cooler. I've told the girls,' he added, passing the cans of beer around. 'The Yank also told me there's a few shops not far from the beach that sell booze, and Polly West is gunna make us some sarnies, so drink up, it's all arranged.'

'And remember to wear plimsolls to protect your feet against sand eggs,' said Dixie, 'digging them out of your feet with a needle is a very painful. Better tell the girls as well.'

During the afternoon most of the ship's company and those ratings off watch were engaged in 'Egyptian PT,' a nickname for catching up with their sleep. By 1700, as if shaken by some unknown hand, one by one they woke up, showered and began dressing in readiness to go ashore.

'While you buggers are busy getting sand behind your foreskins,' Sandy Powel said to Pete Price, 'the boot necks and the rest of us will be in the Britannia Club in the naval base. From what I hear the girls off the *Duncan* get in there, and everything's duty free.'

'Best of luck, mate,' said Pete Price, 'but,' he added, grabbing his crutch over his white boxer shorts, 'I'll think of you when I'm lying in the sand groping Emily Jackson.'

Diana and some of the girls were sitting on the brown leather settee surrounding the lower part of the mess. They had just finished their dinner. The television was switched off and, like the lads, they were enjoying a few cans of beer.

'I wonder what it's like to take a ride on a camel?' sighed Jane Wootton, who was wearing a pink thong and a matching brassier.

'Smelly and bloody uncomfortable,' replied Emily Jackson, trying on a below the knee blue button flared skirt, 'I had a ride on one when I was on holiday in Cairo two years ago. My arse was sore for ages.'

'Anyway, love,' added Lottie Jones, who had just had a shower and had a damp towel covering most of her body, 'those hairy monsters give me the hump.'

'Just like Shady Lane, eh, Lot,' shouted Polly West, gleefully pulling Lottie's towel away.

A few minutes before 1900, Diana, Jane, Emily and Lottie Jones arrived on the flight deck. Behind them came the small stout figure of Polly West breathing heavily while carrying a heavy box of ham and corned beef sandwiches she had lovingly prepared earlier in the galley. Having taken heed of Hailey's orders, under their below the knee, coloured skirts and dresses they wore full body service issue bathing costumes. Each girl, wore thick rubber soled sandals and carried a black shoulder bag stuffed with a towel, make up, money and ID cards. The lads had rolled up towels under their arms and were dressed in an assortment of colourful short sleeved shirts, trousers and trainers. Doing his gentleman act, Shady smiled benevolently at Polly West.

'Can't have you straining yourself, Westie,' he said relieving her of the large box of sandwiches, then, with a salacious grin, added, 'you'll need all your strength for later.'

Having carefully scrutinised them, Bogey Knight, narrowed his pale blue eyes and said, 'I hope you lot remember what the captain said about behaviour ashore. And don't spend all those dinars you drew from the pay office.'

OOW Shirley Mannering stood close by still nursing hangover from last night's run ashore, offered no comment. The time was a little after 1845.

'Here's the taxis,' shouted Shady Lane, watching as two silver Mercedes came down the jetty and stopped near the bottom of the gangway. 'We'll go in the first one, you and the girls,' he added looking at Diana, 'come in the second.' He then turned to Ashir, 'as you speak the lingo, Ash, tell the driver to take us to Tubli Bay and ask him how much it'll be.'

The taxi drivers climbed out of their respective taxis and opened the passenger doors. Both men were tall, swarthy and unshaven wearing white shirts and baggy trousers.

Chattering and laughing like a group of teenagers the girls walked down the gangway and after giving their driver a cheeky smile climbed inside the car.

Ashir touched his lips and breast then addressed the driver with the traditional, 'Salaam Ailaecum and asked, 'how much to Tubli Bay?'

The driver smiled and replied, 'Ailaecum - a - Salaam. For the great Royal Navy, thirty dinars.'

Ashir frowned and shook his head. 'No, no,' he replied, waving his hand, 'too much, fifteen dinars.'

'But effendi,' moaned the driver, shrugging both shoulders and placing both palms up, 'I am a poor man with a large family. Twenty dinars.'

With a satisfied grin on his face, Ashir replied, 'Done,' and they shook hands. Ashir climbed inside and closed the door.

'What was all that jibbering about, Ash?' Pete Price asked as the taxi drove off.

'It's called haggling,' Ashir answered with a grin.

The traffic was quite heavy as the two cars sped along wide roads lined with palm trees and interrupted by a series of roundabouts. The taxis slowed down as they passed through Manama, a bustling city, crowded with tourists, colourful markets and medieval souks alongside modern hotels.

'My goodness, driver,' cried Lottie Jones staring wide-eyed, through the window, 'how can they wear those clothes in this heat?'

Lottie was referring to the Muslim women wearing the hijab, a headscarf covering the head and neck but leaving the face clear. As well as Arabs dressed in dishdashas, the women wore the niqab, a scarf covering all the face except the eyes, while others were clad in the burka, a full face and body covering, their eyes looking inscrutable behind their veils.

'The material is thin and allows the air to get around the body,' the driver replied. 'In England where many live, it is thicker against your cold weather.'

Lottie gave Diana a puzzled look. 'I wonder where they keep their money, Di.'

'I'm not sure,' Diana answered, 'but this cossie I'm wearing is itching like hell.'

'Mine too,' chimed in Polly West, pulling a face and squirming, 'and I want to pee.'

'Maybe we'll be able to take 'em off later when it's dark,' suggested Jane Wootton.

'Now, now,' warned Diana, 'remember the rules . . .'

Everyone laughed and carried on looking outside.

The comments from the lads were slightly raunchier. 'I bet there's no wife swapping here,' quipped Pete Price.

'I'm not surprised,' said Bud Abbott, 'for all you know under their gear they could be fat and doggo.'

'I wonder if they wear any knickers,' Shady whispered to Dutch Holland.

'I doubt it,' Dutch replied, grinning salaciously, 'but I don't fancy finding out.'

After passing stalls selling everything from colourful carpets to stalls overflowing with a variety of fruit and vegetables, Shady asked the driver to stop the taxi outside a large grocery shop. Above the darkened entrance was a sign with words painted in Arabic.

Twenty minutes later, after a lot of haggling, Ashir came out carrying a large carton of Budweiser, a bottle of Bell's whiskey, a bottle of Gordon's Gin and a bottle of Coca Cola.

Tubli Bay was a crescent shaped inlet on the northern edge of Manama. The taxis stopped at a long, narrow sandy path, flanked on either side by wide expanses of lush, green prickly sea grass, dense mangroves and graceful palm trees. As everyone climbed out of the taxi they felt the hot air attack their faces, a stark contrast from the coolness of the taxi's air conditioning.

'My God!' gasped Diana, 'it feels as if we've stepped into an oven.'

'The beach is a hundred yards down there,' said the taxi driver, 'if you look, you can see the sand dunes.'

The time was 1930. Ashir paid the taxi drivers and asked them to return at 2200 to take them back to the ship, 'And there'll be an extra tip if you're on time,' he added with a grin.

The drivers readily agreed and drove off.

Suddenly, darkness descended on them like a black shroud. High above in a cloudless sky, a crescent moon, surrounded by a myriad of twinkling stars, cast a silver glow over the palm trees either side of a wide sandy pathway. A short distance away the colour of the dunes changed imperceptibly from pristine whiteness to a deep, warm bronze.

They reached the end of the pathway and with their feet sinking into the soft powdery sand, ploughed to the top of the nearest dune. The sight that met their eyes was breath-taking. The sea, shining like molten silver stretched as far as the eye could see. A white ribbon of beach curled around the bay before fading into the darkness. Directly in front of them the sand sloped down onto the beach. At the water's edge, the colour of the sea changed imperceptibly from inky black to a stunning translucent green.

'My God,' sighed Emily, 'it's so beautiful. Look at that lovely water it's so clear you can see the fishes.'

'You're right there, love,' Diana, exclaimed, staring upwards, 'I've never seen so many stars. They seem so near you could reach out and touch them.'

'Wow!' exclaimed Shady Lane, taking hold of Lottie's warm hand and squeezing it, 'it looks like a scene from *Lawrence of Arabia*.'

'Hmm . . . you're right there Shady,' Lottie replied, 'all we need is a few camels to complete the picture.'

It's all right for Di,' remarked Polly West, 'she's got Omar Sharif to look after her'

'Jealousy will get you nowhere,' Diana replied, pulling a face at Polly, 'anyway, you can keep your stars and your camels, my dress is sticking to me like glue. The sooner I can take the bloody thing off and get into the water, the better.'

It was a sentiment no doubt shared with the others. However, in their excitement, they failed to notice a Land Rover with two Arab policemen hidden behind a clump of palm trees fifty yards away.

With cries of delight, they felt their feet sinking ankle deep in the warm sand as they ran down the side of the dune onto the beach. Twenty yards away, the surf lapped invitingly along the edge of the water.

'Right girls,' Polly shouted, dropping her bag and hurriedly taking off her dress, 'last one in doesn't get any vodka.' And waving her hands excitedly, ran into the water. 'Come on,' she shouted, feeling the warmth of the water engulf her body, 'it's bloody marvellous.'

The other girls quickly disrobed and joined Polly, yelling and screaming while splashing each other.

The lads were not far behind them. They quickly stowed the beer and spirits at the base of the dune and in a flash discarded their clothes. With their tanned faces standing out starkly against the whiteness of their bodies, they charged into the sea.

'Wow!' shouted Shady Lane, as he made a grab for Lottie, 'this beats Blackpool beach any day.'

'I agree,' spluttered Lottie, 'but take your hands off my tits.'

Meanwhile, Jane, Emily and Polly were frolicking about with Bud, Dutch and Pete, yelling and splashing like exited school children.

'Come on, Ash,' shouted Diana, 'flicking water into Ashir's face, 'give me a kiss.'

Ashir put his arms around her waist with the water lapping against their faces, kissed her warm, wet lips. As they parted, he felt Diana's fingers grasp the band of his shorts and yank them down to his knees. In one swift movement she cupped his testicles and worm-like penis, and gave them a gentle squeeze. Then, with a cheeky grin, swam away and joined the others.

Twenty minutes later, everyone staggered out of the sea, breathless and dripping wet. The hair of each girl was a soggy mess and their bathing costumes clung to them like a second skin. The girls laid out their towels and lay on their stomachs next to each other, allowing the warm air to dry their backs.

Shady opened the cans and passed them around to everyone.

'I don't know about you lot,' Polly said, turning over and sitting up, 'but I could use a drop of that gin.' She then reached across and took out the Gordons. She unscrewed of the top and took a good swig, feeling the liquid burn her insides. 'It'll go down well with the beer,' she said, wiping her mouth.

The other girls heard Polly and turned over, sat up and dusted the sand off their legs.

'After you with the mother's ruin, Westie,' said Diana, who, after accepting the bottle, took a gulp and passed it to Jilly then Jane and finally Lottie.

Not wanting to be outdone, Bud Abbott removed stopper from the whiskey, and everyone except Ashir, who preferred his coke, had a good drink.

After downing the last of the spirits, they had another few cans of beer. Lottie produced a small transistor and, after tuning through some strange Arabic sounds, found some music.

The girls managed to stand up and despite feeling their feet sinking into the sand, they managed to gyrate seductively to the rhythmic sound of an old Beatle song. The lads joined them, holding cans of beer while sluggishly moving their feet. Shady placed his arms around Lottie's waist and pulled her to him. Dutch and Jane stumbled about clutching one another, Bud grabbed Emily and began kissing her while Polly, towering over the small, portly frame of Bud, managed some sort of rhythmic movement. Meanwhile, Diana, with her head resting against Ashir's hairy chest, had hardly moved. Feeling his penis harden, she pushed herself closer to him and gently wriggled her hips. Feeling acutely embarrassed, Ashir moved away.

'Mm . . . don't, Ash,' Diana sighed, pushing harder against him, 'it feels lovely.'

'Err . . . I think I'd better go and have a swim,' Ashir stuttered nervously and took a step backwards.

Taken aback by Ashir's reaction, Diana let her hands slide away from his waist and, cried, 'Right then, I think I'll join you.' And balancing on one foot, managed to wriggle out of her bathing costume then shouted, 'come on girls, the last one is chicken,' then ran down the beach and with her firm breasts bouncing enticingly up and down, splashed her way into the sea.

The sight of Diana's naked white body bathed in bright moonshine immediately attracted everyone's attention. Jane was the first of the girls to accept Diana's challenge. She quickly struggled out of her bathing costume and yelling wildly, dashed into the sea, wading out waist high. Lottie and the others quickly followed suit. In a matter of minutes, the water was churned into a frothy mass as the five girls yelled and splashed each other.

Needless to say the lads, momentarily transfixed by the sudden sight of naked bottoms, divested their swimming shorts and yelling like mad men, charged into the sea. Ashir remained on the beach, his eyes catching glimpses of Diana's nakedness plunging in and out of the water like an excited sea nymph.

After fifteen minutes of kissing and the salacious grabbing of flesh, they returned to the beach, dripping wet and flopped down onto their towels. The moon disappeared behind a large clump of grey clouds leaving the beach in darkness.

'What's the matter?' Shady asked, drying his face with end of the towel, 'don't tell me you're shy?'

'Not really,' Ashir answered, feeling his face redden. 'Muslims are not allowed to go around naked.'

'Is that right, Di,' giggled Lottie Jones, finishing off the remains of the gin, 'or is his willy too big for public display.'

'That's summat you'll never . . .' at that moment a bright beam of torchlight, penetrated the gloom, playing back and forth on the naked bodies. For a few seconds the light blinded everyone. This was quickly followed the mass hysteria as they jumped up and covered themselves with their towels. Then, gradually, the dark outline of two tall figures wearing peaked caps emerged from the darkness.

'Put that light out, you fuckin' perverts,' yelled, Holland indignantly, 'or I'll put yours out.' Like the rest of the lads Dutch was completely naked.

'Who the bloody hell are you?' screamed one of the girls.

Just then the moon emerged from behind the clouds showing two men wearing light khaki uniforms and peaked caps. Both wore shiny leather Sam Brown belts and holsters with the flaps buttoned over their weapons.

The taller of the two, a man with swarthy skin, piercing dark eyes and a black Walrus moustache, glared angrily around. Then, in perfect English, replied, 'I am Sergeant Rasheem al Manir, and this is Private Mohammed el Ragal. We are Bahrain policemen, and you people are breaking the law. In this country nude bathing is a criminal offence for which you could go to prison.'

Emily Jackson almost dropped her towel as one of her hands shot to her mouth.

'*Prison*,' she cried hysterically, 'that's bloody ridiculous. We're in the navy and you can't do that to us.'

'She's right,' Shady Lane added, standing defiantly with his hands on his hips.

'Let me talk to him, Shady,' said Ashir stepping forward and facing the policemen. 'Salaam Aileucum,' Ash went on, bowing slightly while touching his breast and lips, 'please, sir, let me explain,' he added, using Arabic.

Noticing his swarthy appearance, the sergeant replied, also in Arabic, 'Are you a Muslim?'

'Yes, and we are all from HMS *Dawlish*.'

'I am surprised to hear that,' the sergeant replied, 'are there many Muslims in your navy?'

'Yes,' Ashir replied, 'quite a few.'

'Are you Sunni or Shi'ite?' asked the sergeant warily.

'Shi'ite,' Ashir lied.

The sergeant's dark feature broke into a satisfied smile. 'That is good,' he answered.

'Don't you remember, Rasheem,' interrupted Private el Ragal, 'The ship they are from attacked Al Qaeda last week. It was on the radio.'

'Ah, yes,' replied the sergeant, looking approvingly at Ashir, 'you and your crew were very brave. But you have still broken the law, however.' He paused momentarily, then gave his colleague a sly glance. 'We have volunteered for duty here this evening, and, err . . . don't get paid.'

Ashir quickly understood what the sergeant was after.

'I understand perfectly,' Ashir replied with a smile. 'Excuse me for a moment and switch off your torch.' He turned and joined the others who were in the process of getting dressed while waiting anxiously, watching Ashir talking to the policemen.

'Gather round,' he said, beckoning the lads and girls.

'My God, they're not gunna lock us up, are they, Ash?' cried Diana.

'No,' Ashir whispered, 'not if we give them some money.'

'The robbing bastards,' muttered Bud Abbott, 'so that's what this is all about, eh?'

'I'm afraid so,' said Ashir, 'now let's see how many dinars we have, about a hundred should do it.'

With sighs of relief, especially from the girls, a small bundle of dinars was produced and handed to Ashir, who in turn, gave the money to the sergeant.

'I think there's enough to cover the money you should have received for your, err . . . overtime,' Ashir said, lapsing into Arabic.

'You are most kind,' the sergeant answered with a satisfied smile. 'Now, Aileucum - a - Salaam, 'Peace be with you', and please tell your friends to pick up their rubbish and leave. The time is twenty-one-thirty,' he added, after a cursory glance at his wristwatch. 'I'll expect you to be gone within the next ten minutes.'

He and his colleague then left. Shortly afterwards the sound of their Land Rover could be heard fading away in the distance.

'You're a hero,' cried Shady, patting Ashir on the back. 'Just think, without you we might have all ended up in some shitty prison.'

'And God only knows what might have happened to us,' Diana added, giving Ashir a large wet kiss.

With great relief they saw the taxis were waiting. Half an hour later they climbed wearily on board *Dawlish,* each one a dozen dinars worse off.

CHAPTER FORTY-ONE

At 1930, Hailey left his cabin and walked to the flight deck where the ship's officers and duty watch were gathered. Darkness had suddenly descended and the ship's lighting was switched on. High above a bright, crescent moon surrounded by a vast umbrella of glittering stars bathed the base and harbour in a clear white light. Like Hailey, the thirteen officers were dressed in pristine, white uniforms. The exception to this was Somersby, who looked immaculate in tropical khaki.

'Attention,' came the officious voice of Bogey Knight. 'Captain on deck.' Shirley Mannering, the officers and Baggsy Baker immediately snapped to attention and saluted.

'Good evening, gentlemen,' said Hailey, returning their salutes, then glancing at the Knight, said, 'I take it the transport has arrived, Master?'

'Yes, sir,' Knight replied, 'there are three staff cars waiting on the jetty.'

'Splendid,' Hailey replied, and walked down the gangway followed by every officer except Liz Hall, who was in her cabin nursing a hangover from the previous night's run ashore in Manama.

With Hailey and four senior officers in the lead car, the small convoy sped along the jetty and entered the base. A few minutes later the cars stopped outside the Headquarters of the UK Component Command Building. A large coach was parked at the rear of the building. The admiral's aide-de-camp, a tall, naval lieutenant with a deep tan, was waiting at the entrance.

'Good evening, sir,' he said, smiling while giving Hailey a smart salute, 'if you and your officers will follow me.'

The admiral's reception room was reached at the top of three flights of stairs.

The aide turned the handle of a highly polished oaken door and stepped aside allowing the officers to enter. The air conditioned room was larger than Hailey expected. A hub of conversation, interlaced with an occasional burst of laughter gave the atmosphere a pleasant and relaxed feel. The soft strains of Vivaldi emanated from a hidden CD, and from a low ceiling two glittering crystal chandeliers bathed everything in a clear, even light. A lush, dark green carpet covered the floor. On the oak- panelled walls hung a series of romantic desert scenes next to a glass door that opened onto the balcony.

At one end of the room a large ornately framed coloured photograph of Queen Elizabeth and the Duke of Edinburgh hung the behind a long mahogany table on which rested an assortment of drinks and food. A group of women wearing colourful thin cotton dresses, stood in one corner surrounded by several naval officers. Nearby, a small crowd of local dignitaries in evening dress and their well-groomed wives talked sedately while sipping drinks. The tall, heavily tanned, balding figure of Vice Admiral Jones stood in front of one of two tall windows surrounded by three American naval officers and a stout, grey haired elderly lady wearing a loose fitting dark blue dress. All five were holding glasses and chatting amicably.

Meanwhile, male stewards in white dinner jackets hovered about holding trays of drinks. As Hailey and his retinue entered, everyone glanced across at them.

'Ah, please excuse me,' the admiral said, glancing at the elderly lady and the officers, 'our guests of honour have arrived.' He passed his empty glass to a steward and greeted Hailey with a welcoming smile. 'Good evening, Commander,' he said, shaking Hailey's hand, 'wonderful to see you again.' Then, smiling at the other officers, went on, 'It is a pleasure to see all of you after your difficult voyage from England and I'm sure you'll be glad to hear the base PMO tells me your engineer officer is making satisfactory progress and will be sent home to Derriford Hospital in Plymouth when he is well enough to travel.' (PMO – Principal Medical Officer.)

'Yes, sir, that's good news indeed,' Hailey answered, 'Surgeon Lieutenant Smyth here,' he paused and nodded towards the doctor, 'and the chief engineer visited him earlier today and told me.'

Hailey then introduced the admiral to Noble and Smyth then the rest of *Dawlish*'s officers. Just as he had finished, the door opened and in came a small group of people, laughing and talking. Among them were three women, dressed formally in evening clothes, as opposed to the four men who wore coloured shirts hanging loosely outside their trousers.

'Oh, splendid,' cried the admiral, abruptly turning around, 'I see my other guests have finally managed to arrive.' With a gracious smile, he excused himself and made his way towards his late arrivals. As he did so, Hailey overheard Parker-Smith's ribald comment to Dunlop, 'I say, Dunners, look at that brunette, isn't she a smasher?'

Hailey turned around and could hardly believe his eyes. Looking straight at him was his ex-wife, Annabel Sutherland. Suddenly he froze. The shock of seeing the women whose photograph rested in the bottom drawer of his cabin almost made him drop his glass. My God, he inwardly cried, after all these years she hasn't changed a bit. Two strands of pearls adorned her slender neck and she wore her chestnut hair in an attractive chignon and the décolleté of her dark blue, satin dress displayed an exquisite pair of shoulders and an alluring plunging neckline. In one hand she held a small dark handbag and carried a half filled glass of champagne. She looked his way, raised her eyebrows in surprise and slowly walked towards him.

'Hello, John,' she said, staring at him with the beguiling emerald green eyes her remembered so well. 'What a pleasant surprise seeing you again.'

'How . . . why are you here?' Hailey managed to say, regaining his composure. 'I thought . . .'

'You thought I was in America,' Annabel quickly interrupted.

'A bit like de ja' vu,' Hailey answered nervously. 'Remember how we met on board the *Illustrious?*'

'Of course, I do, John,' she said, taking a sip of her drink, 'how could I forget, but it seems so long ago.'

'Eight years and two months to be precise,' he replied. 'But I must say,' he added, staring at her, 'you haven't changed a bit, you're still as beautiful as ever.'

The sight of seeing Hailey again sent an unexpected surge of pleasure running through her, stirring up feelings that had laid dormant since their divorce. She did her best to conceal her pleasure at him remembering the passage of time so accurately by tenderly touching the dimple in his chin, and saying, 'And you're still as handsome as ever, especially with that healthy tan and little bit of grey at each temple.'

'But tell me,' he asked, quickly finishing his drink, 'what are you doing in Bahrain?'

'We're in the middle of a movie about the crusades,' she replied sipping her drink.

'Oh, yes,' Hailey said, as a steward refilled his glass with champagne, 'I read about it in *The Times,*' he paused and cautiously added, 'and about your affair with some actor.'

'Pure publicity,' she said, tossing her head back and laughing, 'the actor in question was one of the biggest homosexuals in Hollywood.'

Hailey was about to say something when they were abruptly interrupted by Vice Admiral Jones.

'Sorry to interrupt you and this lovely lady,' the Admiral said with sly smile. As he spoke his eyes lit up as he glanced admiringly down Annabel's cleavage. 'But you seem to be monopolising the most beautiful woman in the room.'

'I do beg your pardon, sir,' Hailey replied, 'may I present Miss Annabel Sutherland.'

'A great pleasure, Miss Sutherland,' the admiral said, shaking her hand, 'but there are several people dying to meet you. That is, if Commander Hailey can spare you,' he added with a mischievous grin.

'If you insist, sir,' Hailey answered dryly.

Annabel looked at Hailey and raised her eyebrows as if to say 'sorry'. She then turned to the admiral and tried her best to disguise her annoyance at having to leave Hailey, took hold of his arm and said, 'Righto, I'm all yours for a little while at least.' As they walked towards a group of official looking men and women, she glanced coyly over her left shoulder and gave Hailey a cheeky wink.

Dawlish's officers were aware that Hailey had been married to Annabel and had kept a discreet distance allowing them some privacy. However, as soon as Annabel and the admiral left Hailey, Parker-Smith and Dunlop arrived bubbling over with excitement.

'I do beg your pardon, sir,' Parker-Smith stuttered, 'but was that really Annabel Sutherland you were talking to?'

'And are they really making a film out here, sir,' Dunlop added anxiously.

'Yes, to both questions,' Hailey replied, smiling as he accepted a glass of champagne from a waiter. 'Now push off and chat up some of those girls. I believe they're actresses also.'

Hailey was joined by Noble, Somersby and Ashcroft.

'I bet seeing your ex was quite a shock, sir,' Noble remarked as he and the others watched Annabel doing her best to make small talk to a group of dignitaries.

'Indeed, it was,' Hailey answered downing his drink in one gulp.

'What time does all this finish, sir?' Noble asked, giving a bored sigh.

'I'm not sure,' Hailey replied. His eyes were glued to Annabel, who glanced occasionally across at him, with a 'come and rescue me' expression in her eyes.

Finally, half an hour later, Annabel, shook the hands of her admirers, signed a few autographs and re-joined Hailey.

'Whew!' she gasped, accepting a glass of champagne from a steward, 'I thought they'd never stop asking questions.'

'The price of fame,' Hailey replied, then added, 'look, let's get out of here.' With almost everyone in the room watching he took her elbow and guided her across the crowded room towards a large glass door.

'Don't tell me you're going to whisk me away into the desert?' She laughed finishing her drink and placing the empty glass on a nearby table.

'What a splendid idea,' he said, gently squeezing her arm.

The door opened onto a wide wrought iron balcony. In the foreground the lights of the American and British bases shone brightly, while further afield those from Manama lit up the sky.

For a few seconds they stood in silence, listening to the beat of their hearts and feeling the warm breeze gently caress their faces. The tick-tacky sound of crickets along with the exotic aroma of jasmine and spices filled the air.

'It so lovely and peaceful,' Annabel said, taking hold of Hailey's hand and staring up at a panoply of glittering stars surrounded by a dazzling bright crescent moon. 'No matter how many times you see the sky at night, it still moves you.'

'It looks even more beautiful at sea,' Hailey replied, feeling the warmth of her hand and smelling the intoxicating fragrance of Chanel No.5.

Suddenly he turned and taking her into his arms, looked deeply into her eyes and, feeling his heart pounding in his chest, said, 'You know, Annabel, I've never stopped loving you, even . . .'

'Don't say anything else, darling,' she muttered, pulling him close, 'just kiss me.'

It was a long lingering, sensual kiss full of pent- up passion that left them breathless.

'What happened to us, John?' she gasped, nuzzling her head against his chest. 'Where did it all go wrong?'

'The navy, your ambition,' he replied, feeling the softness of her breasts through the smoothness of her dress against his chest, 'a combination of both.'

'Yes, I suppose you're right.' She replied wearily, then looking longingly into his eyes, added, 'how long will you be here?'

'We sail in five days on escort duty then we return to Bahrain,' he replied, noticing how the moonlight caught her eyes making them shine like silver, 'After that we return to Bahrain. What about you?'

'We've a few more shoots to complete,' she answered, feeling the comforting warmth of his arms around her, 'then back to Hollywood for some voice-overs and editing.'

'And another picture, I suppose,' he added with more than a hint of reticence.

'No,' she answered, moving slightly away from him, 'I'm tired of Tinsel Town, with all its conniving and falsehoods,' she paused and took a deep breath as if purging herself of her past. 'Kevin Spacey has offered me a lead part in *The Taming of the Shrew* and as I'll soon be out of contract with Warners' I'm going to accept. Rehearsals start next month. It's at the Old Vic, I think I might have told you about it, do you remember?'

'How could I forget,' Hailey answered with a faint smile. 'De ja' Vu, again, eh?' Just then the door opened and one of the actors came onto the balcony.

'Our coach as arrived, Anna,' his pale blue eyes were slightly bloodshot and his speech was slurred. 'We leave in five minutes,' then with a cheeky wink, he closed the door and left.

Annabel gave a reluctant sigh. 'Looks like I'll have to go, John,' she said holding him closes.

'I expect we'll be going soon also,' Hailey replied. 'Can I contact you when we return?'

'Of course, John,' she answered, 'we're staying at the Bahrain Ritz.' She opened her handbag and took out a notebook and biro. 'Here,' she added, after writing on a piece of paper and tearing it out, 'this is my mobile number. Call me either before or when you return.'

'Thank you, I'll do that,' Hailey answered, folding the paper and placing it his inside pocket.

For a few seconds they stared into each other's eyes and relived that sickening feeling of past good-byes. Then, they kissed with such passion they almost bruised their lips. They parted and without speaking Annabel turned, opened the door and was gone.

Hailey stood and stared at the glass panels of the closed door, wondering if he had imagined the events of the past few hours. However, the lingering aroma of Annabel's perfume and the feel of her warm lips on his told him he was wrong. He re-joined the gathering, many of whom were shaking the admiral's hand and saying their goodbyes.

Noble and the other officers had watched as Annabel opened the balcony door and hurried after her retinue who were leaving.

'We thought you'd got lost, sir,' Noble said doing his best to hide a smile.

Ignoring Noble's sarcastic comment, he walked to the admiral. 'On behalf of my officers and myself, sir,' he said shaking the admiral's hand, 'thank you for a very enjoyable evening.'

'Not at all, old boy, I'm sure you personally enjoyed yourself,' the admiral replied with an impish twinkle in his eyes.

Five minutes later Hailey and the others were on their way back to the ship.

CHAPTER FORTY-TWO

During the following four days, the crew were busy refuelling and replenishing stores and ammunition, including the two Harpoon missies used to destroy the Al Qaeda mother ship. For those ratings wishing to go to Manama, the base provided coaches leaving the main gate each evening at 1700 into the centre of the city, and picking them on the hour up to 2300. However, most of the crew, especially the senior ratings who had been to Bahrain before, used the Britannia Club in the naval base.

On Monday, two days before *Dawlish* was due to sail, Diana asked Ashir to take her into Manama. 'Just to see what it's like' she pleaded, 'and as you speak the language, I won't get lost will I?' she added with a cheeky grin.'

The time was 1200, secure had just been piped and they were now off duty until 0800 the next day. 'All right,' Ashir replied, and in case she might suggest staying overnight at some hotel, he quickly thought up a lie and added, 'but I must be back by twenty-one hundred as my parents are phoning me.'

Diana gave him a suspicious look but didn't reply.

Ashir and Diana left the ship at 1630 along with Shady Lane, Bud Abbot, Jilly Howard, Lottie Jones and several ratings. Ten minutes later after making their way along the jetty and through the naval base they reached the main gate and boarded the coach.

The journey to the city took twenty minutes. As usual darkness suddenly descended, and Manama with its modern buildings rubbing lying incongruously next to narrow winding streets and souks, was now lit up by a neon and electric lighting.

The coach stopped outside the Bahrain Hilton, a white skyscraper edifice, not far away from a tall imposing minaret and mosque.

The driver reminded everyone of the pick-up times. 'And if you miss the last one, you'll have to take a taxi back to the base.'

'I hope you've got plenty of cash on you,' Lottie said, taking hold of Shady's arm, 'you never know, we might miss the last coach, eh Jilly?'

'That wouldn't surprise me in the least,' Jilly grinned, grasping Bud Abbott's hand. 'I hope the beds here are better than the ones in Southsea.'

'Come on, let's go into the hotel and have a drink,' Shady said. 'Are you two coming?' he added looking expectantly at Diana and Ashir.

'No, you lot go on ahead, we're going to have a look around,' Diana replied, with more than a hint of jealousy, 'see you lot tomorrow.'

For the next hour and a half Diana and Ashir cautiously made their way through the narrow souks. The air was heavy with the aromatic aroma of exotic spices and a hint of hashish. Black bearded Arabs, wearing turbans, long white shirts and baggy white clothes, tried to sell them everything from vicious-looking snakes to tiny gaggling monkeys. Eventually they arrived at a large market with stalls packed with multi-coloured rugs, cushions and lush Persian carpets.

Diana stopped near a stall selling a variety of eastern garments. A narrow-shouldered Arab with a face like a shrivelled walnut sat outside rocking lazily and smoking a hookah, (a water-pipe with a smoke chamber and a bowl and hose.)

'Look at those gorgeous caftans, Ash,' Diana cried, grabbing hold of Ashir's arm. 'I'm sure my mum would love one of them. I could keep it until we get home. The expression on her face when she sees it would be priceless.'

For the first time since he joined the ship, Ashir felt a pang of consciousness. The realisation that when he was able to carry out Allah's wishes, she would never see her mother made him feel strangely sad.

'Then let me buy one for her,' Ashir said smiling weakly.

The caftan she chose was made of azure blue silk with long loose sleeves. The back, embroidered in gold metal thread, showed dragons breathing yellow flames surrounded by sparkling crescent moons and stars.

After ten minutes of haggling, Ashir beat the price down from forty dinars to twenty five.

'You drive a hard bargain, effendi,' cried the Arab, displaying a row of uneven tobacco-stained teeth, 'I am a poor man with five children and a nagging wife, but may Allah grant you and your woman a long life and many healthy boys.' He carefully folded the caftan into four small, neat sections and using a sheet of fine scented red paper wrapped it into a neat parcel and tied it in fancy a bow with gold tape. Ashir thanked him and after the customary salutations, gave him an extra five dinars.

'This will probably become a family heirloom,' Diana said, carefully placing the parcel in her handbag, and giving Ashir a hug.

Twenty minutes later they arrived back to the hotel and caught the 2000 coach to the base.

CHAPTER FORTY-THREE

At precisely 0600, on Wednesday 11 September, *Dawlish* slipped her moorings and slowly moved away from the jetty. A cold morning wind blew down river and in the east the sun, rising above the horizon, turned the heavens into a blaze of scarlet and yellow.

As *Dawlish* slowly cruised out of the harbour, Hailey, who was on the bridge sitting in his customary chair, clasped his hands around a hot mug of coffee. Like Noble and those on duty, he wore his blue jacket over his tropical whites.

'Special sea duty men fall out, Number One,' he said, tucking his white muffler around his neck. 'Set the lever at fifteen and increase revolutions one third, please, Number One.'

Noble acknowledged the order and gave a cursory nod to Forbes sitting at the console.

In matter of seconds, *Dawlish*'s two Rolls-Royce Spey engines sprang into action and soon the tall minarets and buildings dominating Manama's skyline gradually faded away in the distance. By 0800 *Dawlish* was twenty miles outside the harbour.

A glance at his small radar screen showed three blips moving slowly south. Hailey leant forward and unhooked the telephone to the Ops Room. Tug Wilson, who was now the ship's PWO, immediately confirmed Hailey's sighting.

'I expect that'll be our convoy,' Hailey remarked, glancing hopefully at Noble, 'alter lever to one, one, zero. We should be off the southern tip of Bahrain in half an hour.'

Shortly before 0900, Hailey and those on duty could see the small convoy half a mile away on the ship's starboard quarter. Even at that distance, they noticed all three vessels were low in the water.

'The big one in the van is the French cargo vessel carrying nuclear waste,' said Hailey, peering through his binoculars. 'The other two are Shell oil tankers probably bound for Tranmere Oil terminal in Birkenhead.'

'Signal the Frenchie, Number One,' said Hailey, 'say, "*Royal Navy frigate Dawlish, Commander John Hailey. Good to see you. Will take station fifty yards on your port quarter*". 'Set the lever at 30,' he added taking a deep gulp of his drink.

Despite their Plimsoll lines being hardly visible, the three merchant ships towered over *Dawlish*. The rusty red hulls of the tankers with their high bridges situated aft and the Shell logos on their white funnels were in sharp contrast to the French vessel's squat funnel and bridge amidships, painted in a dismal black.

'Reply from the French, sir,' said Noble, holding a signal sheet, "*Captain Le Brun. Fleur de Normandy. Bonjour Commander, hope we have a have a quiet voyage*". '

'So do I,' said Hailey dryly, finishing his drink and placing it on the small ledge in front of the console.

In the girls' mess they were enjoying a morning stand easy mug of tea. 'What was the hotel like in Bahrain, Lot?' Diana asked Lottie, a saucy twinkle in her eyes.

'Very expensive,' Lottie replied, sipping her drink. 'It was a good job Shady had his credit card with him or we'd have been thrown out.'

'A pity you and Ash didn't stay,' chimed in Jilly Howard, 'are you sure he's not, err . . . '

'No he isn't,' Diana answered angrily. 'Anyway, he bought me a gorgeous caftan for my mum, so shut up.'

In the seamen's mess, Ashir was sitting sipping his tea, doing his best to ignore Shady Lane and Bud Abbott telling his messmates a detailed description of their run ashore in Manama. Ashir was more concerned with completing his mission and was becoming increasingly despondent at his failure to do so. Now, he told himself, was a perfect time. They were at sea with a full complement. Finishing his drink, he offered a silent prayer to Allah asking for help.

Hailey was sat in his cabin doing his best to write up the ship's log. But every time he tried to do so, Annabel's lovely emerald eyes smiled at him. With a nostalgic sigh he put down his pen and rang for a coffee.

Three days later, the small convoy doing a steady ten knots was fifteen miles from the Strait of Hormuz. The midday temperature was a blistering thirty-eight degrees Fahrenheit, hot enough, according to some old hands, to fry eggs on the fight deck. And high above, in a cloudless blue sky the sun turned the placid sea into specs of sparkling diamonds.

Hailey had shared the middle watch with Noble and was now in his cabin, lying on a settee having a quiet doze. On the bridge, O'Grady occupied the captain's chair. He and Jack Whitton and Bud Abbott were captivated by the antics of pods of dolphins a few yards on the ship's port side, their shiny grey bodies arcing in and out of the sea before disappearing, only to return again some distance away.

'They always seem to be smiling at you, don't they, PO?' Bud asked Whitton, staring out of a window.

'Maybe they know something we don't,' Whitton replied warily.

In the darkened Ops Room, everything was quiet except for the gentle hub of the air conditioning and the occasional comment from weapons electrical operators and radar personnel. Spud Murphy was sat watching his own radar screen in a small recess set apart from the others. He gave a tired yawn and was about to look away when suddenly he saw three tiny black dots appear on his screen. Ashir and Diana also reported seeing them.

'They're about three hundred miles away on our starboard beam, sir,' Diana yelled.

'Yes, I can see that,' Murphy replied. 'I'd better inform the captain.' He then unhooked the telephone connected to Hailey's cabin.

Hailey's tired voice answered. Stifling a yawn, he listened to Murphy's report. 'Three you say,' he said pushing himself up from the settee.

'Affirmative, sir' Murphy replied, 'and they seem to be coming in low as if they're trying to avoid the radar.'

'Try to contact them and ask for identification,' Hailey said, 'and ask the First Lieutenant to join me on the bridge.'

Hailey and Noble arrived on the bridge in time to overhear the stern voice of Pincher Martin, using the bridge radio, saying, '*Aircraft approaching, this is Royal Navy frigate Dawlish, please identify yourself.*'

After repeating the request several times, a husky voice speaking English came over the line shouting excitedly, "*Allah Akbar, God is Great!*" Then the radio went dead.

The words on the radio sent a shiver of fear running through Hailey.

'Great Scott, Number One,' Hailey cried, looking aghast at Noble, 'pipe, Assume Weapons State Monty. These blighters could be the three Mirage fighters stolen from that Base in Libya. You'd better inform Bahrain and *Coral Sea,* telling them we expect to be attacked by them. Take over,' he added sternly, 'I'm going to the Ops Room.'

'Very good, sir,' Noble replied, and nodded to Pincher Martin who immediately followed Hailey's instructions. At the same time, Noble unhooked the ship's tannoy. 'D'you hear there.' Considering the severity of the situation, his voice was remarkable calm and clear, 'This is the first lieutenant speaking. Assume Weapon's State Monty. Three unidentified aircraft are approaching some three hundred miles on our starboard beam. Be prepared for any emergency. Keep calm. I will keep you informed. That is all.'

Noble's words sent an unexpected sense of fear and anxiety running through the minds of the crew. This was quickly overtaken by well-drilled reactive movements as each man and woman grabbed their battle bags and anti-flash gear. In less than five minutes everyone was closed up at their respective stations.

'Bugger me,' muttered Shady Lane, as he and Bud Abbott arrived in the gun bay, 'this is the second time we've closed up for earnest.'

'Yer right there, mate,' Bud replied, breathing heavily, 'after blowing up those Al Qaeda skips and that mother ship, I thought that'd be the end of it.'

'I don't mind being closed up in this fuckin' gun by,' added Dutch Holland, 'it's not knowing what's happening outside that pisses me off.'

This was a sentiment shared by officers and ratings waiting anxiously at their positions throughout the ship.

'How far away are the 'planes, Tug? ' Hailey asked Wilson as he entered the Ops Room.

'Just over a hundred and fifty miles, sir,' Wilson replied, staring at his radar screen.

'Better arm the Sea Wolfs and Vickers,' Hailey said, nervously rubbing his chin, 'that gives us about twenty minutes. If they are those Al Qaeda fighters, I expect they'll be trying to sink one of the ships and block the Straight.'

'The Sea Wolfs only have an effective range of ten kilometres, sir,' Wilson replied cautiously.

'Yes, I know,' Hailey answered, frowning, 'that's the same as the Exocet missies they're armed with, so we'll use the Vickers as soon as you've locked onto them.'

'But if they've come from Syria, sir,' Wilson replied warily, 'won't they run out of fuel for a return trip?'

'Yes, which means only one thing,' Hailey replied, feeling his stomach tighten, 'they don't intend doing so.'

'*My God, sir!*' Wilson exclaimed, '*you mean they're suicide . . .*'

Hailey quickly cut him off. 'Keep your voice down. I don't want to spread undue concern around the ship.'

However, Spud Murphy, Ashir and Diana had already overheard Wilson. Diana loosened her headphone and gently touched Ashir's hand.

'Ash,' she said quietly, 'if anything happens to me, remember, I love you.'

Ashir didn't reply. Instead he squeezed her hand and thought, praise be to Allah, with luck the fighters will do the job for me and I may not have to use the Trysin after all.

'Ten miles and closing rapidly,' Wilson said to Hailey, who was standing watching the radar screen. 'The Vickers are armed and locked onto one of them.'

Hoping the pilots manning the planes might not be used to combat, Hailey decided to take a gamble. If he fired first it might force them take evasive action thus making it difficult for the pilots to compute their Exocets accurately.

'Thank you, Tug,' Hailey answered calmly. 'Fire two Sea Wolfs and open up with the Vickers. With luck we'll take out one of them.'

The shuddering *whoosh* of the Sea Wolfs leaving their silos could be felt throughout then ship along with the *thud, thud, thud,* of the Vickers firing the 4.5 armour piercing shells.

What happened next seemed like an age, but took a mere two minutes.

Noble and the others watched anxiously as two narrow jets of grey smoke zoomed upwards from their silos situated just below the bridge. At the same time a belch of yellow flame emanated from one of the planes as the pilot fired an Exocet missile. With fear etched in their eyes, everyone watched as the missile streaked towards the ship. Then, to their utter relief it suddenly lost height and plunged into the sea some fifty yards away, sending up an explosive mass of white water and bits of black debris. At the same time a bright orange flash lit up the sky as a Sea Wolf along with fire from the Vickers completely demolished on of the planes.

However, Hailey's gamble had not completely paid off. He watched the radar screen and saw the remaining two planes peel off and swoop at the convoy from different directions in an effort to evade the Sea Wolfs and shells. He hurried up to the bridge in time to see one of them bank and level out before firing an Exocet missile at the French cargo ship. It then rose like an eagle into the sky. A deafening explosion quickly followed as a huge umbrella of water and spray hung in the air blanking out part of the for'd section of the French vessel. Then, like a vaporous shroud it gradually collapsed into the sea in a seething mass of frothy bubbles.

'Her bows have caved in but she's still making good headway,' O'Grady cried excitedly.

'Signal her and ask if she need help,' Hailey ordered.

A minute later a reply came. *'Merci, captain, but no serious damage. Can continue unaided.'*

By this time the two fighters had joined forces and began to dive towards *Dawlish.*

'Jesus Christ, sir,' yelled O'Grady, *'they're coming for us!'*

At that moment Wilson's strident voice came over the Ops Room intercom.

'Aircraft approaching rapidly high on the port quarter.'

Everyone instinctively looked up to their left and saw four jet aircraft, their sleek silver bodies glinting in in the sun. In an instant all four fighters dived on the enemy planes, each firing rockets from the underside of their wings.

'By God, they're Americans,' cried Hailey, his binoculars picking out the gold star insignia on their fuselage and wings.'

'They must be from the *Coral Sea,* sir,' yelled Noble.

The attack by the American fighters was over in seconds. Suddenly the two Al Qaeda planes exploded in balls of dazzling yellow flames and black smoke as the rockets hit home. With the exception of Hailey who, with relief etched on his face, slumped into his chair, everyone let out a loud cheer. Then, quickly turning their heads they watched as the American jets swooped down over the convoy before soaring upwards and disappearing over the horizon.

In the Ops Room, Diana ignored the 'no touch' rule and threw her arms around Ashir.

'Thank God for that, eh, Ash? She cried and gave him a wet, warm kiss on his cheek.

'Yes, wasn't it,' Ashir replied weakly, doing his best to disguise his disappointment.

Hailey grinned at Noble and dabbing his sweaty brow with a handkerchief, said, 'That was too close for comfort. Send a signal to the captain of *Coral Sea* and say, "thank God for the cavalry. That's another bottle of Scotch I owe you".' Then, using the tannoy, he calmly told the ship's company to revert to Cruising Station and informed them what had happened, adding, 'Thank heavens it's all over and everyone's safe.'

But he spoke too soon.

CHAPTER FORTY-FOUR

During the night of Monday 16 September, *Dawlish* and the small convoy passed through the Strait of Hormuz into the Gulf of Oman. As the sun rose its rays cast a deep bronze patina over the calm undulating sea. By 0600, as dawn suddenly broke through the dimness of the night. Some ten miles away on the port beam the dark, jagged peaks of Iran jutted through the early morning mist, then, as if someone worked the shutter of a camera, the pale grey sky changed dramatically into a panoply of dazzling blue.

'Looks like another scorcher, sir,' Whitton casually remarked to Gooding who was sitting, hunched up, in the captain's chair.

'Yes, I suppose it will be,' Gooding lazily replied, stifling a yawn, 'another bloody sweltering hot day.'

'When do we meet the Yanks, sir?' asked Mickey Finn who was sat at the console, a bored expression on his round, heavily tanned features.

'Tomorrow about zero seven hundred, all being well,' Gooding replied. With a tired sigh, he eased himself out of the chair and went into the small chart room. 'I'd better check our position,' he said, 'the captain is bound to ask for that and our speed when he comes up after breakfast.'

Sure enough at 0730 Hailey arrived on the bridge followed by Noble and after a cheery 'good morning,' glanced at Gooding, and asked, 'what's our position and speed, Pilot?'

'Longitude fifty one degrees south, latitude thirty, sir. Speed ten knots,' Gooding replied, giving
Whitton a quick, 'I told you so' wink.'

'Thank you, Pilot,' Hailey answered, easing himself into his chair and carefully watching the three merchant vessels moving gently through the calm sea a hundred yards on *Dawlish'* s port bow. 'Any sign of our American cousins?'

'No, sir,' Gooding replied, 'not as yet.'

Shortly before 0800, Morris relieved Gooding, and Harry Lyme took over the watch from Whitton.

'You'd better get to the mess before the gannets eat all the train smash, Mickey,' said Shady Lane, relieving Finn at the console. (Train smash was a colloquial term for tinned tomatoes and fried eggs.)

Ashir and Diana were not on duty until 1200. They and a few ratings were on the starboard side of the flight deck, holding the guard rail, admiring a flock of flying fish skimming in and out of the crystal clear waters like energetic black spiders.

Diana turned and looked up at Ashir's well-defined dark profile. 'Ash,' she said pensively, 'when we get back to the UK, would you like to meet my mum and dad?'

Her question took Ashir by surprise, and for a moment he didn't know what to say. 'But . . . but you told me they lived in Cardiff,' he replied, avoiding her eyes.

'They do, silly,' Diana answered, laughing slightly, 'but I expect they'll be on the wharf along with the other parents when we dock in Pompey.'

Suddenly, Ashir felt a familiar pang of conscience run through him. Little did she realise that she and everyone else on board *Dawlish* would never see home again as he was determined to do Allah's bidding before the ship returned to Bahrain.

'Oh, all right, if you insist,' he replied, smiling weakly.

'You've never told me anything about your mum and dad,' Diana said, allowing her hand to gently brush against his. 'What are they like?'

Not knowing quite how to respond to her question, Ashir took a deep breath and answered, 'they're . . . very kind. Anyway' he quickly added, 'I'd better go below, I've err, got a few things that need ironing before I go on watch.'

'You could always give them to me,' she replied, giving him a mischievous grin. 'I'm sure the girls would love to see your sexy Y fronts.'

Except for a pair of large skips with outboard motors sailing a few hundred yards behind the convoy, the sea was devoid of any shipping.

'That's odd,' Hailey remarked, studying the two small craft, 'they have their nets out, but Arabs don't fish this far from land. Give 'em a wave and let's see what happens.'

Lyme and Morris did as Hailey ordered. .

'No response, sir'' said Morris.

'Yes, I can see that,' Hailey muttered.

'And now they're pulling in their nets,' Lyme added.

'Strange,' Hailey muttered pensively, 'these people know these waters better than we do, so they must realise where they are.' It was then he remembered that Al Qaeda laid their flat mines from such vessels.

'They're hurrying away, sir,' Lyme reported.

'Hmm . . . yes,' Hailey replied, 'better let them go. If we investigated every dhow or skip we met, we'd be late meeting the Americans.'

Just before 0700 the next morning, Wilson in the Ops Room reported seeing two black dots, one large the other small on his radar screen.

'They're about a hundred miles on our starboard bow, sir,' he said, 'one of them must be the carrier.'

'Thank you, Tug,' Hailey replied, 'I've also picked them up on the bridge radar.'

By 0930, the long grey superstructure of the USS *Coral Sea* and the much smaller destroyer, USS *Spruance,* were five miles away.

'Exactly where they should be, sir,' Gooding confirmed after consulting his chart.

'Send a signal to the carrier, Number One, say, "*glad to see you. When do you wish to take over the convoy?*".'

"*Whenever it is convenient and don't forget the whiskey,"* came the reply.

An hour later the aircraft carrier with its massive flat deck, squat shaped island and small funnel was a hundred yards away. By comparison, the destroyer, looking like a dinky toy, lay some distance in the rear.

Hailey ordered Harry Tate, to lower a rigid inflatable and a jury sail to be rigged. (A jury sail is a makeshift sail made from a small mast and a piece of canvas.) Manned by Able Seaman Kennedy and a crew if two, they manoeuvred the inflatable alongside the carrier. A line was lowered from the carriers deck to which was secured a large wooden box. With a friendly wave, Kennedy undid the box, and attached a small bag containing the whiskey. With a final wave he jerked on the line and watched as it was hauled on board the carrier. Twenty minutes later Kennedy and his crew returned with the box containing a large carton of strawberry ice cream and several DVDs, most of which were of a risky nature.

"Thank you for the scotch," came a signal from the captain of the carrier," *we'll take over the convoy. Good luck and a safe trip back to Bahrain.".'*

Hailey swapped goodwill messages with the three merchantmen, then, smiling broadly, he watched as the convoy and their escorts gradually moved away.

CHAPTER FORTY-FIVE

Hailey was in his cabin, sitting at his desk writing up the ship's log when the explosion occurred. The time was 1300. Suddenly, he was thrown backwards, his head struck the carpeted deck and for a few seconds he was too dazed to move. Gradually, he regained his senses and felt the deck had slanted forward. His stout oaken chair was lying on its side and the contents of his desk top were strewn on the deck along with his computer and printer. The door of his wine cabinet had burst open. Broken glasses plus an assortment of bottles of alcohol were strewn everywhere. Books and folders had fallen from the shelves, and even the pair of heavy leather armchairs and settee lay awkwardly on the carpet.

Feeling shaken, Hailey grasped the edge of his desk and staggered to his feet.

'*Good God in heaven!*' He exploded, staring unbelievably at the chaotic mess, '*what on earth was that?*'

The cabin door opened and in came Noble. His face was pale and his eyes looked glazed with shock.

'I . . . I think we've struck a mine or something, sir,' he gasped, holding onto the side of the bulkhead, 'and we're shipping water up fo'rd.'

Hailey didn't answer. His first concern was the safety of the men and the ship. He pushed his way past Noble and despite the awkward cant of the deck managed to make his way to the bridge.

The sight that met his eyes made him gasp with horror.

The ship had lost way and was tilted slightly forwards. The jackstay had broken in two and lay at an acute angle. The fo'c'sle deck was flooded and the guard rails a tangled mess. The anchor capstan was barely visible and seawater was lapping around the base of the Vickers gun and Sea Wolf missile silos.

'Stop both engines, Number One,' snapped Hailey, 'then go and check for casualties and damage.' Glancing guardedly at Gooding, he added, 'Send urgent signals to Bahrain and *Coral Sea,* give our position and say, "*have suffered a severe explosion. Badly damaged. Have stopped. Request urgent assistance.*" Feeling his hand tremble slightly, Hailey unhooked the ship's tannoy.

'This is the captain speaking,' he said, doing his best to control his nerves, 'hands to Emergency stations. The ship has hit something. At the moment I'm not sure what it is, but we are taking in water. Keep calm, wear your life belts, take your ID cards mobile phones and muster in the wardroom. I'll keep you informed,' and replaced the handset.

A few minutes later Pincher Martin phoned the bridge.

'Message from captain of *Coral Sea,* sir, it reads, "*Spruance detached from convoy. Coming full speed. ETA 1900. Good luck.*".'

(The lifejackets are contained in a small pouch in a belt worn around the waist. When required the lifejacket which is attached to the belt is removed and placed around the neck and inflated manually blowing it up. The result is yellow horse-shoe shape similar to the Mae West. Deflation can be quickly obtained opening a small valve.)

The explosion had sent shock waves throughout the ship. The main lights dimmed and the air conditioning stopped as did the electrical supply which automatically closed all screen door and hatchways.

On the bridge, Noble, Gooding and Whitton lost their balance and were thrown on the deck.

The seamen's mess looked like a jumble sale. Lockers had been flung open, scattering clothing and personal belongings everywhere. Large aluminium tea urns, jugs, mugs plus DVDs and broken crockery added to the chaos.

'*Christ al mighty!*' yelled Shady Lane, as he hit the deck, '*what the fuck hit us?*'

'I'm buggered if I know, cried Bud Abbott, who, along with Dutch Holland and Pete Price had been sitting at a table playing cards, and were now a huddled heap on the deck. 'But whatever it was,' he gasped looking in disgust at his cards scattered around the deck, 'it's ruined my hand. For the first time this afternoon I had a full house.'

The marines in the next mess reacted calmly to the sudden chaotic state they found themselves in. Some were sitting around watching a re- run of *Match of the Day,* others were lying on their bunk reading or dozing.

'Come on, lads,' Cassidy ordered, leaping up from his bunk, 'Christ knows what has happened, but everyone get dressed and move yourselves.'

The senior ratings mess was also a wreck. Digger Barnes had been evicted from his chair and lay dazed next to Jock Forbes. Like a few others, they wore startled expressions wondering what had happened.

'Bloody hell, Jock,' Digger said, pushing himself up, 'we'd better get up top and see what's going on.'

The reaction of the stokers in the engine and generator rooms, wasn't so sanguine. Several of them, including Bungy Williams, had slipped on the metal grating but were relatively unhurt.

'Everyone out!' Shouted Vellacott, who was clinging hold of a stanchion, 'and be quick about it.'

'Any idea what's happened, sir?' Bungy gasped, helping a stoker to his feet.

'Don't worry about that now, Chief,' cautioned Vellacott, 'just get the men up top as soon as possible.'

The behaviour of the girls was a mixture of frenzied screaming and shock. Some were still in uniform. Others were clad in T- shirts sweaters and shorts. Magazines, DVDs and books were spread over the carpeted deck along with several chairs. Luckily, the table and settee surrounding the bulkhead were secured to the deck. It took Sadie Thompson a good few minutes to calm them down, during which time Hailey's voice came over the tannoy.

'Do you think we're sinking, PO?' Lottie Jones cried anxiously. Like the other girls she had an expression panic in her eyes and her tanned face looked drawn with worry.

'Of course not,' Sadie replied reassuringly, 'make sure you wear trousers and a jersey. Now shut up, put on your life jackets and do what the captain has said and keep calm.'

In the sickbay the doors and drawers of the medical cabinet were flung open. Surgical instruments, kidney dishes of varying sizes, books and dressing littered the deck. Susan Hughes had fallen against the metal frame of a cot and bruised the side of her face. Dixie Dean, who was sitting at his desk, toppled sideways but managed to prevent the computer and printer from falling on the deck. A few seconds after the explosion Smyth arrived breathless and sweating.

'Bloody hell, sir!' She cried hysterically, while holding the left side of her face, 'what do you think caused that?'

'I'm not sure,' Smyth replied, shaking his head, 'maybe a missile detonated. Anyway, what have you done to your face?'

'Only a slight bump, sir,' Susan replied, 'nothing to worry about.'

'Come on,' said Dixie, standing up, 'we'd better leave this, I expect we'll be needed soon.'

In the ship's office, Liz Hall and Rogers, were busy picking up buff coloured folders, heavy, leather-bound books and files. The computer, printer and lap-top lay at various angles on the deck.

'Please make sure the pay discs are safe,' Rogers said, giving Liz a worried look, 'just in case . . .'

Things were not much better in the Ops Room. Murphy and Wilson had been thrown against the bulkhead but were unhurt. The radar screens remained in position but the weapons electrical systems were dead. Many of the chairs had been thrown onto the deck along with their occupants, including Diana and Ashir.

'Are you all right, Di?' asked Ashir, who was sprawled on the deck next to Diana.

'Yes, thanks,' Diana replied, rubbing her backside, 'only a bruised bum. How about you?'

'No bones broken,' he replied, as he stood up and helped Diana to her feet.

She looked up at Ashir, and with fear etched in her eyes, she said, 'promise me you'll look after me, Ash.'

'Of course I will,' Ashir replied with a comforting smile, 'now stop worrying, you'll be all right.'

'Thanks, Ash,' Diana answered, tenderly squeezing his arm, 'and no matter what happens, remember I love you.'

Meanwhile, on the bridge, Hailey was sat in his chair, anxiously biting his lip while staring out of a window. The temperature had risen and the sky was now a deep, eye-smarting blue.

By now, the fo'c'sle and capstan were almost underwater and the cant of the deck steeper. Noble arrived accompanied by Harry Tate and Bogey Knight. Their faces were wet with sweat and wore life jackets over their tropical whites.

'Nobody's hurt, sir,' gasped Noble, 'but the sonar housing is a complete write off, the beer and , spirit room and sports locker plus the for'd air treatment rooms are flooded.'

'Including the POs' cabins,' added Bogey Knight, 'as well as the Ops Room annex and the for'd fuel tanks.'

'The damage control parties are doing their best to shore up the bulkheads of the auxiliary machine space,' said the Harry Tate, 'but I can't guarantee how long they will hold.'

'All hands are mustered and correct in the wardroom, sir,' said Bogey Knight, 'and if I may say they all look rather anxious, to say the least.'

At that moment Vellacott arrived. His white overalls were streaked with oil, and lines of sweat trickled down the sides of his face.

'If the water reaches the generator and forward auxiliary machine rooms, sir,' he gasped, 'the ship could be in serious trouble.'

Hailey immediately felt the blood drain from his face. 'You mean she could go down?'

'I'm afraid so, sir,' Vellacott answered, a pained expression in his eyes.

The intercom suddenly sounded. Noble unhooked and answered it. After a slight pause, he stared nervously at Hailey and said. 'That was PO Miller, sir, he says the water has burst through into the for'd machine space.'

Noble's words sent an icy chill running through him. Suddenly, Hailey was faced with the most momentous decision of his life. Hailey turned away from Vellacott and for a few seconds stared, tight-lipped out of a window, deep in thought. Without moving his head, he took a deep breath and in a sombre voice, said. 'How long do you think it'll take for the ship to go down, Dicky?'

Vellacott gave a nervous cough, then replied, 'in my opinion, sir, if the two gas turbine rooms become completely flooded this would be enough to increase the ship's angle of tilt.' He paused momentarily, then went on, 'I would say about forty-five minutes.'

'Good grief,' Hailey gasped, glancing at his wristwatch, 'it's nearly fourteen thirty. The *Spruance* won't be here for another four hours. That doesn't give us much time.' Feeling his heart pounding like an express train, he realised he was about to give the order every ship's captain from time immemorial dreaded.

CHAPTER FORTY-FIVE

The tension in the wardroom was palpable. Many personnel glanced nervously at one another and spoke in hushed, worried tones. Suddenly, the conversations abruptly ceased as Hailey's familiar voice came over the tannoy. The time was 1405.

'This is the captain speaking,' he paused briefly, doing his best to control his nerves, 'I regret to inform you that the ship is in imminent danger. I therefore must ask you to report to your abandon ship stations. The American destroyer *Spruance* should be here in about four hours to rescue us. Make sure your life jackets are inflated. When you arrive in Bahrain you will be kitted out and sent to the UK. In Portsmouth you will reimbursed for loss of gear and sent on leave. Good luck.' he paused momentarily, then added, 'Would Lieutenant Somersby and Commander Ashcroft come to the bridge immediately.'

A minute or so later Somersby and Ashcroft arrived. Their deeply tanned faces wore worried expressions and dark sweat stains showed under the armpits of their tropical shirts.

'I'll come straight to the point, gentlemen,' Hailey said sternly. 'I'm sorry to say the ship is too unstable to launch the helo, all heavy weapons are to be left behind as space will be at a premium on board the life rafts and inflatables. Understood?'

'Yes, sir,' Somersby replied, tetchily, 'but they won't like it. They view their L85A assault rifles as an extension of themselves and have used them in action during two tours of Afghanistan.'

'Sorry, old boy,' Hailey answered dryly, 'but there it is.'

'Could we ditch the chopper over board, sir,' asked Ashcroft. 'It would lighten the ship somewhat.'

'Sorry, Jerry,' Hailey replied tersely, 'it would be too dangerous. Please carry on.' He then looked gravely at Noble, and went on, 'make sure there's a seaman in every group that leaves the ship to rig up a jury sail in the life boats. And lower the accommodation ladder on the starboard side for the girls and anyone else to use.' (An accommodation ladder is a portable flight of stairs with rope guard rails, that can be lowered down the ship's side.)

'Very good, sir,' Noble replied. Then, using his hand phone, passed the order to Harry Tate, who along with Jack Whitton, was checking the accommodation ladder.

The ship was now stationary and was rolling awkwardly. Under the watchful eyes of Bogey Knight and Digger Barnes, guard rails had been lowered and scrambling nets and Jacob's ladders placed over the ship's sides. Whitton plus several ratings then loosened the tags on the pods of two port and starboard life rafts. This allowed them to be easily launched and secured alongside the ship by a strong nylon rope to prevent them drifting away. Each raft could hold fifteen personnel and contained a first- aid kit, canisters of water, a Very pistol and six rocket cartridges.

Meanwhile, Dusty Miller and Harry Tate, were supervising the lowering of the two large, rigid inflatables one of which was situated on either side of the funnel. Each of these could accommodate thirty- four men and women as well as a large amount of emergency stores and equipment. The life rafts and inflatables had facilities to enable jury sails to be rigged. With the help of the strong, prevailing westerly wind, these would take them safely away from the suction that would be caused when the ship sank.

With the exception of the marines, the only time the crew had practised using ladders and scrambling nets was during basic training which, for many, was a long time ago.

The strident tones of Noble's voice suddenly came over the tannoy. 'Be careful climbing down the Jacob's ladders and the scrambling nets,' he warned, 'wait for each upward roll of the ship before climbing into your life rafts. When the rafts and inflatables have left the ship try to pass a heaving line to each one and keep close together. This will prevent them from being scattered all over the sea and make rescue easier. Be careful and you'll all be safe. Godspeed.'

The time by his wristwatch read 1407.

Taking heed of Hailey's advice, each rating carefully climbed down into the life rafts or inflatables that were bobbing hazardously against the ship's side. The rigid inflatables were larger and heavier and as such were slightly steadier. The first rating into the craft helped the others down. A jury sail was quickly rigged and when the raft was full, the line was released allowing the wind to carry the craft away from the ship.

One by one, Bud Abbott, Shady Lane, Dutch Holland and Pete Price and eleven other ratings, climbed down onto the scrambling net into the raft, situated , mid-ships on the port side.

'It's at times like these,' cried Bud Abbott, grasping the hand holds, 'that I'd wished I hadn't seen that movie, *Titanic.*'

'Oh, stop fuckin' moanin',' Shady replied, doing his best to disguise his nerves,' or I'll kick you in the arse and throw you overboard.'

By now, Butch Cassidy and the marines along with an assortment of senior ratings, stokers, administrative staff, cooks and stewards, had managed to scramble down into the remaining three rafts. Bungy Williams, Patrick Flynn, Barney Watts, Liz Hall and most of the officers were in the port side inflatable.

Hailey left the bridge and steadying himself against the cant of the ship made his way to his cabin. Here, he quickly collected the leather-bound ship's log along with his mobile phone into his brief case. He hurried away and was now standing by the accommodation ladder next to Noble, who was holding a waterproof bag containing the ship's secret codes. A few yards away Bogey Knight stood alongside Sadie Thompson.

Nearby, the weapons electrical and radar operators and communications ratings waited behind the girls.

'Everyone except this lot,' said Knight glancing them, 'have left, sir.'

'Then they'd better get a move on,' Hailey replied, glancing warily at his wristwatch. 'It's almost fourteen fifteen.'

Sadie Thompson overheard him and doing her best to sound cheerful, looked at the girls and said, 'right, girls, chop, chop, let's get a move on.'

Thompson and the girls, with their shoulder bags slung over across their inflated life jackets, stood waiting pensively, while gazing apprehensively at the large yellow rubber craft heaving up and down in the water six feel below. Behind them the radar, weapons electrical and communications staff also waited patiently.

'It seems a long way down,' Lottie Jones muttered, nervously biting her lip.

'Don't worry, Lot,' said Susan Hughes, giving her a reassuring smile, 'I'm right behind you, so take a good hold of the ropes as you go down the ladder.'

Diana, her face pale and drawn looked behind and saw Ashir. She gave him a slight wave and smiled weakly.

Suddenly, her hand shot to her mouth.

'Good God!' She cried hysterically, *'I've left something important in my locker!'* She turned quickly, brushed past Bogey Knight, and despite the rolling movement of the ship, managed to sprint along the upper deck.

'Where the hell are you going?' Knight yelled frantically, 'the ship's sinking, you daft bugger.' However, his warning fell on deaf ears as Diana disappeared through an open hatchway.

'What the blazes does she think she's doing, Master?' Hailey asked angrily. 'There's only about fifteen minutes left before . . .'

'I don't know, sir,' Knight interrupted, 'but if she's not quick, she'll go down with the ship.'

Remembering his promise to Diana, Bogey's words sent a cold shiver down Ashir's spine.

Thompson's calm voice interrupted his thoughts. 'Come on, girls, get down the ladder into the inflatable. There isn't much time.'

Ashir glanced anxiously along the upper deck hoping to see Diana return. She had been gone over two minutes and still there was no sign of her.

He suddenly remembered what Diana had shouted before she left. He pushed Bogey Knight to one side and dashed along the upper deck and ducked inside the same hatchway Diana had used. Feeling his heart pound like a steam engine, he hurried along the dimly lit starboard passage way. At that moment, a violent shudder ran through the ship throwing him against a bulkhead. He managed to steady himself and arrived at a stairway leading down to the girl's mess.

Suddenly, he froze with fear.

The mess door had been thrown open and dark green seawater was swirling around the room almost covering the mess table. But there was no sign of Diana. He hardly felt the coldness of the water as he waded through the mass of flotsam, desperately looking around and yelling her name. Suddenly, over the dull throbbing of the ship's generator, he heard a muffled cry. He turned and looked down the passage way leading to the girls' sleeping quarters and saw Diana's head and her yellow life jacket poking out of the water along with a hand clutching her shoulder bag.

'*Quick! Quick!*' She screamed. Her face was contorted in pain and her eyes full of fear. '*I'm stuck, my body and one of my arms is trapped. For God's sake help me!*'

'Don't move,' Ashir yelled, ploughing desperately waist high through the water, 'or you might make things worse.' He waded through the murky water and pushed his way to where Diana was lying. He threw away his beret and quickly deflated his life jacket enabling him to move freely. He then took a deep breath and ducked under the water. He blinked a few times and saw the locker jamming one of Diana's arms and lower part of her body firmly against a bunk. He desperately tried to push the locker sideways, but to his horror he couldn't move it. He came up for air and went under again. This time he managed to wedge a foot against the side of the passageway. Using all his strength, he was able to ease the locker away from Diana's body. Luckily, she wasn't badly injured and was able to free herself. With a scream of relief she stretched out a hand grabbed hold of Ashir's arm.

'*Go on ahead of me,*' Ashir shouted, pushing her in front of him, '*and hurry, we haven't much time!*'

She did as Ashir ordered and waded through the water. As she reached door of the mess a huge vibration shook the ship. A thunderous crash nearby made her glance behind, and to her consternation, she saw Ashir. Two lockers had fallen down on top of him. One was lying across his chest and the other one had hit the side of his head. Most of his body was under water all she could see clearly was part of his head and a mass of dark hair floating wildly. His eyes were staring blankly and lines of blood were running down his face.

'*Ash! Ash!*' she screamed and instinctively moved towards him. As she did so she felt a strong hand grab hold of her arm. She glanced up and saw the burly figure of Bogey Knight waist high in the water. His ruddy face was covered in sweat and seawater and his dark, red-rimmed eyes stared down at her.

'Come on, girl,' he yelled, pulling her through the door, 'this bloody ship's gunna go down any minute, so we don't have much time.'

'*But Ash is still there,*' She cried, pointing to Ashir's inert figure lying under the grimy water, '*and he's badly hurt.*'

At a glance Bogey saw that Ashir was dead. 'It's too late for him, now, love, he's gone.'

'*No! No!*'she screamed as Bogey forced her up the stairs, '*it can't be. Please God, no.*'

When they reached the top, Bogey put his arm around Diana's waist and carried her hip-high along the passageway. He lowered her down and pushed her through the open hatchway onto the upper deck. He then grabbed her hand and helped her along to where Hailey and Noble were standing. By this time the fo'c'sle and most of the Sea Wolf and Harpoon silos were completely under water and the ship lay at a dangerous angle.

'For heaven's sake man, hurry up,' Hailey shouted adding, 'where's operator Al Hussar?'

'He won't be coming with us, sir,' gasped Bogey, releasing Diana's hand, 'I'm afraid he's a gonner.'

'I got stuck and he rescued me,' Diana sobbed, 'and now . . . her voice trailed away as she grasped the rope guard rails of the accommodation ladder and carefully began her descent. Below, Sadie Thompson who was having difficulty keeping her balance as the inflatable rose up and down against the ship's side, helped Diana into the rubber craft.

With a forlorn sigh, Hailey looked at Noble, and with a slight gesture of his hand, said, 'After you, Number One.'

'Right, sir,' Noble sombrely relied, and made his way down the ladder and was helped into the inflatable by Bogey Knight.

For a few precious seconds, Hailey glanced forlornly up at the bridge where he had spent so many hours. He slowly raised his right arm and saluted, then, with a heavy heart, walked down the ladder.

The time was 1430.

CHAPTER FORTY-SIX

A scorching sun hung in a clear blue sky and a stiff, warm, westerly breeze quickly moved the inflatable Hailey and fourteen other personnel were in well away from the ship. Shortly afterwards, then other inflatable and four rubber life rafts hove into view linked together by a series of heaving lines.

Dawlish was now a depressing sight. The eyes of everyone in their respective crafts were focused on the ship that been home for many of the crew for the last eighteen months. During that time they had come to know each other intimately and were familiar with almost every part of the ship.

Her pennant number F229, was only partially visible and except for the bridge, mast, yardarms and flight deck the rest of the ship was under water.

'She'll be gone soon,' muttered Bud Abbott to Shady Lane sitting cramped in one of the rafts.

'Aye, you're right there, mate,' Shady quietly replied. 'They say that your last ship was always the best one, and they were right. She was bloody great.'

Meanwhile in the inflatable, Diana and Susan Hughes were lying against the raised rubber bulkhead snuggled up against one another. Diana was sopping wet and shivering despite the blanket Hughes had procured from the emergency stores.

'How are you feeling, Di?' Susan asked, noticing the dejected expression on Diana's face.

'I'm all right, thanks, Sue,' Diana answered, pulling the blanket tightly around her shoulders.

'I don't want to sound nosey, Di,' Susan whispered tactfully, 'but what was it that made you run back to the mess?'

'Just something personal,' Diana replied, tenderly touching her wet shoulder bag.

'What happened to Ash?' Asked Murphy, who was sitting on the other side of Susan.

Tears welled up in Diana's eyes. She shook her head and quickly turned away.

At that moment a deep growling rumble echoing from where *Dawlish* lay, made the inflatable rock violently. This was quickly followed by an ear-splitting explosion. Everyone looked across and saw that the stern of the ship had risen high out of the water. The five huge bronze alloy blades of her twin steel propellers had stopped. Next came what sounded like a miniature earthquake as the helicopter and generators broke free and tumbled forwards smashing though bulkheads. At the same time the mast, a tall thick structure with a mass of radar antennae, folded and crashed forward onto the bridge, taking with it a tangled mess of wires and cables from the yardarm. Behind the mast, the wide, stubby funnel slowly leant forward, then, with a sickening of sound metal snapping, collapsed into what remained of the mast. The last sight everyone had as the ship quickly slid under the water was the White Ensign flapping defiantly from her stern.

When she was gone, Diana and the girls were not the only ones with tears in their eyes.

For what seemed like an eternity everyone sat, cramped and uncomfortable, listening to the sickening squeak of rubber as the inflatable rose mercilessly up and down. Then, suddenly Bogey Knight, who was sitting up for'd scanning the horizon with his binoculars, recognised the unmistakable shape of a warship sending a massive foamy wave curling over her bow about five miles away. A cargo ship and two liners who had heard Hailey's distress message could also be seen some miles away.

'It's the Yanks!' He shouted, waving his arm frantically. 'It's the bloody Yanks, thank God!'

Cheers from the rafts were lost in the strong breeze as everyone, including Hailey and Noble attempted to stand and wave.

'Thank heavens for that, Number One,' said Hailey, whose wristwatch showed 1800.

Ten minutes later the destroyer arrived about fifty yards from the nearest raft, and gradually stopped. The pale grey structure of the ship with its pennant number, D431, painted in black, shone in the strong afternoon sun. In front of a high, enclosed bridge a twin 4.5 gun rested on the fo'c'sle. Then came a large searchlight mounted next to sets of machine guns and other small arms. On her quarterdeck, was a set of guided missile silos similar to those on *Dawlish,* and from her stern the Stars and Stripes fluttered wildly in the strong breeze.

The destroyer's tannoy suddenly crackled into action.

'Now hear this,' came a speaker with a sharp southern drawl. 'Duty watch turn too and lower the accommodation ladder on the starboard side of the fan-tail. Medical officer and staff to stand by. Those off watch, man the side and give assistance to the survivors. That is all.' (The fan tail is the American term for quarterdeck.)

Within twenty minutes, each raft and inflatable were lined up at the bottom of the accommodation ladder. Just then, a tall, broad-shouldered officer came onto the starboard wing of the ship. The three gold bars on the epaulette of each shoulder of his white blouse, indicated a commander's rank. Using a megaphone, the strident tones of his voice boomed across the water.

'Glad to see you. The ship is rolling badly so be careful climbing the ladder. The crew will be at
hand help you. Take your time, I look forward to seeing you all personally.'

Most of the destroyer's crew were leaning on the guard rails waving and shouting encouragement. Many, including several female ratings wore blue trousers and white shirts.. The senior ratings were dressed in pale khaki.

As each rating came on board they were met by a sailor who placed a blanket around their shoulders and ushered them below deck. The girls were taken care of by their counterparts and helped down to their mess and given steaming hot mugs of strong, sweet coffee. The rest of *Dawlish*'s crew were escorted down a set of ladders into the warmth of a large mess and handed the ubiquitous mugs of hot coffee and soup. Hailey and the officers were met by a tall, fair-haired lieutenant commander.

'Harvey Kadinsky, Executive Officer, welcome on board, sir,' he said saluting then, shaking Hailey's hand. 'The captain sends his compliments and asks if you join him on the bridge when you've had a hot drink in the wardroom.'

Hailey thanked him and along with *Dawlish*'s officers followed Kadinsky along a well- lit passageway into the wardroom. As he did so, the pipe, 'now here this. Duty watch stand by to retrieve life boats and inflatables and store them on the fan tail, that is all,' came over the tannoy.

By this time everyone was safely on board and the destroyer got under way. After enjoying a welcome cup of coffee, Hailey left the wardroom and followed a small, dark ensign, up two flights of metal stairs onto the bridge.

Other than the console which was quite large, the layout with its radar screens, wireless, voice pipes and various dials, was similar to that on board *Dawlish,* even the somnolent hissing of the air conditioning sounded familiar

The captain, a forty something officer with a swarthy complexion and close-cropped dark hair, was sitting on a high, oak chair engrossed in thought. A stout chief petty officer sat at the console. Next to him was a radio operator using earphones, listening for any incoming messages.

'Send a message to those merchant ships,' said the captain, to Kadinsky who was stand nearby. 'And thank them for their concern and say we have picked up the survivors and are proceeding to Bahrain.'

'Aye, aye, sir,' Kadinsky replied. He then quickly wrote down the message in a signal pad and handed it to the radio operator.

The captain turned and saw Hailey. As he eased his six- foot frame from the chair, his dark blue eyes creased into a warm smile.

'Welcome on board, Commander, Harvey Ambrose,' he said, proffering his hand. His slow, mid- western American accent was crisp and clear. 'Sorry we have to meet under such tragic circumstances.'

Hailey introduced himself, then added, 'Thank you for being so quick coming to us and for your warm hospitality.'

'A pleasure, Commander,' the captain replied, 'my cabin is at your disposal, and your officers can use my officers' cabins,' he added, giving Kadinsky a sly grin, 'I'm sure they won't mind bunking down in the wardroom for a few days.'

'That's very decent of you,' Hailey said, 'but we don't want to put you out. You've done enough for us already.'

'No problem,' the captain replied, 'I expect to arrive in Bahrain in two days. I have requested transport to meet us and a truck to take the life boats and inflatables to the base. Accommodation, will be provided your officers and crew.' He stopped talking and glanced at Kadinsky. 'Take the con, Harv, while I have a quiet word with Commander Hailey.'

The captain nodded at Hailey and opened a door leading onto the port wing where they were immediately greeted by a stiff, warm westerly breeze.

'I received a secret signal from the captain of the *Coral Sea*,' said Ambrose, staring blindly out to sea. Without moving his head, he went on, 'your ship was hit by what is called a flat mine.'

'I suspected as much,' Hailey replied, taking a deep breath. 'I was warned about them
before we left the UK, but was told it was unlikely we would encounter them as they were very expensive to make.'

'The day after your ship left Bahrain, one of these goddam things was discovered by a minesweeper off the coast of Kuwait,' explained the captain. 'Nobody was sure what the hell it was, but it was brought on board and taken to Bahrain and handed over to the bomb disposal unit. They discovered it was a new type of mine containing a new powerful explosive called Trysin. It was sent to your scientists at Porton Down. They quickly discovered that by using a special microchip inserted into a ship's radar set, the mine can now be detected. These microchips have now been sent to all ships in the Gulf.'

'A pity they didn't discover them earlier,' Hailey replied with a weary sigh, 'had they done so, my ship wouldn't be lying at the bottom of the Persian Gulf.'

The news of *Dawlish*'s sinking was reported by the BBC and ITV. It was also heard on CNN on board *Spruance*. The Royal Navy crew heard this and used their mobiles to reassure parents and loved ones that they were safe.

Noble and Hailey were walking on the fan-tail talking quietly, when Noble's mobile, playing *It's a long way to Tipperary,* echoed from his trouser pocket.

'Probably, my mother,' he said, taking the phone out, pressing a button and placing it to his ear. A few seconds later he almost dropped it.

'*Cynthia*' he cried, 'what a lovely surprise, how are you

'I'm fine, you silly sod,' she replied and burst into tears, 'when I heard about *Dawlish*, I realised if anything had happened to you, I'd die. For God's sake come home quickly and please, please, marry me."

'Of course, darling" Noble replied, feeling his mouth suddenly go dry. 'I'll marry you as soon as I come home. In the meantime, pick out the most beautiful wedding gown you can find. I love you."

Hailey and a few other of *Dawlish*'s officers overheard Noble very romantic conversation.

'Congratulations, old boy,' said Gooding said, slapping Noble on the backs, 'and may all your troubles be little midshipmen.'

Hailey also added his best wishes, then remembered his promise to phone Annabel. Suddenly, he inwardly cursed realising he had left the note she had given him in IBWs.

During the next two days, everyone, including the officers enjoyed unlimited amounts of ice cream, Coca Cola and steaks as thick as their fists. On Friday 20 September, at 0900, with the minarets of Bahrain visible in the early morning heat haze, the USS *Spruance* slowly cruised into Mina Salman and were greeted by the hooting of horns and loud cheering from the crews of a few minesweepers and HMS *Duncan*.

'My God, sir,' Dixie Dean said to Smyth, who was standing next to Susan Hughes, 'you'd think we'd done summat special.'

'I think it's because we survived,' the doctor replied philosophically, 'after all, it could have been one of their ships that was sunk.'

By 1000, *Spruance* was tied up alongside number three berth. Two metal gangways, one on the fan-tail, to allow *Dawlish*'s officers to leave, the other on the fo'c'sle for the crew to the same. Waiting nearby was a lorry and four, blue Royal Naval coaches. After prolonged handshakes and tearful goodbyes from then girls, they, along with *Dawlish*'s crew walked down their gangway, and with a final wave of gratitude to the Americans lining the guard rails, climbed into the first three coaches.

Hailey and his fellow officers stood on the fan-tail, near the top of the gangway. Each one saluted and thanked Captain Ambrose and his staff for their excellent hospitality.

'By the way, Commander,' said the captain, smiling wryly while shaking Hailey's hand, 'you've got an appointment with the admiral tomorrow at ten hundred.' Then every officer walked down the gangway and boarded the last coach.

No sooner was Hailey ashore than a gang of dockyard workers removed both gangways, the thick, nylon hawsers were then taken off the bollards. *Spruance* sounded her horn and gently moved away from the wharf. Hailey, who was the last of *Dawlish*'s officers to leave, turned and gave a final farewell wave to Captain Ambrose and the men on the bridge.

He was about to board the coach when he saw and heard a Land Rover roaring down the jetty.

To his amazement he saw the driver was none other than Annabel. His heart gave a sudden jolt as he watched the Land Rover screech to a halt a few yards behind the coach full of *Dawlish*'s officers.

With her beautiful tanned face wreathed in smiles, she flung the door open and ran towards him. She wore a pair of smart fawn slacks, small brown dessert boots and the vivid red headscarf concealing her short chestnut hair, contrasted sharply with her long-sleeved white cotton blouse.

'*Oh John darling!*' She cried grabbing hold of Hailey's outstretched hands, '*Thank God you're safe.*' As she spoke those lovely turquoise eyes he had seen so often in his dreams, became wet with tears. She let go of his hands and pulled him close. 'I know it sounds silly,' she sobbed, 'but when I heard someone had been killed, I remembered the captain was always the last to leave the ship and thought . . .'

'Well as you can see,' Hailey said, feeling the warmth of her body against his, 'I'm still in one piece.' He then yelled up to the coach driver and told him to leave. As the coach moved away, the officers grinned and waved. Parker-Smith even blew Annabel a kiss and was delighted when she returned the compliment.

'I'm sorry I didn't phone you,' said Hailey, 'but I left your note in my other uniform and . . .'

'Never mind that,' she interrupted, 'I haven't got long, John,' she said, as they walked hand in hand towards the Land Rover. 'Filming finished sooner than I expected and we're off to Hollywood to do those indoor scenes.'

'Then what?' Hailey asked, giving her hand a gentle squeeze.

'Back to London to start rehearsing *Taming of the Shrew,*' she replied. 'I believe I told you I wasn't renewing my contract with Warners. What about you?'

'Portsmouth and a routine Board of Enquiry about the sinking,' he answered with a tired sigh, 'then probably a desk job in MOD.'

Annabel stopped walking and reached up and gently touched the dimple in his chin, and said, 'that means we'll both be back in London then,' she paused, then with a pleading expression in her eyes, added, 'do you think there'll be time for us?'

'We'll damn well make time, darling,' Hailey answered firmly.

'Then don't just stand there, my love,' she murmured softly, placing her hands around his neck,

'kiss me before I go crazy.'

CHAPTER FORTY-SEVEN

Three weeks later after arriving home, Diana left the naval barracks in Portsmouth in a tilly and caught the 0915 train from the Portsmouth and arrived at Waterloo two hours later. Ten days earlier the rest of *Dawlish*'s crew had been sent on leave and Diana remained behind as she had decided she must leave the service. The sight of Ashir lying, blood soaked still kept her awake at night, and the thought she might be sent to sea again made her feel physically sick, as did the sight of a sailor's uniform. She therefore seen her divisional officer, explained her problems and requested to be discharged. After a medical examination by the PMO, she had gone before a panel of officers who had been briefed about her background. After a short, compassionate and conciliatory deliberation, Diana was granted an honourable discharge on medical grounds and given a months' terminal leave, to commence forthwith. When she phoned her parents they were delighted and couldn't wait to see her.

Diana's short brown hair fell lazily against a pink woollen scarf knotted neatly around her neck. Over a fawn sweater, brown, knee-length skirt and matching brogues, she wore a cream coloured coat, thick enough to keep out the harsh north westerly wind. In her right hand she carried a pale green, 'pusser's' suitcase. This and her black shoulder bag were the only clues to suggest she was in the Royal Navy.

During then flight from Bahrain to Heathrow, she had been quiet and withdrawn. This mood of outward silence was in stark contrast to the inner turmoil that had given many sleepless nights. Finally, one evening in barracks when the mess was almost empty, she broke in tears and told Susan Hughes that she blamed herself for Ashir's death.

'Night after night, I can see his face covered in blood staring at me,' Diana sobbed, 'It's . . . it's driving me insane.'

''You mustn't reproach yourself, love,' Susan said, sympathetically holding one of Diana's hands. 'It was that bloody Al Qaeda mine that killed Ash, not you. I'm sure his parents will understand.'

Diana didn't reply. A few weeks earlier a rating in the administrative office had given her the address of Ashir's parents. Now, as she left the train, she was about to find out if Susan's words were true.

After depositing her suitcase in the left luggage department, she studied a map of the underground, then took the Hammersmith and City line to Farringdon and Clerkenwell. With a heavy heart, she realised this was the same journey Ashir had taken every time he came on leave.

Outside Clerkenwell's tube station, she asked an elderly man to direct her the address her friend had given her. A dark beard almost covered most of his swarthy features and like many people she had seen in Bahrain, he wore a white dishdaba and baggy trousers.

'Go down St John's Street, that's the one directly in front of you,' he said. 'Briset Street is the second on your left.'

Diana thanked him and followed his instructions. Ten minutes late she arrived outside number seven, one of the many red-bricked terraced houses lining both sides of the street. Above an oak panelled door was a rounded glass fan shaft embossed with a crescent moon. The mauve curtains of the bay window were drawn allowing Diana to catch a glimpse of a well-furnished room with pale yellow wallpaper. For a few minutes she stood, dry mouthed and nervous. Finally, she took a deep breath and with a trembling hand lifted the latch of the wrought iron gate and pressed the button doorbell.

The door opened and Diana instinctively knew that the small, stout woman standing in front of her wearing a black cotton hijab, was Ashir's mother.

For a few seconds the woman was taken aback at the sight of this smartly dressed young girl, after all, the only visitors she and her husband ever received were fellow Muslims.

'Yes,' the woman said, frowning slightly, 'what is it you want?'

This was the moment Diana had been dreading. How would his parents react when she told them about Ashir, she asked herself?

'My name Diana James,' she said, feeling her heat beat a cadence in her chest. 'I . . . I was a friend of Ashir.'

Noticing the strained expression on Diana's pale face, the woman said, 'I see, then you had better come in.'

With one hand holding her shoulder bag, Diana followed the woman down a short lobby into the room she had seen from the street. It was pleasantly furnished with a brown leather settee and matching armchairs. On one corner, nest to a forty-inch television set, was a tall glass cabinet full of nick knacks and framed photographs of people wearing Arabic style clothing. A colourful Persian carpet covered the floor and gaudily painted pictures of the dessert and eastern cities hung on the wall. But dominating the room was an ornately framed portrait of Mohammad hanging above a white marble mantelpiece under which glowed a gas fire.

'I am, Fatima, Ashir's mother,' said the woman, 'please sit down,' as she spoke, her soft dark eyes and pale brown complexion broke into a warm smile. 'Would you like some tea or coffee?'

'Coffee would be nice, thank you,' Diana replied, lowering herself onto the settee and demurely crossing her legs.

No sooner had Fatima excused herself and left the room, than Diana looked up and saw a tall, dark-skinned man wearing a pristine white dishdaba. She stood up and inwardly gasped. Despite his large black beard hiding most of his features, his upright bearing, aquiline nose and soft brown eyes immediately reminded her of Ashir.

'I am Hussein, Ashir's father,' he said, noting Diana's good manners by rising as he entered. 'I overheard what you said to my wife. Salaam Ailaecum,' he added bowing lightly, 'any friend of my late son is welcome in this house. Please sit down.' His voice was deep, resonant and clear.

He sat down on an armchair and folded his arms across his ample waist. Fatima came in and placed a silver tray with matching cups and saucers. She poured out three cups then handed one to Diana and Hussein, then taking one herself, she sat down on the other armchair.

Diana's coffee was black, strong and sweet. Hussein smiled at her and after taking a sip of his drink, asked politely, 'Please, young lady, tell us about Ashir. The letter we received from his captain, said he was going to be awarded a Distinguished Service Medal, err . . . post, something or other.'

302

'Posthumously, my husband,' interrupted, Fatima, 'it means our son is now with Allah.'

'Ah, yes,' Hussein went on, giving Diana a puzzled look, 'why was he so brave?'

A sense of fear suddenly gripped Diana. Not for the first time she anxiously wondered how they would react when she told them the truth of what happened on that terrible afternoon almost four weeks ago.

Diana finished her coffee and couldn't contain herself no longer. She burst into tears and covering her face with both hands, cried, *'Because he rescued me from drowning. It was all my fault!'*

Her outburst startled Fatima and Hussein. Fatima sat back in her armchair and gave Hussein a look of disbelief.

'We don't understand,' Fatima said, placing her untouched coffee on a nearby table. 'Do we, my husband?'

'No, we do not,' Hussein replied, his cup frozen in his hand, 'perhaps you could explain what you mean. You said you were drowning, how was this?'

Diana removed her hands from her tear-stained face and took out a white, lace handkerchief from her coat pocket. Then, in between sobs, she told them what had happened adding, 'It was rumoured that the mine we hit contained something called Trysin, so you see,' she went on, dabbing her eyes, 'if I hadn't run back to the mess, Ashir would be alive today,' averting their gaze, she added, 'and now, I'll have his death on my conscience for the rest of my life.'

The mention of Trysin immediately made Hussein frown, and give Fatima a wary glance.

Fatima understood and didn't speak. But a few seconds later a puzzled expression spread over Fatima's face. 'But tell me, Miss James,' she asked, 'why did you go back to your quarters?'

Diana stopped crying and was nervously toying with her damp handkerchief.

'For this,' she said, unzipping her shoulder bag and bringing out a slightly squashed parcel covered in shiny red paper with its golden bow still intact. Being kept in her bag had reduced the effect of the water and its contents were undamaged and perfectly dry.

Diana slowly handed the parcel to Fatima, and with a weak smile, said, 'please open it.'

With Hussein looking on expectantly, Fatima gently undid the bow, loosened the gold strings and peeled back the paper.

'By the prophet Mohammad, peace be upon him,' she cried, lifting the slightly creased caftan up,
'Praise be to Allah, look at the golden dragons and crescent moons embroidered into it. Isn't it lovely, what do you think of it, my husband?'

'Yes, my wife,' Hussein replied, doing his best to disguise his displeasure at the garments worldly appearance, 'it is indeed, err . . . very nice,' he added dubiously, 'Allah's hands certainly move in mysterious ways.'

This was the first time Diana had seen the caftan since Ashir bought it for her in Bahrain.

'Ashir gave it to me as a present,' she said, fighting back a tear, 'and now I'd like you to have it.'

'This is very kind of you,' Fatima replied, standing up and placing the caftan carefully against her body, 'but I can't accept such a beautiful gift.'

'Please,' Diana replied, tears welling up in her red-rimmed eyes, 'you see I loved Ashir and despite our different religions and customs, I know he loved me, and I'm certain he would want you to have it.'

'Very well, if you are sure,' Fatima slowly replied, still holding the garment against her, 'it's a little too long but it can easily be altered.' Then, with a tender smile, she went on, 'You must not blame yourself for Ashir's death. It was the will of Allah and he is now at peace. Is he not, my husband?'

'Yes,' Hussein replied with a sad sigh, 'indeed it is.'

With a feeling of relief, Diana zipped up her handbag and stood up, 'and now,' she said, straightening her coat, 'I have a train to catch. I was really worried about meeting you, but after our talk, I'm glad I did.'

With the caftan neatly folded over her arm, Fatima and Hussein escorted Diana to the front door and opened it.

'Thank you both for your kindness and understanding,' Diana said, as he she shook their hands. Then, with a farewell smile, she walked away feeling their meeting had had a cathartic effect on her.

Fatima closed the door and noticed the disgruntled expression on Hussein's face.

'Is there something wrong, my husband?'

'Yes,' he replied gruffly, 'you heard her say it was Trysin in the mine that was responsible for Ashir's death.'

'That is what she said,' Fatima answered, nodding her head slightly.

'And not the Trysin I gave him. How very strange,' Hussein added, pensively stroking his beard, 'And furthermore,' he went on, 'the girl said Ashir loved her, but surely this is impossible. Under no circumstances could a Muslim and a Christian infidel ever love one another. Is this not so, my wife?'

A faint, suspicious smile played around Fatima's lips. She gently ran a palm over the soft, silkiness of the caftan, and quietly replied, 'Of course, you are right, my husband, but was it not you who said Allah's hands moves in mysterious ways . . .?'